MORMONVILLE

MORMONVILLE

by
Jeff Call

CFI

Springville, Utah

ISBN: 1-55517-618-6
e. 2

Published by Cedar Fort Inc.
www.cedarfort.com

Distributed by:

Typeset by Kristin Nelson
Cover design by Adam Ford
Cover design © 2002 by Lyle Mortimer

Printed in the United States of America
10 9 8 7 6 5 4 3 2 1

Printed on acid-free paper

Library of Congress Cataloging-in-Publication Data

Call, Jeff, 1968-
 Mormonville : a big-city reporter spends a year in Utah to uncover the truth about the LDS Church, but uncovers truths about himself / by Jeff Call.
     p. cm.
 ISBN 1-55517-618-6 (pbk. : alk. paper)
1. Journalists--Fiction. 2. Mormons--Fiction. 3. Utah--Fiction. I. Title.
 PS3603.A44 M67 2002
 813'.6--dc21

                    2002006663

Dedication

To my wife CherRon,
and my sons Ryan, Brayden, Landon,
Austin and Carson.

PROLOGUE

From the second-story window of the apartment he shared with his mother, 11-year-old Luke Manning watched the police car pull up to the curb. Such was a common occurrence in this run down, low-income housing district in Syracuse, New York. Only a couple of weeks earlier, a murder had been committed a couple of floors up. This time, though, Luke sensed that the cops were coming for him.

He turned off his favorite television program, *The Dukes of Hazzard*, and heard an authoritative knock at the door. "Luke, it's me, Mr. Grich, from the Department of Social Services," said Luke's case worker. "Please open up."

Luke figured his days as a full-time latchkey kid were about over, but he wasn't about to surrender without a fight. He peered out the peephole. "I know you're in there," said Mr. Grich, who sported a handlebar mustache, bushy side-burns and a charcoal-colored three-piece suit. "We need to talk about your mom. She's in some trouble."

Luke hadn't seen his 26-year-old mother, Sheila, in about a week. As a single mom, she did the best she could to make ends meet, but it was never easy. Damon Manning, Luke's father, abandoned the two of them when Luke was seven. Luke counted that departure as one of the highlights of his life.

When he wasn't working, Damon whiled away the hours at a nearby bar, either until he passed out or was kicked out, whichever came first. He frequently came home drunk and physically vented his many frustrations on Sheila. Though just a young boy, Luke intervened on his mother's behalf and he often wound up black and blue because of it. One night, Damon became enraged and began striking Sheila repeatedly in the face. Luke quite possibly saved his mother's life by slamming a Mike Schmidt-signature model baseball bat on his father's head, knocking him unconscious. Luke and Sheila got out of the apartment for a few days and by the time they returned, Damon had left without a forwarding address.

After that, things improved—comparatively speaking.

Money was scarce and Sheila couldn't hold down a job. Luke didn't receive birthday presents and Santa Claus never came on Christmas Eve. Luke was lucky to get three square meals a week.

Then Sheila met a stranger who introduced her to ways that she could earn enough money to provide for herself and her son with relatively little effort. The man also introduced her to substances that helped her forget all her troubles. Sheila entered a new world that took her away from Luke for long periods. On the one hand, the Mannings' standard of living improved dramatically—there was food on the table and the electricity wasn't cut on a regular basis for failing to pay the bill. On the other hand, Luke noticed the light in his mother's eyes had faded away. She never smiled anymore.

Long before *Home Alone* was a movie, it was a lifestyle for Luke. He worried about his mother, but felt helpless. At the same time, he enjoyed his independence. He preferred being on the streets to staying in the apartment. Before disappearing each month, Sheila placed a few dollars on the rickety kitchen table for Luke. She typically returned home in the middle of the night and then slept for 14-16 hour stretches. When she awoke, she sat him down and apologized and cried, promising that things would be different from then on. And, within a couple of days, the process repeated itself.

Where she went, Luke didn't know, though he had some ideas. A few times, he rummaged through her purse and found it filled with illegal drugs.

Following every term, Luke forged his mom's signature on his report card—not because he didn't want his mom to see his grades (despite everything, he was a solid B student) but because she wasn't around much. When she was, she was barely coherent and Luke didn't want the teachers at school snooping around. When people from the school called for her, he lied, explaining she had gone to the store. He wasn't about to tell them the truth—that he hadn't seen her for several days or that she had passed out on the bathroom floor. Teachers asked him about his home life and he painted for them a rosy picture—until a social worker named Richard Grich dropped by the Mannings' apartment and discovered Luke was practically raising himself. Sheila was arrested on misdemeanor child neglect charges, went to court and was told that she would lose custody of her son unless she made some changes. Sheila promised the judge, and Luke, that she would.

She didn't.

That's why Luke knew Mr. Grich and the cops at the door weren't making a social call. His mom had slipped up again, he thought, and nothing short of an executive pardon from President Carter himself could save her, or him, now.

"I've got two police officers here with me," said Mr. Grich, who continued pounding the door. "We want to help you, Luke. We're on your side. We're your friends."

"Don't make us use force to come in there," said a cop. "If you don't come out on your own, we will come in after you."

Luke opened the window and looked down at the pavement below. He grabbed a thick rope his father had left behind in a closet and, after tying one end to a metal pipe, he tossed the other end down to the sidewalk. Holding the musty rope in his right hand, he stuck his left leg through the window and rapelled down the face of the building. Once he reached the ground, he sprinted down the street.

His hands were bleeding from the rope burns, but he didn't care. He ran for several blocks, past the pharmacy, past the corner market, past the magazine stand, and past the school. Up ahead, he saw the stately old church where his mother used to take him years earlier on Sundays. That was one place Luke thought he might be safe. He bounded up the steps and opened the heavy, wooden door. Once inside, he made his way through the empty chapel and to the front pew. While catching his breath, he gazed at the stained glass windows and the towering arches that rose up to the lofty ceiling.

Luke recalled his mother reading him passages from the Bible and praying in that church. "A lot of good that did her," he said quietly to himself. Scared, and knowing nobody on earth could help him, Luke sought a higher power.

If there's a God, he thought, *he'll bring my mom back to me.* Luke lowered his head and whispered: "Don't let them take me away from her. Please let us be together again. Help us to have a better life . . ."

Suddenly, the church door creaked open and Luke saw the two policemen and Mr. Grich enter. He crouched down onto the floor. "Luke," Mr. Grich called out, "don't make this harder than it has to be. Please, let's talk."

Luke crawled under the pews and somehow he reached the back of the church undetected. He stood up to make his escape but Mr. Grich was blocking the doorway. A cop collared Luke from behind, but he broke free. He eluded his three pursuers for a while, but the second police officer finally caught Luke and tackled him to the ground. Luke was taken into protective custody and he rode to the juvenile detention center in a police car. Mr. Grich told Luke that Sheila had been arrested the previous day on felony charges.

"Oh yeah? What did she do?" Luke asked defiantly.

"I'm not at liberty to say," Mr. Grich replied, adding that she was probably going to prison for a while.

At the courthouse early the next morning, Luke appeared before an Onondaga County judge, who made the boy a ward of the state of New York.

Until he was eighteen, Luke bounced from one foster home to another and in and out of trouble. During the first few months of being in foster care, Luke secretly harbored the hope that God would bring him back to his mother. But soon that hope of a reunion with Sheila deteriorated into a deep resentment for her (as well as just about everyone else he met). She had let him down. If he couldn't trust his own mother, he concluded, whom could he trust?

Maybe that's why Luke Manning became a newspaper reporter. It was a profession that allowed him to ask questions and get answers. It allowed him to challenge authority, to challenge the establishment that he felt had robbed him of all he had cared about. Luke yearned to expose the truth and hold people accountable for their actions. After a childhood where he could control nothing, he felt he had a measure of control as a journalist. Luke vowed not to rely on anyone, or anything, ever again.

CHAPTER 1

It was while desperately searching for a bar in Helaman, Utah, on a sweltering Sunday afternoon that Luke Manning realized he had accepted the worst assignment in the history of journalism.

Head pounding, brow beaded with sweat—the air conditioner in his cherry-red Corvette had gone out—and his mouth drier than the local liquor laws, Luke wanted a stiff drink more than he had ever wanted anything in his life. He felt disoriented and trapped in this dreary wasteland where Prohibition, apparently, had never been repealed. But what else could he have expected from arguably the most conservative town in the most conservative county on the planet?

Despite the wide-open spaces around him, he felt like he was suffocating. Sure, looking for a place to buy a beer was part of his research, but he knew it was also needed in order to preserve his sanity.

As he drove through the nearly deserted streets, he punched the buttons of his car stereo but couldn't even find anything decent on the radio.

He threw in a CD of Jimmy Buffett's *Greatest Hits* and cranked it to eardrum-shattering levels. As he stopped at a red light, the only one in town, a dilapidated minivan pulled alongside his sports car. Luke glanced over and noticed a gaggle of restless children—he stopped counting at six—strapped in their seats. An infant had cracker crumbs on her face, while another child pressed his runny nose against the window. Two haggard parents sat in the front seat, staring straight ahead as if in a daze. On the side of the van was a faded bumper sticker that read, *"Families Are Forever."* The children stared at Luke's car, entranced by the clamor that shattered the quiet Sunday afternoon. As the light turned green, Luke flashed them the peace sign and sped away, wheels squealing.

When Luke finally found an open convenience store, he ran in, grabbed a six-pack of beer, and took it to the counter. Seeing his intended purchase, the clerk informed him the store could not sell alcohol on Sunday. "Sorry, buddy," the man said. "That's the law around here."

Luke slammed his fist down on the counter. "I'll give you fifty bucks."

"Can't do it. Like I said, it's the law. Besides, we're on surveillance camera. I'd get fired."

Luke cursed as he stomped out of the store. "What kind of a place is this?" he shouted at the camera. When he returned to his car, he pulled out his notebook and wrote, "This place should have a sign on it, *'Welcome to Utah County. Please Set Your Clocks Back to 1912.'"*

The unrelenting heat, the lack of liquid refreshment, and the sober surroundings were causing his stomach to do flip-flops. He couldn't shake this fear that the towering Wasatch Mountains were going to crumble and bury him alive.

Other than that, Luke was enjoying his stay in Utah immensely.

Just twenty-four hours earlier, he had moved to Helaman, which would be his home for the next twelve months. After residing the previous eleven years in New York City, the jolt was almost too much to endure. That first night in Helaman, a parade of visitors had come to his door, bearing gifts ranging from homemade zucchini bread to Rice Krispy Treats to potted plants. They treated him as if he had a terminal illness—or had won Publisher's Clearinghouse.

This assignment was the only thing that could have brought him to Utah. He longed to pack up and catch the next flight to the East Coast, but he knew he couldn't do that. He had a job to do. As burdensome as this task was, it would also be lucrative. But now he was wondering if all the money on earth would be worth this kind of aggravation. He had heard stories about how difficult it would be to buy liquor in Utah, but this was absurd. Back in New York, locating a watering hole had been the least of his concerns.

As a star reporter and columnist for the *New York Post*, Luke had bar-hopped with professional athletes and high-profile politicians, not to mention other well-known journalists. He hung out with the rich and famous at chic taverns and trendy dance clubs. He caroused at wild parties, and there had been plenty of cavorting with leggy cheerleaders, gorgeous supermodels, and aspiring actresses. In the span of two months, he had dated most of the women in last year's *Sports Illustrated* swimsuit issue.

It wasn't uncommon for him to do lunch with movie stars. He was an occasional guest on local radio and television news talk shows, and was on a first-name basis with the mayor and every other influential public figure in town. Enamored with the glitz, glamour, and bright lights, Luke was a tabloid king in the greatest city on earth. Millions knew his name. His chiseled mug, in fact, was plastered on billboards and dozens of New York City buses.

"He's the Man!" read the ads, trumpeting his column. *"Get the quick and*

dirty with Luke Manning of the New York Post."

Luke very much enjoyed the clout and prestige that came with being a reporter in "The City That Never Sleeps." Naturally, he was a bonafide insomniac. In New York, after all, he was working in the hub of the universe. His column ran on the weekends, and during the week he averaged one eyebrow-raising story a day. Addicted to the adrenaline rush of scooping the competition, he thrived on seeing his name in print. He saw himself as a crusader, a renegade, a Dirty Harry with press credentials. During his years at the *Post*, he had reported on cold-blooded murders, mafia wars, gang violence, kidnappings, terrorist bombings, police brutality cases, political scandals, dead bodies surfacing in the East River, and of course, the horrific aftermath of the World Trade Center bombing. Subscribers from Harlem to Queens, from Brooklyn to Yonkers, would snap open their copies every morning looking for Luke Manning's byline.

One time, he bagged an exclusive interview with a man who was sentenced to twenty years in prison for attempting to strangle his employer with strands of dental floss. The interview ended with the man lunging at him after Luke asked him if he was "mentally disturbed or just plain stupid?"

In self-defense, Luke knocked him silly. In his column the next day Luke wrote, *"The guy has no heart, no brains, no guts—and a weak right hook."*

On another occasion, Congressman Curtis Strahan absentmindedly told Luke during an interview that he sometimes enjoyed walking around the privacy of his house in women's dresses.

"What size?" Luke asked.

"Six," the congressman replied, chuckling. "But that's off-the-record, of course."

"There's no such thing as off-the-record, after-the-fact," Luke said. "You said it, I'm printing it." The congressman became the laughing stock of the city, not to mention the nation. Funny thing, the congressman's re-election bid a couple of months later didn't go so well.

Luke Manning was the best journalist of all time. If you didn't believe it, all you had to do was ask him. As far as he was concerned, his life couldn't have gotten much better.

But that was before The Assignment.

The Assignment had lured him to Utah with promises of big bucks and a *New York Times* bestseller. But right now Luke would trade it for the companionship of a cold beer. And to think that before arriving in Utah, Luke Manning knew practically nothing about the Mormon Church.

CHAPTER 2

Luke had learned about The Assignment on a bright, crisp April day. He had taken the subway into midtown Manhattan, feeling as though he had just conquered the world—or at least a good portion of it—having almost single-handedly brought down the most powerful government official in the state.

Sitting inconspicuously in his seat, Luke hid behind designer, wraparound sunglasses and smugly observed the crowd of passengers, their eyes riveted on their copies of the *Post*, lapping up the titillating details of his story in that day's first edition.

GUV'S A GAMBLER! screamed the headline on the front page, next to an unflattering photo of Governor Geoffrey Sharples. *Sharples linked to high-stakes wagering scandal*, it read below. New York City was buzzing about the shocking revelation.

Acting on a tip he had received weeks earlier, Luke relentlessly pursued the story. He dug into the governor's life and established a connection between Sharples and an organized crime family. One of Sharples' bookies, Tommy "Hacksaw" Biancalana, informed Luke that the governor made wagers on everything from meaningless regular season games to the Super Bowl. Hacksaw had a jewelry box full of receipts to prove it. As part of his investigation, Luke discovered that years earlier, the governor had even helped orchestrate a point-shaving scandal by a local college basketball team for his own financial benefit.

Sharples was a compulsive gambler who had maxed out enough credit cards to wallpaper the governor's mansion and was $335,000 in the hole. Hacksaw did not smile kindly upon those who failed to make good on their debts. Instead of the conventional route, which involved kneecaps and a tire iron, Hacksaw chose a more painful approach—leaking an exclusive about the governor's dirty little secret to the most hard-nosed, cold-hearted investigative reporter in New York City.

After weeks of researching and writing, Luke contacted the governor for a response before the story went to press, calling him at 8 p.m. at his home.

Sharples, happily married with three children, was horrified and humiliated to learn that his soiled laundry was about to be aired in public. He knew he had disgraced the family name and his political career was over. Still, he denied everything.

"You're lying to me, Governor," Luke responded coldly.

Sharples stuttered for a moment, then tried intimidation tactics. Luke just laughed. Sharples begged Luke to give him a little time before publishing the report. "The story is running tomorrow," Luke said. "You have your job, Governor, and I have mine. Or, at least you *had* your job. By the way, I've got a little advice for you," he added before hanging up. "I'd put my money on the Knicks tomorrow night."

Not long after the papers hit the streets, the governor solemnly scheduled a press conference in Albany to announce his resignation, but Luke wasn't going. Earlier that morning he had appeared on *The Today Show* and a couple of other major network news programs to talk about his big scoop. Now he figured he deserved a break and his editor gave him his first day off in months. Luke had one year of paid vacation stored up and he was set to go on a two-week leave-of-absence.

Not, however, before he took care of a mysterious appointment downtown.

A few days earlier, Luke had fielded a phone call from Jack Kilborn, vice president of Halcyon Publishing, Inc., a multi-billion-dollar publishing empire. Kilborn had been cryptic during their conversation.

"I've got a big story for you that I would like to talk to you about, in person," he said, inviting Luke to his office. Luke was mildly interested, since he frequently received new tips from all sorts of people, not just mobster types. So he scrawled the appointment into his planner.

Luke expected his sources to keep appointments, so he always kept his. Still, he wanted to get this one over with as quickly as possible. He wanted to go to Queens to catch a Mets-Dodgers matinee game, then hit Atlantic City for a little poker and blackjack. The next day, he might meet a gorgeous girl in Soho and take her to Las Vegas. Or Bora Bora. Didn't really matter where.

When the subway screeched to a halt at its designated stop, Luke made his way off with the masses, climbed to the top of the stairs and onto the bustling New York City streets. He drew a breath of the morning air and entered a coffee shop for his daily fix, a cup of cappuccino to go. Then he ambled a couple of blocks, weaving in and out of the sea of people, and into the towering Halcyon

Books Building, located in the heart of the Manhattan business district.

Once inside, Luke removed his sunglasses, ducked into the elevator, and punched the button that carried him to the forty-second floor. When the elevator doors opened, he strolled into a plush lobby.

The receptionist stationed behind the desk almost fainted at the sight of him. Luke was, as always, impeccably dressed, today in pleated slacks and a tailored tweed blazer over a navy blue turtleneck. His ruggedly handsome appearance— thick, collar-length black hair and athletic build—struck her immediately. She clearly recognized him and his bright blue eyes from his TV appearance that morning as well as his picture that ran with his column, and like many women meeting him for the first time, she was smitten.

"Luke Manning," he announced, stroking his immaculately trimmed goatee, "and I have a ten o'clock appointment with Jack Kilborn."

The young woman ran her trembling finger down the appointment book. "Please take a seat," she replied, her voice quavering. "He'll be right with you."

Luke smiled, revealing his dimples. "Thanks," he said. She blushed.

It was 9:54 a.m. He was punctual, as usual. Checking out the elegant surroundings as he sipped his coffee, he could see the young receptionist couldn't resist stealing a glance at him. Laughing inwardly at her coy behavior, he suddenly shot a look her way and when the two made eye contact, he winked. She blushed again.

Luke flipped open his cell phone and checked his messages. Then he perused the box scores in the newspaper. The longer he sat, the more agitated he became. He couldn't believe he was being forced to wait. Why would Kilborn, a top exec with a publishing behemoth, want to talk to him in the first place? he wondered. The whole thing struck him as odd, to be summoned by one of the country's most powerful publishers. This had better be a *big* story, he thought.

The appointment smelled like a setup. He was accustomed to people who had ulterior motives or hidden agendas. Second-guessing people's actions was second-nature to Luke. Then it came to him. Kilborn was probably angry about a book review he had done. Earlier that year Luke blasted an overhyped Halcyon Books crime novel he described as "literary tripe destined for an eternal shelf life in the bargain books bin at Barnes & Noble," by an author he called "a Jell-O-brained, John Grisham-wanna be." The book was a flop and Luke proudly felt responsible. If that was why Kilborn had requested to speak with him, then he welcomed it. Nothing like a little confrontation and psychological warfare to get the blood going in the morning. Besides, maybe a good column would come out of it.

But he detested waiting. Luke brushed back his coat sleeve and glanced at his watch again. It was 10:02. He shook his head in disdain. After sitting idly for another minute, tapping his foot, Luke took out a notebook and pen, which he carried with him at all times, from the inside breast pocket of his jacket.

"Mr. Manning," came the receptionist's voice, "Mr. Kilborn will see you now."

Luke lifted himself off the sofa and strutted toward a spacious office where Jack Kilborn and his steel-toed, alligator-skin cowboy boots awaited him in the doorway. "Son," Kilborn exclaimed in his baritone voice, "it's a pleasure to meet you."

He offered his calloused right hand, which clasped Luke's like a bear trap.

"Likewise," Luke said as he entered Kilborn's lair, surveying the surroundings. He saw a Browning rifle mounted next to rows of awards, plaques and autographed pictures of famous authors on the wall. "Nice place you have here," Luke said. "You'll have to give me your decorator's number."

Kilborn was lean, with a craggy face, steely eyes, and a tuft of coarse hair on the back of his scalp resembling a Brillo pad. From what Luke had heard about him, he had all the charm of a traffic cop with a case of the gout. Luke saw past his pleasant veneer instantly, knowing this greeting had to be an act.

"You probably can't guess why I've brought you here," Kilborn said after closing the door behind them.

"We're not into guessing in the newspaper business," Luke shot back as Kilborn ushered him to his seat. "I'm a reporter, not a soothsayer."

Kilborn unleashed a booming laugh from his leather chair behind the mahogany desk. "You're a very talented reporter, among the best I've read. I've admired your work for some time. Great story again today. You've managed to accomplish what the Republicans have been trying to do for years—get rid of the governor."

"Believe me, I wasn't trying to do the GOP any favors," Luke said. "I just report the truth." He let out a bored sigh, stifled a yawn, and gazed out the window at the panoramic view of the hazy New York City skyline. Then he looked at his watch. "Would you just get to the point? I know you didn't bring me here to wax my ego."

Kilborn removed a Cuban cigar from the credenza. As he lit up, he continued, "Like I said, I've been reading your stuff for quite a while. You've been at the *Post*, what, eleven years?"

Luke nodded without interest.

Kilborn placed owlish bifocals on the bridge of his nose and opened a thick file of Luke's newspaper clippings. He thumbed through the stack. "Your five-part series on NYPD corruption was riveting," he said. "Nominated for the Pulitzer, as I understand."

"Should have won it, too," Luke said. "I was robbed like a little old lady walking through Central Park at midnight."

"I enjoyed your story about that evangelist minister who was bilking his congregation too. I loved how the minister confessed his crimes in a church meeting and how the cops carted him off to prison afterwards to the sound of the organ playing 'Amazing Grace' in the background. You've certainly got a flair for the dramatic and I really liked this column here, where you made fun of figure skating. It was hilarious. I heard you got about 12,000 angry e-mail messages on that one."

"And a few death threats. Even one from Tonya Harding."

Kilborn reached into a drawer. "I even have my own personal copy of your book about those Arab terrorists who threatened to blow up the Statue of Liberty a few years ago. As I recall, it was on the *New York Times* bestseller list for a few weeks, right?"

"Four to be exact."

"I've heard about your reputation. I understand your colleagues call you the 'Pit Bull.'"

"Hopefully not because of my looks," Luke said. He leaned back, folded his arms and defiantly propped his size twelve suede shoes on top of Kilborn's desk.

"I did a lot of research on you before I called you. I know all about you. You were named one of the city's most eligible bachelors. You finished in the top ten percent of your class at Syracuse University. You acted a little bit in college. You are agnostic. Or is that atheist?"

"A little of both, actually. What is this, anyway? *This Is Your Life?* Did you hire a private investigator or something? Well, you get an 'A' for your homework. Look, I haven't had a day off since about 1993, and I'm not about to miss the first pitch at Shea Stadium."

Kilborn rested his cigar in a marble ashtray. "What I'm not doing a very good job of saying is, I want to commission you to write a book for us."

8

"What, my memoirs?"

"No," Kilborn said. "About the Mormons."

Luke halfway expected the crew of Candid Camera to appear from under the desk. He was puzzled. And insulted.

"A few years ago, I attended a strange religious conference at Madison Square Garden," Kilborn said, puffing away madly. "Gordon Hinckley, the leader of the Mormons, spoke. I trust you've heard of the Mormons."

Luke shrugged. "I don't own any Mormon Tabernacle Choir CDs, if that's what you're asking. I've met a couple. I've read a little about them. They're the polygamists, right? I believe their motto is 'Seven brides for every brother.'"

Kilborn roared with laughter. "Great sense of humor. I like you, son. This is going to work out splendidly."

"What are you talking about?"

"Here's my plan. I want you to live in Utah for a year, get to know the Mormons, earn their trust, join their cult. Get on the inside. Write about your experiences. I can feel a best-seller."

"A best-seller, coming out of Utah? About Mormons? Please. I think you've been smoking too many of those cigars. Congratulations, Jack. You've cornered the market on crazy. You want to banish me to Utah, to live among the Mormons and study them. Like Jane Goodall and the chimpanzees? Look, I've covered the O.J. Simpson murder trial, the Summer Olympics, and the Super Bowl. And you want me to monkey around with Mormons?"

"Son, if you'll just let me explain."

"No, let *me* explain. First, don't call me 'son.' Ever. Second, is this what this meeting is about? I'm flattered, *really*, but I'm working for the *Post*, not some church newsletter. You think I'm going to throw my career down the sewer to write a book about some cult from Utah? Well, save your breath and your time. I'd rather move to Pennsylvania and write about the Amish. I'm not doing your book report, Jack. Thanks for the laughs."

Luke arose from his chair, spun around, and had his hand on the brass door handle when Kilborn lobbed a bombshell: "I'll pay you $250,000 up front."

Luke froze. Then he turned around slowly. *"Whaaat?"*

"A $250,000 advance and another quarter million upon completion. And that's not including future royalties."

Luke found his way back to the chair. The absurdity of the offer was enough to make him listen a little longer.

"You want to be rich, right?" Kilborn asked. "You want to win the Pulitzer, right? It's all within your grasp. I'm handing you the chance at a Pulitzer on a silver platter. I am willing to pay you $250,000, right now, if you agree to do it, plus another quarter million when it's done."

For perhaps the first time in his life, Luke was speechless.

"Now that I've got your attention, let me tell you that I'm a patient man," Kilborn continued, his voice rising gradually and the purplish veins in his neck bulging. "I wouldn't invite you here unless I was very serious about this. I don't bring in thirty-two-year-old prima donnas like you off the street for my health. There are hundreds of guys out there who would cough up their gall-bladder right here on my carpet for the chance I'm offering. You have a lot of talent. I can't believe it's wasted on such a self-absorbed idiot. You're irreverent, insolent, and arrogant . . ."

"Don't try to flatter me, Jack."

". . . and that's exactly why you're perfect for this project. I like your slash-and-burn style. If there's anybody who can find the chinks in the Mormons' armor, it's you. I've got a plane ticket to Salt Lake City for two months from today, and I've made arrangements for you to drive a nice car and live in a nice house. I'll pay you a generous monthly stipend, too. All you have to do is examine Mormonism, incognito, from the inside-out and write about your experiences. You'll bring Mormondom to its knees. Then you'll collect a hefty paycheck and, maybe, win a Pulitzer. After that, the *Post* will be begging you to come back. By then, you'll be able to write your own ticket to any news organization you want. We'll even sign you to a long-term book deal, if you'd like."

Luke tried to make sense of it all. He had heard a little about Mormons when he was growing up. He remembered that a bunch of them seemed to descend on Syracuse every summer to attend a nearby play about their religion. But he never paid much attention. "Why Mormons? Who cares about them? Why not, say, a book on pro-wrestlers-turned-politicians?"

"Because we already did one of those. Mormonism is fresh material for us. The Mormons make up the wealthiest, most powerful religious cult in this country. They believe they are going to rule the world some day. One expert projects that in eighty years, Mormon membership will reach 260 million people. Their designs are to make this country, and the world, a Mormon Empire. They won't be satisfied until they impose their beliefs on every human being. They are bent on brainwashing everyone they come in contact with. They say they have nothing to hide. Well, I say that is an open invitation for scrutiny. You ask 'Why Mormons?' So, I ask you, Luke, why not the Mormons?"

Luke's curiosity was somewhat piqued, but, of course, he was still skeptical. Kilborn returned to his chair and rocked back, fishing for some sort of response. Luke was leaning forward, head down, arms resting on his knees, staring at the floor.

Kilborn forged ahead. "The Mormons like to tell this story. In the 1800s in upstate New York there was a boy who wanted to know which church he should join. According to the legend, he went into a forest, prayed, and claimed to receive a visitation from God and Jesus. Did you hear that? God and Jesus! That boy's name was Joe Smith, founder of the Mormon Church."

"I'm familiar with the name," Luke said, looking up. "There are a lot of crackpots who claim to have visions. If I had a nickel for every apparition of the Virgin Mary at a certain 7-11 in Queens I've heard about, I could buy the Vatican."

"My point exactly. This is the biggest hoax in the history of the world. Millions of people have bought into it. Now's the time to expose the Mormons for the frauds they are. The Mormons are taking over influential positions all over the country. Steve Young's a Mormon. The Marriott Hotel chain is owned by Mormons. Larry King is married to a Mormon. For crying out loud, Gladys Knight is a Mormon."

"What about the Pips?"

"I don't know, but I'll expect you to find out. I do know our government actively recruits Mormons for the CIA. Mormons are crawling everywhere in the FBI, too. Hundreds of books have been written about the Mormons, but nothing like this one. You'll weave everything together, the fascinating history of the Mormons, along with a first-person account of the modern-day rank-and-file. With your writing ability, people will eat this stuff up with a spoon."

Luke was somewhat swayed by Kilborn's passionate monologue. Of course, the $500,000 dangling carrot had something to do with it, too.

"Once the book's finished, you'll go on book-signing tours. You'll hit all the major talk shows," Kilborn said. "We'll negotiate the film rights."

Luke was interested, mainly in the money and fame. "Whoa, Jack," he said. "I'll have to think about it."

"By all means, think about it," Kilborn said, flashing a wily smile. "Take all the time you need. Just give me your decision within the week." He slid an envelope across the desk. "Open it."

Enclosed were two checks made out to Luke Manning totaling $500,000. He counted each and every zero. Twice. Kilborn snatched the checks back and placed them in a drawer. "This is yours, as soon as you say the word."

"I'll be in touch," Luke said.

CHAPTER 3

Considering this new development in his life, Luke didn't go to Shea Stadium that day, and never mind Atlantic City. Reeling from Kilborn's stunning offer, he canceled his plans and returned to his apartment on Manhattan's Upper West side.

Luke turned on the television and mindlessly watched Governor Sharples, pasty white and visibly shaken, grovel before the people of New York, admit his gambling habit, and apologize for his mistakes and connections with the under-world. As cameras whirred, the governor vowed to pay his debts and receive professional help for his addiction. Then, with his family by his side, he announced his resignation, effective immediately. He did not field questions from the media afterward. Indictments and prison time were likely for the governor of the great state of New York. The Justice Department had already opened up a federal investigation. Letterman and Leno were probably already cranking out the one-liners about it for that night's monologues.

Ordinarily, Luke would have taken great delight in witnessing this scene—having a hand in a public official's ignominious undoing. But on this day, given the circumstances, he had practically forgotten all about it. He had a decision to make.

Luke never believed what anyone said; he never took anyone at face value. He had to verify everything for himself. In this case, he made numerous phone calls to find out about Kilborn and his publishing company. He was suspicious of the offer, but he knew Halcyon was a respected, big-time publishing house. As far as he could tell, everything was legit.

But spending twelve months of my life in Utah? Surely the ransom should be more than $500,000, Luke thought. So he called Kilborn and reminded him that Hillary Rodham Clinton had received a seven-million-dollar advance on one of her books. "And you gave the mayor three million for his," Luke said. "I won't do it for less than one million. A million to you guys is pocket change anyway. I'll need that kind of money because I may need serious therapy when I'm done."

A part of him was hoping Kilborn would withdraw the offer. Then he'd be off the hook and he could resume his life. Kilborn was reluctant at first, but to Luke's surprise, he eventually caved in. "Okay," he said, "one million dollars it is. But it had better be a million-dollar book."

Luke still didn't commit, though. For two days he contemplated Kilborn's pet project. It was his chance to make some serious money. But was all the cash in the world worth putting his career and his life on hold for one year? One minute, he wanted to call Kilborn and tell him to stick that check in his mouth and smoke it. The next, he wanted to use that check to buy a house in the suburbs.

Maybe, he thought, this book would catapult him to national stardom. Maybe the place to find the story that would make his career was in, of all places, Utah.

But why Mormons? he wondered. He had met a few. He knew Dave Checketts, the former president and CEO of Madison Square Garden, was a Mormon. He remembered that a Mormon, Mitt Romney, made big news when he ran against Senator Ted Kennedy in Massachusetts years earlier. Then again when he saved the Winter Olympics. He also recalled the ruckus basketball player Dennis Rodman caused when he used profanity to describe the Mormons during the NBA finals. Like Rodman, Luke was sure he couldn't survive in Utah, light years from the East Coast.

If he were to masquerade as a Mormon for a year, that would mean a temporary hiatus on some of his favorite pastimes—namely baseball, drinking, and chasing women (not necessarily in that order). Then he remembered that check. And Kilborn's promises. The idea of book-signings and making the rounds on the talk show circuit appealed to him. This Mormon gig intrigued him. After it was over, he could work wherever he wanted and continue to write best-sellers. There was no doubt in his mind that he could put together a fascinating tome on any subject, even Mormons. He had always believed writing books full-time was the next rung on the career ladder. Perhaps the time was right to make the jump.

Late that afternoon, he left the confines of his apartment and strolled around Central Park. Taking in the New York City sights and sounds and smells, he couldn't imagine the thought of living in a Mormon environment, whatever that was. He could only imagine. A convent came to mind. This Mormon Assignment would be unlike anything he had ever done before.

Anytime Luke wanted to do some serious thinking, he'd go to a baseball game alone. He sat in the box seats in Shea Stadium on a Saturday afternoon with a hot dog and a beer. A scorecard rested on his leg. It was all very relaxing. Until Peter Bartholomew showed up.

"Mind if I sit down?" Peter asked.

"Yes, I mind. This is a baseball game. You're dressed like you're going to a funeral."

"Well, the way the Mets have been playing," Peter said with a pitying smile, "I think I'm dressed appropriately."

Peter Bartholomew worked for the rival *New York Times*. He and Luke never did get along. Not since the night they met at a university journalism awards dinner while they were in college. Peter, a gaunt blond with a surfer's 'do, was attending Columbia University and up for the same award as Luke. Peter won the plaque and the check. Luke finished second. Peter was not exactly gracious in victory, droning on about himself being the next Woodward *and* Bernstein. A couple of months later, Luke landed a job with the *Post,* and Peter got on with the *Times*. Luke went head-to-head with Peter and beat him on most stories. But when the Pulitzer Prize was handed out, it was Peter who won it, for a story that Luke felt he had lucked into. Peter gloated about it at every opportunity. On that afternoon at Shea, or on any afternoon, Bartholomew was the last person Luke wanted to see.

"I don't see why we can't get along," Peter said, taking a seat next to Luke, whose eyes were fixed on the baseball diamond. "You must still be upset about the Pulitzer. Are you?"

Luke made a notation in the scorecard, then took a sip of beer. "Did you say something?"

Peter stretched out his legs. "You're just jealous."

"What do you want from me? I'm trying to watch a ball game here," Luke said. "Take your two-bit writing skills and your Hollywood studio teeth and let me enjoy this game in peace. You know the only reason why you won the Pulitzer over me is because you're a preppy Ivy League boy. Your daddy bought out the committee. I can outwrite you with the left side of my brain tied behind my back. You know it and I know it. So why don't you go home and polish your lovely awards."

"Like I said, you're jealous."

Luke flipped his hand, knocking his beer onto Peter's lap and soaking his pants.

"Looks like you had a little accident," Luke said as Peter jumped to his feet, shrieking. "If you didn't know where the bathrooms were," Luke added, "why didn't you just ask?"

"I'm sending you the cleaning bill for this!" Peter yelled as nearby fans jeered him. "This is an expensive suit!"

"Sit down, you pantywaist!" screamed a fan wearing a bright blue wig and a Mets logo painted on his chest. A brawny stadium security guard chugged toward them. "Mr. Manning, is this guy bugging you?"

"Yeah, but he was just leaving. Take it easy on him. He's got this bladder control problem."

"You'll pay for this," Peter said. "And I'm not just talking about the suit." With that he made a hasty exit.

That incident put a whole new spin on his decision. If he wrote a best-seller, that in and of itself would probably drive Peter to the grave. *For that reason alone, maybe going to Utah is the right thing to do*, Luke thought.

After three agonizing days of weighing all of his options, he experienced an epiphany of sorts while eating a Philly cheesesteak at a deli in Greenwich Village, even though on principle Luke didn't believe in epiphanies. The answer was clear. He enjoyed taking risks and he wanted to prove to himself, and everyone else, that he could do it. Besides, he had a million little reasons to take the offer. Luke knew it would be tough to abandon stories about murder and mayhem for one about Mormons. But he relished the challenge.

So he picked up the phone to deliver the news to Kilborn. He was going to Utah.

CHAPTER 4

At first, Luke didn't tell anyone else about his career move. Not that he had any real close friends to confide in. Besides, he couldn't tell people what he was doing, or he'd jeopardize his cover. Luke told his colleagues at the paper he had to get away and that he was going to work on a personal project for a while.

When Luke informed his *Post* employers he was taking a leave of absence, they were not amused. For two hours a group of editors and even the publisher discussed his future with him, but Luke held firm. The paper offered him a substantial pay raise as well as other benefits. But they didn't come close to what Kilborn was giving him.

Luke met with Kilborn at a posh Manhattan eatery, Smith and Wollensky steak house, to seal the deal. Over drinks and medium-rare steaks the size of manhole covers, they talked about the book. Luke read over the contract, even scanned the fine print. He considered hiring a literary agent to look it over, but how complex could it be? He was getting $500,000 up front, and an agent would just skim about fifteen percent right off the top. Besides, he took a business law class in college. After a few minutes of eating appetizers, he affixed his signature to the contract.

"You'll be living in a place called Helaman, a town about fifty minutes south of Salt Lake," Kilborn said.

"How did you say you pronounce that?" Luke asked.

"Hell-a-man, I believe."

"I couldn't have made up a better name."

"It's a perfect setting, too. I hear you can't sling a dead cat without hitting a Mormon there. Utah County is always making news for being backward. They tried to run a lesbian school teacher out of town. They have laws against nudes posing for art classes. They don't drink or smoke. They don't dance. They don't watch R-rated or even PG movies."

"Sounds like they are trying to live in the '50s," Luke said. "The 1850s."

"Every other week Utah County is making national news for one reason or another," Kilborn said, wiping his mouth with a napkin. "There's never a shortage of controversial stories coming from there. I want you to 'become' a Mormon so you have a view of Mormonism from a front-row seat. They have a very closed society. If there's anyone who can infiltrate the 'Latter-day Ain'ts,' it's you. Did you know they frequently excommunicate members who criticize church leaders? I hear some members have disappeared without a trace."

"It's probably the Mormon mafia." Luke narrowed his eyes as he considered this.

"Wouldn't surprise me. With all that money, there's got to be scandals and cover-ups and power struggles in there somewhere."

Luke fondled his glass of expensive wine. Scandals and coverups. He might like this assignment after all.

"Scandals can be found if you look in the right places," Kilborn continued. "You'll expose them for who they really are. You'll explain them to people like only you can. You know, this book will make you the Mormon Church's version of Salmon Rushdie. But at least you can be reasonably sure they won't put a bounty on your head and try to kill you. I think."

"Unless the Mormon mafia gets me," Luke said. "So, what kind of digs will I be living in during my stay in Utah? Deluxe accommodations, I'm sure."

"Not bad. But I want you to fit in with the average, middle-class Mormon family, just without a brooding wife and a brood of kids. I've got you a decent house with a view of the mountains. We don't want it to look too suspicious. But I've allowed you one toy. I bought you a used Corvette. Anyway, the house and car are all paid for. Plus, like the contract states, I'll give you $2,500 a month. On that, you'll live like a king in Utah."

"That's not saying much," Luke said. "A Corvette, really?"

"Really." Kilborn picked up his glass of red wine and decided to propose a toast. "To you, to us, and to *My Year Among The Mormons*. May this be a successful venture," he said as the two men clanked their glasses.

"My year among the Mormons?" Luke asked before taking a prolonged swallow.

"That's your working title—*My Year Among The Mormons: The inside story of America's most powerful cult.*"

"Thanks for consulting me," Luke said. "I haven't even left yet and you've already got the book jacket written. I guess that title will do until I think of something better." He paused. "So you really think we're sitting on a best-seller?"

Kilborn motioned the waiter for the check.

"You'll *make* it a best-seller. I've got boxes of books and pamphlets on the Mormons, written by Mormons and anti-Mormons. It'll give you something to do in the next few weeks."

"As if I can't think of anything better to do before commending my soul to Mormon purgatory."

In the days before going to Utah, Luke deposited Kilborn's check and paid off his credit card debts. Most of the money he used as a down payment on a house in Greenwich, Connecticut, not far from New York City. Most of his house payment, he figured, would be taken care of by Kilborn's monthly checks. Anyway, it was a dream come true. Growing up, he had always heard stories about the rich people living in Connecticut. To him, that was a sign of having arrived. He couldn't wait to return in a year to live in the nine-bedroom, five-bathroom estate complete with a gourmet kitchen and three marble bath tubs. There was a library upstairs and a tennis court in the backyard. He knew it was way too big for his needs—except for parties, of course—but it was a status symbol. It was the mere fact that he could buy such a place. At the very least, it was a good investment.

Luke spent his final night in New York City hitting all of the dance clubs. In the wee morning hours, he packed and moved out of his apartment. Ready or not, he was going to make the trek to Utah.

He never liked to go into a story with preconceived ideas, but in this case, it didn't look good for the Mormons, whom he deemed to be woefully misinformed and misguided. *The Mormons don't know what they are in for,* Luke thought. He almost felt sorry for them. Almost.

CHAPTER 5

Luke considered himself well-traveled, but he had never been to Utah. Not that he ever felt a void in his life because of it. Two months after that first meeting with Kilborn, he boarded a plane bound for Salt Lake City. He was a little wistful as he walked through JFK Airport, knowing he wouldn't be back for a full year. He felt as though he might as well be going to Mozambique. On the plane he sat in first-class—Kilborn insisted and Luke, for once, did not put up any fight—and started flirting with the young flight attendant before takeoff. Somewhere over the midwest, he ordered a Bloody Mary and started reading an anti-Mormon book that he found compelling. There were tales of bizarre Mormon practices and beliefs. Stuff about strange underwear.

As the plane descended into Salt Lake City International Airport, Luke peered out the window. It was a resplendent, cloudless Saturday afternoon in June. He marveled at the regal mountains and gazed down on the Great Salt Lake, though, from what he could see, there was nothing great about it. Luke realized, while taking in an aerial view of Utah, that this was going to be a major adjustment.

After deplaning, he spotted a portly, bearded man in a Hawaiian shirt, Bermuda shorts, Birkinstocks, and a diamond stud in his right ear. The man held up a sign that read, "Luke Manning."

"I suppose you're my ride," Luke said as he approached. "You must be one of Jack's henchmen."

"So you're Luke Manning. Heaven help you," said the man. "I'm Woody Elfgren. I'll be your escort to Happy Valley."

"Happy Valley?"

"That's where you'll be spending the next year."

"Talk about oxymorons."

"You got that right."

Woody worked for Halcyon Publishing's Los Angeles-based offices and was somewhat familiar with Utah, but no more than he had to be. "Let me take you on a tour of Salt Lake City while we're here."

"Is that a threat?"

"C'mon, it'll only take five minutes," Woody said as they retrieved Luke's baggage. "No extra charge."

"As tempting as that sounds, I just want to get settled. I'm sure I'll get up here eventually."

"I'd bet on it," Woody said. "After a couple of days in Utah County, this will look like paradise."

That doesn't bode well, Luke thought.

They walked to the parking lot and got into a silver Cadillac. During their journey south down I-15, Luke noticed the Stockton-to-Malone car dealership and a billboard with the smiling visage of LaVell Edwards.

"They call this the Point of the Mountain," Woody said, pointing up ahead. "You can just consider this your Point of No Return."

"You really have a gift for making people feel comfortable," Luke said.

"You know how you get to Utah County from Los Angeles, don't you?" Woody asked. "Travel north until you smell it, then go east until you step in it."

"So you're a comedian, too."

On the right side of the freeway was the state prison. "That's where they lock up people who don't go to church on Sundays," Woody said. Luke thought he was being facetious, but he couldn't tell for sure.

Minutes later they passed Thanksgiving Point. "That's Johnny Miller's golf course," Woody said. "Mention my name and you should be able to walk right on."

"How bad is it here?" Luke asked.

"Let me put it this way. I wouldn't drink the water. I try to stay away from the Mormons myself while I'm here, but I guess you've got no other choice. The Mormon influence is everywhere in this place. It's scary."

Scary wasn't the adjective Luke would have used to describe Utah, upon first impression. More like sterile. Boring. Empty. Just mountains, miles of open space, pastures, suburbs, and a few shopping malls.

"Do you ever worry about those mountains crumbling to the ground while you're here?" Luke asked.

"Naw," Woody replied. "I'm from California. We don't worry about anything. We've lived through earthquakes and Rodney King. By the way, Utah is due for a doozy of a quake here soon."

"I'm making a new rule," Luke said. "Don't talk anymore."

Woody merged off the freeway and headed west. Eventually, they were welcomed by a small sign on the side of the road. "Welcome to Helaman. A Little Piece of Heaven." Luke laughed aloud as he copied down the words in his notebook.

Soon, Luke and Woody saw a herd of cows grazing inside a fenced area. Then they passed a family of four riding horses down the middle of the street. Woody had to swerve to avoid hitting them.

"Jack never told me I was being sent to a dude ranch," Luke said. "I left my cowboy boots, belt buckle and ten-gallon cowboy hat in my other suitcase at home."

Woody made a left turn off the main street, where there stood a row of modest, two-story brick houses with well-manicured lawns. He pulled into a driveway that had a red Corvette parked out front looking terribly out of place.

"This is it," Woody announced.

"Is that my car?" Luke asked.

"All yours."

Luke looked at the house. "Maybe I'll just live in the car," he said.

Still, Luke liked the idea of living in a place with its own yard and its own grass, even though he didn't even know how to operate a lawnmower. He got out of the Cadillac and grabbed his luggage from the back seat and the trunk. The place was so quiet, he could almost hear New York. Soon, the stench of manure filled his lungs and his allergies started acting up. He sneezed three times in a row.

"Should have brought a gas mask," he muttered to himself.

After putting his suitcases down, he ran his hand across the hood of his new car. "Wow," he said. "I think I'm in love."

"Here are the keys to your car and your house," Woody said. "Good luck. I'd love to stay and throw you a house-warming party, but I've got to get out of here. I'm starting to develop a rash."

The two men shook hands and with that, Woody got back in his car and disappeared down the road.

Standing alone, and feeling very alone, Luke felt the sun beating down. He ventured up the driveway, unlocked the front door of the house, pushed it open and was greeted by a blast of cool, damp air. The smallish abode, built in the early 1960s, wasn't luxurious by any stretch of the imagination, especially compared to his apartment in Manhattan. For some odd reason, the place smelled of liniment and prune juice, as if it had been the AARP headquarters. He pulled out some cologne from his suitcase and sprayed it liberally throughout the living room.

All in all, the house wasn't anything to e-mail home about. The living room was well-furnished, complete with a leather couch, a couple of recliners, and a big-screen television. It wasn't spectacular, but very livable. Just fine for a bachelor's pad. He kept reminding himself it was only for one year. He walked in the kitchen and found a refrigerator stocked with food. Down the hallway was the master bedroom, featuring a king-sized bed.

One more room beckoned—a den with a cherry wood desk, leather chair, computer, printer, fax machine, and a view of the mountains. Next to the mouse pad was an envelope with his first monthly check inside. A handwritten message was scratched on an attached note. *Hope you like the place. Go get 'em.* It was signed *Jack*. Next to the computer was a cigar.

Luke unpacked his belongings then flopped on the couch and took a two-hour nap.

CHAPTER 6

When Luke awoke, he flipped on the television and raced through the stations until he found a baseball game. Hearing a gentle rapping at the door, he was tempted not to answer it, but the knocking would not cease. He dragged himself off the couch, looked out the peephole and saw a clean-cut man, about his age, wearing faded Levis and a BYU T-shirt that said, "1997 Cotton Bowl Champs." In his hands was a plastic jar. Standing next to him was a young girl with freckles, big brown eyes, and pig tails. *Must be selling Girl Scout Cookies,* Luke thought.

He reluctantly swung open the door. "Hey," he said, "what do you need?"

"Hi, I'm Ben Kimball. I live across the street," said the man, gesturing toward his house. He stood a good four inches shorter than Luke and sported glasses, short-cropped hair, and a lopsided smile. Luke thought the man possessed the most honest face this side of Opie Taylor. Ben reached out and shook Luke's hand. "And this is my daughter, Brooklyn."

"I'm Luke. Luke Manning," he replied.

The young girl was staring up at him with trepidation.

"Your name is *Brooklyn*?" Luke said, looking down at her. "You know, there's a borough in New York by that name."

"I've always loved the Dodgers," Ben explained. "I didn't tell my wife that the Dodgers used to play in Brooklyn; otherwise she would have never gone for it. Are you from New York?"

"That's right."

"Wow, New York," Ben said. "This has got to be quite a shock to your system, huh?"

"About ten thousand volts worth. You must be the official welcome wagon. Don't waste any time, do you?"

"I saw the moving van a couple of days ago, and the movers told me you'd be arriving this weekend. How was your trip out here?"

"Long and uneventful. Tell me something. Does it always smell like this here? I mean, like a rodeo?"

"Pretty much," Ben replied, taken aback by Luke's manner. "But we like it here. In time, you'll like it here, too. What do you do for a living?"

"I'm a freelance writer. I thought this might be a good place to work. Nice and quiet. How about you?"

"I work at Kimballs' Market on Main Street," Ben said. "Lowest prices in town. Of course, we're the only market in town."

Luke did not laugh at Ben's attempt at humor. "How long have you lived in Helaman?" he asked.

Ben snickered. "Actually, it's pronounced Heal-a-man."

"Not Hell-a-man?"

"Afraid not."

"Thanks for setting me straight."

"No problem. Well, I don't want to take up your whole afternoon. I just wanted to stop by and meet you. If you ever need anything, just ask. Oh, my wife made these treats for you. Hope you enjoy them." Ben handed over the jar filled with chocolate chip cookies.

Luke couldn't remember when anyone had ever made him cookies before. What he had read in Kilborn's materials appeared to be right. These Mormons sure liked killing people with kindness. "Thanks," he said. "But it might take me until Christmas to eat all of these."

"Daddy," Brooklyn said quietly, tugging on Ben's pantleg. "He talks funny."

"That's not nice to say, Brooklyn."

"Sorry Daddy," she said. "But he does talk funny."

"*I* talk funny?" Luke said, laughing. "You're a spunky one."

"What's spunky?" she asked.

"It means you're a handful," Ben said.

"A handful of what?" she asked again.

"Are you married?" Ben asked. Luke just laughed and shook his head.

"Do you have other kids?" Luke asked Ben.

"Would you believe three others?" Ben said. "Brooklyn's our oldest."

"Never a dull moment at your place, I imagine."

"Never," Ben said. "Nice car you have."

"It looks like a spaceship," Brooklyn said.

"Maybe I'll give you a ride in it sometime," Luke said.

"Can I, Dad?"

"I guess so, as long as the spaceship has seat belts," Ben said.

Luke started to get the feeling he would need a court order to remove these people from his porch. "Thanks for the cookies," he said again.

"You're welcome," Ben said. "It was nice meeting you."

"Likewise."

"Bye," Brooklyn said, taking her dad's hand and skipping toward the sidewalk.

Luke closed the door and stood there momentarily, chuckling to himself, then marched directly to the den. Inspired, having met Utah Mormons for the first time, he sat down at his computer, rested a pen behind his ear and started typing the word *MORMONVILLE* along the top of the screen. He liked that title better than *My Year Among The Mormons*.

Luke had officially begun his book. In celebration, and in tribute to Kilborn, he lit the cigar.

The rest of the day and into the evening, Luke worked on a rough draft of the first chapter. *Utah is a world shrink-wrapped in old-fashioned idealism,* he wrote. *But beneath the rose-colored facade lurks the dark side of Mormonism.*

Too stuffy, he thought as he highlighted the words and punched the delete key.

So he began again. Luke opened with his arrival in Utah and an overview of Mormon history, gleaning information from books, then retelling the story by spicing it up with his own acerbic commentary. He only wished someone had published a book called Mormonism For Dummies to save him some time.

Meanwhile, a steady stream of shiny, happy people arrived at his door in about ten-minute intervals, dropping off house-warming gifts and disrupting his work. Before long, his kitchen counter was filled with pastries and plants. Each encounter gave him more material to work with.

In the den, he was surrounded by dozens of LDS-related books provided by Kilborn, written by Mormons, non-Mormons, and anti-Mormons. His favorite LDS material, though, was by an old-time General Authority named J. Golden Kimball. Luke instantly had the utmost respect for a Mormon who wasn't afraid to curse every now and again.

The more he read about Mormons, the more interested he became. Here was one of the most powerful religions in the world that sprouted after a simple farm boy claimed to talk to deity. After that, tales of mystery followed. There was a story about gold plates, delivered by an angel, no less, which allegedly detailed the discovery and history of America. *If this stuff were true*, Luke wrote, *it would be the biggest story in the history of the world*. The fact that nearly 12 million Mormons actually claimed to believe this stuff amazed him.

Certainly, there were plenty of controversial topics to write about. He included overviews of the persecution of the Mormons, the pioneer trek across the country led by Brigham Young, the establishment of Utah, the Mountain Meadows massacre, and polygamy, for starters. Some of the stories he came across, like the one about the seagulls eating the crickets in the Salt Lake Valley, he found to be apocryphal. Yet he knew full well that the key to this book being a success was his own personal experiences among the Mormons.

As much as he loathed having to hang out with these people, he knew it was the only way. He had to find out the inner workings of the church and the experiences of the regular church membership, to discover what they honestly felt and thought. Which was why no one could know his real purpose in Utah.

Certainly, Luke had strong opinions on the subject of religion. He had attended various church services over the years, mostly on assignment, and it only confirmed what he already believed—that religion was a fruitless, time-wasting endeavor. The only good thing was that religious zealots usually made for entertaining reading. He had won an award for his coverage of the fiery destruction of a cult years earlier in a town he not-so-fondly called "WACK-O," Texas.

This was the gospel according to Luke Manning: He did not believe in God and thought people who did were weak-willed. Cowards prayed. He believed those who had to rely on faith or intangible, illogical beliefs were foolish. He whole-heartedly endorsed all the adages about religion being a crutch and opiate of the masses. He didn't need it. Religious people looked for excuses for when good things and bad things happened. Religious leaders played to people's insecurities, preyed on their gullibility, and profited from them. He had seen it countless times. He had no use for people who were self-righteous and narrow-minded. Aside from that, religious people were hypocritical. And if there was one thing he despised, it was a hypocrite.

Life had dealt Luke a bad hand, but he'd played it out all right. He didn't need a family to get him to where he was. He was a self-made man. He saw in himself the classic, American rags-to-riches story: a boy born in challenging circumstances who had grown up to be a difference-maker. As a journalist, he altered the way people looked at life. And he loved it—poking around the underbelly of controversy, discovering something new, and telling the world about it. He had painstakingly cultivated a network of well-placed sources throughout the city, state, and country, and he tirelessly worked the phones in search of stories. He had a flashy, distinctive writing style—which is one reason the *Post* hired him out of college.

He also had a knack for getting what he wanted, by lulling people—manipulating them, really—into a false sense of security. Before they knew it, they were revealing to him trade secrets or intimate personal experiences. Sure enough, the next day those secrets and experiences would show up in the paper for public viewing. Just by walking into a room, he could scare PR spin doctors right out of their silk ties. He made press agents cry on a regular basis. He had given the mayor's press secretary a permanent facial tic.

Depending on who you asked, Luke was one of the most popular and most loathed reporters in New York. His goal was to expose the truth. If doing so made people angry, which it often did, so much the better. But mostly, he didn't care what anyone thought of him or his work. He relished the search for unseemly facts on people and organizations. He enjoyed being among people, studying them, carrying on with them a brief, impersonal relationship, milking them for information, chronicling their tale and moving on. And that was exactly what he planned to do in Utah.

After writing for several hours, Luke finally fell asleep in the chair. At 5 a.m., he awoke and stumbled into his new bed.

CHAPTER 7

Next thing Luke knew, he was awakened by bright sunlight pouring into his room. He peeked through the blinds and squinted at a cloudless, powder-blue sky. Much to his dismay, moving to Utah had not been a bad dream after all. He put on a bathrobe and headed for the kitchen. It was almost ten o'clock, Sunday morning. He turned to CNN to find out what was going on in the world, since he felt like he was on Neptune.

While eating cold cereal, he was startled by a knock on the door. Luke was unshaven and tired of the constant interruptions. A smiling, middle-aged woman holding a large paper sack stood on the doorstep. Luke was not in the mood.

"Good morning," the woman said brightly. "I hope I didn't disturb you."

"Oh, not at all," Luke replied, rubbing his eyes. "I love to have visitors on Sunday mornings."

Not appearing to hear the sarcasm in his voice, she continued.

"I'm Monica McGown, president of the Ward Welcoming Committee."

"Luke Manning," he replied. "President of the Leave Me Alone Committee."

Sister McGown's smile froze. "I understand you just moved in and wanted to welcome you to the neighborhood. You wouldn't by chance be LDS?"

"No," Luke said, "but I once tried LSD."

Sister McGown glared at him. "Just a hunch—you don't have many friends, do you? I brought this booklet for you with important information about the city," she continued curtly, handing Luke one thing after another. "This is a magnet for your refrigerator. It has the name and phone number of the bishop, if you ever need to talk to him. And this fruit basket is for you, since you probably haven't had time to do any shopping yet."

Luke stood in the doorway with an armful of trinkets. "What, no key to the city?" he asked.

Sister McGown began to walk away in a huff. "Our church, as you can see, is just down the street. Our meetings start at ten, if you think you'd like to come out sometime."

29

Luke laughed as he placed the magnet on his fridge. Bishop Samuel T. Law, Helaman 6th Ward, it read, with the bishop's home and work phone numbers listed underneath. Included in the stack of literature he received was a ward telephone directory, a copy of the ward newsletter, a ward calendar, and a brochure about the city of Helaman. It featured black-and-white pictures and a brief history of Helaman. Luke grabbed a banana from the fruit basket and started to read.

"Our fair city of Helaman (pop. 4,076) was founded in 1853 by a group of intrepid Mormon pioneers seeking a place to settle, for 'a little piece of heaven.' After seeing the fertile valley, picturesque mountains, the fresh-water stream and sego lillies, they decided to call this locale of exceeding beauty their home. Helaman is named after that righteous Book of Mormon prophet and military commander of the same name."

Looking out his kitchen window, Luke witnessed a procession of well-dressed people walking past his house, making their way to the church. Dozens of people, mostly kids, filed into the church building carrying books and bags. It was as if they had rolled off the Brady Bunch assembly line, he snickered to himself.

He knew he had to get out of there. Besides, he couldn't wait to try out his new set of wheels parked in the driveway. It was the first time in his life that he'd had a car at his disposal. Back in New York, Luke always had to take the subway or taxi cabs if he wanted to go somewhere.

He showered, threw on a pair of shorts and a T-shirt, and tossed his golf clubs in the back of the car. Wherever he went, there was little sign of life beyond the Mormon churches. Restaurants and shops posted signs that read "Closed." Few pedestrians were on the streets and those he did see were dressed in their Sunday best. On nearly every corner, it seemed, he spotted a Mormon church with a parking lot filled to capacity. It was early, but he needed a drink. That was when he tried unsuccessfully to buy a six-pack of beer. So he meandered out of Helaman and continued until he reached State Street, the major thoroughfare in Utah Valley. From time to time, Luke would veer off the main road, hoping to find a golf course. The two golf courses he did manage to find were, naturally, closed.

While driving along some roads in a residential area in Orem, Luke nearly rear-ended a car in front of him whose driver failed to turn on his blinker on a right turn. Luke slammed on his brakes, jumped out of his car, and like any proper New Yorker, screamed obscenities at the driver, who was blithely cruising away. Glancing up at the street sign, Luke read, Courtesy Way, and grimaced.

Then the air conditioning in his car went out. So he rolled down the tinted windows and a steady, furnace-like breeze blasted in his face.

After a while, his stomach began to rumble. Maybe he was hungry. Or sick. He wasn't really in the sightseeing mood, but since he was in the area, he figured he might as well check things out. Following the signs, he wound up in Provo at the campus of Brigham Young University. He was sure he wouldn't find alcohol at the Mormon Church-owned school, but he might as well do some research while he was here. He strode through campus and saw a smattering of students dressed in suits and dresses. They seemed to be staring at him.

On one part of campus, he approached a red-headed co-ed in a floral print dress sitting alone on the grass beneath a tree, reading what appeared to be a Bible, although Luke could only guess.

"Excuse me," he began, trying hard to be polite, though it was against his nature. Startled, the girl looked up at him.

"Can you tell me if there's a bar around here?"

"Excuse me?" She looked at him suspiciously.

"A bar," he repeated.

"You mean, to drink alcohol? I wouldn't know," she sniffed.

"Well, you might try it sometime. It would loosen you up. What do you people do around here for fun?" he asked.

"Well," she said, as if trying to muster all the Christ-like feelings in her soul, "there's a fireside tonight at the Marriott Center."

"A fireside?" he said. "Like a cookout? Does anyone bring a keg?" He loved making people squirm.

The girl smiled awkwardly as she stood up. "Good luck finding whatever it is you're looking for," she said as she hurried away.

Luke returned to his car and started driving again, feeling thirstier than before. He was hot, sweaty, and nauseous. *There's got to be a place to find a drink somewhere in a college town*, he muttered to himself. Then he reminded himself this was not your average college town.

At that moment, Luke decided he officially despised this place. He knew he couldn't live life in slow-motion, surrounded by a bunch of closed-minded people. As he thought about his new house in Connecticut, one year seemed so far away. After a much-longer drive than he would have liked, he found a convenience store in Salt Lake County that actually sold beer. He bought three six-packs. And a bottle of Pepto-Bismol. When he returned to Helaman, he spent the rest of the night drowning his sorrows with both. After reading the fine print on a can of beer, he figured out that beer sold in Utah could have only a maximum of three percent alcohol, compared to five percent back home. He felt cheated.

On the desk in his den, Kilborn had left a one-year calendar. Luke pinned it to the wall and turned the pages. It depressed him. One year seemed like an eternity. He drew a big red "X" over the day he arrived, and he couldn't wait to do the same the following day. He decided it would be a ritual he would perform every day until he returned to New York City.

Then the phone rang. It was Kilborn.

"How's my good 'ol Mormon boy?" he cracked.

"Don't ever call me that, Jack."

Kilborn chortled. "I knew you'd be seriously homesick about now. I'm calling you from Yankee Stadium. It's the bottom of the eight, two outs nobody on, Yanks up 5-2 on the Twins."

Luke was seething. "I may be miserable, but I guarantee you I am going to write the best book that has ever been written on the Mormons. Then I'm going to kidnap you and leave you here for a year. Just to see how you like it. And another thing. That car you got me—the air conditioning has already gone on it."

"Well, what do you expect from a used car?" Kilborn said. "Fix it and send me the bill."

"I'd like to fix you," Luke said.

Kilborn laughed again. Luke hung up.

And to think that it was only his first full day in Mormonville. Three-hundred and sixty-four days to go.

CHAPTER 8

That first week in Utah County turned out to be the longest of Luke's life. There weren't even any cappuccino shops, that he could find. Didn't anyone in Utah County drink cappuccino, or was he as rare an individual in Utah as an English-speaking cab driver was in New York City?

Luke was suffering from some serious Happy Valley Blues, and he felt engulfed by some sort of weird Mormon karma. As far as he was concerned, he might as well have been sentenced to a year at Alcatraz. Utah was the closest thing he'd experienced to being in a Communist country. He'd turn on the radio and TV and there would be all sorts of Mormon propaganda. He'd hear the talk shows that had people defending conservative positions on abortion, capital punishment, and welfare. It made Luke want to scream at his radio, to the point where he had to turn it off. He read the views expressed in letters to the editor in the local paper, and he'd end up tearing it to shreds.

Things got worse one afternoon when he went to a video store in Orem—the one he'd gone to in Helaman did not carry R-rated shows—and checked out a few movies to relieve his boredom. By the time he had returned home, he realized his wallet was missing and remembered leaving it on the top of his car while he opened the door. Immediately, he called his credit card company and the police. Then he drove back to the parking lot, scouring the premises for his wallet. Luke didn't think he'd ever see it again.

That night, he was pacing the hallways of his house, recognizing the irony—that in all his years living in New York, the Pickpocket Capital of the World, he had never lost his wallet. He had to go to Utah to do that. About 7 p.m., a boy dressed in a Boy Scout uniform paid him a visit.

"Excuse me, sir," the teenager said. "Are you Luke Manning?"

"Who wants to know?" Luke said.

"My name is Eric Thomas. Is this your wallet?"

Luke was dumbfounded. "Thanks, kid," he said, taking the wallet. He saw that the $120 in cash was all there and accounted for.

"Where did you find it?" Luke asked.

"I was riding my bike in a parking lot and saw it. I looked through your wallet and saw that you were from New York. Then I found this address on a piece of paper. So I rode my bike up here."

"That's quite a ways to ride a bike," Luke said.

"Yeah," the boy replied. "I think I've earned the cycling merit badge today."

Luke tried to give him fifty dollars as a reward, but the boy wouldn't take it.

"This is my daily good turn. If I took that money, my parents would probably ground me."

"Well, we wouldn't want that."

"Have a good night," the boy said as he rode away.

From then on, Luke rarely, if ever, locked his door at night.

Nevertheless, he missed Manhattan. He even missed Newark, and he deliberately hadn't been there in years. He missed his daily cappuccino, the slices of cheese-laden, greasy pizza he used to buy on the street corners. He missed the rats. He missed the array of chalk outlines on the city sidewalks. He missed the constant din of police sirens. Heck, he missed the pungent odor of the subways.

To keep himself from going stir-crazy, he resolved to keep busy. He obtained a membership to a local gym, which, of course, was closed on Sundays. On his first visit, while doing some bench-pressing, he could sense that a man, possibly in his early forties, was checking him out. When Luke went to the treadmill, the man followed him. As Luke removed a bottle of mineral water from his bag, the man, dressed in a tank top and shorts, approached him.

"You're new here, aren't you?" he said.

"You'll have to be a little more creative than that," Luke said.

"I'm Brock Morton."

"Luke Manning."

The two men shook hands.

"You're not a Mormon, are you?" Brock said.

"You can tell that by the way I shake hands?" Luke said.

"I can just tell."

"I suppose you want to tell me all about your Mormon Church. No offense, but I don't have time for that right now."

Brock began laughing. "I'm not Mormon, either," he said, pulling out a crucifix from underneath his tank top. "It's great to find someone who's not one of *them*. It's like being in a Nazi prison camp and you're the only American.

Then one day you find another American and you feel an immediate bond."

Luke couldn't believe his good luck. Without even trying, he had found another source for his book. "What's it like here?" he asked, trying to get the man to unload, which he did.

"You obviously haven't been here very long, have you?"

"A few days."

Brock shook his head sympathetically. "I need to warn you," he said. "Do you want to go to lunch?"

Luke agreed, knowing he could get some good material this way. He showered, changed and met Brock at a nearby Italian restaurant. Of course, being from New York, Luke had eaten authentic Italian food, but he would settle for what they served at this place.

"So what's so bad about being a non-Mormon in Utah?" Luke asked again after ordering his food.

"How much time do you have?" Brock asked.

"All day, if necessary." Luke clandestinely turned on his tape recorder, which sat on his knee under the table.

"For starters, when I first moved out here from Philadelphia a couple of years ago, the people were so nice. Overly nice, if you know what I mean. They invited me to outings and other social events. I didn't think much of it. I just thought they were friendly people. But that's the trap they set."

"Trap?"

"They just want everyone to be a Mormon. But, when they realize you're not going to convert to their religion, they dump you like yesterday's garbage. You feel ostracized. You're an outcast. I have a friend here who isn't a Mormon either, and the Mormons won't let their kids play with his kids. There's absolutely zero tolerance in this place for anything or anyone who's different from what they believe. When they find out you're not Mormon, the Berlin Wall goes up between you and them. You can tell by the expression on their faces. It's like they don't trust you, just because you're not Mormon. Mormons trust other Mormons implicitly. And you know, for some of these people it isn't enough to be a Mormon. You have to be a Republican, too. As if the Republican Party was God's Party."

Luke had struck oil. "Wild," he murmured encouragingly, shaking his head.

"I grew up in a suburban, middle-class neighborhood outside Philly," Brock continued. "Here I am, a white guy, and I feel like a minority. A foreigner. If you don't have a certain hairstyle, or if you have tattoos or body-piercings, they just categorize you. You know how Utah is shaped like a box?"

"You mean like a square."

"Exactly. Well, if you don't fit into that box, people try to make you fit. If you resist, they'd just as soon put you in a box six feet under the ground. Trying to get a date around here is almost impossible. That's why I always go to Salt Lake for entertainment. It's a little better up there. But down here, if I buy beer I get these strange looks, like I'm going straight to hell. Women hide their children from me. Like I'm the devil himself."

"Ever think about getting out of here?" Luke asked, chomping on a bread stick.

"Sometimes. It can get lonely. But my business is going really well. And I love the recreation opportunities this place has, with all the mountains and bike trails and skiing and waterskiing. Plus, I'm getting used to it. It's funny, growing up I never was religious. My mom used to drag me to mass and I hated it. But since I came out here, in a weird way, I've found God."

"So He is in Utah, then."

"What I mean is, in trying to avoid all the questions and the proselyting attempts, I've actually gotten involved in the Catholic Church. I get so tired of people asking me what ward I'm in. When I can, I wear this cross. It usually wards off the Mormons. On Ash Wednesday, I put ashes on my forehead. That also does the trick."

"Thanks for the tips," Luke said.

"Say," Brock added, "a group of us meet at the church in Orem every week. We go bowling, to the movies, things like that. There are some cute women in our group, too. Would you like to come on Friday night?"

The last thing Luke needed was to go to one church while trying to get into another. One religion was more than enough for him.

"Maybe some other time," he said.

That night, as Luke was about to sit down at his computer to write about his insightful conversation with Brock, Kilborn called again.

"So, how close are you to being a Mormon?" he asked.

"Jack, I've only been here a week."

"From what I understand, it's easier to become a Mormon than it is to get a library card. What I can't understand is how they can have so many converts. Why are so many people being duped? That's what we have to find out."

36

"Maybe the Mormons give away a free toaster when they convert," Luke said.

"On the contrary. They require members to pay an income tax. Ten percent of all they make goes to the Church. They're all about brainwashing and financial exploitation of their members. From what I've read, this church is merely a tax-exempt business. Their financial holdings are in the billions. I'm telling you, Mormonism is a strange religion, full of deceptions. I was reading some more about them last night. The Mormons have power. They have money. They have influence. They're on the cusp of controlling the world if we're not careful. They're meddling in politics. They've spent millions fighting a proposition to make gay and lesbian marriages legal. They've crossed the line. We're going to hammer those Mormons."

"Sounds like this is personal, Jack." Luke said. "Um, Jack, are you at all familiar with the phrases 'conspiracy theory' and 'journalistic fairness'?"

"I'll tell you one thing, Manning, there's a story to tell there. I'm all about two things—getting the truth and selling books."

"Me too."

"Good. We see eye-to-eye on this. I know that the Mormons have a lot to hide. They blindly follow a so-called prophet, Gordon Hinckley, like sheep. He's in his nineties! And claims to be a prophet. Like Moses! If you get the chance to meet this man who claims to be a prophet, why don't you ask him to part the Great Salt Lake?"

"You're scaring me, Jack," Luke said, turning on his computer. "Did you forget to take your medication today? By the way, what's with this Mormon fetish? Most men your age have obsessions with their prostates, 401ks, and Viagra. Yours seems to be Mormons. What gives?"

Kilborn paused for a moment. "It started about two years ago. I came home one rainy night, earlier than usual, about eight o'clock, and there were these two very plain women in their twenties, wearing nametags sitting in my living room, talking to my daughter, Audrey. She was seventeen at the time. I asked who they were and they told me they were missionaries for some church I had never heard of. I told them we weren't interested in buying anything and to get out of my house. My daughter defended them anyway, saying they were her friends. Well, religious freaks are not welcome in my house.

"I found out later they were Mormons. Then my daughter tells me she wants to join their cult. I told her over my dead body. They gave her this book, a

Mormon Bible, and I tossed it into the fireplace."

"Imagine that. Mr. Book Publisher burning a book," Luke said. "What are you, Jack, a neo-Nazi?"

"I had to get rid of it. Just the sight of that book made my skin crawl. Audrey is the love of my life. She's what I live for. I was just trying to protect her. Anyway, she was upset. She ran to her room and cried. Didn't talk to me for about a week. She's a headstrong girl."

"Gee, I wonder where she gets that."

"Anyway, a few days later, she went back to live with my ex-wife—I call her 'Number Three'—in California. Wouldn't you know it? My daughter became a Mormon out there. Her mom gave her permission. I think Number Three did it just to spite me. After I calmed down, I realized I couldn't do anything about it, so I decided I would find out about the Mormons. If I had enough background on them, I knew I would be able to talk to my daughter rationally. Know what? The more I learned about the Mormons, the more interested I became—as a topic for a book. I thought somebody ought to write about it. And it might as well be us. I guess it's like they say, good things can come from the worst situations. We're going to take the Mormons down."

"Jack, look, I don't have a vendetta here, like you," Luke said. "I don't care about the Mormons. In fact, I treat Catholics, Mormons, presidents of the United States, homeless people, and mass murderers all the same way. I'm a skeptic. I've got a job to do, to find the truth and to tell a story, and I'm going to do it. I don't like getting emotionally involved with my work. But I'll tell you one thing: I'm going to write you a million-dollar book. I guarantee it."

"That," Kilborn said, "is what I like to hear."

CHAPTER 9

Luke obtained a prescription to counteract his allergies and went running almost every morning. At first, the open spaces spooked him, but he quickly began to like them. Unfortunately, Luke had to share the roads with a pack of hearty women. He learned later that after they sent their children off to school, they met at a selected sister's house in the ward to eat bran muffins and drink cocoa while they discussed the scriptures. Then they went on five-mile jaunts through town. Folks in the ward, Luke discovered, called these women "The Mormon Battalion" for the way they marched up and down the streets. For his book, Luke nicknamed them "The Mormon Battleaxes."

The purpose of Luke's daily jog was twofold: to exercise and to learn more about the area. Breathing in relatively clean air might even do his body some good, he thought. But it wasn't his body that he was most concerned about. It was his mind. And he feared he just might go out of it before the year was up. During his jogs around town he'd venture up a hill in Helaman, not far from his home. The higher he went, it seemed, the newer the houses were, the wealthier the people were. He found well-scrubbed subdivisions filled with brick homes with sport utility vehicles, plexiglass basketball backboards in the driveway, gnomes, and an array of flower beds on the front lawn.

One large house in particular always caught his attention. All sorts of women would go in and out, carrying books or food or babies or all three at once. He only saw one man, and he seemed to preside over the chaos. Luke noticed the name McMurray on the mailbox. So polygamy does still exist! he thought. That was a chapter right there, just waiting to be written.

Luke lived down below the hill, in the older section of town, filled with average homes on larger lots. It was farm country—with every imaginable live-stock. One yard was populated by llamas.

No matter where he went in town, Luke received a lot of stares, though folks always gave him a cheesy grin, a friendly wave, and a cheerful "hello." The people were kind and courteous. It was like being at a Boy Scout Jamboree. It made him sick.

Still, he tried to stay focused. Though he didn't like the idea, he wanted to become well-versed with everything Mormon. He resigned himself to the fact he had to become All-Mormon, All-The-Time. He wanted to know more about the Mormons than the Mormons themselves, all the while remaining undercover. Not that he was too worried about pulling off the charade. He prided himself on being an accomplished actor. And he discovered right away that becoming a member of the Mormon Church wouldn't be a problem.

Within ten days of arriving in Utah, he was the recipient of two copies of The Book of Mormon. It was a book Kilborn had not given him—the Mormon Bible.

Luke received one while waiting in line at Kimball's Market. If there was one thing he detested, it was grocery shopping, especially at a place that did not sell beer. Since he figured it would be the ideal location to study Mormons—and the fact that his neighbor, Ben, worked there—Luke went anyway. Besides, with the dearth of good restaurants around town, he was stuck having to prepare many of his own meals.

A portly woman noticed Luke in the frozen food aisle and caught up to him in the check-out line. "I've seen you around. You moved into the Winters' house, across from the Kimballs, right?" the woman said. "I'm Sue Fidrych. You must be new in the ward."

"Ward?" Luke replied, playing along. The only ward he was familiar with prior to this assignment was that of the psychiatric variety. He thought it was an apropos term.

"Oh, you must not be a member of the Church," she asked.

"What church?"

"You know, The Church of Jesus Christ of Latter-day Saints. The Mormon Church."

"No, and I plan to keep it that way." He couldn't believe people could operate under the assumption that everyone was Mormon. "Who did you say used to live in my house?"

"Fred and Barbara Winters," she said. "They're an older couple, in their seventies. They're on a Church mission in Nauvoo for the next eighteen months."

That would explain the liniment and prune juice smell in the house, Luke thought.

Sister Fidrych had pledged a couple of days earlier in Relief Society to place a copy of The Book of Mormon into the hands of a non-member. That very morning, she had fasted, hoping to find someone. Then she remembered the newest neighbor in the area wasn't a member of the Church, and so she had followed him from his house to the store.

"You're more than welcome to visit us at church," Sister Fidrych said. "Our meeting house is on Main Street. We meet at ten on Sunday mornings. By the way, there's a book I feel you might be interested in . . ."

"I don't have any change with me," Luke said.

She patted his hand. "I want to give it to you. For free," she said, removing it from her purse. "Just promise me you'll read it."

"I will," he said, "if you promise to leave me alone."

Sister Fidrych later told one of her friends she hadn't been that offended since her daughter, Chloe, wasn't chosen to play Mary in the ward Christmas pageant. But she explained that she looked past that. "I've seen him before somewhere," Sister Fidrych told her friend.

As Luke left the store, he noticed those McMurray women, and their children, filling carts to the brim with groceries—which reminded him he needed to check into this polygamy thing.

He received another copy of the Book of Mormon while he was at a car shop in Provo waiting for the air conditioner to get fixed. The mechanic was a nice enough guy and gave him a good deal on the work and replacement part. He even checked the tires, vacuumed the floors, and washed Luke's car for free. Then, somehow, the mechanic deftly changed the subject of conversation from radiators to religion. It was as if Luke had the word Non-Mormon engraved on his forehead. Luke was given a copy of the Book of Mormon with his receipt.

He had read about, and visited, the Bible Belt. But it had nothing on the Book of Mormon Belt. Luke already despised being surrounded by these apple-cheeked people. They seemed pushy and provincial, oblivious that there was a cruel world out there beyond the mountains. Every fifteen minutes or so he would curse Kilborn's name.

While doing some research, Luke read about an early Mormon pioneer who was commanded by Brigham Young to locate from Salt Lake to Provo. "I'd rather go to hell than go to Provo," was the reply. Luke could relate. As he drove aimlessly through Provo, the giant Y on the mountainside haunted him. He figured it must stand for "Yesteryear."

But it wasn't just Provo that he poked fun at. One afternoon Luke went for a drive in his Corvette to explore Utah County. Most of the people looked like they were lifted off a G-rated movie set. He mocked the city names every time he came across a new one. American Fork? Spanish Fork? Santaquin? Goshen? Pleasant Grove? Lehi? He thought they should rename the whole place Dullsville. Better yet, he concluded, they should burn it down and start over.

Utah County is closed on Sundays, and from what I've seen, it should be shut down the other six days, too," he wrote. *Nightlife in Utah County is an oxymoron of Biblical proportions. There is nothing to do here after eight in the morning. What these people here lack in caffeine they more than make up for in saccharine. . . . Utah's principal export is nineteen-year-old missionaries. Average age in Utah: six. It's a "pretty great state," if you're a toddler. Or in the Federal Witness Protection Program, for that matter . . . I've been to Amish bergs that have more diversity than this place.*

As it turned out, Woody Elfgren was right. Salt Lake City was Luke's respite. There, he found several nightclubs and bars. It was still one of the most lifeless towns he had ever been in, but compared to Utah County, it was like Mardi Gras. He also checked out Temple Square, the Church Office Building, and the Great Salt Lake. He had hoped to float in the Great Salt Lake, as he had read was possible, but when he showed up, it stunk like rotten eggs and unwashed socks. Luke's hometown, Syracuse, held the nickname "Salt City" because of the abundance of salt deposits in that region. But at least Syracuse didn't smell nasty.

This much he had to give to Salt Lake: the wide streets were easy to drive and the linear addresses were easy to find. It didn't take him long to figure out that the center of this town was the Salt Lake Temple, with everything numbered from South Temple, North Temple, West Temple and State. *Which is convenient, if not particularly imaginative*, Luke thought.

What wasn't convenient was trying to get a drink. Brock educated him on the Utah liquor laws—that a person had to buy a membership to a private club first. *Just a classic example of the monotheistic culture and the lack of separation of church and state in Utah,* Luke thought. He purchased a membership to a private club, where he sat next to a twenty-something University of Utah student named Lane, who was between classes. Or frat parties.

Lane sported a mop of orange hair, a tattoo of a Chinese symbol on his left arm, a nose ring, and an earring that could have doubled as a hula hoop.

Finally, Luke thought, *a normal person.*

42

Lane thought it was cool that Luke was from New York.

"Dude, you live in Utah County?" Lane said, laughing. "That sucks. You need to get out of Zoobieland."

"Zoobieland?"

"Yeah, that's what we call BYU and anywhere within a fifteen-mile radius of BYU."

"Why Zoobieland?"

Lane chugged his mug of beer, then wiped the foam from his mouth. "You know, I have no idea. It just fits them. That place is just weird, dude. I don't consider it part of the rest of this state."

"Do you ever get used to living with all these Mormons?" Luke asked.

Lane smiled and said quietly, "Don't let this get out, but I'm a Mormon myself."

"You had me fooled," Luke said.

"I was raised a Mormon," Lane explained. "When I was in high school, I partied it up, dude, you know what I mean? I haven't been to church in about six years. My parents still cry when they see me. My dad's a stake president. Maybe someday I'll go back to church. I'm just taking a sabbatical from religion right now. After all, I've got to learn about life for myself; I'm not just going to rely on what a bunch of old guys say. I guess I'm a Jack Mormon, someone who doesn't practice the religion. I'm not ruling Mormonism completely out. Right now, I just don't consider myself Mormon. Every month I get an invitation to attend the Institute at the U. But that would really mess me up. If I don't go to church or institute, there's no guilt involved. I'm much happier this way. Besides, church, I've found, really interferes with my drinking and partying."

In Lane, Luke found volumes of valuable information. He was a great source. Luke even went to one of his keg parties up the canyon one Saturday night. There was a bonfire, cases of beer, and dozens of U students. Everybody got drunk, even the designated drivers. While going back down the canyon, the car Luke was traveling in weaved back and forth down the two-lane highway, narrowly missing trees and other cars. It had been more than ten years since his college days and he was too old for this, he told himself. They returned to where Luke had left his car at the canyon entrance and he stumbled out, then slept in the back seat of his car until morning, when he was sober enough to drive himself home.

After arriving home, Luke once again observed the weekly church pilgrimage phenomenon outside his front door. With a hangover as big as the Goodyear Blimp, he decided he would just stay indoors. It was safer that way. He made up his mind that he wouldn't spend time with Lane again, as much as he enjoyed getting the information for his book. He could have been killed going down that canyon. The last thing he wanted was to die in Utah.

CHAPTER 10

About one fifteen that afternoon, he was stretched out on the couch, ice pack on his head, watching a baseball game, when his neighbor appeared at the front door again.

"Hi, Luke," Ben said, "I know it's short notice, but we were wondering if you'd like to come over for dinner."

Luke hadn't had a home-cooked meal in who-knew-how-long, and the Utah County restaurant fare was getting old. Besides, he hadn't eaten in a while. "All right," he said, "but you're really twisting my arm here." This was perfect for his book. Field research and free food. Two time-honored tenets of journalism.

When he arrived at the Kimballs' home, his head still throbbing, Brooklyn greeted him with a bashful smile.

Next, Luke met Ben's other three children, Jared, four; Megan, three; and Rebecca, eight months. *This guy probably never heard of birth control,* Luke thought.

Then Ben introduced Luke to an attractive woman in a blue-flowered dress with a white bow on top of her brown hair; she was stirring a pot of mashed potatoes in the kitchen. "This is Stacie, my wife," Ben said.

"Is she the only one?" Luke asked.

"My other three wives are out back, feeding the chickens," Ben replied with a straight face. Stacie burst out laughing.

"Just a joke," Ben said.

"So this is what a Mormon family looks like," Luke said.

"Yep," Ben said. "What gave us away?"

Stacie entered the room carrying a bowl of gravy. She placed it on the table. "I think we're ready," she said.

Once the kids were settled down and seated, Ben offered a blessing over the food. Luke didn't close his eyes and he didn't know what to do with his hands. He noticed that the three oldest kids folded their arms and closed their eyes right on cue.

Luke thought the food was great—roast beef, corn, and mashed potatoes. He thought the red jello with carrot shavings was a little exotic.

"How long have you been Mormons?" Luke asked.

"All our lives," Ben said. "Born and raised."

Perfect, Luke thought. *Just what I was looking for.*

"What does 'Mormon' mean, anyway?" he asked, salting his potatoes.

"It comes from a set of scriptures we believe in—the Book of Mormon," Ben said. "Ever heard of it?"

"I hadn't until I came here," Luke said. "Now I own two unsolicited copies."

"The real name of our church is The Church of Jesus Christ of Latter-day Saints," Ben added.

"Quite the tongue-twister. No wonder you guys shortened it."

Stacie and the kids were uncharacteristically quiet during dinner, while Luke and Ben talked about sports and politics. Brooklyn listened intently to every word. After a while, the kids' initial bashfulness diminished, and Stacie had to keep the younger ones from starting a food fight.

"So, what do you do, Stacie?" Luke asked.

"Pretty much what you see me doing now. I'm a stay-at-home mom," she said, wiping Jell-O stains off Megan's cheeks.

"That's more work than a full-time job," Ben said.

"How do you guys survive on one income?" Luke asked. "That's pretty much unheard of these days."

"Stacie is a whiz at cutting coupons," Ben said. "She's got the callouses to show it."

"Don't you get bored? Don't you ever want a career?" Luke asked Stacie.

"I'm never bored," she replied, giving the crying baby a pacifier. "Believe me."

"Tell me about your job," Ben asked Luke. "What exactly do you write about?"

"Oh, a little of everything," Luke answered, trying to be as vague as possible. "How do you like working at a grocery store?"

"The most exciting part of my day is a price check on mangos," Ben said. "But I like it."

"He's the manager," Stacie chimed in, pouring Ben a glass of water.

"I've been to your store a few times," Luke said. "You guys leave watermelons outside overnight. Don't you have a problem with people stealing them?"

"Not yet," Ben said.

Ben and Luke spent the remainder of the day talking about everything—but religion. They intentionally skirted around that subject, not wanting to get into that prickly topic so early on. Of course, Luke secretly wanted to talk about the Mormon Church, and Ben secretly wanted to bring it up. But for the time being they were having too much fun to let religious issues get in the way. By nightfall, they were talking as if they were long-lost brothers. They discussed baseball, basketball, and football, quoting stats and recalling memorable games, coaches, and athletes. Luke was knowledgeable about BYU and the Utah Jazz, which impressed Ben, and Ben knew all about the Mets and Knicks, which impressed Luke.

Both were amazed at how well they got along. It was as though they had known each other all their lives. Or longer, Ben thought. Luke's explanation? Sports was the world's secular religion, which had the power to connect any two people. Over the next couple of weeks, they got together frequently. For Luke, it was great material for the book, a way to establish an inside source. On the other hand, he knew Ben wasn't the type to lead him to any scandals. At least not wittingly. Ben was so clean, he squeaked when he talked.

For Ben, it was a chance to do missionary work, or at least a chance to enlighten a non-member. And he went the extra mile to do so. Since he had a lawnmower and Luke didn't, Ben mowed his lawn for him. Luke was relieved. He didn't want to be bothered by mundane outdoor chores anyway.

On the Fourth of July, Ben invited Luke to a family barbecue at the Helaman City park. Actually, it was the third of July. The Fourth fell on a Sunday that year, so all the parades and barbecues and fireworks in Utah County were changed to Saturday, the third.

Luke would have preferred spending the day going to a pool and getting a tan, or tuning into a baseball triple header on TV, or watching the grass grow, but, he realized this experience would be his indoctrination into Mormon culture. He met Ben's extended family, including his parents, siblings, aunts, uncles and cousins. There were tables with potato salad, hamburgers, hot dogs, brownies, cookies, and fruit punch. Luke was surprised by how everyone eyed him cautiously, as if he were a sideshow freak. *And in this cage, all the way from New York City, we give you a non-Mormon!* Luke wrote later. *Please feed him whatever you'd like! Especially the potato salad!*

They asked him all sorts of questions about New York. They meant well, but they drove him crazy. Especially all the children.

Still, meeting Ben's relatives certainly gave Luke some new insights. He heard some names he had never heard of before, at least not outside the ghettos of New York. Uncle *LeVan*. Aunt *LaPriel*. Maybe *LaVell* Edwards' name wasn't an anomaly after all, he thought. At least not in Mormonville.

Late that afternoon, the group traveled to Provo and sat on blankets on the Provo Temple grounds to watch a fireworks show. Luke, Ben, and Ben's brothers played frisbee football and board games while waiting for it to begin. Uncle LeVan, owner of Kimballs' Market, cornered Luke and began regaling him with one story after another. He had a glass eye, caused, Luke later found out, from an injury sustained in a farming accident. Luke never knew what he was looking at when he talked. And, boy, could he talk. He was a human filibuster. LeVan told him about his family's polygamist roots in Mexico, which Luke found interesting—more material for the book. LeVan reminisced about "The Big War," memorable BYU games from the 1980s with Jim McMahon, Danny Ainge and Steve Young, and particularly scintillating high council meetings. Fortunately for Luke, Brooklyn came running, frantically, asking Luke to retrieve a ball that had been kicked in some bushes. He was able to escape for a time. If only he could escape from Utah as easily.

CHAPTER 11

Ben was proud of his family, glass eyes and all.

He was the fourth child of Wayne and Edna Kimball's nine children—five boys, four girls. The Kimballs traced their Mormon roots back to the earliest days of the Church. Their ancestors had known Joseph Smith personally. One had even wrestled the Prophet Joseph. It was the family's claim to fame.

Ben's name reeked of Mormonism. Benjamin was bestowed on him in honor of King Benjamin in the Book of Mormon, a fact his father liked to remind him of often. His middle name, Woodruff, was for late Church President Wilford Woodruff. All of his brothers' middle names came from last names of latter-day prophets. And, of course, Ben shared the last name of another late Church President, Spencer W. Kimball, though he wasn't related to him, at least as far as the four-generation family group sheets showed. In any event, it was a power-packed name. Benjamin Woodruff Kimball knew he had a lot to live up to.

He was as square as a Relief Society quilt. He was the kind of guy who got weepy-eyed when he took his kids to Primary. In his store, he placed coverings over displays of magazines like *Elle* or *Cosmopolitan*, with their scantily clad women and provocative headlines, leaving only the magazine's title visible. He instructed his employees to hand out inspirational quotes to customers at the store with their receipts, which was very popular in Helaman.

Ben grew up in Helaman and had the typical credentials of a thirty-two-year-old Mormon male. He was a returned missionary (served in France), a BYU graduate (in business), a father (of four children), and a husband (to one wife). Ben and Stacie had met in their BYU ward and theirs was a four-month courtship. At the time they met, both were serving on the ward activities committee. Ben, a recently returned missionary, was assigned to bring punch to the ward's opening social and Stacie, in her first year out of the freshman dorms, the cookies. As they served refreshments, they became acquainted. A couple of days later, he asked her out and during their first date, they pretty much knew where their relationship was headed. Stacie liked to joke that Ben had put something in the punch.

Ben hadn't planned on getting married at twenty-one, just months after coming home from his mission. Stacie had barely turned twenty. But it was already too late. They had been bitten by the BYU marriage bug. Besides, they were in love.

Like most young married Mormon couples, they fretted over how they would pay their bills, especially when Stacie got pregnant during their honeymoon in Cedar City. Ben had nearly three years of school left and a stack of student loans to pay off. But they had at least two things going for them: an unwavering faith in the Lord and a promise that Ben would have a full-time job after graduation at Uncle LeVan's grocery store. While he was going to school, he stocked shelves at the store and did a little of everything. And up until the first of her three ensuing miscarriages, Stacie worked as a checker. Somehow, they survived. Uncle LeVan gave them all the demo products they could eat. They practically lived off of Top Ramen noodles, Saltine crackers, and Malt-o-Meal.

When Ben finished school, his uncle promoted him to store manager because he was so diligent and such a hard worker. It wasn't Ben's idea of a dream job, but he was grateful. Finally, after three years of unsuccessfully trying to have children, Brooklyn Marie was born. She had bright eyes, and Stacie swore that her little girl had smiled the first time she held her in the delivery room. Before Ben and Stacie knew it, eleven years had passed since they were married and they had four children, a mortgage, a minivan, and a year of food storage in the basement. Ben enjoyed being a store manager and under his watch, the store turned remarkable, unprecedented profits. Every morning, at six sharp, Ben and Stacie led the family in scripture study. Then Ben would leave to open up the store. On Sundays, he taught Primary and Stacie served on the homemaking committee. Life was good.

But Luke's arrival began to turn Ben's relatively calm life upside down somehow. Having a non-Mormon move in next door was quite an event, especially in Helaman. Sharing the gospel was something Ben believed strongly in, yet it was also his greatest fear, simply because his track record in that department wasn't exactly outstanding. Although he had served an honorable, two-year mission and was a model missionary who kept every rule down to each jot and tittle, had worked tirelessly, and perfected his command of the French language, the fact that he had never had any convert baptisms during those two years haunted him. It left him feeling unfulfilled. He often wondered if he had done everything he could have. He experienced a recurring bad dream almost monthly. He would be dressed in white clothing and standing all alone in an empty baptismal font. The only thing that was wet when he awoke was his body—with sweat.

It got to the point that he avoided talking about his mission all together. In his mind, he had no tangible proof that he had been successful. Zero baptisms. He could have stayed home and gotten that many. Actually, he had come close to having one, once.

Fairly early in his mission, he and his French senior companion, Elder Cormier, were teaching an aging widow, Madame LeDoux, in a small town. She seemed receptive, although she never asked questions. She just nodded her head and said, "*Oui*," a lot. Ben wasn't sure if the discussions were penetrating past her blue hair, but he and Elder Cormier weren't picky about their investigators. At least she wasn't like the majority of other French people, who cursed Americans and turned them away while hurling insults and setting their dogs on them.

After a month or so of teaching Madame LeDoux, Ben and Elder Cormier felt she was ready for baptism. She had given up smoking cigarettes, after all. She was reading the Book of Mormon every day. Without saying more than a handful of words, she passed the baptismal interview. A date was set for the blessed occasion. She told the missionaries she wanted Elder Kimball to baptize her. Madame LeDoux wanted the ordinance to be performed by an American— she was a big Jerry Lewis fan.

When the day arrived, Ben was ecstatic. He thanked the Lord for this blessing of being able to baptize and believed it would be the first of many conversions during his time in France.

About an hour before their Sunday meetings, Ben and Elder Cormier went to Madame LeDoux's house to walk her to church, just as they had done on previous occasions. They knocked on the door and waited. No answer. After ten minutes, Elder Cormier, Ben's senior companion, began to panic. He started pounding on the door. Still nothing.

"Hey! We know you're in there," Elder Cormier said in French. "Open up!"

"Elder," Ben said, "take it easy. I'm sure there's an explanation..."

Turned out, there was. A young woman in her thirties surprised the elders from behind.

"Who are you and what are you doing?" she demanded.

"We're looking for Madame LeDoux," Elder Cormier said.

"She's not here," she said. "She is my mother. She died last night."

Ben's heart fell into his forward thruster shoes. But Elder Cormier apparently thought the woman was lying through her nicotine-stained teeth.

"Where is she *really?*" he asked. Ben was horrified by his companion's lack of sympathy. "We know she's here somewhere. She's not going to stand us up like this." Elder Cormier had been on his mission long enough to have heard zillions of excuses for not going to church or getting baptized. He was completely jaded, as far as missionaries go. To him, this was the most elaborate, and the ultimate, excuse of all time.

The young woman began crying hysterically. "My mother is dead!" she exclaimed, then proceeded to call the missionaries a couple of names that Ben didn't understand—words he hadn't been taught at the Missionary Training Center. "Are you calling me a liar?"

Ben wasn't especially fluent at that point of his mission, but he spoke up. "No, no, we believe you," he assured her in his broken French. "We're so sorry. Your mother was a friend of ours. She was such a wonderful woman. In fact, she was going to be baptized a member of our church today."

His words calmed the woman, who had no idea her mother had been talking to the missionaries. Ben boldly told her that he knew of a way she could be with her mother again someday. But Madame LeDoux's daughter rebuffed his invitation to meet with them. She had heard one too many nasty rumors about the Mormons and Elder Cormier's behavior didn't help.

Dejected, the missionaries went to church. Ben felt guilty, thinking that maybe they should have baptized Madame LeDoux the previous week, before she had to meet the Lord. Little did he know at the time, that would be as close as he would come to a baptism during his mission.

While most missionary homecoming talks are filled with inspiring stories about people who overcome great odds, change their lives, and convert to the Church, Ben's was different. In his homecoming talk, he barely mentioned his mission. The only story he told was about a man who had had a dream that was almost identical to the description of Christ's appearance to the Nephites in America, as chronicled in the Book of Mormon, even though he had never heard of the book. The man had the dream the night before Ben and his companion knocked on his door. What Ben did not mention to the congregation was that the man did not get baptized because he couldn't give up wine or his mistress.

So, Ben had some issues when it came to missionary work. That passage in the Doctrine and Covenants, section eighteen, played in his mind from time to time. "And if it so be that you should labor all your days crying repentance unto this people, and bring, save it be one soul unto me, how great shall be your joy with him in the kingdom of my Father!" That struck him like a cement truck. He felt deflated. Joyless, at least in terms of missionary work.

Occasionally, Ben would remove a well-worn piece of paper from a white envelope containing the words of his patriarchal blessing. About midway through, his eyes stared at the words he had read so many times before. It said he would be a faithful missionary, and through his example he would bring many souls into the Church. Many times he wondered how different things would have been had he been called to serve in, say, South America, where people lined up and took a number at the baptismal font. As a youngster, not long after he memorized the words to "I Hope They Call Me on a Mission," he had fantasized about baptizing thousands of souls.

The day before he left to return home from France, he talked about his deep-seated disappointment with Elder Burghoff, who had been one of his roommates at the MTC. Since they were leaving the mission field at the same time, they spent a lot of time the day of their departure reviewing their two years of service and talking about their experiences and their future plans. Elder Burghoff had been an Assistant to the President and had baptized a good number of converts. Ben was ashamed that he had not led even one person to the waters of baptism.

"Our time in France as full-time missionaries may be over," Elder Burghoff had told him as they walked together around Paris, "but our missions are never really over. When I get home, I still plan to set yearly goals for convert baptisms. There are people out there the Lord has prepared for the gospel, if we just ask for His help."

Ben felt somewhat encouraged. He and Elder Burghoff made a pact, right in front of the Eiffel Tower, that they would baptize at least one person a year for the rest of their lives.

In the eleven years since that agreement, the gregarious Elder Burghoff had been wildly successful. As a computer science student at Cal-Berkeley, he had baptized a couple of hippie non-conformists and even a philosophy professor. After graduation, he settled in southern California and routinely met poor, Latino families who were receptive to the gospel message. After every baptism, Elder Burghoff would send Ben a Polaroid of the white-clad converts and a brief letter about their conversion story. In every picture, Elder Burghoff was wearing a size

XXXL grin. He was like the Pied Piper of missionaries. Converts followed him into the waters of baptism in droves. By Ben's count, Elder Burghoff had seventeen baptisms since his mission. Ben had had exactly none, though Elder Burghoff was doing enough for the both of them singlehandedly. *Why can't I have just one experience like that?* Ben wondered.

Elder Burghoff wasn't boastful about his success, and Ben was happy for him. But Ben's frustration intensified. In his weaker moments, he started to wonder if he was jinxed. *I may have Wilford Woodruff's name*, he'd say to himself, *but I'm no Wilford Woodruff.* Of course, he had a built-in excuse for not having any post-mission baptisms. While a student at BYU, he rarely ran into non-members. And in Helaman, his opportunities to spread the gospel were limited as well. Whenever the store hired someone he knew was not a member, he tried to be a friend, but he had a hard time going from first impression to first discussion. It took him weeks or months to muster up the courage to talk to the employee about the gospel. Finally, when he felt the time had arrived to do so, he always cut himself off at the pass. He didn't want to fail again. Any time he brought up the Church in a subtle manner, Ben sensed their reluctance and he would swallow his tongue. He swore he felt hives covering his body. Whenever he came in contact with non-members he would try to be a good example. But that was it. The fear of rejection gripped him.

When the subject of Ben's mission came up between them, Stacie consoled her husband. "You're such a worrier. Let it go," she'd say. "You will never know the impact you had on those people in France. Who knows, maybe some of those people you taught have since joined the Church. You planted seeds and maybe those people weren't ready then. That was your test. You passed it. Besides, when we get older, we'll go on a mission together. And we'll have a lot of baptisms."

Ben appreciated his wife's support and encouragement, but it didn't remove the sting of failure. He longed to be instrumental in bringing someone into the Church, before male pattern baldness and Alzheimer's set in.

While he wanted to introduce the gospel to Luke, he certainly didn't want to rush things. He didn't want to ruin a budding friendship. Besides, not only did Luke seem like the antithesis of a golden investigator, he didn't seem like a candidate for Mormonism at all. That took a lot of the pressure off.

"Are you going to set Luke up with the missionaries soon?" Stacie asked Ben one night, in the way that only wives can.

"Um, sure," Ben said, brushing his teeth. "I'm just establishing, you know, that relationship of trust."

"I think you've got that part down," Stacie said.

"This process will take a while. He doesn't strike me as the religious type, you know? We'd have to clean up a bunch of things. He seems like a decent guy, though."

"You can never judge who will accept the gospel," she said. "Why don't you invite him to the church party next week?"

Ben swallowed hard. "We'll see."

One Saturday afternoon, Luke invited Ben over to his house for another type of religious experience—watching the Mets-Braves game on TV. In the name of sharing the gospel, Stacie relented, although there was house cleaning and yard-work to be done.

"It's a big sacrifice," Ben said, suppressing a smile as he walked out the door.

"Uh-huh," Stacie said, rolling her eyes.

Stacie made Ben promise that he would invite Luke to the ward party—and as he walked to Luke's house he tried to think up every segue he could. He knew he couldn't just mention it out of the blue. He didn't want to come across as fanatical.

Luke, meanwhile, thought Ben was fanatical, regardless. And eccentric. But Luke genuinely enjoyed his company. He would never have believed he would actually get along so well with a Mormon. Nevertheless, work came first. He knew he needed to focus on his book and Ben was his link to the Mormon Church, especially since Luke had seemed to alienate about everyone else in town—word of his confrontation with Sister McGown had gotten around.

Luke tidied his living room and ordered a pizza. He decided he would bring up religion and conceived the perfect way to do it without being too obvious. When Ben arrived, Luke had him take a seat on the couch, right in front of the big screen TV.

"Hey," Luke yelled from the kitchen, his head poking out of the refrigerator door, "Wanna beer?"

"No thanks," Ben called back. "I'm going to be walking home later."

"Oh, I bet you don't drink," Luke said. "Is that a Mormon thing or personal preference?"

"Both."

"Ever tasted beer?" Luke asked, opening a can for himself.

"Nope. Never had the desire. I've never been hip on marinating my brain in alcohol."

"Don't knock it until you've tried it," he replied.

"Got milk?" Ben asked. "Or how about root beer?"

"Is that the Mormon version of a brewski?" Luke said, returning to the kitchen. "Sorry, I'm all out. How about some non-alcoholic orange juice?"

"Sounds great. Make it on the rocks. I like to live dangerously."

As the game went on, they paid little attention. Their chat about alcohol consumption led to a conversation about the Word of Wisdom. By the top of the third inning, they had launched into a full-blown discussion about Mormonism, touching on a variety of topics, including polygamy, the Book of Mormon, tithing, priesthood, prophets, temples, Relief Society, and Deseret Industries. Ben felt like he was back in the mission field, without the French.

"You guys must be Orthodox Mormons," Luke said.

"Why do you say that?"

"I can just tell you really believe that stuff and live it."

Ben thought that was one of the finest compliments he had ever received. "Thanks," he said. "We do take it seriously. Three hours of church every Sunday pretty much says it all, right?"

After a while, Ben asked Luke if he wanted to attend the ward party. "Thanks for the invitation, but I've got plans," Luke said. In reality, Luke knew he should go for his book's sake, but he already had decided to drive to Salt Lake and visit a dance club he had heard about. He needed a break, after all. He was only human.

Several hours later, after the baseball game had ended, Ben returned home and told Stacie that Luke couldn't go to the party. "But he's not totally opposed to the gospel," Ben explained happily.

After that night, Ben started brushing up on his missionary skills. He skimmed *Truth Restored* and *Mormon Doctrine* and looked up his old notes from BYU religion classes. Luke threw out some wild, and sometimes deep, questions and Ben wanted to always have the right answer. He liked the challenge. He was surprised that Luke had so much interest in the Mormon Church. But, Ben figured, Luke was a writer with a curious mind. What else was he going to talk about when it came to Utah culture? Fry sauce?

CHAPTER 12

The next week, Ben took off work early one day to go golfing with Luke. Ben wasn't very good, but he liked playing. Luke, on the other hand, was a scratch golfer who used to participate in media/celebrity golf events. He had even won a couple and told Ben as much.

"Say, where'd you get those clubs?" Luke asked.

"They were my grandfather's. He was an insurance salesman. When one of his long-time clients died, his wife didn't know what to do with them, so she gave them to him. He passed them down to my dad, who gave them to me."

"Was that client named Fred Flintstone by chance?" Luke said. "Those things look like they belong behind glass at a museum."

Ben smiled as he approached the first tee. He took a couple of practice swings. Then he swung his club forward and whiffed. Nothing but air. Ben was humiliated. He took a step forward, acting as if it were only a practice swing, and tried again. This time he topped the ball, which rolled about twenty-five yards. "I told you that I wasn't very good," Ben said.

"Take another one," Luke said.

"No, I'll keep that one. At least it was straight. That's all I ask."

"So you don't believe in mulligans. I should have figured as much. Suit yourself, Captain Honesty."

Luke wore a designer glove, a Nike visor, and spiked shoes. He carried $1,500 clubs that he had recently purchased. His first drive sliced left, which wasn't bad, considering his ball landed on the fairway. Ben would have given up root beer for a month to hit a drive like that. Still, Luke threw his club on the ground and let out a blue streak, causing Ben's face to turn every shade of red in a box of Crayolas. Ben looked around, hoping nobody he knew was within earshot. He wanted to find a shovel and bury himself in a sandtrap.

As they walked down the fairway, Luke appeared to notice the change in Ben's hue. "I guess you're not comfortable with my language," he said, which was his way of apologizing. "I'll try to tone it down."

Luke drilled his second shot perfectly—high, long, and straight, onto the green, and not far from the hole. He punctuated his beautiful shot with more curse words, this time in a joyful tone. When the ball stopped rolling, he again said he was sorry about his language, but it was a battle not to use certain phrases that were so entrenched in his vocabulary. Being around Ben was like swearing in front of a five-year-old kid. Speaking of kids, no way Ben wanted Luke talking like that around his children, but he was glad that he was making an effort to curtail the swearing.

"Don't make me wash your mouth out with soap," Ben joked.

"I've been talking this way all my life," Luke told him. "Those words just come out naturally."

Ben didn't want to come across as self-righteous or judgmental. "Being a writer, I'm sure you know a lot of other words you could say instead, if you put your mind to it," he said. "You must have a thesaurus at home."

For a while, Luke tried substituting innocuous words for curse words, but with little success. Ben suggested "fetch" or "flip" or "dang."

"*Those* are offensive words where I come from," Luke said.

As they were walking to the fifth hole, Luke said, "I guess if I'm going to live in Utah, and hang out with you and your family, I'd better clean up my language." On the back of the scorecard, he wrote down a lengthy list of swear words. There were many more than the traditional dirty words, including some Ben had never heard of. "Tell me which ones are considered swear words around here, so I won't use them."

Ben scanned the list. "I think you pretty much covered them all," he said.

"Okay, then. This is going to be tough. I know I can't stop cold turkey. I'll have to use some sort of 'step down' method. You know that big cookie jar at my house you guys gave me? Every time I swear, I'll put twenty-five cents in that jar."

"A Swearing Jar?" Ben asked. "You must be a wealthy man."

"I can afford it," Luke said. "In fact, I'll donate the money to charity. Hey, I'll give it to your church. Not that you guys need it."

As they played, they talked about sports, about life, about Ben's mission.

"France?" Luke said when he found out where Ben had served. "I've been there. They can't stand Americans, let alone Mormons. Did you have much success over there?"

"Not really. But it was a great experience. I learned a lot."

"What did they pay you?"

"Nobody paid us," Ben said after Luke struck the ball and took out a divot the size of the golf pro's toupee. "In fact, all expenses came out of our own pocket."

"You're kidding me," he said, replacing the divot. "How old were you when you left?"

"Nineteen."

"How long were you over there?"

"Two years."

"Two years? You're out of high school, ready to have a good time, and you go to a foreign country for two years, and they don't even pay you? Well at least it must have been fun sightseeing. The French Riviera is great. How much time did you guys spend doing church work?"

"We usually had 14-16 hour days, mostly knocking on doors."

Luke stared at Ben incredulously. "That's insane. Why would anyone want to do that for two years?"

Ben had never really considered that question before. He'd always known going on a mission was just something he was supposed to do. And once he was in the mission field, he just knew it was where he was supposed to be.

"We believe that what we're teaching is true and that it can help people live happy lives."

"Yes, but how do you *know* it's true?" Luke asked. "There are no guarantees in life. Wouldn't you just be bummed if you died and found out that the Hare Krishnas actually had the truth? Ever consider you've been brainwashed? That you're merely conforming to social pressures?"

Ben tried to think up something profound. But there wasn't time. "It all comes down to faith," he said. "There's no way I can convince you that what I believe is true. Only God can convince you of that. It's something everyone has to find out for themselves." Ben stopped, thinking that Luke was probably not ready to hear his testimony.

"I've heard you guys believe that you can become gods yourselves," Luke asked.

Ben thought for a moment about how he had answered that while he was on his mission. "Let me put it this way," he said as he silently prayed for help, translating from French to English. "What do puppies grow up to be?"

"Is this a trick question?"

59

"No. Just answer the question. What do puppies grow up to be?"

"Dogs."

"And kittens?"

Luke shook his head at the infantile nature of this exercise. He felt like he was on an episode of *Sesame Street*.

"Cats."

"So what do the children of God grow up to be?"

Luke paused. "I knew it was a trick question." But this was great stuff for his book. He couldn't wait to write it all down when he got home.

"We believe that God loves us so much, he wants us to become like He is. Growing up, didn't you want to be like your dad?"

"Never. Actually, I never knew him. But from what I do know, my old man was a bum, a lush. A loser. I don't want to talk about him. I've seen a lot of sorrow in the world. Why would a God who's supposed to love His children let them suffer so much? Why would He, a so-called perfect being, allow so much chaos?"

"You mean like my golf game?" Ben joked.

"Religion, in my opinion, is a waste of time. No offense," Luke said, getting into this. His life had been rather quiet lately. He'd missed a good verbal battle. "All religions do is argue over which interpretation of it is right. Everyone believes the way they want to. My problem is when people try to impose their beliefs on others—"

Then Luke caught himself. He didn't want to create a gulf too wide between them. "But Mormonism does interest me," he added. "I think you guys talk a lot of sense, from what I've heard, although you do have some strange beliefs and traditions. Like this thing about having a lot of kids. Don't you ever wish you were unshackled, free to just travel and go to baseball games, drive nice cars?"

"You're saying my minivan isn't nice?"

"Why are you guys Mormons, anyway? Do you feel obligated? Is there a Mormon fun police who monitors you?"

"I couldn't imagine not being a member of the Church, just like I can't imagine my life without my wife and kids. I mean, sure, I haven't had a good night's sleep in about, oh, seven years. I don't even have to set my alarm anymore. My kids wake me up every morning at 6 a.m., like clockwork, and ask me to fix them breakfast. I've purchased so many diapers I think I've single-handedly kept Huggies afloat. But in some warped way, I wouldn't trade it."

"It doesn't seem worth all the trouble," Luke said. "All the meetings you go to. You don't drink. I hear you give away ten percent of your income. You probably spend the equivalent of Guam's gross national product in kids clothes. Don't you ever look at your life and say, 'Enough's enough'? Don't you ever want to tell your church it's full of it? Or are you expecting some sort of eternal payoff?"

Ben silently prayed for help to give Luke the right answers. He didn't want to come off sounding holier-than-thou, but he wanted to say something that would touch Luke's callous heart. Thinking on his feet was never one of his strong suits, but he surprised himself.

"I do believe there is an eternal payoff. But there's more to it than that. Living the gospel has its own immediate rewards. Like just spending time with my kids. I just want them to be better than I am. I want them to avoid the same mistakes I've made."

Luke laughed as he sunk a putt. "Next thing you know, you're going to tell me you once killed a guy. I know you better than that. What have you done that's so terrible?"

"Don't you remember my tee shot on the fourth hole? I could have killed someone with that. Listen, everyone has personal demons they have to deal with in life. Members of the Church are no different. I have my fair share of them myself, which I try to overcome. The only way I can overcome them is with God's help. That's why I go to church on Sundays, to become a better person."

Ben felt good about what he had said. He awaited a reaction—a sarcastic comment from Luke—but it never came. Instead, as they went to the next hole, Luke gave Ben some tips on his back swing and putting. It seemed to help a little. But Ben was relieved when the round was over. Luke added up the scores. It was embarrassing.

"I must say, you did pretty well toward the end," Ben said.

"Pretty well?" Luke said. "I birdied the last three holes."

"Who said I was talking about your game? You really toned down your language. Thanks."

"So what's the Swearing Jar damage?" Luke said.

"Two dollars and fifty cents," Ben said. "But who's counting?"

As they walked through the parking lot, Luke handed Ben the scorecard. "You don't mind if I rip this up, do you?" Ben asked.

"No, why? Because I beat you so badly?"

"Yeah, that, and I don't want Brooklyn finding your list of swear words."

CHAPTER 13

Stacie and Ben invited Luke over for dinner the following Monday night. He accepted the invitation. After eating, Luke and the Kimballs moved from the kitchen into the living room.

"Are you staying for Family Home Evening?" Brooklyn asked.

"Family Home what?"

"Every Monday night we spend time together as a family, with no interruptions," Ben said.

"Well, I don't want to interrupt your family time, then," Luke said.

"You're invited to stay, but don't feel like you have to," Ben said.

Luke decided to stay, for his book's sake. Ben figured it would expose Luke a little more to the Church. They sang songs and prayed, and then while Ben gave a lesson, the children sat quietly on the couch.

"How do you get your children to be so well behaved?" Luke asked later.

"It's called bribery," he said. "They know there are no treats for those who misbehave."

Brooklyn requested they sing "We'll Bring the World His Truth" for the closing song. It was her favorite song, especially the part that said, "We are as the army of HELAMAN." She always shouted that word.

"Let's have Luke say the closing prayer," she announced before refreshments were going to be served.

"Honey, let me call on someone for the prayer," Ben said.

"Why?" she asked. "Luke, you do want to say a prayer, right? You've got to learn sometime."

"I'm glad you're not in charge," Luke said, laughing.

"Brooklyn, why don't you go ahead and say it?" Ben said.

"Okay, Daddy."

She bowed her head, folded her arms, and scrunched up her eyes. Luke folded his arms and watched her at first. Then, out of respect for the family, he closed his eyes.

"Heavenly Father," she began, "we thank thee that Luke could come over and learn about Jesus."

Brooklyn was so sincere, she sounded as though God Himself was in the room. Luke opened his eyes briefly and glanced at the couch, just to make sure He wasn't sitting there.

"Please bless Luke that he will learn how to pray. Bless him that he will go home safely. Bless the Mets, that they will win, so he will be happy. And bless me, that I will get to stay up until 8:30, and bless the refreshments. In the name of Jesus Christ. Amen."

During the game-and-refreshment portion of the night, the children carried on like lab rats injected with No-doze. Brooklyn gravitated toward Luke, wanting to sit by him and talk to him. She begged him to read books to her and play hide-and-go-seek. Luke obliged. He had never spent much time with kids in his life, but he thought Ben's were fun to hang out with. There was just something about the Kimballs' house. There was an unassailable peace amid the bedlam. One thing was certain, he'd never had that feeling when he was a kid.

Luke took a special liking to Brooklyn and he enjoyed teasing her. He even went to her soccer games and piano recitals. She was enthralled by his New York accent. Brooklyn liked imitating the way he said "New Yawk." She was intrigued by his goatee, too.

"You forgot to shave again," she'd say.

"Oh yeah? And you forgot a few of your teeth," he'd reply.

Brooklyn had a hard time believing a grown man didn't know anything about the Book of Mormon or Nephi or Heavenly Father. She had always figured everyone in the world knew that stuff. Of course, she had always figured that everyone in the world was a Mormon, too.

While Stacie and the kids were dishing up dessert, Luke turned to Ben. "That was quite a production."

· "This is what being a Mormon is all about. It's all about spending time with family. Being a member of the Church provides us with happiness, security, and stability," Ben added, carrying a soiled diaper to the kitchen garbage can, "though it may not show all the time."

After downing ice cream and brownies, Brooklyn ran to her bedroom and returned moments later. She playfully approached Luke and told him to close his eyes and stick out his hand. So he did. She placed something wrapped in toilet paper in his palm.

"What's this?" he asked.

"Honey," Ben said with caution, bordering on panic, "what *is* that?"

"Luke has to open it to find out!" Brooklyn said with a squeal.

Luke slowly unwrapped the gift. "It's a ring," he said, somewhat bewildered.

"A CTR ring!" Brooklyn exclaimed. "I bought this with my own money. Mom helped me pick it out. It's for you, because you don't have one. Since you don't know how to pray yet, I thought you could use it. CTR means 'Choose The Right.' Just wear it on your finger, like me, and you'll always make the right choices. Put it on. You will wear it, won't you?"

Ben was a little embarrassed. "Uh, Brooklyn," Ben said sheepishly, "he doesn't have to wear the ring..."

"Sure, I'll wear it," Luke said, impressed by the young girl's gumption. He shoved it onto his pinky finger.

Brooklyn was thrilled. She taught him Primary songs, complete with the actions. Before Ben knew it, Brooklyn and Luke were singing "Popcorn Popping on the Apricot Tree."

After the kids trundled off to bed, Luke, Ben, and Stacie played a game of Scrabble. While laying down his tiles to form the word "quagmire," Luke decided it was time he got serious about this Mormon thing. He had been in Utah a little more than a month. How else would he be able to uncover juicy scandals unless he was on the inside? It was time to quit being a bystander. He felt he had the Kimballs' trust.

"How would I go about learning more about your church?" he asked. Ben and Stacie almost face-planted into the chip dip.

"Well," Ben said, "I could make arrangements for you to receive some formal lessons about the Church from the missionaries."

"You have missionaries here?" Luke asked. "In Utah? Isn't that preaching to the choir?"

"There are more non-LDS people here than you think. If you'd like to really learn about the Church, you can meet with the full-time missionaries. They teach discussions to those who want to investigate the church. Six in all."

"Six missionaries?" Luke asked.

"Discussions."

"Sounds serious."

"It is serious. And fun."

"Why don't you come to church on Sunday with us?" Stacie asked.

"Sure," Luke said. He was smiling on the outside and cringing on the inside. But he knew this step was unavoidable. He could feel himself being sucked deeper and deeper into the Mormon quagmire.

"So, should I invite the missionaries over next week?" Ben asked.

"What the heck," Luke said, showing he had command of the Utah vernacular. "Let's do it. If I'm going to live in Utah, I might as well learn about the predominant religion."

"I'll make arrangements," Ben said. "Weekday evenings okay?"

"As long as it doesn't conflict with a Mets game."

Ben couldn't stop smiling that night. "He must have felt something," he told Stacie later. "Boy, my lesson on gratitude tonight must have really gotten to him."

"That's probably what it was," Stacie said. "Your daughter is quite the missionary, too."

"I'll say. Everything is happening so fast," Ben said. "I know this doesn't mean he's going to join the Church, but I can't believe he's interested."

"I have a real good feeling about this," Stacie said.

"Let's not jinx it. Let's just take it slow and not get our hopes up. But wouldn't that be great if he actually got baptized?"

Every night, he prayed that it would happen.

CHAPTER 14

Church started at ten a.m.

Luke awoke early and surly that Sunday morning. Of course, he woke up surly on a regular basis, but even more so on this occasion. It was nine a.m. and when it came to Sundays, he acknowledged only one nine o'clock—and the a.m. variety wasn't it. Sundays, after all, were for sleeping in late, relaxing, watching sports, and getting inebriated. The only thing he ever did religiously on Sundays was watch NFL games at Big Apple sports bars.

He stared at his collection of clothing hanging in the closet and picked out his favorite suit, an olive-green Armani number. Begrudgingly, he threw on a tie and cinched it up. It might as well have been a noose.

Luke hated the idea of going to church. Any church. To mitigate the dread of this experience, he decided not to look at it as three hours of ecumenical ennui, but rather as three more hours of field research—for which he was being paid gobs of money. Couched in those terms, he thought he would be able to endure his first formal encounter with the Mormon Church. Besides, he knew the best way to write about an asylum was to spend time among the inmates. This way, he could gather material that would provide texture and color to his book. It didn't mean he had to like it. And he knew he wouldn't. He placed his notebook and tape recorder in his suit coat pocket.

Ordinarily, Luke tried to avoid religion like a case of botulism. If he didn't know better, he might believe he was psychosomatically allergic to anything religious in nature. When he was first hired at the *Post*, one of the editors had dispatched him to write a review of a Christian rock music concert. It gave him a month-long migraine headache. Later, Luke was in Mexico on assignment to cover the Pope's visit. While there, he bought a burrito from a street vendor that gave him diarrhea for six weeks. Ever since, every time he saw anything papal, he darted to the nearest bathroom.

Why would the Mormon Church be any different? What malady or injury would he be inflicted with this time?

By 9:40 Luke had drunk a pitcher of coffee, read the *Post* online, and watched a little CNN and ESPN. He slipped his shoes on and shuffled off to the Kimballs' house in the dry, desert heat.

When he arrived, Brooklyn gleefully invited him inside. She was wearing a blue dress and her hair was festooned with curls and bows. She was so excited about him going to church, she had awakened at five a.m. Then she had bathed, got dressed by herself, and fixed her younger siblings breakfast. "Come sit down," she said, grabbing his hand and leading him to the living room. "Aren't you glad you're coming to church with us?"

"I can't tell you how glad I am," Luke said, plastering a counterfeit smile on his face. Suddenly, a piercing scream came from one of the rooms. It was Megan, throwing a fit, almost drowning out the sound of a Mormon Tabernacle Choir CD playing in the background. Ben entered the room, somewhat startled to see Luke.

"I wasn't expecting you so soon," he said. For Ben, everything had gone wrong that morning. He and Stacie had been up all night with Megan, who was sick. The three of them were operating on about two hours of sleep. "We may be a few minutes. I've got to change Megan's diaper and Stacie's getting ready. Sorry we're running late."

"Don't worry about me, I've got all day," Luke said. "Why do you Mormons go to church so early, anyway? I don't think God even gets up this early."

Just then, the baby spit up a white, sticky liquid all over Ben's suit. "Stacie warned me to put on a burper," he said, heading quickly out of the room. He was especially nervous and wanted the day to go well. But everything seemed to be conspiring against him.

"Are you wearing your ring?" Brooklyn asked, grabbing Luke's right hand again.

"Sure am," he said. He almost forgot he was wearing it, though he couldn't take it off anyway. Earlier in the week he had spent a good hour trying to, using soap, water, butter, and thirty-weight motor oil. But the thing wouldn't come off his pinky finger. He was sure gangrene would eventually set in. "I wear it all the time," he said.

Brooklyn beamed. "Guess what?" she said. "Last night my tooth came out." She grinned, revealing a large gap in her smile.

"Did somebody steal it?" Luke asked her.

"No, silly," she said. "It fell out by itself. Then I left it under my pillow and the Tooth Fairy left me a quarter."

"Don't spend it all in one place," Luke said.

"I won't. This morning, daddy and I figured it out. We pay Heavenly Father ten percent and keep ninety percent. So I owe two-and-a-half cents in tithing. That gives me twenty-two-and-a-half cents to keep."

"How do you spend a half a cent?"

"Actually, I won't keep the half a cent. My dad traded me my quarter for twenty-five pennies, and I'm going to give the bishop three of them. My dad says that with the Lord, we should always round up."

Megan and Jared appeared from the kitchen. Megan was pulling up her dress and caterwauling. Jared was tugging at his miniature tie and sporting a giant cowlick, roughly the size of a Banzai pipeline wave, in his hair. He wore a black nametag on his little white shirt that read, "Future Missionary." Ben called into the room. "Hey, Luke," he said, "would you mind putting Jared's shoes on for him?"

"Sure," Luke said as he took Jared's leg. Jared squirmed and squealed. Luke had to hold down his leg to keep his foot still, as if he were hog-tying a sheep, then he stuffed his foot into the shoe and tied the laces.

"Stacie will be out in a second, then we'll go," Ben said, straightening Megan's dress. Stacie entered the room, looking as pretty as ever. "Sorry I'm running a little late," she said to Luke.

Then the baby spit up again on Ben's suit, forcing him to change into his third different ensemble of the morning. Which, unfortunately, was the extent of his wardrobe.

"Dad, can Luke come to our class today?" Brooklyn asked Ben after he returned. Ben taught her Primary class, but today he had arranged for a substitute so he could take Luke to Elders Quorum.

"No, honey," he said, as they hustled out to the minivan in the garage. "Luke will be with me."

Ben and Stacie each carried two or three bags with them. "Are we going to church," Luke asked, "or backpacking across Europe?" The process of quickly strapping the kids into their car seats was nothing short of a Summer Olympic event.

The Kimballs lived close enough to the church to walk, but with all the bags and little people it was easier, and faster, to drive. Luke squeezed in middle seat, in between Megan and Jared. Megan grabbed Luke's $120 silk tie and immediately began sucking on it.

When they got to church, Luke felt his stomach tighten and he cursed Kilborn under his breath. At 10:03 they walked through the front doors, along with other obviously winded families. Luke wondered if his watch was fast. Ben introduced Luke to Brother Sweeney, the ward executive secretary, as they entered the chapel.

"Luke moved into the Winters' home," Ben explained.

"How are you?" Luke asked Brother Sweeney.

"Best day of my life," Brother Sweeney replied, writing down Luke's name in his palm pilot. "I'll be sure to check on your records."

"I'm no criminal, believe it or not," Luke said.

"Uh, Bob, he's not a member of the Church," Ben said.

"Would you like to be?" Brother Sweeney asked Luke.

"Thanks, but I like to keep my Sundays free," Luke said.

Brother Sweeney patted Luke on the back. "Welcome," he said.

Ben led his family and Luke to the second row from the front, which was never occupied. Ordinarily the Kimballs sat in the back so they could make emergency exits with the kids when necessary. However, Ben decided he would give Luke a good seat for his first meeting. For all Ben knew, it might be his last.

Sister McGown got whiplash from doing a double-take when she watched Luke walk in. "He's got a lot of nerve, showing up here," Sister McGown said to her husband.

Sister Fidrych was so proud of herself. She was sure it was her encounter with him at the store, and the Book of Mormon she gave him, that had prompted him to investigate the Mormon Church.

Sister Winkler played the prelude music on the organ. Luke looked around and was surprised more by what he didn't see than what he did see. First, the chapel was only half-full and it was after ten o'clock. There were no crosses, no statues of Joseph Smith, no stained glass windows, no candles burning, no people wailing or dancing. "Hey," Luke whispered, "don't you guys have tambourines or guitars?"

"Just at the annual ward talent show," Ben said. "And Brother McMurray can really wail on the glockenspiel."

All in all, Luke found the church rather dull and austere. That same description fit the people. Half the women he saw appeared to be pregnant. The other half, he could see, had been pregnant at some point. The men all wore a variation of the same outfit: white shirts, conservative ties, dark slacks, and sensible shoes. With the number of kids that abounded, the place could have passed for a daycare center. The infants were bedecked in fancy kids clothes, complete with color-coordinated pacifiers. Like the Kimballs, other families hauled in diaper bags filled to the brim.

Why the fascination Mormons had with large families, he wasn't completely sure. But he figured that they wanted to overpopulate the world. And with the way they lived, the Mormons would probably outlive the rest of society, too. Maybe Kilborn was right about the Mormons taking over the world.

As the strains from the organ faded, a short, avuncular man approached the pulpit. The congregation hushed. "That's Bishop Law," Ben whispered to Luke. "He's the leader of the ward."

"He doesn't look like a preacher to me."

"Well, like everyone else in the Church, he's a layman," Ben said quietly, tying Jared's shoe for the third time in ten minutes. "He volunteers his time to preside over the ward."

"What's his full-time job?" Luke asked.

"He drives a tow truck."

"You're kidding."

"It's true. He owns his own towing company."

"We'd like to welcome you all out to sacrament meeting this fine summer morning," Bishop Law said with a slight drawl. The second counselor, Brother Sagapolu, forgot to lower the pulpit, so all that really showed was the bishop's glimmering, balding pate. The congregation chuckled at the scene as the pulpit was lowered. "I seem to be shrinking by the week," the bishop said.

Luke couldn't believe the Mormons had chosen this country bumpkin—a tow truck driver of all things—as their leader. Luke thought he had all the charisma of a tree sloth.

After checking his watch again, for about the one hundredth time that morning, Luke looked over his shoulder and saw that the chapel was now nearly full, with more families trickling in.

"Brothers and Sisters, I woke up this morning and looked out my window and saw beautiful Mount Timpanogos," the bishop continued. "It made me think of the words of that wonderful hymn, 'High on a mountain top, a banner is unfurled.' I drove over here and saw the horses grazing in Brother Woodard's pasture. Beautiful animals. Then I pulled into the parking lot and thought, 'What a beautiful building we have to meet in.' We are so blessed, brothers and sisters."

He paused. "I apologize that I'm not much to look at."

This is going to be a long three hours, Luke thought.

"We'll begin with some announcements. Brother and Sister Timmons welcomed a baby boy into their family last Thursday. Mother and son are doing fine. I wish I could say the same for Brother Timmons, who I understand had a water leak that flooded his basement late last night. We'd like to thank those who helped him out. So if you see a few brethren nodding off during the meeting, just know that they have an excuse today.

"Wednesday, the Relief Society will be tying a special quilt to commemorate the 24th of July. The theme is 'Modern-day Pioneers.' On the 24th, the Primary will hold a parade. Children can decorate their bikes and wagons. Sister Watkins wanted me to announce that no roller blades are allowed. Last year, you may recall, we had an unfortunate incident involving some children on roller blades and Sister Kraven's three-tier 24th of July cake. We want to avoid all foolhardy stunts this year.

"Tomorrow, the Scouts will be leaving for the week for summer camp. Mothers of the scouts, please hold your applause. We would like to remind the boys to meet here at the church at seven a.m. in full uniform with their backpacks and gear. Brother McNabb tells me that the food for the troop has already been purchased and stowed. Now, I know that a scout is 'trustworthy, loyal, helpful, friendly, courteous, kind, obedient, cheerful, thrifty, brave, clean and reverent.' They are also hungry. Boys, Brother McNabb has purchased enough food to feed the entire stake, so there is no need to bring your own. I went up to scout camp one day last year and some of the boys were roasting Twinkies over an open fire rather than eating the delicious Dutch oven roast that had been prepared. What a shame!

"Well, I believe we will enjoy a spiritual feast instead of a spiritual Twinkie today. We'll begin by singing hymn No. 284, 'If You Could Hie to Kolob.' After which, Sister Alice Wilmsmeyer will offer the invocation."

All I want to do is hie out of here, Luke thought.

The organ swelled and Ben grabbed a hymnbook and held it open for Luke, so he could sing along if he wanted. Luke didn't want. He would rather have Pavarotti sit on him than sing dirges in public. Ben's voice was no bargain, but he sang anyway. It was enough to make Luke's eardrums curl. Luke read the words of the song and leaned over to ask Ben a question. "Where in the world is Kolob?"

"As far as you know, it's in southern Utah," Ben said. "I'll explain it later."

When Sister Wilmsmeyer hobbled to the pulpit to offer the invocation, members of the congregation bowed their heads and closed their eyes. Luke refused, at first, until he realized it was a good chance to catch a cat nap. Then he noticed a strange, odoriferous smell emanating from the pew, quite possibly from Megan.

Sister Wilmsmeyer's prayer took more than five minutes, during which she thanked God for everything imaginable, including the birds, the sky, and her artificial hip. Brooklyn had to elbow Luke in the ribs to wake him up when it was over. He pried his eyes open and the bishop was at the pulpit again.

"Would Ammon Adams please come forward," Bishop Law announced as Stacie took Megan to the bathroom. "While he's coming up, let me take this opportunity to say what a fine young man he is. Now that he is of dating age, I must tell the young women of the ward that he is simply a tremendous young man."

Ammon stood next to the bishop and they shook hands. "I guess I'd better watch what I say since you're twice my size. I understand you're quite the basketball player." The boy shrugged his shoulders. "I have interviewed Ammon and found him worthy to be advanced to the office of priest. All of those who would support Ammon Adams in this priesthood advancement, please manifest by the uplifted hand."

Luke sat with his arms folded amid a flurry of raised hands. *A priest, at his age?* he wondered.

"Any opposed, manifest it by the same sign," the bishop said. "Thank you."

After another hymn came the sacrament. A cadre of young boys dressed like junior Republicans began passing out bread on metal trays. Then water. Stacie returned with Megan following the sacrament, but moments later had to take Megan out again because she wouldn't sit still. Taking trips to the foyer was usually Ben's job, but Ben wanted to stay by Luke's side. Luke, meanwhile, wished he could join Stacie and Megan outside.

Brooklyn sat quietly on the pew, reading an animated version of the Book of Mormon. Jared entertained himself with an Etch-a-Sketch. Luke noticed parents wrestling with their children and trying to stuff them full of dry cereal out of plastic bags to keep them quiet. Jared suddenly declared in a loud whisper, "Dad, I need to go to the bathroom again!"

Ben turned to Luke. "Would you mind holding the baby and watching

Brooklyn while I take Jared?"

"Sure," he said. "I've got nothing better to do."

Fortunately for Luke, the baby was fine for the first few minutes. Then little Rebecca began wailing at the top of her lungs. The congregation wondered what Luke had done to the poor little child to make her scream like that. Luke didn't know what to do, except to bounce her in his arms. Brooklyn took her off his hands. By the time Ben and Jacob returned to their seats, Rebecca had calmed down.

Meanwhile, the bishop stood at the pulpit again and told a quaint story about the power of prayer. He expressed his love for his wife, said he knew that Joseph Smith was a prophet of God, and that the Book of Mormon was true. When he finished, he turned the balance of the meeting to the congregation. At once, a group of children marched to the stand, including Brooklyn.

Boy, do the Mormons start the brainwashing young or what? Luke thought.

When Brooklyn's turn arrived, she confidently stepped up to the microphone. "I want to berry my testimony that I know that the Church is true. I know the Book of Mormon and Doctor and Covenants are true, too. I love my mom and dad. And my brother and sisters, even though they mess up my room sometimes. I'm also thankful for my new friend, Luke. He is not a member of our church, yet. I'm glad he could come with us today. He's learning about Heavenly Father and Jesus."

Ben smiled proudly. Luke gave a bemused smile.

After the children finished, mostly women went up to the microphone. They sobbed continuously. The bishop finally placed a box of tissue on the pulpit. There was so much crying going on, Luke wished he had worn a rain poncho. They cried about their children, the Book of Mormon, their neighbors, their pets. It was hard for Luke to tell if they were shedding tears of joy or sorrow.

What was also hard for him to understand was why these people didn't talk about world peace or politics or abortion or the corruptive government. At least taking some sort of political stance would have livened things up. Didn't these Mormons read the papers? For him, the meeting was excruciatingly boring. He'd been to wakes that were more exciting.

To break up the monotony, Luke leaned over to Ben. "Hey, I haven't seen any collection plates being passed around," he said.

"We don't have those."

"Then how do they get your money from you?"

Ben pulled out a gray envelope sticking out of his shirt pocket. The envelope had the bishop's name and address on it. He opened it and showed him the tithing receipt.

"That's pretty ingenious," Luke said. "That's something you can show to the IRS to prove you deserve a tax-write off, that you paid a donation to a charitable organization."

"That's one way to look at it," Ben said.

Luke was silent, trying to think of all he knew about churches. Then he leaned over to Ben with another question.

"Do you guys play Bingo during the week?"

"I'm afraid not," Ben said. "We do play basketball, though." Luke liked the sound of that.

Toward the end of the meeting, Sister Margaret Stimple arose from her chair. It was as predictable as the rising of the sun. She always bore her testimony every fast Sunday and she had an uplifting story for every meeting, every lesson, every situation. For ten minutes, she talked about her own experience during a baptism for the dead at the temple, saying she felt a kinship with a woman, for whom she acted as a proxy, who was born in the 1700s.

"This woman's name," Luke said to Ben, "isn't Shirley MacClain, by chance?"

"I'll explain it all later," Ben said.

"You've got a lot of explaining to do."

All things considered, it was completely unlike any church service Luke had ever attended.

Following sacrament meeting, Ben introduced Luke to other ward members and Luke politely shook their hands. One person after another came to meet this new visitor. In Sunday School, Brother Hemphill, the teacher, had Luke stand up so that Ben could introduce him. The Doctrine and Covenants lesson dealt with the law of consecration. Brother Hemphill did a fine job, considering the subject matter, but Ben almost took Luke home at that point.

Ben then took Luke to Elders Quorum. Again, Ben had to introduce Luke to the group, which he was asked to do before the announcements were given. What followed Luke's introduction was about five minutes of Mormon humor.

"Brethren," said Brother Monson, the Elders Quorum president, "I under-stand that a few of you anonymously mowed and trimmed Brother Evans' yard last Wednesday. He said he saw three men working in his yard. Many of you know that Brother Evans has been very sick lately. Doctors have told him to lay flat in bed. As a result, he hasn't been able to care for his yard. His eyesight isn't too good anymore and he couldn't reach his glasses, so he couldn't recognize the faces of those who were helping. He wanted me to pass along his gratitude. If you're here, I hope you know that it was very appreciated. I presume those mysterious helpers were from our ward." He paused. "Or maybe they were the Three Nephites."

That elicited a laugh from the brethren of the quorum. Luke didn't get it.

As for the lesson, Ben felt like he was accompanying a kindergartner to a university lecture on the theory of relativity. The teacher might as well have been speaking in reformed Egyptian, for all that Luke got out of it.

Ben thought maybe he should have let Luke go to Primary with Brooklyn, after all. The lesson dealt with revelation, and the discussion turned toward, as fate would have it, blacks and the priesthood and polygamy. *Of all the topics to come up on Luke's first Sunday,* Ben thought. He hoped Luke wouldn't be completely spooked.

"Feel free to ask me questions," Ben said. "You've probably got a few."

"You have no idea," Luke said.

When church ended, Sister Fidrych approached Luke and asked him if he remembered her. "You're the one who gave me a Book of Mormon at the grocery store, right?"

"Yes!" Sister Fidrych said. "I just wanted to welcome you to church. If you have any questions, I'm in the ward directory."

As Ben and Luke made their way to the parking lot, a man in a gray pinstripe suit tapped Luke on the shoulder from behind.

"Excuse me," he said, "I just had to meet you. I'm Brother Zimmerman. Everyone calls me Doctor Z. Brother Z at church."

"Nice to meet you," Luke said. "Are you really a doctor or do you just play one at church?"

"I work at Utah Valley Regional Medical Center," Brother Z said, "in the emergency room. I just wanted to tell you that even though you're not a member, you have this aura about you."

Ben wanted to grab Luke and whisk him away in his minivan.

"Aura?" Luke said. "I have an aura? I'd better get that surgically removed."

Brother Z laughed. "No, that's a good thing. When I saw you walk through the doors today I knew that you were someone special. When I found out you weren't a member, I told Sister Z that you would be one day."

"Well, you know, Brother Z, we've got to get going," Ben said. "The home teachers are coming over this afternoon and ..."

"Good enough," Brother Z said. "Brother Manning, we'll talk again soon."

"I'm sure we will," Luke said. He hated that the doctor had called him "Brother." In fact, he was angry that anyone would presume that he would join the church like that, even though he knew he would actually have to if he was going to do this assignment right.

"Why don't you come over for lunch this afternoon?" Ben said. "Stacie's making pork chops with rice."

"Thanks, but I'm not feeling so well," Luke said. Instead, he went home and washed down a couple of Tylenol tablets with a cold beer.

As for Ben, well, he certainly wasn't ashamed of the gospel, but the day reminded him how peculiar the Church and its members are. Ben wondered if Luke would cancel his appointment with the missionaries and forget the whole thing.

"You never know," Stacie said. "Maybe he liked it."

"Liked it? This guy is sophisticated and worldly. It must seem so weird to him." Ben started to feel more relaxed since there was no way Luke Manning would ever be interested in the Church.

Late that afternoon, the phone rang. It was Luke. "Ben? Hey, we're still on for Wednesday, right? The missionaries."

"You bet," Ben said after a prolonged pause. "I'll have everything ready."

"Good. I'm looking forward to it," Luke lied.

Ben told Stacie what Luke had said. "See, he must really be prepared to receive the gospel," Stacie said.

"If he is," Ben said, "he sure has fooled me."

CHAPTER 15

Ben contacted Brother Davis, the ward mission leader, and set up an appointment with the missionaries at the Davis home. Wednesday night, Stacie sent the kids to her parents' home for the night, even though Brooklyn begged to come along. The Davises always had investigators over for dinner for the first discussion. It was a tradition—if you can count one other time before that a tradition. They thought it was a good idea to break bread together to allow everyone to get to know each other beforehand.

Luke was looking forward to the meeting like a spinal tap, so he took a few swallows of vodka—he had brought it with him to Utah in case of such emergencies—before arriving at the Kimballs' home to localize the anticipated pain.

The missionaries, Elders Webster and Petrovic, were partially intoxicated, too—with joy. They were almost as happy about the food—Sister Davis had quite a reputation around the mission—as they were about an appointment with an investigator who had already been to church. Ben considered telling the missionaries about Luke's background prior to the meeting, but he decided against it. He didn't want to color their judgment going into the discussions.

Just after 6 p.m., they all converged at the dinner table. Elder Webster was tall and as straight as the part in his hair. He grew up on a Moscow, Idaho farm and had just a few weeks left on his mission. His companion, Elder Petrovic, hailed from Moscow, Russia. He was plump, had a ruddy complexion, and recognized the smell of vodka on Luke's breath. His grasp of English was only so-so, and he had just two weeks of experience in the mission field, so he mostly kept quiet and thought longingly about Tolstoy and borscht.

Luke looked at this Muscovite pair of emissaries of the Mormon Church and wondered how they could possibly believe they could convince him, or anyone, for that matter, to join their cult. He decided that if he had to suffer through these lessons, he was determined to have a little fun with them.

During dinner, Ben, Brother Davis, Elder Webster, and Luke did most of the talking. Elder Webster asked Luke about himself. Luke told him he used to work for a newspaper.

"What type of work did you do?" Brother Davis asked.

"I sold papers on the street corners."

Ben forced a laugh so that everyone would know he was joking.

Luke, on the other hand, was merciless in his line of questioning.

"Are you guys, as missionaries, unionized?"

"Do you have to sleep in your ties and nametags, too?"

"Do you ever get sick of each other? I mean, don't you ever just want to strangle your companion with your bare hands?"

"You mean you guys don't date? So you're kind of like priests?"

"Nineteen is a weird age to go on a mission. Did you know that's when men reach their, um, how should I put this, the peak of their manhood and virility? When I was nineteen . . . well, never mind."

Elders Webster and Petrovic kept glancing at the Kimballs and Davises, wondering how to react. They had never experienced an investigator this colorful. They didn't know whether to be amused or insulted.

"Luke," said Ben, who was sweating profusely, "hasn't anyone ever told you to respect your elders?"

That broke the tension. For a minute. "Luke, would you like some more chicken?" Brother Davis asked.

"Sure," Luke said. "This isn't bad."

Brother Davis figured if he kept Luke's mouth full of food it would keep him quiet.

"Sorry," Brother Davis said, "looks like this piece was left on the barbecue too long. It is a little black."

"That's okay," Luke said. "I'm not a racist."

This isn't going well, Ben thought.

Brother Davis had a notion to throw Luke out of his house. But he remembered that the Lord had put up with all sorts of faithless souls when He was on earth.

"You say you can't see your family while you're out here?" Luke asked the missionaries.

"Haven't seen them since I left for the MTC," said Elder Webster.

"What's the empty sea?" Luke asked.

"It's where we go for missionary training, the Missionary Training Center. M-T-C. It's in Provo."

"It's boot camp for missionaries," Ben said.

"Sounds like fun," Luke said.

"Yes, sir," Elder Webster answered.

"Please, don't call me 'sir.' I'm not that much older than you. So why are you on a mission, anyway?"

"I felt that going on a mission was the right thing to do," Elder Webster replied. "It's been worth it. I've made a lot of friends and I've had a lot of unforgettable experiences. I'll admit that when I found out I was coming to Utah, I wasn't that excited. At first."

"You mean you didn't pick Utah?"

"No," Elder Webster said with a chuckle. "The Presidency of our Church makes the assignments, each individually."

"What does he do, throw darts at a map?"

"He prays and chooses the place where we're most needed," Elder Webster said.

"Sounds like the Mormon version of a lottery to me," Luke said.

Ben tried to keep from wincing while listening to the exchange.

"What did you guys do before your missions?" Luke asked.

"We both went to college," Elder Webster said. "I majored in pre-med at the University of Idaho. Elder Petrovic attended a college in Russia."

"What did you major in, Slim?" Luke said, firing a glance at Elder Petrovic. "Lunch?"

Elder Petrovic, who had a mouth full of food at the time, looked as though he wanted to crawl under the table, curl up in the fetal position, and weep.

"Luke's quite a kidder," Ben said.

Luke took another helping of orange Jell-O. "Why are you Mormons so nuts about Jell-O? What's up with that? Is Jell-O some sort of corporate sponsor of your church?"

"No, it just seems that way," Ben said.

"Bill Cosby isn't a Mormon, is he?"

"No, but give us some time," Ben said.

"Say, Elders, how did your P-day on Monday go?" Brother Davis asked, hoping to circumvent Luke from the conversation. He should have known better.

"Pee day?" Luke asked. "You mean they only let you go to the bathroom on certain days?"

Stacie kept excusing herself to go in the kitchen, ostensibly to check on the brownies. But it was to escape the embarrassment. The brownies were cooling on the counter. She and Sister Davis had lost their appetites.

After dessert, the group adjourned to the living room, where the missionaries unpacked their scriptures and flip charts. "You guys aren't messing around," Luke said.

The first discussion hadn't even begun and tension was already running high. Ben wondered if this was all a big mistake. Was he just setting himself up for another letdown? And what about the missionaries? Was he just wasting their precious time?

Sister Davis offered the opening prayer and Elder Webster began the discussion. "We appreciate you making time for us, Luke," he said. "To begin, we have a question for you. What do you think about God?"

Elder Webster and the rest of the group braced themselves for the response.

"I don't think a lot about God, to be honest," Luke said. "I just wanted to meet with you guys because I thought I was going to get a free set of kitchen knives." After a pause, he added, "It's just a joke, fellas." Luke couldn't help it; acting like a jerk came so naturally to him.

The Davises began to think seriously about asking the bishop to release them from their callings. Ben and Stacie were dying a slow, painful death.

Elder Webster took a deep breath and on went with the discussion. The missionaries taught about Jesus Christ, Joseph Smith, and the Book of Mormon. Luke sat expressionless and took copious notes.

"We've never had anyone take notes before," Elder Webster said.

"Didn't think you were 'noteworthy,' did you?" Luke replied. He figured if he was going to pretend to be a Mormon, first he'd better pretend to be interested.

The thirty-minute lesson was stretched to more than two hours because Luke continuously assaulted them with questions and comments.

"Where are those gold plates now, did you say?"

"An angel named Moroni, the same person who buried the plates, took them," Elder Webster said.

"That's one strong angel. Where did he work out in order to carry those gold plates, Gold's Gym?" Luke asked. "C'mon. You guys really believe that stuff?"

"Yes, we do," Elder Webster said. "We believe this with all our hearts."

Luke was just getting started. He deliberately used five-syllable words and referred to ancient philosophers, stuff he had learned in college but never thought would come in handy. Until this night.

Ben had a pit the size of the Bingham Copper Mine in his stomach. Things were shaping up to be a federal disaster area. Why did this always happen to him? He couldn't help but think of Elder Burghoff in California, who had investigators he was teaching by the busloads. Not Ben. No, it was never easy for him.

When Luke finished his line of questioning, the exasperated elders thanked him for his time. Elder Webster glanced at his watch, apparently nervous about making it home by curfew. Elder Petrovic looked like he wanted to catch the next flight to Siberia. The missionaries gave Luke a copy of the Book of Mormon and invited him to read a couple of chapters.

"I'll add this to my extensive Book of Mormon collection," he said. Ben offered the closing prayer.

The elders were stunned, not to mention appalled, when, as they were walking out the door, Luke asked, "So when's our next meeting?"

"Excuse me?" asked Elder Webster, who had been thinking this had been a one-and-done affair. It had gone down as the worst discussion in his two years in the mission field.

"Ben told me there are six of these lessons. I'd like to hear all of them. You guys are more entertaining, and a lot nicer, than the Jehovah's Witnesses, I'll give you that."

Elder Webster reluctantly removed his day planner from his backpack and searched for an open day. "Friday?" he asked, hoping Luke was busy.

"Perfect. But I'm afraid we'll have to cut it a little shorter that night, guys. The Mets are playing the Giants on the left coast."

"Okay," Elder Webster said. "We'll talk to you again under one condition. This is the most important message you'll ever hear and what we ask is that you do your part. I'm going to ask that you read from the Book of Mormon before our next visit. I've marked Third Nephi, Chapter 11 for you to read."

"Boy, you guys are sticklers, assigning homework and all," Luke said.

Afterwards, when the elders left, Ben walked home with Luke, knowing he had to talk to Luke about his behavior.

"Hey, I rented *Saving Private Ryan* today," Luke said. "You game?"

"No thanks, I—"

"How about tomorrow? It's a five-day rental."

"Well, actually, Stacie and I don't watch R-rated movies."

"You must not watch many movies then."

"You're right," he said. Ben's idea of a wild evening consisted of root beer floats, a pepperoni pizza, and a rousing game of Monopoly.

"You guys aren't allowed to have any fun at all," Luke said, shaking his head.

Ben wanted to know why Luke wanted to listen to the discussions if all he was going to do was mock everything he heard. When Ben expressed his concern, Luke was surprised. He was used to having fun at others' expense, but he had never intended to upset Ben. After all, Ben made this whole Mormon experience bearable. It was amazing to Luke that someone tied down with four kids and a wife could act so, well, happy. Luke decided he'd better change his attitude, or he was going to blow this chance to become a Mormon insider. They walked into Luke's house.

"I didn't mean to insult you and your beliefs," Luke said, turning on the Dodgers-Mets game. "You know, I've never been a religious guy by any stretch of the imagination. But, for some reason, I find Mormonism fascinating. You Mormons are different. I want to know why. I want to know why when the world goes one way, you go the other. Like this thing about families. You guys are big on families, when most people these days don't seem to be. I spend most of my waking hours trying to forget I even have parents. My mom was fifteen when she had me. It's a wonder I survived."

"Don't you ever think about getting married? Having a family of your own?"

"Nah. That's not for me. It works for you and that's great. You're a good dad with good kids. I'd be lousy as a father, just like my old man. My mom was a drug addict. Why create another dysfunctional family? That's one thing the world needs less of."

Ben had a lot of faith, but, he thought, maybe not enough to believe Luke could ever accept the gospel. Luke was never getting baptized, Ben decided. Period. Why worry about it anymore? If he wanted to keep listening to the discussions, fine. But Ben wasn't going to stress about it. He had done his best. Just another unsuccessful conversion attempt.

The Dodgers-Mets game had already started, and although Ben was a Dodger fan, he could relate to the Mets—it just wasn't their night. The Dodgers were up 6-0 in the bottom of the third inning. Luke cursed after every bad pitch and after every Dodger hit. Each time he used a profane word, true to his word, he stood up and walked over to the Swearing Jar and dropped in a quarter. He had actually gone to the bank and purchased ten rolls of quarters. By the fifth inning, the Dodgers had extended their lead to 13-1 on a grand slam home run. Luke was so frustrated, he didn't say a word. He just walked over to the jar and dumped out a whole roll at once.

"That," he said, "is for what I'm thinking."

CHAPTER 16

For their next appointment, Elders Webster and Petrovic visited Luke at his home. Ben and Stacie also showed up. The Davises were invited, but they said they were busy, for at least two or three months.

Luke had skimmed the assigned pages of the Book of Mormon, and after that first discussion, he made a conscious effort not to be so caustic. In fact, Ben, Stacie, and the elders could hardly believe it when Luke agreed to prepare for baptism during the second discussion. "If I find out this stuff is true," Luke said, "I'll do whatever you want. Within reason."

The missionaries decided to exercise a little more patience. As the elders taught Luke, they challenged him to live every principle they taught. And Luke challenged the two missionaries right back on every principle they taught.

The Book of Mormon—"How do you know that Joseph Smith just didn't write it himself? Why doesn't your church get those gold plates back from the angel, put them on a bus and have them tour the world? You might have more converts that way."

The Angel Moroni—"So, that's the guy who blows a trumpet and graces the tops of your temples. Is he considered the Saint Peter of the Mormon Church?"

Revelation and Living Prophets—"That's a tough one to swallow. You're telling me there is a prophet, like the ones in the Bible, living on earth today? If that were true, wouldn't he at least have his own twenty-four-hour-a-day cable network? His own web site, with pictures of him talking to God?"

The pre-mortal existence—"You're saying we all lived together before we were born? That we all chose to come here? If God is all-powerful and all-knowing, like you say he is, then why would he allow people like Hitler, Mussolini, and H. Ross Perot on this planet?"

Temples—"Why not open them up to the public? They'd make nice home-less shelters."

Eternal marriage—"Let me get this straight. You'll be with the same woman throughout your life, then on throughout eternity. Forever. And you're trying to pass that off as something positive?"

Tithing—"Explain something to me. If God is all-knowing, all-powerful and all-everything like you religious types say he is, and if he created everything on earth too, then why does He need money?"

Baptisms for the Dead—"Pretty macabre stuff, if you ask me. Sounds like the premise of a Stephen King novel."

Polygamy—"I can't really blame you Mormons for giving up the practice. I've learned the hardest thing in the world is keeping a woman happy. I can't imagine being responsible for making more than one woman happy."

The Word of Wisdom—"You're telling me if I drink coffee I'm going to hell? I don't see why God would care if someone chooses to toss back a cup of coffee now and again. Your Doctrine and Covenants say nothing about caffeine. It does say no hot drinks. Does that mean hot chocolate, too?"

"No," Elder Webster said. "Hot chocolate is fine."

"You're confusing me. What about drinking beer? It's one of life's greatest pleasures. If God didn't want us to drink beer, he wouldn't have given us barley. And if He didn't want us to drink wine, he wouldn't have given us grapes, right?"

The Ten Commandments—"I've decided you Mormons don't believe in the Ten Commandments."

"We don't?" asked Elder Webster.

"No. It's more like the Ten Thousand Commandments."

They went round and round on all these topics and more. They revisited different issues. Elder Petrovic told his companion after the discussion, that his testimony was being shaken.

After a couple of weeks, the elders knew they could not go any further with Luke unless he gave them a firm commitment to be baptized. "We've taught you everything we can to this point," Elder Webster said. "We have a baptismal service scheduled for the first weekend in September. Will you be baptized on that day?"

"You expect me to change my life, and my lifestyle, just like that?" Luke asked.

Ben knew this was the moment of truth.

"Then I guess you're on your own," Elder Webster said. "Like we've told you before, what you need to do is ask our Heavenly Father if what we are teaching you is true. That's the only way to clear up your doubts."

At that point, Ben spoke up. "Luke, I was born into the Church, as you know, but there comes a point when every person needs to find out for himself if the Church is true. You can only rely on the testimony of others for so long. I have received my own witness of the truthfulness of this Church. It's a wonderful gift from Our Heavenly Father, that we can find out for ourselves if it is true."

"We care about you and want to help," Elder Webster said. "If you ever need to talk, or if you have more questions, please contact us."

Over the next few days, Ben noticed something of a change in Luke. He was putting fewer quarters in the Swearing Jar. He went to church on his own.

Of course, Luke drew heavily on his acting abilities to appear to be sincerely interested. Plus, he stopped drinking and he had the headaches to prove it.

After church one Sunday, Luke started watching a baseball game. That's when Ben called. "Gordon B. Hinckley, the president of the Church, is speaking at the Conference Center in Salt Lake tonight. We're going. Would you like to come with us?"

Luke knew he couldn't pass up this opportunity to see the Mormon prophet. On the drive up, Brooklyn rattled off information about President Hinckley as if she were reading the back of a baseball card. "He was born on June 23, 1910," she said. "He went on a mission to England. He's the fifteenth president of the Church. . ."

Not long after they found their seats in the top row of the Conference Center, the entire congregation of 20,000-plus rose when President Hinckley and his wife made their way to the stand. President Hinckley took a seat and motioned for the crowd to do likewise. During his address, Luke found himself entertained, for the most part. President Hinckley told stories and spoke about the importance of praying daily, being honest, and serving others. Then he issued a challenge to anyone investigating the Church to pray about its truthfulness. It was as if he were speaking directly to Luke, who decided he was probably the only non-Mormon in attendance.

While returning to Helaman, Luke praised President Hinckley for his speaking skills. "He's even better than Billy Graham," he said.

"That's because he's a prophet," Brooklyn said.

Luke knew the clock was ticking on his book. It was already mid-August and he needed to infiltrate the LDS Church. There was only so much he could do on the outside. Luke had been putting off the inevitable. This was his chance.

The next morning, Luke and Ben met at the golf course. On the second hole, Luke dropped the news after hitting a sweet little nine-iron shot onto the green.

"Ben, I've decided to get baptized," he said without much emotion. He might as well have said, "Ben, I've decided to order the ham-and-cheese on rye for lunch."

"Did you say something about getting baptized?" Ben asked. "I'm not sure I heard you right. I think the sun was in my ears."

"You heard right. I'm taking the plunge," Luke said. "Literally."

Ben obviously didn't know what to say. "Are you sure?" he stammered. "I, well, I just figured that you weren't ready for this yet . . ."

"From my conversations with the missionaries, and with you, I just feel like it's the right thing to do," Luke said, faking sincerity the best he could. "I think I would like to be a member of your church. I feel this is what God wants me to do. I'm going on faith here."

Luke thought that if there really was a God, He would probably strike him dead with a lightning bolt, right out of the cloudless sky, for telling such a big lie.

"Congratulations, Luke," Ben said, smiling. "I know it's the right decision."

"Hey, you can baptize, right?"

"Yes," Ben said.

"Well, would you mind doing the honors?"

Temperatures were in the mid-eighties, but Ben had goose bumps. "It would be my pleasure. I'm happy for you," he said, giving him a hug. Luke looked around to make sure no one was watching.

Ben believed in miracles and this was the biggest one he had ever been a part of. The more he thought about it, the more it made sense. Certainly, Ben thought, President Hinckley's talk had worked wonders.

"Now that I'm going to be a Mormon, does this mean I have to sell my Corvette and buy a minivan?" Luke asked.

"No," Ben replied. "Not until you get married. Just wait 'til the missionaries find out you're getting baptized. They'll be ecstatic." Truth was, nobody was more ecstatic than Ben. He knew it was a blessing from the Lord. After tribulation, he thought, come the blessings.

CHAPTER 17

Elder Webster was supposed to finish his mission that week and return home, but he obtained permission from the mission president to change his plans and remain a few more days so he could witness Luke's baptism. Unless he saw it with his own eyes, he would never have believed it.

Luke was interviewed for baptism by the district leader, Elder Chamberlain, and he was able to fake his way through most of the questions. Elder Chamberlain wasn't sure if Luke was bragging or confessing during the course of their interview. But the missionary gave Luke the benefit of the doubt. Luke told him he had given up liquor and women, although the very words were painful for him to say. Luke had decided earlier that if he was going to become a Mormon, he had better act like one in order to be convincing. He knew the Mormon women would produce no temptation for him. While taking the discussions, he fought off the urge to buy beer and instead stocked up on Pepsi and Snickers bars, to which he developed an immediate addiction.

At church, ward members congratulated him on his decision. Brother Z walked up to Luke as he entered the chapel. "I knew it," he said, smiling. "I told you that you would join the Church. Didn't I?"

Luke swallowed hard. "Yeah, you did," he said. "You're a regular Nostradamus."

"Naw," Brother Z said. "I don't shop at that store. But I had this premonition about Bishop Law being called to be our bishop a week before it happened. I'll have to tell you about it sometime."

"I'll be waiting on pins and needles," Luke said.

When Sister McGown caught wind of Luke's decision to join the Church, she was aghast. "They must be letting anyone into the Church these days," she said to her husband as they sat in their seats.

"If he can change," Brother McGown responded, "then anyone can."

"We'll see about that," she said.

Brother T.J. Sagapolu, the hulking Tongan second counselor in the bishopric, opened sacrament meeting by putting his lips close to the microphone and booming, as he usually did, "Aloooooooooo-HA!"

"Aloha," the congregation mumbled.

"C'mon, brudders and seesters," Brother Sagapolu said. "You can do better than dat. Is everyone asleep dis morning? Alooooooooo-HA!"

"Aloooooooo-HA!" the congregation echoed.

"Bettah. We have a very special meeting dis morning," Brother Sagapolu continued, gesturing to the thirteen-member McMurray family seated behind him. "We will be pleased to be addressed, and sung to, by the very talented McMurrays. Where I come from, we had villages smaller than dis family. If we could, we would extend sacrament meeting to three hours to listen to them."

"These guys are incredible," Ben whispered to Luke. "This should be a good meeting."

"I'll try to contain my enthusiasm," Luke said. "Aren't they polygamists?"

Ben laughed. "I don't know what they told you in New York about us, but we don't practice polygamy anymore. Honest. Where'd you get an idea like that?"

"I've been by their house before," Luke said. "There are all these women around."

"Brother and Sister McMurray have their own singing group, but it's part of a larger family group," Ben explained. "Sister McMurray has six sisters herself. They meet at the McMurray house almost every day to practice. They perform everywhere. They perform in concerts and have their own CDs. They're a great family."

Luke counted all eleven kids. He looked at the program and read their names, starting with the oldest: Joseph, Celestial, Daniel, Nephi, Sariah, Elizabeth, Samuel, Timothy—and the triplets—Faith, Hope, and Charity. They ranged in age from eighteen to three. They were the Mormon version of the Von Trapps. According to a page-long description on the back of the program, they sang, they danced, they played musical instruments, they clogged, they traveled the world over, and they owned synchronized watches. They were disciplined from the tops of their jelled hair to the tips of their spit-shined shoes. The family began their presentation by singing a stirring rendition of "Come, Come Ye Saints," including one verse sung in Spanish and one in Japanese, that nearly brought the entire congregation to tears. Except for Luke, of course.

All eleven kids spoke, even the three-year-old triplets. Between the quoting of scriptures and the singing of hymns, Luke didn't catch exactly what they were all talking about. The older McMurray children talked as if they had swallowed a Book of Mormon whole.

The proud parents followed. Their messages were replete with old-fashioned values, homespun homilies, and scriptures. Sister Pauline McMurray talked about how blessed she was to be "A Mother in Zion," recounting experiences she'd had with her children and their travels around the world entertaining people. They had sung at the White House. They had sung for dictators, magistrates, and emperors. She told how they arose at 5 a.m. every morning to sing hymns, read scriptures, and do chores together. Brother Paul McMurray told about how he grew up on a pig farm in southern Utah and how he learned responsibility by caring for pigs, a work ethic he tried to instill in his children. "Those days on the pig farm are brought to mind every time we sit down to a meal together," he said.

"Yeah, right," Luke said to Ben. "I bet they have their kids enrolled in etiquette school."

"Actually," Ben said, "they *own* an etiquette school."

So much for a chapter on a polygamist family, Luke thought.

During sacrament meeting, Sister Fidrych was racking her brain. Luke looked so familiar, but she couldn't figure out why. It was beginning to eat at her. She was the type of woman who would go into a bookstore and read the last page of book just so she could tell people what happened. She couldn't stand not knowing everything. Before going into Relief Society, she cornered Stacie by the water fountain.

"Did Luke ever work at Disneyland, by chance?" Sister Fidrych asked.

"I don't think so," Stacie replied. "Why?"

"I know I know him from somewhere."

"Maybe you knew him in the pre-existence," Stacie said.

Sister Fidrych was sure she had seen him since then. She was determined to get to the bottom of it.

"Don't you find it a little strange that someone like him from New York would move to our little town?"

"Maybe he's looking for a different type of life."

"If he is," Sister Fidrych said, "then I guess he came to the right place."

CHAPTER 18

The night before his baptism, Luke found two cans of beer in the refrigerator and reluctantly poured them down the sink. He didn't feel at all well, which he thought was understandable, considering what he was about to do. Luke had no appetite and he hadn't eaten in a few days. Nor did he sleep much on account of his stomach hurting so severely. The sharp pain in the right side of his abdomen coincided with his arrival to Utah, so he didn't think much of it. Plus, he figured it was a natural by-product of giving up drinking and swearing.

To look convincing, Luke showed up at the church that Saturday morning for the baptismal service clean-shaven. It had been years since he had gone without the goatee look and he felt naked without it. He had even got a hair cut dangerously close to missionary standards. As a result, people in the ward barely recognized him.

Luke wanted to look the part of a Mormon, though his heart certainly wasn't in it. His philosophy was: When in Mormonville, do as the Mormons do. Like it or not, he had to appear to be a man reborn. He didn't believe a baptism had any real meaning and figured it was similar to being initiated into any other organization, like the Elks Club or something. Luke would be a full-fledged, if not silently hostile, member of the Helaman 6th Ward. He knew the hard part was just beginning. Now he had to be nice and cheerful all the time and smile until his cheekbones ached. As soon as this charade was over, he would have his records and his name expunged from the Church's records. He had read that was possible.

Luke showed up at the church at 9:15 a.m., as he was told to. The only person in the whole building at that time was Brother Sweeney, who was filling up the baptismal font.

"How are you?" Luke asked, knowing the response in advance.

"Best day of my life," he said.

"Hope that water's warm."

"It's nice and toasty," Brother Sweeney said. "Like a hot tub. Say, are you feeling okay? You look a little pale."

"I feel a little pale, too."

Luke looked at his watch. For some maddening reason he couldn't comprehend, no one was ever on time in this church. He just wanted to get this formality over with, go home, and lay down. As he paced around the chapel, the pain in his stomach worsened. He went into the bathroom and began vomiting. He put his hand on his forehead. He felt as if he were burning up. He guessed he had a temperature of 103. Never in his life could he remember being sick like this. Not to mention, he had more important things to do than be in a church on a Saturday in September, what with an abundance of college football games on TV. As Luke splashed cold water on his face, Brother Sagapolu walked into the bathroom wearing a navy blue suit and flip-flops.

"Here you are," he said, revealing his gap-toothed smile. Brother Sagapolu gave Luke a bear hug, which caused Luke to groan. "Congratulations again on your baptism, Bruddah Manning." Then he placed a lei around Luke's neck. "You're about to become a new man, my bruddah."

A crowd of people finally showed up, almost all at once. Many of them came to see if this stranger from New York City was actually going to get baptized. About seventy-five people sat down in the chapel for the service, which included the baptisms of three eight-year-olds in the stake. Luke felt a little out of place during the group picture.

Brooklyn carried a special drawing she created for the occasion. Nearly every day, Brooklyn went to Luke's house to give him a picture. This one depicted Luke standing next to Jesus, with the sun shining in the background.

"I'll be sure to hang this on my refrigerator," Luke said, "with the others."

Just before Ben and Luke began changing into their white clothing in the dressing room, Ben gave Luke a quadruple combination, with his name monogrammed on the front, as a gift. Luke thanked him for the gesture. He hated to see them waste their money.

Walking into the room where the others were, Luke could hardly carry the book due to the pangs in his stomach. Suddenly, he had a whole lot of respect for pregnant women.

"You've done this plenty of times before, right?" Luke asked Ben.

"You mean perform a baptism?"

"Yeah."

"Never."

Luke nearly fell over backwards.

"I've never baptized anyone in my life," Ben said. "You'll be the first."

"What on earth did you do on your mission?"

"Everything but baptize. I never had much success that way. The only time I got wet was my weekly shower."

"Now you tell me. Just don't drop me."

"Look, I want to thank you for this opportunity," Ben said. "I've waited a long time for this. It really means a lot to me, more than you'd ever know. It's a real privilege, a blessing, to be able to baptize you—"

"You're not going to start blubbering on me, are you?" Luke asked.

Ben marveled at the change Luke had undergone in the three months since he met him. His dream had come true. He had finally helped lead a soul to the waters of baptism. A burden had been lifted off his back. That morning, he read a scripture from the Book of Alma: "And behold, when I see many of my brethren truly penitent, and coming to the Lord their God, then is my soul filled with joy; then do I remember what the Lord has done for me, yea, even that he hath heard my prayer; yea, then do I remember his merciful arm which he extended towards me."

Finally, he could taste the fruit of his labors. A few days before the baptism, he had removed his white baptismal pants, something he never used during his mission, out of the bottom of his dresser drawer and tried them on. They were a little snug, but they still fit.

At last he understood the joy of missionary work described in the Doctrine and Covenants. He couldn't wait for Stacie to take a picture of both of them so he could send it to Elder Burghoff. Ben vowed to continue working with Luke for the rest of his life and to help him progress in the church. Then, as was his wont, Ben began to worry, hoping he wouldn't ever go inactive.

The baptismal service began and Bishop Law conducted. Sister Dunn struggled on the piano with the opening hymn, "There Is Sunshine in My Soul Today." During the singing, Luke's head began spinning, then everything went dark on him. Ben watched him pass out, right there on the front row, onto the floor, midway through the second verse. The eight-year-olds sitting next to him giggled.

Ben bent over and laid Luke down flat. Before Ben could turn around and ask for help, Brother Z had rushed to his side. After checking Luke, Brother Z called the hospital on his cell phone.

"He's burning up," Brother Z announced.

"The Lord's probably burning the sins out of him," Sister McGown said quietly to her husband, "like He did to Zeezrom."

Luke came to for a moment, to the sight of Brother Z kneeling over him. "We've got to get you to a hospital," he said. The doctor and Ben accompanied Luke there in an ambulance. After arriving, Luke underwent an examination and Brother Z returned his diagnosis.

"Just as I thought. You've got acute appendicitis," he said. "We need to operate immediately, before your appendix bursts."

Operate? Luke thought. *No way is this quack touching me.* But there was no time for a second opinion. He just wanted the intense pain gone.

Brother Z and Ben offered to give him a blessing. It sounded mystical to Luke, but he figured anything might help.

"We bless you that you will be relieved from the pain you are suffering and that you will fully recover from this illness, according to your faith," Ben said. Luke didn't have faith in anything, but he was almost delirious with pain and barely heard what Ben said.

The surgery went well. Ben waited at the hospital until it was over, and later Stacie, Brooklyn, and the other kids visited Luke, bringing balloons and a get-well card. That night, Elders Webster and Petrovic stopped by. Elder Webster was going home from his mission in a couple of days. "When you do get baptized," he said, "let me know, because I'm coming back for it."

Getting baptized didn't seem like such a good idea to Luke anymore. As he lay in the hospital bed, he remembered what the missionaries, and Ben, had told him about baptism—that it was like a contract with God. And regardless of whether there was a God or not, Luke didn't want any part of it. Luke wondered if the appendicitis attack was God's way of stopping him before he went through with it. Besides, even Luke couldn't be that cruel to his friend Ben. If he got baptized, Ben would be devastated later to learn that it was in vain.

There had to be another way he could get inside the Mormon Church without actually becoming a card-carrying member, he thought.

Sunday morning, Bishop Law was the first to visit him, before heading to church meetings.

"We've never had a baptismal service like that before," the bishop said. "How are you feeling?"

"Like ten bucks," Luke groaned.

"The ward is fasting and praying for you. When you get feeling better, we'll set up your own baptismal service," Bishop Law said.

"Bishop," Luke said, "about my baptism. I just don't feel I can take such an important step in my life right now."

Bishop Law nodded sympathetically. "I understand. You've been through a traumatic experience. Brother Z told me you should be back to normal in a few days. How about a week from Saturday?"

Luke shook his head. "I just can't commit to getting baptized, at least not for now."

"The missionaries feel you're ready," the bishop said. "You took the discussions, you passed the baptismal interview. Is there something you'd like to talk about?"

"No," Luke replied. "You have to understand. Before I moved out here, I had a pretty wild lifestyle. I need some time to adjust. But can I still be involved in the Church? Can I still come to the meetings and activities?"

Bishop Law smiled and placed his hand on Luke's shoulder. "Of course," he said. "This covenant you're going to enter into is between you and the Lord, and I'm glad you are taking this so seriously. You work it out with Him. Take whatever time you need. I am happy about your willingness to be involved. Just do one thing. Try fasting and praying about your baptism as soon as you are able. Why don't we meet together every so often to track your progress and to talk. Would that be okay?"

Luke agreed, reluctantly.

Even without being baptized, he knew he could pass himself off as a Mormon, though it wouldn't be easy. If he was to ever fully gain the Mormons' trust, he was going to have to act like the best Mormon alive. In other words, he'd have to be a Ben Kimball clone.

Later that day, he told Ben about postponing his baptismal plans. Ben hoped the anesthesia Luke had received hadn't completely worn off yet.

"I'll be ready when you are," Ben said, trying to mask his disappointment.

As he left the hospital, Ben wondered what he had done wrong. It was worse than the Madame LeDoux episode.

Ben went home and told Stacie. "I told you I was jinxed," he said. "I can't catch a break."

"I, I, I. Sounds to me like you have an 'I' disease," Stacie said. "You can't see what the Lord sees. Maybe He wants you to learn something here. This hang up with not having any baptisms—maybe you're focused more on the glory of yourself than the glory of God."

It was as if Ben was being reproved by the Angel Gabriel himself.

"Besides," Stacie added, "in just a few months, you'll be able to baptize Brooklyn. I don't think there's anything that could top that. Do you?"

Ben knew his wife was right. "No," he said. Stacie had a way of putting things in perspective.

Late that night, Ben went into the kitchen alone, opened the scriptures, and did some soul-searching. He realized that he had been too caught up in his desire to get a baptism. At the same time, he promised the Lord that he would work as hard as he could to help Luke Manning get baptized. Someday. From that day on, he vowed, he would get Luke so entrenched in the Church, there would be no way he could resist baptism.

That night, Kilborn called and found out Luke had undergone an emergency appendectomy. "Why didn't you tell me you were in pain?" he said. "I could have flown you out here for surgery. They're so primitive out there compared to what we have here, medically speaking. And what if you had said something to blow your cover while you were sedated?"

"Jack, this isn't Bolivia," Luke said. "Everything went fine. Besides, if I would have let you fly me out there, I wouldn't have wanted to come back."

CHAPTER 19

A couple of days after the surgery, Luke was back home, where, for the next week, Stacie helped out. She did his laundry and cleaned his house, except for his den. "Everything's just the way I want it in there," he told her.

His appetite returned and the Relief Society arranged to bring him meals. Luke stayed in bed and worked on his book. It was like being at Club Med. Every night, like clockwork, someone in the ward would bring dinner to him. When it was the Kimballs' turn to bring a meal, Stacie left a casserole in Luke's kitchen. One day she left Brooklyn alone with Luke as she ran home to bake some biscuits.

"Luke," Brooklyn asked, "will you listen while I read this?" She pulled out a copy of an illustrated book titled, *My Book of Mormon Storybook* from her bag. The particular story she turned to was about a missionary cutting the arms off of thieves who were trying to steal a king's herd of sheep.

Luke scanned the story. "Are you sure your parents let you read this stuff?" Luke asked. "This is pretty graphic. This is as violent as any R-rated movie."

"What's an R-rated movie?" Brooklyn asked.

"Forget it."

Then Brooklyn saw Luke's wallet on the nightstand and started going through it.

"Why don't you have any pictures in here?" Brooklyn asked.

"There's a picture on my driver's license."

"That doesn't count. Where are the pictures of your family?"

"I don't have any pictures of my family."

"Why?"

"Because I really don't have a family."

Brooklyn had never heard of such a thing. "Everyone has a family. Where's your mom and dad?"

"My mom and dad both left me when I was a kid," he said.

Brooklyn thought for a moment. It was the saddest thing she had ever heard.

"You lived by yourself?"

"No, I lived with other families—a new one every month."

"Maybe your mom and dad are looking for you. They probably miss you. Why don't you try to find them?"

"It's not that simple," Luke said.

"I'll be right back," Brooklyn said, running out the door. She returned moments later, picked up his wallet again, and placed a small school photo of herself in the first clear-plastic sleeve.

"There," she said proudly, "now you'll never be lonely. I'll always be with you. If anyone ever asks about your family, you can show them this picture."

Stacie came back and began dishing up dinner.

"Why aren't you baptized yet?" Brooklyn asked Luke.

"You think I should be?"

"Of course," she said. "Everyone needs to be baptized. If you don't, you can't live with Heavenly Father again. I would never see you. That would be a sad day."

Brooklyn paused as an idea came to her. "Hey! I'm getting baptized in February, just after I turn eight. We could get baptized together!"

Luke hated to break her heart. "I can't promise you anything," he said. "I'm not ready for that yet."

"Well, let's get you ready!" Brooklyn picked up her pad of paper and crayons. "I'll explain it all to you," she said, drawing five big circles. "This is the place where we were before we were born and this is the earth," she added, pointing to the first two circles. "Before we were born, we lived with Heavenly Father. There was this war there, but without guns. We took sides. All the good people, like us, we were on Jesus' team. The bad people were on Satan's team. Our team won and we got a prize—a body and a trip to earth. Before that, we were just spirits, floating around, with Heavenly Father. To get our bodies, we had to get inside our moms' tummy for a long time. It must have been very squishy in there. On earth we have all these tests, like in school. While we're here, we're supposed to go to church every Sunday, get baptized, and help other people. When we die, our body goes into the cemetery, the one next to the park. Our spirits go to the spirit world. All the good people will go to this place called Pair of Dice. The bad people go to another place. I can't remember the name, but it's like a jail. It's like sitting on your bed and having a very long time out. Kind of like what you're doing now. After Jesus judges us, he tells us where to go. The people who go to these bottom two circles have to live by themselves without their families. You wouldn't get any Christmas presents. Nobody would know when it was your birthday. That's why you need to get baptized. The people who are very good get to go to this circle, the biggest and prettiest of all. This is the celestial kingdom. You can live here with your family forever. That's where I'm going."

"What will the people do there?" Luke asked.

Brooklyn was pensive for a moment. "We'll probably go to Primary every day and get to eat ice cream and play games with Heavenly Father. I think He'll tell us stories and teach us how to do things."

"So I'd really be missing out, then."

"Yeah. My dad told me I needed to read all of the Book of Mormon before I get baptized. So we read it together last spring. My dad gave me a dollar when I finished it. I'll give you a dollar, too, if you read it all."

"That's a magnanimous gesture, but you keep your money," Luke said. "I'm going to read all of the book, eventually. I just can't keep all the stories straight. It's confusing."

"I know," Brooklyn said. "That's why I like to read this one with all the pictures. I'll help you."

While Luke ate dinner, Brooklyn told Luke about a couple of dozen people from the Book of Mormon. Luke got confused about the wicked King Noah. "Noah's good in the Bible," he said. "And you're telling me this one is bad?"

"Yep," Brooklyn said. "And he doesn't build an ark, either."

Luke also got tripped up by Alma and Alma the Younger. Then there were the Sons of Mosiah, the Stripling Warriors, and the Brother of Jared. These new characters all seemed to blend together. Brooklyn helped him sort it out, or at least she tried to.

While recovering, he stayed in the house to write. After several days, though, he set up a tee time with Ben.

"You sure you're up to it?" Ben asked.

"I can still beat you without my appendix," Luke replied. "In fact, I can beat you using my appendix as a golf club."

Two weeks after surgery, Luke was working on his book and plotting his next move, when he received a phone call from Brother Sweeney.

"Brother Manning," he began, "how are you?"

"Doing better, thanks. And you?"

"Best day of my life."

Luke hated it when he said that.

"Say, the bishop would like to meet with you tomorrow morning before church, say 9:20, in his office. Can you make it?"

Luke wanted to say he was busy, but he knew he couldn't. "Okay."

"Great. He'll see you then. Have a good evening."

Though disgusted that he had to get up even earlier than usual the next morning, Luke knew the key to getting on the inside of the ward was through the bishop. At least now, he thought, he was getting somewhere. The better acquainted with the Church leaders he became, the easier it would be to uncover scandals. He was determined to take advantage of his near-member status in whatever way he could.

When he awoke, he shaved and showered, but decided not to eat breakfast. Luke remembered he had promised the bishop he would fast, so he thought he'd try it, for the book's sake. He didn't have time to eat anyway.

Luke pulled into the church parking lot bleary-eyed. There were few cars there, among them Bishop Law's tow truck.

As soon as Luke entered the building, his brand new quadruple combination in hand, he spotted the bishop standing outside his office, reading his own scriptures. Bishop Law shook Luke's hand. "Thank you so much for coming, Brother Manning," he said.

"Wouldn't miss it," Luke said.

"I'm impressed," the bishop said. "You're even a little early."

They entered the modest office with imitation wood paneling on the wall. Bishop Law closed the door and pulled out a chair for Luke, then sat behind his desk. What Luke couldn't figure out was how this guy, a tow truck driver of all things, could be the most powerful man in the ward. Luke knew that in the ward there were wealthy businessmen and doctors, men who were a lot smarter, and a lot richer, and had more charisma than the bishop.

"I've had a couple of thoughts since we last spoke," the bishop said. "I wanted to ask you if you would be interested in attending the single adult ward in the stake."

"Trying to get rid of me, huh?" Luke asked.

"Not a chance," said the bishop. "It's a ward for unmarried singles like yourself. They have activities geared for singles. You might feel more comfortable there. Just wanted to let you know it's an option."

"It sounds like a Mormon singles bar," Luke said. "I think I'll stay where I am."

"That's great," the bishop said. "I'm glad to hear it."

Luke had this uneasy feeling come over him, as if the bishop's piercing green eyes could see right through him, could see every sin he had ever committed in his life. Luke began to wonder if the bishop knew exactly what he was up to.

"I've talked to the missionaries about you and they've entrusted you into my hands," the bishop went on. "I promised them, though, that I will let them know when you get baptized."

Luke nodded.

"I understand you are a writer," Bishop Law continued. "Ben tells me you graduated from Syracuse University. That's a fine school."

"It is," Luke said. "Where'd you go to school?"

"Helaman High. I never went to college," the bishop said. "I got married after my mission and started working instead. Sometimes I wish I would have gone to college."

"But you have your own business," Luke said.

"Yes, and I enjoy my work," Bishop Law said. "Speaking of work, even though you're not baptized—yet—the Lord has a great work for you to do. If you're obedient, you can accomplish great things in this Church. And there's no time like the present to get started, while your enthusiasm for the gospel is so strong. We want you to be involved in the Kingdom right away."

Luke cleared his throat. "Kingdom? What do you have in mind?"

"We'd like to call you to serve in the Primary as a teacher."

"Primary? Is that the thing with all the kids?"

"That's right."

Luke laughed nervously. "Um, one thing you should know. I've never dealt with kids before. Plus, I don't know everything about the Church."

"Brother Manning," the bishop said with a smile, "there is a first time for everything. I understand you are close to the Kimball family, and they are quite fond of you. Brother Kimball, as you know, teaches the seven-year-old class. Brooklyn is in that class, too. I'd like you to be Brother Kimball's assistant. If you don't feel comfortable teaching, you don't have to. You'll be there to help with the children. It can be a rowdy class sometimes, from what I hear."

"So you want me to be a bouncer?" Luke asked.

"Don't think of it that way," the bishop said, laughing. "This is what the Lord wants you to do. Will you accept that calling?"

Surely, Luke thought, *given his talents and abilities, the bishop should give him a more important position than being a babysitter.* But, he realized, as long as he was seen as a non-member, it would have to do.

"Do you realize that just a couple of weeks ago, when people told me to meet at the stake center, I thought they were talking about Sizzler?" Luke said. "I don't feel prepared for this."

"Few people ever do feel prepared for the callings they receive. What you need to understand is, this calling doesn't come from me. It comes from the Lord. The gospel is simple. You're an intelligent young man. Teaching the children is one of the most important callings in the Church. I've always believed that if the Lord were to come to our church meetings on Sunday, the first ones he would visit would be our Primary children. The Lord believes in you. I believe in you. Now, will you do it?"

What was Luke supposed to say to that?

"I'll give it a whirl," he said. "What do I have to do?"

"Sister Watkins, the Primary President, and Brother Kimball will meet with you and give you a copy of the lesson manual. Even though you won't be teaching, you'll be better able to help Brother Kimball with his lesson and the children. You and the Spirit of the Lord will do the rest. You can start next week. Go into Primary today and get to know the children in your class."

The bishop asked if they could close with a word of prayer. Luke said yes, then the bishop got down on his knees. Luke did the same. Bishop Law offered a prayer asking for Luke to be blessed in his calling. After that, Bishop Law gave him a Salt Lake Temple tie tack.

"The bishopric gives one of these to everyone who gets baptized," he explained. "Of course, since I've been bishop, we've only given them away to eight-year-old boys. You're not baptized, but I have faith you will be soon. When you wear this, I want you to remember the importance of baptism."

Let's see, Luke thought, *a CTR ring and a temple tie tack. What's next? An Angel Moroni waterproof wristwatch?*

As Luke walked around the church waiting for sacrament meeting to begin, he couldn't believe this was happening. His stomach was growling. He wanted to eat. Anything. Even a bowl of Jell-O sounded good. He couldn't believe the Mormons expected him to actually do something—and he wasn't even baptized.

He couldn't believe the Mormons would trust him, a non-member they didn't even know, with their children, without an FBI background check. Luke hated the whole idea of being a babysitter. It was insulting. Why couldn't they at least have him write and publish the ward newsletter? Surely they could put him to better use than being with *kids*, he thought.

On the other hand, he realized, he had his foot in the Church.

As usual, Luke found a seat next to the Kimballs. For the opening hymn of sacrament meeting, the congregation sang all seven verses of "A Poor Wayfaring Man of Grief."

"This must be the *War and Peace* of church songs," Luke said to Ben.

The bishop made Luke stand up so the ward could sustain him in his calling. Brooklyn was ecstatic when she heard the news. "Wow, you're my teacher!" she said. "Now I have two teachers, you and my dad!"

Luke recognized the irony. After all, a lot of what Luke knew about the Mormon gospel he had learned from Brooklyn.

Ben and Stacie were excited that Luke had accepted the calling and they were grateful for the bishop's wisdom in giving it to him. At first, they wondered if Luke should attend the gospel essentials class. But that was taught by the Davises and they didn't want to be involved in any more teaching settings with him. Besides, Ben thought, if Luke has a lesson manual and has to read up on the lessons, surely he would feel the Spirit. The seven-year-olds were preparing for baptism, too, so it was a perfect place for him.

Not everyone agreed with the decision to give Luke a church calling.

"I don't think a non-member should be teaching our children," Sister McGown said to her husband. "What if he teaches them false doctrine?"

"Bishop Law knows what he's doing," Brother McGown replied.

Following sacrament meeting, Brooklyn took Luke's hand. "I'll show you where to go for opening exercises," she said.

"Opening exercises?" Luke asked. "What are we going to do—pushups and squat thrusts?"

"No, silly," Brooklyn said. "That's where we sing and play games and learn how to be reverent. Let's hurry so we won't be late!"

Along the way, everyone smiled and glad-handed Luke as if he were a politician. He was relieved when he got to the Primary room, which was filled with kids who didn't know who he was or cared that he was a non-member. He was just the guy who passed out before his baptism. One kid from another class, Byron Pierce, threw a spitwad that thwacked Luke in the back of the head. Luke wanted to take the kid outside and teach him a lesson that had nothing to do with turning the other cheek, but he refrained.

"This is our new teacher," Brooklyn announced to her class. "He's my friend, Luke. I mean, Brother Manning."

"Teacher's pet," said Danny Silcox.

Sister Watkins welcomed Luke to Primary and handed him a thick manual. The chorister conducted singing time, which was followed by sharing time. Thanks to Brooklyn, Luke was somewhat familiar with the songs.

When opening exercises ended, Brooklyn and the other eight children in the class stood up in unison, folded their arms and led Luke to their classroom, where they sat in miniature seats. Boys on one side, girls on the other.

"Oh no," Ben said upon entering the classroom. "I forgot to get some chalk. I'll run to the library. Luke, um, Brother Manning, maybe you could get acquainted with the children while I'm gone."

Luke stood up in front of the kids. "So, how are the Moonbeams today?" he asked.

The class erupted in laughter. "Not Moonbeams. *Sunbeams!*" Brooklyn exclaimed. "And we're not Sunbeams. We're CTRs. We're seven years old. The Sunbeams is Jared's class. They're four."

"Why are they 'Sunbeams'?" Luke asked.

Brooklyn didn't miss a beat. "Because Jesus wants them to be."

Luke had the children introduce themselves. All of them did, but one—a boy who was sitting backward, sucking on the top of his chair.

"What about you?" Luke asked. "What's your name?"

"That's Oliver Cluff," Brooklyn said. "He doesn't talk much."

"That's because he's retarded," Danny said.

Brooklyn stood up. "No he's not! He's just a little slow. My dad says he's very special and we'd better be nice to him."

"All he does is sit there and put things in his mouth and make weird noises," Danny said. "I don't know why he comes to church."

"I don't know why you come if all you're going to do is say mean things about Oliver. Stop it."

"Who's going to make me?"

"Me," Luke interrupted. "Please, let's keep it down. I've got a headache."

Ben finally returned and began the lesson. Luke had to keep jabbing himself with his new tie tack to stay awake.

How he was going to pull this off every Sunday for the next eight months, he didn't know.

CHAPTER 20

As soon as they found out that Luke was a new member—more or less—of the ward, the Munchaks were all over him like flies at a ward picnic.

Tim and Lisa Munchak owned a lucrative family business called "Millennium Musts," which was advertised on a Main Street billboard that proclaimed, "Ask us about our Garden of Eden specials." They referred to Helaman as "the worldwide headquarters of Millennium Musts." They sold dehydrated food under the brand name "Munchak's Munchies." They reasoned it was more marketable, and palatable, that way.

The Munchaks, who had six children, lived and worked out of their nine-bedroom house in the most recently (and expensively) developed part of Helaman. Having struck it rich in the emergency preparedness industry, they felt that their business was their livelihood and their way of life. It was hard for them, or anyone else who knew them, to distinguish one from the other. They were also charter members of the Homeschoolers Association of America. Sister Munchak was a licensed midwife. They ate only whole-grain foods, fresh fruits and vegetables, and vitamin supplements. Meat was a four-letter word to them. Preservatives were downright evil. For Halloween, they would pass out home-made rice cakes to trick-or-treaters (needless to say, they didn't have many visitors on that night). They made their own bread every day. Sister Munchak sewed all their clothes—by hand. They had a large garden in the back yard that provided many of their meals. They had a local, weekly radio show, "Munching with the Munchaks," teaching listeners how to prepare lintel beans and other healthful foods in "fun and exciting ways."

The Munchaks spent their evenings delivering in-home presentations on their vast array of products, including gas stoves, wool blankets, and combination radio-flashlights. Every month, they would go a whole week without electricity, just for practice; they encouraged everyone else to do the same. On fast Sundays, Brother and Sister Munchak would alternate taking turns at the pulpit. One or the other would discuss the Last Days, quote some verses from

Revelations, and describe how their business had blessed so many lives. It always made Bishop Law a little uncomfortable. They talked a lot about natural disasters, quoting fatality figures from the latest earthquake or mudslide or hurricane. In fact, they had a book, which members of the ward called "The Munchak's Big Black Book of Death and Destruction," which was filled with newspaper clippings featuring stories about natural disasters and other calamities from around the world.

"It's not a question of if it will happen to us," they liked to say, "but *when*."

Needless to say, they were charming folks. One day after church, Brother Munchak, wearing suspenders and a bow tie, approached Luke, extended his hand, and said, "Tim Munchak."

"Gesundheit," Luke said.

Brother Munchak cocked his head and gave Luke a bewildered look.

"It sounded like you had sneezed," Luke said. "It's a joke."

"That's very funny," he said with a straight face. "My wife, Lisa, and I were wondering if we could visit you this week."

"I don't see why not," Luke said. "Everybody else does."

Luke accepted their offer to listen to their presentation, for the book's sake.

He had noticed that everyone in Utah was obsessed with hoarding food. Ben told him that at his store, some families bulk-shopped 'til they dropped, so he held case lot sales on a regular basis. Families wheeled out hundreds of dollars worth of groceries in the form of canned green beans, corn and fruit cocktail, and sacks of flour the size of Toyota Corollas.

"What do you Mormons do with all that food?" Luke once asked Ben.

"Well, we take it home, put it in a storage room and then keep it for five years, until we eat it or until it spoils—whichever comes first. Then we replace it."

"Makes perfect sense to me," Luke said.

Though the Munchaks typically didn't schedule appointments with unmarried men, they figured it was just a matter of time before Luke joined the Church, and that a wife and children couldn't be far behind. They showed up—fifteen minutes late—wearing pioneer attire, for effect. They parked a handcart on Luke's front lawn.

"I didn't know it was Halloween already," Luke said as he opened the front door.

"We just want to make the point that someday we may have to return to living like the pioneers did," said Brother Munchak, who wore a floppy hat, a ruffled shirt, and wool trousers. Sister Munchak wore a bonnet and floor-length dress.

"Someday," she said, "we may return to living completely off the land, like Adam and Eve did."

"I thank you for not showing up in fig leaves," Luke said.

The Munchaks were shrewd, energetic salespeople. They started their presentation by quoting homespun homilies and reading scriptures dealing with being prepared. It was like one of those late-night infomercials, except it was live, which meant Luke couldn't turn them off with his remote control.

"If we fail to plan, we plan to fail," Brother Munchak said, enunciating the words like a Baptist preacher. "We don't know what kind of trouble we may be in one day. You read the papers. Terrorism. Oil shortages. Energy blackouts. Wars and rumors of wars. The United Nations. The government is falling apart before our eyes. In the Doctrine and Covenants, it says members of the Church will save the Constitution of the United States when it is hanging by a thread."

"Is that right?" Luke asked.

"Oh, yes," said Brother Munchak, moving up to the edge of his seat on the couch. "Things are bound to get worse. Our existence is precarious. I don't tell this to just anyone, but I'm digging a twenty-by-fifty-foot trench in the backyard. When it's finished, it will be a state-of-the-art bomb shelter. We'll have all the essentials in there. Toilet paper, food, guns. You can never be too prepared for disaster."

Luke's eyes lit up. The Munchaks were about to write yet another chapter for his book.

They handed Luke a stack of brochures, showing him all types of products, from a Bucket O' Flour ($25.95) to a hand-operated wheat grinder ($74.95) to a 72-hour kit ($89.95).

They tried to whet his appetite for dehydrated foods by bringing out a propane stove and cooking a meal for him, right on his kitchen counter. The dehydrated linguine had a rancid aftertaste, and the dried milk nearly made him heave.

"I'll let you know if I'm interested," Luke said. *When the telestial kingdom freezes over*, he thought.

"What do you do for a living?" Brother Munchak asked.

"I'm a writer."

"A writer? Did you hear that, Lisa?" Brother Munchak rubbed his hands. "Brother Manning, we're looking for someone creative to help us with our business. A little marketing, if you're interested. I know a writer's hours are flexible. Maybe you could help us sell our products. You could make a lot of money. And with your connections in New York, wow! That's an untapped market out there! If you could put us in touch with some potential distributors out there . . ."

"You folks wouldn't be operating a pyramid scheme, would you?" Luke said.

"There's nothing illegal about what we do," said a rankled Brother Munchak. "I'm a very busy man and I'm trying to help others find financial independence, like I've found." Before leaving, Brother Munchak gave Luke a business card that included a phone number and a website address, munchak-munchies.com.

"By the way, on my site, if you click on the little icon on the bottom, the icon next to the one that says 'Armageddon,' you'll find some information about my candidacy for governor in November."

"Governor? Of Utah?"

"Yes sir."

Luke scratched his head. "Governor Munchak. It just rolls off the tongue."

"I think so, too."

"I had no idea about this," Luke said.

"You must not be reading your free copies of the *Helaman Times*."

"Yeah, I stopped getting it a while back. So what party do you belong to?"

"The American Constitutionist Party."

"What's your platform?"

"I'm glad you asked, Brother Manning." Brother Munchak pulled out a couple of pamphlets from his satchel. "These explain in detail what I believe. I'm hoping to have a few TV spots before the election. The short answer is I believe that, as a nation, we've forgotten God. I want to put 'one nation under God' back into the Pledge of Allegiance. If elected, I will call for the Pledge to be recited at every school and workplace in the state every day. Also, families are falling apart due to the plague of divorce. Traditional marriage must be restored. We're awash in immorality. We're ignoring the Constitution of the United States, which made our country great. We need to create more private schools with a curriculum based on good values. I believe the United Nations and the IRS are evil organizations created and run by nefarious, corrupt men. We must be self-sufficient. If

I'm elected governor, I'll cut taxes to the bone. Think of me when you vote."

"How could I not?" Luke said. "But, unfortunately, I'm not a resident of Utah yet. I can't vote for you, though you know I would if I could."

"Hmmmmm," Brother Munchak said, lifting the brim of his hat. "In that case, would it be okay if I got those pamphlets back? They cost me sixteen cents each."

Luke returned them. Then he offered the Munchaks a Snickers bar before they left. They were not amused. Luke watched out the window as they pushed their handcart back down the road.

Everything seemed to be coming together nicely for his book, Luke thought. He couldn't have dreamed up scenarios and people like the ones he was finding here. Every once in a while, he would drive to bookstores in Orem and Provo to imagine what it would be like seeing his book on the shelves. He dreamed of all the money he'd get, all the talk shows he would do when he returned to New York. Only 247 days to go.

CHAPTER 21

Before Luke knew it, it was Sunday again.

Ben had asked for his help on the lesson, so he flipped through the manual during breakfast that morning. The topic? Baptism. *How hard could it be?* he wondered. He had just been taught everything there was to know about baptism.

Since he was trying hard to act like a member of the Church, he didn't show up until a few minutes after sacrament meeting was scheduled to start. Although Luke had learned more than he thought possible about the Mormons, he had committed a social gaffe when, following a special musical number—Sister Nielsen and her eleven-year-old daughter, Maggie, sang "His Image In Our Countenance" while being accompanied by Sister Abrams on the violin—he instinctively started clapping at the end of the selection. Everyone smiled at him forgivingly.

After Primary opening exercises, Ben, Luke and the kids were walking to their classroom when a copy of *Sports Illustrated* fell out of Luke's lesson manual. Brooklyn picked it up and gave it back to him before anyone else saw it.

"Is our lesson about football?" she asked.

"I wish," Luke said.

In class, Ben talked about the importance of baptism to the children and reminded them that they were only months away from being baptized like Jesus was.

Then Sister Paultz, from the nursery, showed up at the door with Ben's son Jared, holding him under his armpits. "I'm afraid he's had a little accident," she said. "His britches are soaked." Ben sighed and turned the time over to Luke for a game. "I've got to take him home," he said.

The only kids' game Luke knew was hangman. He chose words like "immersion" and "John the Baptist." Every time they guessed a correct letter, the kids, especially Oliver, screamed with delight, which echoed down the corridors of the building. They were so loud, they kept the high priests awake. Some had to turn off their hearing aids.

There came a knock on the door. The Primary president peeked in and smiled.

"Mind if I join you?" Sister Watkins asked.

"Not at all," Luke said.

Sister Watkins sat down and spoke up. "Brother Manning," she said, "since you are preparing for baptism yourself, why don't you share your personal feelings about that sacred ordinance with the children?"

Luke could have punched the woman in the nose.

"Okay," he said in mock delight. He could feel Sister Watkins boring a hole in his chest. Knowing he only had a few minutes left, he started telling the children about a memorable baseball game, as if he were going to draw an analogy. Before he knew it, the final bell had rung. "I guess I'll save the rest for next week," he said. He excused the children. But they sat still. Then Brooklyn raised her hand. "You forgot to ask someone to say the prayer," she said.

"Okay, why don't you say it?"

Brooklyn gave thanks for the Church and the bishop and Sister Watkins and the lesson that her dad and Luke had spent so much time preparing for them.

As everyone left, Brooklyn gathered up the chalk. "Do you like teaching our class, Luke?" she asked.

"Love it," he said.

"Oliver really likes you."

"How can you tell?"

"Usually, he tries to climb out the window during lessons," Brooklyn said. "And he's usually eating something. He's always hungry."

"Guess I'll have to start bringing food," Luke said.

"We're not supposed to have treats in Primary," Brooklyn said.

Brooklyn followed Luke into the hallway until she found Stacie. As always, Luke tried to get out of the building as quickly as possible. Before he could, Sister Fidrych hemmed him in by the wall. "Say, Brother Manning," she said, "did you ever live in Duchesne?"

"What is that, a planet?"

"No, it's in eastern Utah."

"Then the answer is no."

"You are so funny. Were you ever a stand-up comedian?"

"Not that I can remember."

"You look so familiar to me. It's driving me nuts. One of these days I'm going to figure it out."

"Good luck with that," Luke said. Then he escaped before anyone else could buttonhole him.

At home, he took the phone off the hook and didn't go out of the house the rest of the day. He ate two frozen pizzas and a bag of potato chips and swigged a liter of Pepsi while he watched football games.

Before going to sleep, he marked another X on his calendar.

Over the next few weeks, Luke was the most popular man in the ward, much to his dismay. After all that emphasis in the discussions about agency, Luke soon discovered that in the Mormon Church he had no free time whatsoever. There was barely time to work on his book.

Ben and Jared invited Luke to the ward fathers and sons outing up American Fork Canyon. It was the first camping experience for both Luke and Jared. When it came time to leave, Jared cried and begged to stay in the canyon for another week. Luke, on the other hand, was cold and hungry the entire time. His left hip ached from sleeping on top of a rock. He would have begged to go home if he had to. Then, as soon as he returned home Saturday afternoon, tired, dirty, and smelling like a burned marshmallow, Brother Sweeney called and asked him to help clean the chapel.

"Don't you have janitors who do that?" Luke asked.

"Not anymore," Brother Sweeney said. "The Church has instituted a policy of having the members take care of the maintenance of the buildings. It's a blessing for us. The three hours go really fast. It's an invigorating experience." Luke begged to differ as he vacuumed, scoured the bathrooms, and swept dirt from around the building.

While Luke muttered to himself the entire time, Brother Sweeney whistled church tunes. He was just so darn perky, it made Luke want to close off Brother Sweeney's windpipe. He hated the way Brother Sweeney, and all the other Mormons, didn't pronounce the word "foyer" correctly. *It's not foy-ER, it's foy-YEA,* he thought. But he kept the thought to himself.

Another weekend was marred by something called the Primary Program, an annual event, or so he was told. Sister Watkins asked Luke to serve as the narrator of the program. That required him to read an uplifting, spiritual text and scriptures. He agreed to do it. It seemed better than having to wrestle the kids, especially Oliver, on the stand. Either way, he had to spend Saturday afternoon with the children at a singing practice at the church, keeping him from watching college football games. Again. The actual program on Sunday went relatively well, except for the two Sunbeams who started screaming for their mothers while Luke read the words to a hymn titled, "In Our Lovely Deseret."

That the children may live long, and be beautiful and strong
Tea and coffee and tobacco they despise,
Drink no liquor, and they eat but a very little meat;
They are seeking to be great and good and wise.

Hark! Hark! Hark! 'Tis children's music —
Children's voices, oh, how sweet,
When in innocence and love, like the angels up above,
They with happy hearts and cheerful faces meet.

The activities and meetings and service projects—Hark!—never ended. Not only was Luke invited to Family Home Evenings (which meant he could never watch Monday Night Football) and ice cream socials, Ben dragged him to one service project after another. Luke laid sod, raked leafs, and washed windows. He was certain by the time he made it back to New York, he would be looking for a chiropractor. Or shopping for orthopedic shirts.

And that wasn't all. One day, Ben and Stacie took him to the Lindon Cannery, where they canned beans and fruit for an entire afternoon. He was also asked to pinch-hit on daddy-daughter night when a young girl's father had to go out of town at the last minute.

When several young women in the singles ward who had seen Luke at church invited him to sing hymns on a Sunday night on the Mount Timpanogos Temple grounds, he respectfully declined. "I have this throat condition," he said. "My doctor told me to stay off it for a few years."

Still, the invitations kept rolling in. Brother McNabb, the ward scoutmaster, asked him to speak to the troop and help them pass off the journalism and communications merit badges. Luke did it, though he couldn't maintain the boys' attention for more than thirty seconds at a time.

Sister Watkins asked him to dress up as Nephi for sharing time in Primary and tell the story of Lehi's Vision. Luke had no clue about the story she was talking about, so he solicited help from Ben and Brooklyn, who explained it to him. After sacrament meeting, Luke dressed up in sandals and a leather skirt he found at Deseret Industries. He wore no shirt. The kids, not to mention the women in attendance, were so distracted by his appearance that they barely noticed that he didn't know the story very well.

Luke also attended Brother Sagapolu's ward luau at the park. Brother Sagapolu had poi roasting on a spit, rugby games, grass skirts for everyone, hula dancing, and ukelele-playing. At the end, he twirled a stick alight with fire on both ends, and received a hearty standing ovation for that. Almost every night, Brother Sagapolu would drive up and down the streets on his motorcycle wearing shorts, flip-flops, and a Hawaiian shirt, dropping in on random souls, bringing cheer and his goofy grin.

Luke was assigned hometeachers, too. They were Brother Monson, the Elders Quorum president and a seminary teacher, and Brother McGown, the Young Men's president and a computer guru. His hometeachers brought Luke a copy of the *Church News* and set him up with a subscription to the *Ensign*. The trouble for Luke was, they didn't limit their visits to once a month. It was more like once a week. During one visit, Brother McGown asked Luke if he wanted to help him and Ben coach the priests' basketball team, and Luke agreed to do it. What they didn't tell him, at first, was that the team practiced on Saturday mornings at 6 a.m.

By now, Luke had discovered the reason Mormons didn't sin. They didn't have time to.

While Ben was pulling weeds in the yard one Saturday afternoon, listening to a BYU football game on the radio, he spotted Luke, who was taking out his garbage.

"I see the Laurels and Mia Maids struck again," Ben said, wiping sweat from his face.

"Your Maids? What maids?"

"Those plates of cookies you keep getting on your porch. They're from the Laurels and Mia Maids, the teenage girls in the ward. You must notice that they always stare at you at church."

"They do?" Luke asked. "Why?"

"Face it, Luke. You're the ward matinee idol," Ben said, laughing. "But you won't have to worry about that next week. You know that general conference is coming up, right?"

"General what?"

"General conference," Ben said. "It's a weekend when the general authorities and the prophet speak to the members of the Church worldwide. No regular Sunday meetings."

"You mean, like a church holiday?" Luke asked, trying not to sound too happy. "These meetings, where are they held?"

"In the Conference Center in Salt Lake."

"All you Mormons can fit in there?"

"No, but it's on TV. You're invited to watch it at our house."

"Do you need a satellite dish to watch it?"

"No, it's on regular TV."

"What is it, a couple of hours?"

"Let's see. Six hours on Saturday, four on Sunday."

That was worse than going to church, Luke thought. "What time should I come over?"

"If you're here at nine, you can eat our traditional pre-conference brunch with us," Ben said, thinking that maybe the words of the apostles and prophets would convince Luke he needed to be baptized.

Luke decided he would go to the Kimballs, for the book's sake. When he awoke Saturday morning, it was raining hard. Not having an umbrella, Luke sprinted to the Kimballs and arrived soaking wet. As Ben gave Luke a towel to dry himself with, Luke suggested that maybe God had made it rain because he wanted all the Mormons to stay in their homes to watch conference. Ben and Stacie laughed. "There's probably more truth to that than you realize," Ben said.

The kitchen table was covered with plates of pancakes and fruit and pitchers of hot chocolate. After breakfast, Ben built a fire in the fireplace, clicked on the television, and had everyone gather around. Ben and Stacie cuddled on the couch. Brooklyn and Jared sat quietly on the floor with a large, laminated card featuring twenty-five squares. Each square contained a gospel-related picture and word or phrase on it, such as prophet, food storage, tithing, baptism, and Bible. Next to the card was a bowl of Smarties. Every time they heard one of those words or phrases, they would place a Smartie on the square. "If we get a Bingo," Brooklyn explained to Luke, "we get a scripture sticker." Jared had about five Smarties stuffed in his mouth.

This was not the way Luke wanted to spend another fall Saturday afternoon. Knowing that college football games were on TV, and not being able to watch them, was torture. Especially knowing that Syracuse, his alma mater, was playing on another channel.

Luke fought to stay awake. "What's up with all the speakers using their middle initials?" he asked.

"It sounds more dignified that way, I guess," Ben said.

"I bet you don't know what the B in President Hinckley's name stands for," Brooklyn said.

"You've stumped us," Stacie said with a smile.

"Bitter," Brooklyn replied proudly.

"Bitt-ner," Ben corrected.

"I know your initial," Brooklyn said to Luke.

"What is it?" Luke said.

"It's a D."

"What does it stand for?"

"Damon."

"How did you know?"

"My dad was practicing saying your full name before he was going to baptize you," Brooklyn said. "When you get baptized and if you become a General Authority, you'll be Elder Luke D. Manning."

Stacie and Ben tried not to laugh.

"The day that happens," Luke said, "is the day the Cubs and Red Sox play each other in the World Series."

Confused, Brooklyn went back to her Bingo card.

Luke was so bored, he started keeping track of the color of the tie of each speaker. By the end of the first two-hour session, he had tallied three red ties, one blue and one lavender. What that meant, he did not know.

Between the morning and afternoon sessions, Ben turned the channel to the Syracuse game before going to help Stacie with lunch. Syracuse was playing Miami, and the Orangemen were down 35-14. Brooklyn talked Luke into playing a Book of Mormon trivia game, though Luke had most of his attention on the TV. As he watched, Syracuse chipped away at Miami's lead. Brooklyn skunked Luke, of course, so she explained all about the Anti-Nephi-Lehies to Luke between the commercial breaks.

Then tragedy struck. Just after Syracuse drove for a touchdown to tie the score at 35 and force the game to overtime, Ben turned the channel. "Time for conference to start again," he said cheerily, then called everyone into the living room. During the opening hymn, Luke began fidgeting. He just had to find out the final score. Five minutes into the afternoon session, Luke discreetly motioned for Brooklyn.

"Can you do me a favor?" he asked.

"Yeah," she said. "Why are you whispering?"

"I'm not whispering," he whispered. "I need you to find out the score of the football game we were just watching. Can you go turn on the TV in your parents' room and find out for me?"

Brooklyn smiled mischievously. "Okay."

Luke gave her a piece of notebook paper and a pen. Then she tiptoed out of the living room as nonchalantly as possible.

"Where are you going, Brooklyn?" Stacie asked. "Conference has started."

"I have to run a quick errand," she explained.

She returned moments later and handed Luke the folded-up paper. Ben and Stacie exchanged quizzical glances at one another. Luke held the paper for as long as he could stand, so as not to act too anxious. Then he slowly unfolded it. In a seven-year-old's handwriting, he read, "41 to 35."

Perplexed, he called Brooklyn over again. "Which team won?" he asked.

"I don't know," she replied. "You just said you wanted the score."

Luke sighed and stewed in his agony. Conference dragged on and on. His misery was far from over, even when it finally ended. "I'll pick you up at 5:45 for the priesthood session," Ben said.

Luke hurried home and, after learning Syracuse had lost, stomped around for a while, convinced that things would have turned out differently had he been able to watch the game. He had to put it out of his mind, though, because the next challenge confronted him. His beloved Mets were about to play the Atlanta Braves in the Major League Baseball playoffs. Luke always loved October, when so many exciting sporting events converged. But even Ben, who loved sports, seemed almost oblivious to it all. *This guy has his priorities all out of whack,* Luke thought.

No way was Luke going to miss this game. Before Ben picked him up, Luke had an idea. He grabbed a transistor radio with an earpiece. It took him about fifteen minutes to rig up the contraption to make it as inconspicuous as possible. He placed the radio in his shirt pocket, slipped on his jacket, and threaded the wire through the back of his coat and around the neck of his shirt.

They arrived at the stake center and found seats next to Ben's dad and brothers. Luke made sure he sat next to a wall so Ben wouldn't notice the earpiece. As soon as the conference broadcast began and the lights were dimmed, he turned on the radio inside his jacket. At first, things were going swimmingly. The Mets took a 2-0 lead on a two-run home run in the fourth inning. While Luke wanted to leap off the pew, shout, and high-five somebody, he instead sat quietly. No one suspected a thing. His radio died in the top of the ninth inning with the score 2-1, bases loaded. He had forgotten to refresh his batteries. So he had to sit through the rest of the session and listen to the talks.

After the meeting, he spent an hour at the Kimballs' home, sipping cocoa and chowing down on scones with Ben's extended family. That, he found out, was a family tradition after every priesthood session. Everyone got together, ate scones and reviewed the meetings' highlights.

As for the highlights he was interested in, Luke returned home to watch SportsCenter. That was when he found out the Mets had lost and had been eliminated from the playoffs. In a way, he was relieved. He wouldn't want the Mets to win the World Series with him in Utah. That would be too much to bear.

In eight months, Luke would be back in New York. He would no longer have things like general conference interfering with his life.

CHAPTER 22

The following Sunday, it was back to the old grind. Ben got sick on Saturday, so he called Luke and asked if he could teach. He actually read the manual.

Somehow, between the Primary room and the classroom, Oliver got lost. The problem was that Luke didn't realize it until he was five minutes into his lesson.

"Hey," Brooklyn asked while Luke was explaining the differences between the National League and the American League to the children, "where's Oliver?"

Luke took a look around the room and his face turned a shade of alabaster. He remembered seeing him in opening exercises. Oliver was gone.

"Everybody, stay here," he told the class. "If any of you get off your seat, I'll put you in a lion's den, like what happened to that guy Daniel. Brooklyn, you're in charge."

Luke walked up and down the hallways, but there was no sign of the boy. So he went out one of the side doors of the church and scoured the area. Moving briskly around the building, he searched in and under every car in the parking lot. He rummaged through the bushes. He checked the banks of the creek that ran near the church. All sorts of worst-case scenarios popped into his head, including a few involving lawsuits. When he walked back into the building, Sister Watkins happened to stroll by. Seeing Luke, she panicked.

"Brother Manning," she said, "where's your class? Is everything okay?"

"Everything's fine except for one little thing," Luke replied. "I can't find Oliver."

Sister Watkins began hyperventilating. "Oliver's missing? We need to find the bishop! We need to call the police! We need to find someone to sit with your class! We need to find Oliver's parents! Oh no! I'm going to be released!"

Luke had been hoping he would find Oliver before it became an incident. At that point, it was too late.

"Calm down," he said to Sister Watkins. "We'll find him."

Word of Oliver's disappearance traveled fast. Church leaders, and the boy's parents, were called out of their classes to help conduct a search. Brother Budd, the Helaman City Police Chief and first counselor in the bishopric, was pulled out of a priesthood meeting. Within minutes, police cars surrounded the area. Nets were out, ready to drag the creek for a body. Dogs from the K9 unit were released to sniff around the building. Parents worried that there was a kidnapper on the loose, as unlikely as that seemed in Helaman. With the aid of a bullhorn, Brother/Chief Budd instructed people to search whatever room they were in for the missing child. Pandemonium ensued as parents tried to locate their own children first.

Meanwhile, Luke remembered Brooklyn telling him that Oliver liked to eat constantly. So he went to the only place he knew of that had food. Entering the empty chapel, he walked up to the sacrament table. As he quietly approached, Luke heard a muffled sound beneath the sacrament table. It was Oliver, stuffing his mouth with bread. Luke lifted him in his arms just as police officers stormed the chapel.

"He's okay," Luke said. "Just hungry, apparently."

The police officers grabbed Oliver from Luke and handed him to Oliver's parents. Brother and Sister Cluff cried as they embraced their son, who had crumbs on his shirt and pants.

"Thank you, Brother Manning," Brother Cluff said.

"Don't thank me," Luke said. "I'm the one who lost him in the first place."

Bishop Law tussled Oliver's hair. "You gave us scare, young fella," he said.

"This never would have happened," Sister Fidrych told the other members of the Relief Society Presidency, "if the bishop had a real teacher in there."

Luke expected a lecture from the bishop but didn't get one. In fact, nobody said much of anything to Luke the rest of the day. Except Stacie.

"Are you okay?" she asked.

. "I will be, eventually," Luke said. He turned to Brooklyn. "I need your help. From now on, you're Oliver's buddy. Please don't ever let him out of your sight, okay?"

"Okay," Brooklyn said.

"I can't believe I almost lost a kid," Luke said to Stacie. "I was scared to death."

"It happens to everyone."

"Has that happened to you? Have you ever lost a kid at church?"

Stacie thought for a moment. "Actually, no, I guess I haven't."

"I don't know what I would have done if something had happened to him," Luke said. "He's such an innocent kid. Why would God punish him like that? You Mormons say that we're here on earth to be tested. Why does he need to be tested?"

"I don't think the test is for him," Stacie said. "It's for us."

"Well," Luke said, "I flunked mine today."

Everyone returned to class. Almost everyone. Sister Watkins was hoisted onto a stretcher by her husband and Brother Sagapolu. As they lifted her inside the ambulance, she was babbling incoherently.

"She just needs some rest," her husband told Brother Sagapolu.

Luke couldn't wait for the day to end. After three hours of church, he was physically and emotionally spent. It had been one of the most draining days of his life. This masquerade was getting tougher and tougher.

Stacie had invited Luke to eat Sunday dinner with them again, but he felt like a leech, so he said no. Besides, he just wanted to go home and relax. He was about to sit down with a bowl of Wheaties and watch a football game when Ben called.

Ben said he was feeling much better after eating a bowl of Stacie's home-made chicken soup, and that he had great news.

Luke didn't like that excited tone in Ben's voice. It was never a good sign.

"A couple of weeks ago, I asked the bishop if you could accompany me on hometeaching visits," Ben said. "Brother Dunn just called to tell me we're home teaching companions."

"Somebody pinch me." Luke was not enthused, but Ben didn't seem to notice.

"We've been assigned three families in the ward to visit every month. Since it's the 20th already, do you mind if we drop by our families today?"

"Today? Right now?"

"I'll give the lesson this time, and you can do it next month. I'll pick you up at five."

Luke groused as he changed back into his church attire. So much for thinking Sunday was a day of rest. It was the most tiring day of the week, as far as he was concerned. Luke wondered which of his many sins he had committed to deserve this.

So, on a crisp, autumn Sunday afternoon, Ben and Luke set out to their appointments. The visits with the Larsen and Pearce families went relatively well, though Luke was miserable. He was sure he was going to come down with some dreaded disease after allowing the Pearce kids, who all had something, to climb all over him. Brother Pearce didn't say anything about the kids being ill until he and Ben arrived. "They have pinkeye," he explained, "but I'm sure, being our home teachers, the Lord will keep you from getting it. Just in case, I'd wash your hands with bleach when you get home."

At the Larsens' home, the family dog—a golden lab named Shasta—kept sniffing Luke and placing his head on his lap. Luke was sure his allergies would start acting up and, sure enough, he started sneezing violently.

After they left the Larsens, Ben told Luke they needed to keep track of the birthdays of each member of their three families. With each birthday, Ben suggested, they could deliver a birthday card and cake. Luke did the math in his head. Twenty-three people.

"Is this normal," Luke asked, picking dog hair off his pants, "or are you going for Home Teacher of the Year?" Ben laughed. Luke was going to have to ask Kilborn for a raise just to buy gifts for all those people. "Can you get a discount on cakes at your store?" Luke asked.

"Yes," Ben replied, "and we can have the baker individualize each one."

The third and final appointment, with the Gruber family, was not scheduled. As Ben and Luke crunched their way through the orange and yellow leaves that blanketed the sidewalk leading to the Grubers' front porch, Ben explained that this particular family was "inactive."

"Inactive in the sense that they don't exercise regularly?" Luke asked.

"No," Ben said, "more like, an inactive volcano ready to erupt. As in Mount St. Helens. They probably won't appreciate this visit." He explained the plan was just to make contact with them—that in and of itself, he said, would be a major challenge.

They removed their ties in the car when they arrived at the Grubers' house, so, Ben explained, as not to look "too churchy." Ben knocked on the door, but there was no response. He and Luke could hear the muted din of an NFL game on television. The bone-chilling wind and a chance to talk to a disgruntled church member gave Luke ample motivation to get inside that door, and maybe catch a few minutes of the game.

Ben knocked again.

When he had received the assignment of hometeaching the Grubers, Ben felt the pressure. The Grubers hadn't been to church, as close as anyone could figure, since sometime during President Ezra Taft Benson's administration. The whole scene, Ben thought, was somewhat reminiscent of his mission. Here he was, with his trainee—though this one was a non-member—showing him how it was done, waiting for a door to be slammed in his face.

The Grubers seemed like decent people. Ben saw them around the neighborhood, and he always went out of his way to greet them. They usually responded with a half smile and a look like, "Come any closer and I'll get a restraining order" on their faces. At the store, they'd see him coming and hide behind the rutabagas. Of course, the Grubers felt like The Ward Project, especially Brother Gruber, who, if you actually called him "Brother Gruber" to his face, was liable to slug you in the molars.

So ward leaders called him by his first name, Lloyd.

Lloyd was in his fifties. He was lanky, thinner than a lightpost, and had black hair flecked with gray. There was perpetual grease under his fingernails. As the long-time owner of an auto mechanic shop, he was an expert on brakes, alignment, rotors, state inspections, emissions testing, the works. If the man had gone to college, he would have earned a doctorate degree in Automotive Repair, with a minor in Gruff. When people were the least bit impatient with him, he had this little habit of yelling at them. Customer service was not one of his strong suits. But he usually did such a good job servicing their cars, customers literally lined up around the block. People came from as far away as Provo to see him. They scheduled appointments with him like they would schedule an evening at an upscale restaurant. You needed to have an appointment a week in advance for him to even look at a car.

Why the Grubers stopped attending church was anybody's guess. And almost everybody in the ward had an opinion on the subject. One rumor purported that he was upset when the bishop called him to be a scoutmaster and that was the end of his church-going days. Others thought that because Lloyd and his wife had five daughters, he was angry at God for not sending him any sons to carry on the family name and run the family business. Some claimed Brother Gruber was an alcoholic.

Ben wasn't sure about any of those theories. Having grown up in Helaman, Ben vaguely remembered when the Grubers were active. Lloyd had been the Sunday School president at one time, in fact. Sister Gruber had once been Ben's Primary teacher. From what he observed, their business had started to take off, and they began going to the shop here and there on Sundays to catch up with their workload. They hired more help and bought a boat and a motor home. After that, they were gone every other weekend and stopped attending church altogether.

For years, a litany of church leaders had paid visits to the Grubers in an attempt to re-activate them, to no avail. High priests, Elders Quorum presidents, stake presidents, and even a general authority had attempted to coax them back into the Church. The Grubers went through hometeachers like a box of Kleenex. Finally, one day Lloyd exploded and told them never to come back. That was eleven years earlier, just after Ben had returned from his mission. The way he heard it, Brother Newell and a fourteen-year-old companion stood at the front door, and Lloyd, wearing red boxer shorts and a tanktop, made quite a scene, saying that he didn't want anything to do with the Mormon Church again. According to the boy, beer cans were strewn throughout the house, which led to the rumors of Lloyd's alleged alcohol problem. Ben could just imagine a repeat performance, with Luke, the man he was trying so hard to be a role model for, at his side, witnessing it all.

Brother Monson had told Ben he felt the ward should try fellowshipping the Grubers again. Ben and Luke, he said, were the ones for the job. He felt "strongly impressed" to send them to the Grubers. But the longer he spent in front of that door, Ben was feeling "strongly impressed" to get off Lloyd Gruber's porch.

As for Luke, of course, he was new to this home teaching thing. While he thought it sounded quite sophomoric, he was curious. He'd never heard of a religion where parishioners made formal house calls on their fellow church-goers. Personal curiosity aside, however, Luke knew it was mandatory for his book that he get to know people who had stopped practicing Mormonism. This would give him a different perspective. He hoped that they would have some particularly nasty things to say about Mormons because he needed some juicy quotes for his book. Maybe they had some dirt on the Church that he could use.

Ben decided to knock one final time.

"Would somebody get the door!" Lloyd yelled from the living room, just a few feet from the door. A few seconds later, the door creaked open slightly. Lloyd's wife, Martha, appeared, looking like a frightened rabbit.

"Hi," Ben said uneasily. "I don't know if you remember me or not. I'm Ben Kimball."

Martha nodded. "How are you?" she asked quietly.

"I'm doing fine," he said, trying not to sound too enthusiastic. "This is Luke Manning. He moved into the, um, neighborhood recently." He consciously tried not to use the word "ward" or any church-related words at all. "Can we speak to your husband?"

Her face sunk like a cheap soufflé "I don't think that would be a good idea right now. He's watching football. The Raiders are on and he's a big Raiders fan."

"MARTHA!" Lloyd bellowed from his barcalounger. "Shut the door! We're not paying to heat the whole outdoors."

"Lloyd," she said, "Ben Kimball and a friend are here to see you."

Lloyd cast a baleful glance their way and shook his head in disgust. "Whatever they're selling, we don't want any."

"They really want to talk to you," Sister Gruber said.

Lloyd slammed a beer can on the table. After he stood up from his chair, he watched the Raiders kick an extra point, then stomped over to the door.

"What do you want? Mormons are not welcome here. I thought I made it clear I don't want anything to do with you. Or didn't you get that church memo?"

Luke liked this guy very much.

Ben hated confrontations. He kept thinking about that scripture in Alma, something about being bold but not overbearing. He introduced Luke to Lloyd.

"Like I said, what do you want? The game's about to come on again. Unless our house is on fire, get off my property. I've got a gun. Don't make me use it."

"Well, you see, I, um, we . . ." Ben stammered.

Lloyd was about to shut the door on his visitors when Luke, who didn't want to miss this opportunity to interact with an apostate, addressed him. "Hey," he interrupted, peering inside the doorway, "aren't the Raiders playing the Jets?"

"Yeah. So?"

"I'm a big Jets fan."

"Well, pretty boy, your Jets are getting their keisters handed to them today," Lloyd said, "twenty-four to nine."

"You're kidding. What quarter is it?"

"Middle of the fourth," Lloyd said.

"I'll bet you twenty bucks the Jets win this game."

Ben was pretty sure the Lord frowned on intermingling gambling and home teaching. But he remained silent. He knew Luke was onto something. Namely, he had at least momentarily stopped Lloyd from committing a double homicide.

"Nobody comes back on the Raiders. Not in Oakland."

"Okay then, do we have a bet?"

"You're not from around here, are you, boy?" Lloyd said.

"No. I'm from New York."

"*New York?* Figures. Twenty bucks it is. I don't take checks or credit cards, just cash."

"You've got a deal," Luke said.

Lloyd opened the door wider and returned to his easy chair. Ben and Luke walked in, shut the door, and sat down on the couch. Ben was astonished. Luke's methods were a little unorthodox, but Lloyd had let them into his living room. There had been some high rollers in the Church who hadn't gotten that far.

"You boys want a drink?" Lloyd sneered, brandishing a beer in front of their noses.

Luke wanted very badly to take him up on the offer.

"No, thanks," Ben said.

Luke acted like the biggest Jets fan in the universe. Following a long pass, New York had the ball first-and-goal at the Oakland five. Luke evoked names like Joe Namath, Mark Gastineau, and Weeb Eubank. "J-E-T-S! Jets! Jets! Jets!" he yelled at the TV.

Lloyd shifted in his chair as he gripped a beer can. "Keep it down, will you? I'm trying to watch a game here."

Luke secretly coveted that can of beer, but kept his attention on the game.

On the following play, a New York running back took a handoff, dodged a cadre of tacklers, and raced into the end zone untouched.

"Twenty-four to sixteen!" Luke exulted, pumping his fist. "My Jets are coming back!"

Lloyd crushed the empty beer can on his forehead. Martha poked her head out of the kitchen. She had her phone in hand, apparently ready to push 911 at a moment's notice.

Ben grew worried. If the Jets were to come back and win, Lloyd would be irate and likely never invite them back. That was the kind of man he was. He was a sore loser. On the other hand, come to think of it, he was a sore winner, too.

"Hey, I thought you guys didn't watch football on Sunday," Lloyd popped off during a commercial.

"Well," Ben said, trying to come up with something clever, "the Jets have a Mormon player on their team. We're just supporting a fellow member."

True enough. Linebacker John Flynn was a returned missionary from BYU who was in his second year with Jets. Of course, he only played on special teams. Ben could just imagine what Lloyd was thinking, that the Mormons had gone lax on some standards since his last trip to church.

Luke changed the subject. "Ben tells me you're the best mechanic in town."

"Well, he's got that right. I've had my own business for twenty-seven years."

"You know," Luke said, "I've got this Corvette that I've had some trouble with. It makes this harsh, grating noise when I turn on the ignition. You think you could help?"

"Bring it in to me," Lloyd said. "I'll look at it tomorrow."

"Tomorrow? Ben tells me you're booked weeks in advance."

"I am. But I like you. You're not like the rest of those Mormons. Come in at 8 a.m. and I'll see what I can do."

Lloyd Gruber never admitted to liking anyone. Ben silently thanked the Lord.

"Thanks," Luke said. "I'll be there."

"If the Jets win," he said, "it's on the house."

"Good enough," Luke said.

Seeing how easily Lloyd was charmed and disarmed by Luke, Ben felt about as useful as an ashtray at a ward yard sale. Turned out, the Raiders won, 31-23. Luke pretended to be crushed as he handed over twenty dollars to Lloyd.

Before they headed out the door, Lloyd stopped them. "Why did you guys come over here, anyway?" he asked.

"We just wanted to get to know you better," Ben said.

"I just wanted to get my car fixed," Luke said.

As usual, Ben thought, Luke knew just what to say.

"You guys can come over again next Sunday, to watch football," Lloyd said, laughing. "You bring the beer."

After saying good-bye, Ben opened his car door. "I didn't know you were such a Jets fan," he said to Luke.

"I'm not," Luke said. "I'm actually a Giants fan."

CHAPTER 23

As planned, Luke took his car to Lloyd's shop that next morning. Lloyd identified the problem in about thirty seconds. While Lloyd worked, they talked. Luke discreetly turned on his tape recorder.

"The Church must really be getting desperate if they're sending people all the way from New York to visit me," Lloyd said proudly.

Then Luke told him he wasn't even a member of the Church.

"What are you doing hanging around the Mormons, then?" Lloyd asked. "Do you have a death wish or something?"

"I'm investigating the Church," Luke replied.

"Not only did they send someone from New York, they sent me a non-Mormon. Wow, I really have been out of the Church for a while. Well, I'm glad you're talking to me before you join. I can stop you from making a big mistake. You wouldn't have found out until it was too late."

"What do you mean by that?" Luke asked. "Why did you stop going to church?"

"To begin with, they're always pestering you," he said, his head under the hood, examining the engine. "They don't know how to take no for an answer and leave people alone. Besides, you can't trust them. Especially the leaders. They're hypocrites. Besides, as long as that man is the bishop, I'll never set foot in that church."

A large red flag starting waving in Luke's journalistic head. *Maybe the bishop isn't as scrupulous as he appears,* he thought. Wanting to give Lloyd a hug, Luke turned up the volume on the tape recorder in his jacket pocket.

"You mean Bishop Law?"

"Who do you think I mean?" Lloyd snapped, picking up a socket wrench.

Luke couldn't imagine anyone disliking the bishop. He was just a down-to-earth, humble man. Or so it seemed.

"What beef do you have with him?" he asked. "Did you guys have a falling out or something?"

"He tows cars in here all the time, but I refuse to speak to him."

"Why?"

"I've said too much. If you join the Mormon Church, you'll find out for yourself."

Finally, Luke had a lead. He was determined to keep an eye on Bishop Law.

Lloyd fixed Luke's car in a matter of minutes. He didn't even charge Luke a dime for his services. "I wouldn't feel right about taking more money from you," Lloyd said.

Soon, fall settled on Helaman and temperatures dropped like a 350-pound pole vaulter. Snow covered the tops of the Wasatch Mountains and Luke enjoyed the view. He didn't mind the change in weather. It kept him inside and spurred him to work more on his book.

Kilborn occasionally called, usually at the most inopportune times. It was as if he disregarded the two-hour time difference between New York and Utah. Luke would be asleep at 7 a.m., and Kilborn would wake him up, seemingly just to irritate him. Or Luke would be watching a ball game or a video, and Kilborn would call and ruin his evening. Luke pretty much cringed every time the phone rang. It was either Kilborn or somebody in the ward, usually Ben, asking him if he needed anything or if he would help with one thing or another. Mostly, Luke let his answering machine take care of the phone.

Of course, Kilborn always asked Luke how the book was coming. "It's a real page-turner," Luke always replied. Whenever he finished a chapter, he would e-mail a copy to the editors at Halcyon Publishing, who would then let Kilborn read it. Sometimes, Kilborn would quibble with a few things, mostly about nit-picky grammatical usage. One time, Luke tried in vain explaining the difference of the verbs "affect" and "effect." Another time, they got into a heated argument about dangling modifiers, to the point where Luke wanted to take a dangling modifier and use it to tie Kilborn to a train track.

But when it came to the content, Kilborn was thrilled. Luke portrayed the Mormons as teetotaling, minivan-driving, Jell-O-eating, food storage-collecting fools. Luke did not spare any harsh indictments, which, according to his research, were justifiable. To Kilborn, all shots taken at the Mormons were justi-fied. Kilborn especially enjoyed hearing that gubernatorial candidate Tim Munchak, in order to draw media attention to himself, was sleeping in a tent outside the State Capitol building in Salt Lake City.

The one element both Kilborn and Luke knew their book needed, though, was a scandal. What better way to sell gobs of books and ensure that it would be on the *New York Times* bestsellers list? Luke knew that discovering a scandal usually happened as a result of both hard work and serendipity. One day while driving aimlessly around Helaman, Luke thought he had stumbled upon a motherlode of a scandal.

It was a week before Halloween and Luke saw Bishop Law park his tow truck in front of a run-down apartment complex, the only run-down apartment complex in town. Wearing his navy blue jumpsuit, with a "Law's Towing" patch on the back and his name embroidered above the shirt pocket, Bishop Law entered the complex with a large box. Remembering what Lloyd had said about the bishop, Luke stopped to check it out. He waited for the bishop to come back out. Twenty minutes passed. Then forty-five minutes. An hour. The longer he was in there, the more suspicious Luke became. One thing was certain, he wasn't there to tow a car.

Luke knew there was something odd about the bishop, besides his slight lisp and gnarled hands. He was different from most religious leaders he knew. No fire-and-brimstone speeches. No ostentatious garb. No fancy cars. When he wasn't driving a tow truck, he drove an '83 Honda Accord.

While Luke sat in his car, listening to Jimmy Buffett, several men, shady characters in Luke's estimation, went in and out of the building. Finally, when the bishop appeared, so did a Latino woman. She hugged him, as did three small children, one by one. Bishop Law then got into his truck and drove away.

Luke's imagination started going berserk. Just the scandal his book needed. That night, he decided to investigate further.

"The bishop sure gets around, doesn't he?" Luke asked Ben.

"What do you mean?"

"I see him all over the place."

"That's his life," Ben said. "In fact, this afternoon, he was in our store. When I first saw him, I thought there was a ward emergency. It's the first time he's been in in a while. He said he just had to pick up a few things. But I know he's not one to shop."

"Like what?" Luke asked.

"That's what was weird about it," Ben said. "He bought some cough medicine, a bunch of cleaning products, and some cookies. I asked him jokingly if he was having a party and he just laughed."

Late that night, about 1 a.m., Luke dressed in disguise, putting on some old clothes, a wig, and a pair of sunglasses that he had purchased at Deseret Industries. Using black shoe polish, he darkened his face.

When he arrived at the apartment complex, he saw an unusual number of people going in and out, so he decided to snoop around. Inside the building, paint was peeling, floor tiles were loose, garbage was strewn to and fro. Many of the windows were covered up with cardboard. There was a distinct smell he recognized. He had done a story months earlier about methamphetamine labs abounding in the West, and the bitter odor struck him immediately. Soon, it caused his eyes to water and his throat to burn. He went back outside and opened a garbage can. Inside he found broken glass bowls, a pile of stained rubber gloves, some eyedroppers, empty boxes of medicine, and empty cans of cleaning products.

Luke added everything up and came to a stunning conclusion: the apartment complex was one giant methamphetamine kitchen. Bishop Law, Luke figured, was the head chef.

Luke returned inside. Peeking between cracks in the doors, he saw equipment to create fake identifications and all sorts of items that had probably been stolen.

Suddenly, a middle-aged man accosted him. "What are you doing here?" he asked menacingly.

Luke pretended to be drunk, lost, and confused. "Hey man, got some crank?" he asked, remembering the street term for meth.

"You got money?" said the man, who had a handgun tucked in the waistband of his pants.

"Not on me," Luke said.

"You produce some cash, then we'll talk."

Then the man called for a friend and they grabbed Luke by the lapels of his greasy coat and escorted him outside, throwing him into the parking lot. Luke didn't care. He had found the break he was searching for, and he could hardly believe his good fortune. The bishop was in the middle of something big. And bad. Maybe he was on the verge of a Jim Bakker fall-from-grace story. Luke loved writing those. It wasn't every day that a religious leader was found subsidizing a meth lab. Lloyd was right. Bishop Law was a hypocrite.

Luke decided he would keep following the bishop around for a while. Sure enough, almost every day around lunchtime, he saw the bishop go inside the apartment complex and stay for about an hour. Luke had a pretty good idea of what was going on.

He planned to proceed with caution. First, he would have to come up with some hard evidence. Who knew where a drug ring would lead? Maybe all the way to the hierarchy of the Mormon Church. This scandal consumed him to the point that he put his book on the back burner, knowing if he could break this open, it could take a whole new turn. Using a computer program he had from his days at the *Post*, Luke looked up criminal records on Bishop Law. He found nary a speeding ticket.

The following afternoon, Brother Sweeney called.

"How are you, Luke?"

"Fine. How are you?"

"Best day of my life. Say, the bishop would like to see you Wednesday night."

Perhaps the bishop knew that Luke was on to him. But Luke welcomed the opportunity to find out more about the bishop.

Luke showed up at the scheduled time, Halloween night. It worked out well, since he preferred not being bothered all night passing out candy. Before he left for the church, Brooklyn and Jared showed up. She was dressed as a pioneer girl. Jared was dressed as Brigham Young, fake beard and all. Luke dumped a package of beef jerky he had lying around into their buckets and left for his appointment.

As usual, Luke arrived early and approached the bishop's office. The door was cracked slightly and he could hear voices inside.

"We've got to make the distribution on the night of the 24th," he heard Bishop Law say, "and we've got to make sure all the goods are collected by the 15th, at the latest. Make sure to keep things under wraps."

"That won't be a problem," said a voice belonging to Brother Budd. Luke hurried and ducked around the corner just before Brother Budd walked out.

The cops are involved, too! Luke thought. *It is almost too good to be true.*

After waiting for Brother/Chief Budd to leave the building, Luke knocked on the bishop's door and Bishop Law invited him to sit down.

"Brother Manning," the bishop said, leaning forward, "is everything going well in your life? You seem a little tense." Luke felt as though the bishop was looking right through him again. It was an eerie feeling. Yet Luke also felt as though he was looking right through the bishop.

"I'm fine," Luke said. "I just have a lot on my mind."

"Is there anything I can do to help?"

"No, don't think so," Luke replied, trying to mask his annoyance.

"I hope you've given more thought to your baptism. Has your life changed at all since you've been participating more fully in the ward?"

"Believe me, my life has changed completely," Luke said.

"Glad to hear that."

Then the bishop's cell phone started ringing.

"I'm sorry, Brother Manning," the bishop said, "I usually turn this off when I'm here. Will you excuse me?"

"Sure," Luke said, thinking it might be one of the bishop's dealers on the other end.

The bishop mumbled something, wrote down a couple of notes, then hung up.

"Luke, I apologize, but there's an emergency I need to take care of," he said, picking up a copy of the Book of Mormon. "I've got someone stalled on I-15. If you'd like, we could reschedule for Sunday morning or, if you don't mind waiting, I should be back in twenty minutes."

First off, Luke did not want to have to get up any earlier than already necessary on a Sunday. Second, it was a chance to do some digging.

"I'll wait," Luke said.

"You're welcome to read my scriptures while I'm gone," the bishop said. Then he thanked Luke for his patience and excused himself. Luke was surprised that the man would leave him alone in his office. He started searching for documents, for any evidence, linking the bishop to anything criminal. He found nothing, but, he realized, even this guy wouldn't be dumb enough to leave evidence in his church office. *Maybe it's a ploy,* Luke thought, *to get me to believe that he's innocent.* Then he heard someone whistling in the hallway. Luke hurriedly cleaned up Bishop Law's desk again. Brother Sagapolu entered the office.

"Hey, bruddah," he said, shaking Luke's hand. "How are you doin'?"

"That's quite a grip you have."

"That's from picking pineapples when I was young," Brother Sagapolu said, showing him his massive wrists. "This is what happens when you grow up in Hawaii."

"You ever play football?"

"You betcha, bruddah. I played a little football about ten years ago at BYU."

"What position?"

"Defensive lineman."

Surely, Luke thought, *this guy is in on the bishop's sordid operation, too. Every crime ring needs an enforcer, after all. This guy certainly fits the bill. The bishop probably sent Brother Sagapolu over to check on me,* Luke thought. *There is a Mormon Mafia after all.*

Brother Sagapolu left as soon as the bishop returned. The bishop's white shirt and tie was blotted with dirt and grease. "Sorry about that interruption," he said.

"You look like you just took a swim in a vat of motor oil," Luke said.

The bishop laughed. "I had to help a man with a flat tire. He was a nice guy. From Arkansas. I'm at the beck-and-call of AAA."

"I noticed you took a Book of Mormon with you when you left."

"Every time I go out on assignment like that I like to take one with me, in case the person I help isn't a member of the Church. This guy wasn't. He took the book. Maybe he'll read it. Anyway, let's get back to you. How are you doing with your Book of Mormon reading and your personal prayers?"

Luke couldn't believe the man had the gall to ask such things. "That's kind of a personal question, isn't it?"

"Yes, that's the point," Bishop Law said. "I'm here to help you. If there's one thing that I would advise you, as your bishop, to always do, it's to pray, fervently and humbly, every day. Do that, and I promise you that you will be blessed. It takes work, I know. But it pays big dividends. Especially when you need help from above. And remember, you can't offer a fifty-cent prayer and expect a million-dollar answer."

The bishop didn't stop there.

"You're a fine member of our ward and I want to see you continue your progress. I understand your reservations about baptism, but I have been impressed with what I have seen from you. You're at all the ward functions, and you're always volunteering for service projects. A lot of members of the ward can learn from you. We just need you to become an official member of the Church. Baptism, as you know, is an important step. You may feel unworthy to receive this ordinance, but I assure you, once you're baptized, you'll understand that the Lord forgives. Just as this dirty shirt will become white again after my wife washes it, you too can become clean through baptism."

As far as Luke was concerned, the bishop was the biggest hypocrite he'd ever known.

"Yes, I understand the importance of baptism," Luke said. "When I decide to do it, you'll be the first to know."

"Good enough," the bishop said. Then he asked questions about Luke's work, but Luke revealed little. He also did a little prying of his own, hoping the bishop would let something slip.

"Your first counselor is quite a guy."

"Oh, he is," the bishop said. "T.J.'s our gentle giant."

"He said he used to play football."

"Is that all he told you? He's so modest. That's typical of him. He was all-conference at BYU. He was, uh, I don't recall what position. Left fielder? I'm not much of a sports fan. But he was recruited for the NFL."

"He was drafted?"

"Drafted, yes."

"Did he actually play in the NFL?"

"I don't know. He was drafted by the Cowboys, but he never talks about playing in the NFL."

"What does the T.J. stand for?"

"Thomas Jefferson. His mom was a big fan of our third president, I guess. Say, before you go, Sister Law and I would like to invite you over for dinner next week. How's Wednesday night, seven o'clock?"

Sure, Luke thought, *what a perfect place to poison me.* "I'll be there," he said.

He went back home and got on the Internet to do some research. Sure enough, Thomas Jefferson Sagapolu had been drafted in the third round by the Dallas Cowboys. Luke also discovered that as a youth in Hawaii, Brother Sagapolu had a police record. Arrested for grand theft auto. The tow-truck driving bishop, the ex-con Tongan football player, and the Chief of Police had a crime ring going on, Luke just knew it. He was so excited about his discoveries he could hardly sleep.

Early the next morning, an hour before dawn, the phone rang. Luke figured it was Kilborn, but he decided to answer it anyway. It was Ben. "Sorry to call so early," he said. "Some of the men in the ward are needed to shovel the snow on the sidewalks and driveways of some widows' houses. We've organized a Ward

Snow Patrol. I know this is a funny time to be asking for volunteers, but we're a little short of manpower. Would you like to join us? I'm going in about ten minutes."

"You mean it snowed last night?" Luke said, opening his blinds. "It was fifty-five degrees yesterday."

"Vintage Utah weather," Ben explained. "It is November. We got about two feet outside."

Luke wanted to say he had malaria, or come up with some sort of excuse that sounded plausible, but he knew he had to show up, for the book's sake.

In the early morning darkness, Luke trudged through the snow to Sister Wilmsmeyer's house. Brother Sagapolu was already there, wielding a shovel and wearing a thick coat, shorts, and flip-flops. "We don't get weather like this in Hawaii, bruddah," he said.

Just as Luke was wishing he were in Hawaii, Ben showed up, carrying an extra shovel for Luke. As they worked moving piles of snow, Luke couldn't stop thinking about the bishopric's exploits. While Brother Sagapolu shoveled the sidewalk, out of earshot, Luke struck up a conversation with Ben about Brother Sagapolu's past.

"I hear he played pro football," Luke said.

"Actually, he didn't," Ben said. "He was drafted by the Dallas Cowboys, but his career ended in training camp before his rookie year."

"Injury?"

"Yes, but not his own."

"You're going to have to explain that one to me."

"During practice one day with the Cowboys he hit the fourth-string quarterback so hard, the quarterback's helmet came off. Gave him a concussion," Ben explained. "T.J. felt terrible about it. The next day, he returned to camp, turned in his helmet and the rest of his equipment. He told the owner that God was putting him on waivers. He didn't want to play anymore. He decided he didn't want to hurt another player or play on Sundays. He returned his signing bonus and voided his contract. Man, were the Cowboys mad. The owner and general manager screamed obscenities at him for an hour, upset about wasting a draft pick on him, on a quitter. Then his agent screamed obscenities at him, upset about losing a client. I think T.J. cried. He felt so bad about the whole situation, he sent the Cowboys organization a box of pineapples every year—until they started winning Super Bowls again. He figured they had forgotten about him by then."

"What does he do now?" Luke asked.

"He directs those Church public service announcements. You know, the commercials that show people helping each other and families being together, with the sentimental music in the background. They're very good."

"Yes, I've seen them," Luke said. "I weep every time I see them."

What a story this was shaping to be, he thought. He could just see it—the three leaders of the ward, being fitted for orange jumpsuits and checking in for an extended stay at the gray-bar hotel. Kilborn would be so thrilled.

CHAPTER 24

When Bishop Law announced to the congregation that a special meeting would be held in one week, at 6 p.m., the ward started buzzing. "I can't tell you exactly what's going to happen at this meeting," he said, "but I would advise you to be there, especially if you're hoping to have a new bishop."

Luke wondered if the bishop was planning to resign, a la Richard Nixon.

Members of the ward knew exactly what was happening. Ben explained to Luke that the meeting had to do with splitting the ward. "They've been talking about that for about a year," Ben said. "But it has to go through all the church-related red tape first. It takes time."

Rumors ran rampant that week. There was speculation about who the bishop of the new ward would be and where the new boundaries would be. On Tuesday night, Ben paid Luke a visit. Luke was working on his book in the living room and quickly hid all of his notes and books when he saw Ben was at the door.

"I'm not really one to engage in gossip and rumor-mongering...," Ben began.

"Thanks for the disclaimer."

"Stacie was talking to Sister Fidrych and, well, it appears the ward may be splitting down our streets."

"Meaning that we wouldn't be in the same ward anymore?"

"Afraid so. You might be in the new one."

Luke was steamed. All this work, all this time invested in the ward, and now it looked as if he would have to start over.

"That's the dumbest thing I've ever heard," he said. "Why split it here?"

Ben was afraid of that reaction. The last thing he wanted was for Luke to be mad, to feel disenfranchised, and never return to church at all. "Well, it's not official, of course. But I just wanted to prepare you. I hope it doesn't happen."

"If it does, can we appeal? We can overturn it, right? Sign a petition? Go to court? Who do we need to talk to? The stake president? I'll take it to President Hinckley if I have to."

"Well," Ben said, feeling like he was going to be cursed for taking part in this conversation, "things in the Church don't exactly work that way. If it happens, we just have to believe it's the Lord's will. Besides, just because we're in different wards doesn't mean we can't associate anymore. We'd still see each other at stake conferences twice a year." Ben smiled.

Luke figured the bishop was behind all this, trying to run him out of the ward. If the bishop suspected Luke might be on his trail, what better solution than to conveniently cut him out of the ward boundaries? The more he thought about it, the angrier he became. *How can these Mormons just accept their leaders' decisions so blindly?* he wondered. *Why does everyone feel the need to conform? Haven't they heard of democracy?*

Then it occurred to him: why should he worry? He wasn't even a member of the Church, let alone a member of the ward. He would attend whatever ward he wanted. Just the same, Luke was going to bring it up during his dinner with the bishop the next day.

While he ate at the Laws' new dining room table—Luke learned that the bishop had recently bought it for his wife—he tried to pin Bishop Law down on what was happening with the ward split. But Bishop Law was as inscrutable as a CIA agent. If he knew something, he wasn't telling. Luke tried the bishop's wife next.

"I'm married to the man and I don't have any idea what's going to happen," Sister Law sighed. Luke was sure, too, that the poor woman was blissfully unaware of her husband's secret life.

As they finished eating, the bishop was called out on a work assignment again. Luke thought it was suspicious. "Honey, save some dessert for me," the bishop said as he hugged his wife and kissed her cheek.

"We'll try," she said.

Naturally, Luke took advantage of the opportunity to talk to Sister Law. She gave him a quick tour of the living room and showed him the pictures of relatives on the wall.

"So," he said, "you don't have any children?"

"No. But how we wish we did," Sister Law said. "We've had some foster children in our home from time to time, but we've never adopted. We tried all our married lives to have children of our own, but I suppose it just wasn't the Lord's will for us. Before we got married, I told Sam I probably couldn't have children because of a medical condition I have. But he told me he loved me, no matter what. I feel so bad for him, because I know how much he would like a son or daughter. I think that's why he loves to be with children so much. Sam has never complained to me or to the Lord about not having children. I know it rips his heart out, like it does mine sometimes, but you'll never see it. There's not an angry bone in his body."

"The bishop sure seems to keep busy," Luke said, changing the subject.

"He sure does," she said. "It's not uncommon for him to receive calls at two o'clock in the morning. He answers the phone and leaves, and I never know until the next day whether it was church-related or work-related. He's gone quite a bit. I can hardly keep track of him these days."

If only you knew where he's been and what he's been doing, Luke wanted to tell her.

"Nice TV," Luke said, pointing to a big-screen TV in the living room.

"Thanks. Sam bought it for me for our anniversary. It's so out-of-character for him. He's the least materialistic person I know. I'm not sure how we could afford it. Maybe we're being blessed for paying our tithing," she joked.

You keep thinking that, Luke thought. Everything was making sense.

When Sunday arrived, the main topic of conversation, of course, was the impending ward changes. "There's no greater intrigue in the Church," Ben told Luke, "than the creation of a new ward and changes in ward leadership." Luke found himself caught up in the speculation. Anticipation increased to a fever pitch. At church, the parking lot was filled, even more than usual. Members of two wards in Helaman were invited to the meeting, since the split would affect both. President Mathis, who was a millionaire real estate developer, stood at the pulpit and thanked the congregation, which stretched to the back of the cultural hall, for coming. There were hundreds of people sitting on folding chairs in the overflow area. The meeting began with an opening hymn and prayer.

These Mormons can't go to the bathroom without a song and prayer, Luke thought.

After quoting some scriptures found in the Doctrine and Covenants, President Mathis announced the changes. Fortunately for Luke, he was to remain in Bishop Law's ward, along with Ben and most of the other people he was writing about. His relief was short-lived, though. At the end of the meeting, the stake president told members of the 6th Ward that they had the assignment of taking down the folding chairs. Luke helped out, with Ben by his side.

"Glad you're still in our ward," Ben told him. The feeling was mutual.

After Ben and Stacie had tucked the kids into their beds one snowy evening, Brother Glenn, a member of the high council, invited Ben and Luke to play basketball over at the church with some other people in the ward. Brother Glenn figured it would be a good way to integrate the old and the new members.

Luke hadn't shot hoops for months, and he was happy to do something competitive for a change. It was a chance to unleash his many aggressions brought on by a deprivation of alcohol and women; a chance to teach these Mormon boys how to play the game. Besides, it would do him some good, he thought, to let his mind take a break.

Not surprisingly, he had never played basketball at a church before. He'd been bred on the mean blacktops of Syracuse, having played against a number of future college players. He was used to shooting at rusty, creaky rims with metal nets, and courts surrounded by a twelve-foot-high chain-link fence. In the background, sirens blared, and gunshots and rap music filled the air. No one dared call a foul without producing a death certificate.

Little did Luke know, he'd be right at home in ward ball.

Ben and Luke arrived with four other ward members. A couple of them he had already met, the others he didn't know. Luke expected these guys to ask permission before driving the lane. *I would like to penetrate into the paint, Brother. May I?* No way. Here were men with temple recommends, multiple dependents, and receding hairlines jockeying for position in the paint, wearing kneepads and diving for loose balls.

Ben and Luke were on the same team for the three-on-three game, and Luke drew the defensive assignment on Greg Dunbar. Ben knew a little about Dunbar, a fiery stockbroker, and sensed trouble. Dunbar lofted the ball toward the rim almost every time he touched it. He had an annoying little gesture that he made after each shot that went into the basket. He would pump his fist and swagger back down court, his blond hair flapping. He whined and called a foul every time Luke so much as breathed on him. He reminded Luke of another Mormon basketball player, one of greater repute, Danny Ainge. Dunbar was getting on Luke's nerves. He wanted to knock that smirk right off his face.

Dunbar had a patented, turnaround jump shot that Luke couldn't stop. He hit three in a row and talked smack all the way back down court. So Luke went right back at him with driving reverse layups and talked right back. "Luke, it's just a game," Ben told him while they ran down court.

"Stay out of this, Ben," Luke said. "This is personal."

That's what Ben was afraid of.

Dunbar hip-checked Luke on one drive, but Luke decided to let it go. The game turned into a one-on-one show. Dunbar would score, and then Luke would return the favor. Ben started getting nervous their duel would flare up. The other four guys, who on this night couldn't hit the basket with a Mac truck, just tried to stay out of their way.

When Luke tried to post Dunbar up, Dunbar reached around and hacked him on the wrist. Luke didn't say anything. When Luke skied up and dunked the ball, Dunbar about took out Luke's legs from under him. Luke tumbled hard to the floor, but, after glaring at Dunbar, got right back up. When he caught Dunbar cherry-picking for a breakaway layup, Luke knew he couldn't let him go untouched. As Dunbar went up toward the basket, Luke wrapped up on him and sent him careening head-first into the padded wall.

"Hey! What was that?" Dunbar screamed as he stood up, blood dripping from his nose.

"Good defense!" Luke yelled back.

Before Ben could react, Dunbar ran at Luke, diving into his midsection and both players crashed to the floor. Luke quickly flipped Dunbar on his back and both started slugging wildly. The other four men tried to break up the melee, without much success. Luke and Dunbar were wrestling on the hardwood and exchanging punches for what seemed like several minutes. There had been fights at the MGM Grand that hadn't seen that much action. Bruce Woodard, a high priest in his fifties, grabbed Luke by the scruff of his neck and tried pulling him up by his shirt.

"Let go of me, old man!" Luke barked.

"Cool it, you hothead!" Brother Woodard barked back.

Brother Woodard continued to pull on Luke's shirt as Luke broke free from Dunbar's grasp. Luke's flailing hand hit Brother Woodard's mouth, causing his front tooth to fly out of his mouth and skid across the floor.

Bishop Law heard the commotion from his office and strolled into the cultural hall. Upon seeing the bishop, the players froze almost immediately. Just like that, the brawl subsided. The bishop didn't need to say a word. After looking around for a spell, he finally spoke up. "So, who's ahead?" he asked dryly.

All six players were stupefied. "Um, sorry, bishop," was all Ben could get out of his mouth.

"Cold water should remove those bloodstains from the floor and the wall," the bishop said before turning around and heading back to his office. Quietly, the players filed into the bathroom, grabbed paper towels and started wiping up the smatterings of blood. Dunbar removed his shirt and placed it over his bleeding nose. Luke had a cut above his eye and a sore tailbone. Brother Woodard stooped down and picked up his tooth. Then they all parted ways without saying a word. Luke went home and showered. Ben accompanied Brother Woodard to the emergency room.

"That was a nice getting-to-know-you party, wasn't it?" Luke said to Ben later that night. Ben did not respond.

The following Sunday, The Brawl was the talk of the ward. Word of it had spread like a case of head lice. Brother Woodard, Sister Fidrych, and others, suggested Luke not be invited back to play again.

Brother Richards, the high priests group leader, Brother Monson, and Brother Sagapolu gathered the fracas participants in a room to clear up the matter. Brother Monson adjusted his glasses, broke out the scriptures, and started talking about brotherhood within the quorum—of which Luke, of course, was not a member.

"Brethren, the Lord doesn't tolerate fighting in His House," he said solemnly.

Luke rolled his eyes, over one of which he sported a Band-Aid. After Brother Monson's discourse, all the brawlers shook hands, even Luke and Dunbar. When Luke shook hands with Brother Woodard, though, Brother Woodard squeezed his hand especially tight, as if he were trying to crush every bone. Ben informed Luke that Brother Woodard had to get a fake tooth.

"You don't mess around with Grit," Ben told Luke later.

"'Grit?'"

"That's Brother Woodard's nickname. He's the toughest man I've ever known. They say once he was deer hunting and went off by himself to, well, you know, relieve himself. He put his gun down and started taking care of his business. Next thing he knew, a mountain lion started growling at him from only a few feet away. Brother Woodard wrestled with that lion for a good twenty minutes before he could grab his gun and shoot it. I remember he came to church that next Sunday with scratches and claw marks all over him, but acted like it was no big deal."

"Sounds like a regular Davey Crockett," Luke said. "I'll watch out for him."

There was no directive from the bishop or stake president, but those weeknight basketball games ended abruptly. Ben decided it was about time to retire from ward basketball pickup games altogether. No sense in risking a further loss of dignity, not to mention a loss of teeth.

With Thanksgiving approaching, Ben invited Luke to join in the Kimball family festivities. They went to Uncle LeVan's house for the traditional flag football Turkey Bowl game in his sprawling backyard. The game was an elaborate set-up, with T-shirts for both sides that read "Kimball's Market" on the front and "Best Prices In Town" on the back. The two teams were divided up, blue and red flags for each side, orange cones marking the sidelines and end zones. Uncle LeVan refereed. Ben quarterbacked one of the teams, and Luke was one of his receivers.

After the donnybrook at church, Ben was a little leery of Luke's aggressive nature when it came to sports. At the same time, Ben wanted to win the game since, as part of the Kimball family tradition, the losing team had to clean up the Thanksgiving dishes. And with eighty-one people showing up for dinner, there was no shortage of motivation. Luke wound up catching the winning touchdown pass from Ben in the final quarter, but the other team protested because Luke wasn't a relative through blood or marriage. Ben settled the dispute by offering his services, and Luke's, to cleanup detail. Brooklyn showed Luke how to scrub the plates and save leftovers. By the time he was through, Luke never wanted to eat turkey again for the rest of his life.

That night the Kimball clan, with Luke tagging along, traveled to Temple Square in Salt Lake City to see the Christmas lights. "No wonder you guys have to pay so much tithing," Luke said to Ben. "This electric bill's got to be a killer."

A couple of days after Thanksgiving, being the 24th of the month, Luke staked out the apartment complex, hoping to gather more evidence against the bishop and his accomplices. He knew something big was about to happen. Luke was prepared to wait all night for something to happen and he almost had to. At about 4 a.m., Luke saw a group of people enter and exit the complex. With the aid of binoculars, Luke saw they were carrying something, perhaps drugs. Unfortunately for him, none of those people included members of the bishopric. But Luke did not stop his investigation.

During the first part of December, Luke did everything he could to avoid malls and Christmas music. He had never been much of a fan of holidays. Brooklyn was excited for Christmas, of course, and Luke promised her he would buy her a present. One day Brooklyn came over and scolded him for not having a Christmas tree. He took her to a Christmas tree lot and she picked one out for him. She even decorated it.

With the holiday season having arrived, Luke could only imagine how these insufferable Mormons might be. Most of them acted like every day was Christmas as it was. But he was hip-deep in "Bishop Lawgate," which kept him occupied.

One afternoon, Sister Fidrych arrived at his doorstep selling Christmas candy for her son's school. Luke bought some just to get rid of her. But before he knew it, she and her son, Blake, were sitting on his couch. Sister Fidrych jabbered between bites of candy and Luke realized he might as well take advantage of her gratuitous information. Within forty-five minutes, he learned all of the gossip going on in the ward—for instance, that Sister Adams' husband was in prison.

"For what?" Luke asked.

"Embezzlement and check-kiting," she said. "He was the accountant at his business. He was also the financial clerk before he was sent to prison."

He's about to get an extended visit from the bishopric, Luke thought.

Sister Fidrych droned on about Sister Jenkins, who hadn't been to church in three months because she was associating with another "denomination," about Sister Evans, whose mother had recently passed away, about Sister Thomas and the wart she had removed from her big toe the previous Thursday.

For all the time they spent in church, these Mormons certainly have their share of hang-ups, Luke thought, *but none bigger than the one that belongs to Bishop Sam Law.*

CHAPTER 25

One bitter-cold evening, about nine, the sound of a gunshot, followed by police sirens, echoed throughout Helaman. Someone had called from the rundown apartment complex to report that a man was brandishing a gun and threatening to kill someone. That someone was Bishop Law.

The story that circulated after the fact went like this: the bishop had gone over for one of his visits. A man with glazed-over eyes and unruly hair had confronted the bishop as he made his way up the stairs.

"Is there anything I can do to help you?" Bishop Law asked.

"Get away, or I'll shoot you!" the man said, slurring his words.

"There's got to be a better solution than that," the bishop said. "What's your name?"

"Victor!" he screamed.

"Victor, our Heavenly Father loves you. Whatever is wrong, He can help you. Let's calm down and talk about it."

The man suddenly pulled a gun and demanded the bishop give him his wallet. The bishop removed it from his pocket and placed it on the ground. As the man reached for the wallet, he tumbled down the icy stairs and the bishop tried to break his fall. But the man was too heavy. The man's gun went off and ricocheted off the stairs. By the time he hit the bottom, the man was knocked out cold. The bishop tried to revive him. While all this was happening, a bystander saw the commotion and called the police. Several officers, including Brother/Chief Budd, arrived. They questioned the bishop and checked the man. They entered one of the apartments and discovered, just as Luke suspected, a massive meth lab operation. Four arrests were made. The Utah County Major Crimes Task Force evacuated the complex to prepare for decontaminating the building.

As the cops hauled people out in handcuffs, Luke and Ben arrived. So did other ward members, including Sister Fidrych and Brother Sagapolu. The bishop was being taken to the police station for further questioning, but not in handcuffs.

At the time Luke had been sure that all of his suspicions about Bishop Law were about to be confirmed. Bishop Law had fought the law and the law had won.

"Ben, T.J., Luke," the bishop called from the squad car, "could you please go help the Mendozas? They're going to be staying at my home for a while."

"Sure, Bishop," Ben said.

"Who are the Mendozas?" Luke asked.

"A family in the ward that lives here," Brother Sagapolu said.

Luke recognized Sister Mendoza and her children as the ones he had seen with the bishop at the apartment so many times before. But Luke had never seen Brother Mendoza, who was being pushed by Brother Sagapolu and Brother Budd in a wheelchair.

Since the Mendozas were being displaced from their home, Bishop Law made arrangements for them to move into his basement. Ben, Luke, and Brother Sagapolu helped them move their possessions. It didn't take long.

Luke was baffled.

While they carried a few items out of the Mendoza's apartment, Ben told Luke that Brother Mendoza and his wife had been baptized in Chile soon after they were married. Their dream was to live in Utah. Brother Mendoza had immigrated to the United States and left his family behind. For years he worked in California on an orange ranch, plus held down two or three other jobs, in order to earn enough money to bring his wife and children to the United States. He slept in fields and on park benches. Finally, he took all of his savings and sent for his family. They arrived in Utah and found a cheap apartment in Helaman.

A few weeks later, Brother Mendoza was involved in a serious car accident while he was traveling to California with some friends. It left him paraplegic.

Luke met Brother and Sister Mendoza and their three children, an eleven-year-old boy, a nine-year-old boy, and a six-year-old girl. "The beeshop is a very, very good man," Brother Mendoza kept saying. He told how Bishop Law, who had served a mission to Mexico, spoke Spanish with the family. He visited often, playing games with the children, teaching English to Sister Mendoza, for whom he had arranged some cleaning jobs around town to help them pay their bills.

So much for the scandal. To Luke's disappointment, Bishop Law had gone from scoundrel back to saint.

After Ben and Luke helped the Mendozas get settled in the basement, they went upstairs. Bishop and Sister Law had just returned from the police station. The bishop acted as if he had just got back from a ward outing. Sister Law, though, was lying on the couch, trembling.

"I knew being a bishop was tough, but I never thought of it as being life-threatening," Ben said.

"Oh, it's no big deal," the bishop said. "My wife's taking this harder than me."

"So should we refer to you as Bishop 007 from now on?" Luke asked.

"No, my crime-fighting days are over. I hope."

"Bishop Law never ceases to amaze me," Ben told Luke as they left. "Just when I thought I knew everything about him, something like his happens. He is always giving to those in need, quietly and anonymously. He tows people's cars for free sometimes. I don't know how he can make a living. He's never had much interest in money. When it comes to friends, though, he's as rich as Bill Gates."

If all that wasn't enough evidence to convince Luke of the bishop's innocence, Ben and Luke ran into Brother Budd.

"You're going to the meeting tomorrow night, right?" Brother Budd asked Ben.

"I'll be there," Ben said.

"What meeting?" Luke asked.

"Brother Budd and the bishop are in charge of the ward's annual sub-for-Santa project," Ben said. "They organize it every year. Brother Budd collects toys from his police officers and ward members. They have a party, complete with a turkey dinner, and give the presents to needy families on Christmas Eve. Hey, would you like to be involved? Maybe we could help a family together. How about it?"

At that point, Luke felt like Ebenezer Scrooge. He realized what the big distribution on the 24th was. It was the 24th of December, and it had nothing to do with drugs and everything to do with toys. "Sure," Luke said. "You might as well sign me up."

When Luke got home, he took his files on the bishop and tossed them in the garbage. The next day in the local papers the bishop was called a hero for breaking up a crime ring. Police confiscated $400,000 worth of drugs during the bust. That meant Luke had to rewrite pages and pages of material about Bishop Law.

Kilborn was furious. "It's time to find a new scandal," he huffed.

Luke decided to start with Brother Gruber. That second weekend in December, Ben asked Luke to set up a hometeaching visit with the Grubers.

"Have you been baptized yet?" Lloyd asked when Luke called.

"Nope."

"Good for you. Keep holding out. But why are you doing all these Mormon things if you're not a member?"

"I'm just easing my way into the Church," Luke said.

"Like the *Titanic* easing into the ocean," Lloyd said, laughing. "Be careful. And you can tell your Mormon friends up front that I am never going back to Church. I want to make that clear. If you guys still insist on coming over, you have to promise that we won't talk about the Church."

"Tell you what," Luke said. "We'll only talk religion for five minutes. That's it. I promise."

"Two minutes."

"Three."

"Two-and-a-half."

"It's a deal."

When Luke informed Ben about the compromise, Ben didn't mind too much. Growing up, he often had to deliver two-and-a-half minute talks. They arrived at the appointed time and Lloyd told his family to leave the room. Then Lloyd set his watch. "You've got 150 seconds," he announced. "When the alarm sounds, no more talk about religion."

Ben tried to prepare the most uncontroversial topic he could think of—prayer. If he could get Lloyd to start praying again, maybe he would feel the Spirit, and he'd realize what he and his family had been missing out on for so many years. Ben culled the best quotes he could find on the subject and crafted a perfect message. But it didn't matter. While Ben talked, Lloyd stared at his watch as if he were keeping the official time of an Olympic track and field event. Ben felt as though the stuffed moose head above Lloyd's chair was gleaning more out of it than Lloyd was.

"Time's up!" Lloyd shouted as the alarm sounded. Ben was stopped mid-sentence during a profound comment.

"Hey, did you guys see that game the other night?" Lloyd asked.

Ben and Luke stayed for nearly an hour. They talked about sports, the weather, Lloyd's business, and, finally, about ward business.

"I heard about what happened to Sam Law," Lloyd said. "How is he doing, anyway?"

"As good as ever," Ben said.

Lloyd looked at Luke. "When we talked about him at my shop a while back, I probably left you with the wrong impression about him," Lloyd said. "I may have led you to believe he was dishonest in his business practices. Sam Law is a lot of things, but dishonest isn't one of them. For some reason, ever since I told you that, it's been bugging me. I'm still not on speaking terms with the man, but I thought I should tell you that."

"What is it about the bishop that bothers you?" Ben asked.

"It seems kind of silly now," Lloyd said, itching the back of his head. "A long time ago, my business wasn't going very well. We had some financial setbacks. I told my daughters before Christmas that year they wouldn't be receiving any gifts. Well, on Christmas Eve, kinda late, I heard a commotion at the front door. I opened it and there, sitting on the porch, was a pile of gift-wrapped boxes."

"That's neat," Ben said.

"I didn't think it was," Lloyd snapped. "I don't believe in handouts. I took those presents, loaded them in the back of my pickup truck and left them at the church. I knew someone in the ward was involved and I was angry. To me, it was an insult, as if someone was saying I wasn't good enough to provide for my family. I was bound and determined to track down the culprit. It took me about four months, but I finally figured it out. Sam Law, who was the Elders Quorum president at the time, was behind it. I was spitting mad. I confronted him about it and I've held a grudge ever since." He paused. "Like I said, seems kinda silly now."

Ben saw Lloyd Gruber's rock-hard exterior start to crack. Luke saw Lloyd slipping away.

Digging up dirt on the Mormons, at least on the ones Luke knew, was tough. Especially now that the holiday season was approaching. Even Lloyd was losing his Grinch-like tendencies. Maybe it was the foul weather, or the fact that his theory about Bishop Law had fallen through, but Luke's mood was growing more foul by the day. Blinking Christmas lights festooned the houses around his, lighting up the street like the Las Vegas strip. The Kimballs had a plastic Santa Claus and eight tiny reindeer sitting on their lawn. As a form of silent protest, Luke deliberately kept his porch light off, leaving an empty black hole at night where his house sat.

Naturally, Ben invited Luke to participate in the ward's twelve Days of Christmas service project. One family or ward member would take a night and deliver a gift to a widow or shut-in in the ward. Luke agreed to do it, begrudgingly. His volunteered to do Day One to get it over with quickly, so he showed up at an assigned house carrying canned pears—symbolizing a Partridge in a Pear Tree—that he bought at Kimballs' Market. He felt ridiculous as he rang the doorbell. A nurse in a white outfit answered the door and looked at him suspiciously.

"Hello," Luke said. "My name's Luke Manning. I'm here to visit Mable Sterling."

"Does she know you?" the nurse asked.

"Actually, no. I live down the street, and I'm helping out with this ward service project."

"She's asleep right now, but you're welcome to come in," she said. "Wait just a moment."

When the nurse returned to the living room, she wheeled Mable out in a wheelchair.

"Are you sure this is okay?" he asked.

"Oh, yes. She loves visitors. She's ninety years old and she doesn't walk too well anymore. Her children tried to get her to go to a nursing home, but she wanted to stay at home."

"I have a small gift for her, if you want to give it to her when she wakes up."

"I'll do that," she said. Then Mable started to stir. She slowly opened her radiant blue eyes and looked directly at Luke.

Luke told her who he was and explained he had something for her. "It isn't much," he said. Then the woman grabbed his hand. It startled him at first. Her hand was warm and her grip surprisingly strong.

"Thank you," she said weakly. "What's your name, young man?"

"Luke Manning," he said.

"So nice to meet you."

On a table was a black-and-white picture of a happy couple. "Is this you?" he asked.

Mable smiled.

"That's her with her late husband, Elder Robert B. Sterling," the nurse said. She waited for Luke to react, but he didn't. *"The* Robert B. Sterling. You know, the General Authority."

"A General Authority?" Luke asked.

"You must not be a member of the Church," said the nurse.

"No, I must not be."

"That's okay," Mable said. "I wasn't a member either when I met my husband."

Luke didn't know what it was, but he knew he had to get to know this woman, for his book's sake. "I'd like to come back another day and talk to you," he said. "Would that be okay?"

"I'd like that."

"She loves to have visitors," the nurse said.

"Thank you so much for your visit, Luke," Mable said.

He shook Mable's hand again and looked into her eyes. They were shining with unshed tears. Luke couldn't afford to keep the holiday spirit he was beginning to feel.

CHAPTER 26

Two weeks before Christmas, Luke awoke to three-foot snow drifts and a phone call from Ben, reminding him of his duty as a member of the Ward Snow Patrol. He spent two hours shoveling. Just his luck, it was the harshest winter in Utah in a decade. The snow fell heavily that morning and didn't let up all day. The prevailing festive attitude didn't make Luke feel any better about being in Utah.

After unthawing and straightening his back, he spent the day in the Helaman City Library researching and reading. It was not a large library, so he managed to glean something from every Mormon-related book there. All in all, he considered it a productive day. By late afternoon, blizzard conditions had hit the valley, and a heavy blanket of white covered the streets. The commute home was agonizingly slow on the icy roads. With every delay of traffic, he muttered under his breath, "Stupid Utah drivers."

Before he reached his street, he noticed bright lights flashing from an ambulance and a row of police cars parked in front of the Kimballs' house. All of a sudden, in the space of a week, peaceful, boring Helaman had turned into an episode of *NYPD Blue*.

Luke stopped on the corner without shutting off the engine and got out of his car. Negotiating his way through the snow and the crowd of people, he made his way past his driveway and into the Kimballs' yard. He spotted Ben and Stacie, talking to paramedics next to the ambulance. Before he could get over to them, though, he was intercepted by a grim-faced Brother Monson.

"It's Brooklyn," he said, grabbing Luke's shoulders. "She's hurt bad."

Luke felt like he had been hit in the abdomen with a baseball bat. "What happened?" he demanded.

"She was hit by a car."

As Luke surveyed the scene, he saw several medical personnel hovering over a stretcher. During his journalistic career, he had covered a handful of accidents like this one. Now, for the first time, he took it personally. Luke watched helplessly as medical personnel lifted Brooklyn's unconscious body into the ambulance. Ben and Stacie climbed in behind. Then the vehicle raced away, sirens howling.

His reporter's instincts kicked in. He found the eyewitnesses and pieced together what had happened. Brooklyn and Jared had been in the front yard, building a snowman, when Jared wandered into the street. Brooklyn helped him back onto the sidewalk, then Jared pointed to the glove he had left in the road. As she retrieved it, she slipped and fell. A speeding car slid on the ice and struck her.

Luke returned to his car and drove, albeit slowly because of the weather, to the hospital in Provo, but he couldn't find Ben. He found a familiar face, though. "Dr. Z," Luke said, "where's Brooklyn?"

"We've life-flighted her to Salt Lake," he said. "She'll be at Primary Children's Hospital."

To Salt Lake he went. The roads were terrible. After a couple of hours, he arrived to find Ben, Stacie, and their relatives sitting in the waiting room.

"How's Brooklyn?" Luke asked Ben.

"Not good. The doctors don't know if she'll ..." Ben's voice cracked. "She's in surgery right now. Her liver and spleen were punctured. My brother, my dad, my uncle, and I gave her a blessing. I don't know what's going to happen. Pray for her, Luke."

Pray for her? Luke knew that was an exercise in futility. But for Brooklyn, he could try it. After debating about it in his mind for about fifteen minutes, he found an empty bathroom and entered a stall. He bowed his head and closed his eyes.

"God," he whispered, feeling as though he were talking to himself, "I don't necessarily believe in your existence. But I feel like I need to do all I can for Brooklyn. You can't let her die. She's got a lot to live for. There's so much senseless loss and destruction in the world. Cut her a break, okay?"

He was about to exit the stall when he stopped and looked up. "Amen."

For the next several hours, he paced the hallways. By 2 a.m., he found an empty couch and slept fitfully until dawn. That was when Ben woke him.

"How is she?" Luke asked.

"Well, she came out of surgery about thirty minutes ago. It's too early to tell, but the doctors are optimistic. It looks like she's going to make it."

Luke was relieved, but he didn't believe for more than three seconds that his inept prayer had anything to do with it. "Do you mind if I see her?" he asked.

"Sure," Ben said. "Come in with me."

He slowly pushed open the door to her room and saw Brooklyn's limp body lying in the bed. Stacie sat on a chair next to her, holding her hand. Ben's parents and other members of the extended Kimball family were there, too. Brooklyn had tubes coming out of her body every which way.

Luke went home to shower and change clothes, but returned to the hospital late that afternoon. Brooklyn was awake by that time and, upon seeing him, she smiled faintly.

"Hi, Luke," she said.

"How's my girl?"

"Fine."

The ward held a special fast on Brooklyn's behalf. Luke even participated and didn't complain to himself once.

CHAPTER 27

Over the next week, Luke made the trek from Helaman to Primary Children's Hospital daily. Each morning, he would buy a handful of children's books and take them to Brooklyn. They read and played games and watched TV and talked until visitors' hours were over. Nurses had to kick him out of the room.

Brooklyn had so many books that she started sharing them with other patients. Soon, all the children looked forward to Luke's visits. He actually kind of enjoyed it. It was like being Santa Claus, minus the red suit and fake beard.

"We're thinking about naming our hospital library after you," a nurse told him.

Luke bought a small Christmas tree and placed it in her room. Brooklyn told him what she wanted for Christmas and what she missed about being at home. He pulled a present for her out of a bag and placed it beneath the little tree.

"Can't I open it yet?"

"Not until Christmas."

"I wish I could get you a present," Brooklyn said.

"You already have."

"I can't wait until I get better. I'm getting baptized in February. You can do it with me."

Luke quickly changed the subject and decided to ask about the accident. He was a reporter, after all.

"Do you remember much about it?"

"Not really," Brooklyn said, coloring a picture.

"Were you scared?"

"No. I remember going into the street and picking up Jared's glove. I felt something hit me. It really hurt. Then the angels started helping me."

Luke pulled his chair closer to the bed. "Angels?"

"Yeah. Three of them. They were very nice. Heavenly Father sent them."

"That must have been quite a dream," Luke said.

"It wasn't a dream," Brooklyn insisted. "It was real."

"Tell me more about the angels. What did they look like?"

"One was an older man, like a grandpa. The other was a grandma. Another one was younger, like a boy. But older than me. They knew my name and everything. They smiled a lot and talked to me. They were very nice angels, just like the ones on TV."

"What did they say?"

"They told me they loved me and that I would be okay," she said.

"What did you and the angels do?"

"We were here, at the hospital, watching everything. I saw the doctors cutting me open. I saw Mom and Dad crying. I saw you."

"Me?"

"Yeah. You were praying for me in a bathroom."

Luke's skin went clammy.

"I tried to talk to all of you, but you couldn't hear me."

"Did you tell your mom and dad that story?" Luke asked.

"No."

"Why?"

"They didn't ask."

"Ask what?" Ben said, walking into the room with Stacie.

"About me and the angels," Brooklyn said.

The following day, Christmas Eve, Ben and Stacie brought the kids along with them and a couple of photo albums. They asked her to look at the pictures.

"Hey," she said, stopping at one particular page. "These look like two of the angels."

"Are you sure?" Ben asked.

"I'm sure."

Tears welled up in Ben's eyes. "That's your Great-grandmother and Great-grandfather Kimball," he said. "That's my grandma. She died a couple of years before you were born."

"Your grandpa talked like he swallowed a whistle," she said.

"That's right!" Ben exclaimed. "He lost part of a tooth once when he bit into one of Grandma's biscuits."

"What about the third angel, honey?" Stacie asked.

"He looked familiar, but I didn't know him," she said. "He kind of looked like dad."

Ben hurriedly turned to a specific page of the album. It was filled with old pictures. "Here, look at these," he said. "See if you can find him."

In a matter of seconds, she pointed to a young boy. "That's him," she said. "That's the third angel that helped me. Who is he?"

By this time, both Ben and Stacie could barely speak. Luke was spooked.

"That is your Uncle Brett," Ben said quietly. "He died when he was twelve."

"He was so funny," she said as she turned pages of the album.

Since it was Christmas Eve, Ben and Stacie gave each of the kids a present to open. Brooklyn received a pink coat with goose-feather lining, the one she had picked out at the mall before her accident. She was thrilled when she saw it. But moments later her face lit up even more. "Mom, Dad," she said, "you know that sub-for-Santa you're doing for the Mendozas?"

"Yes, honey," Stacie said.

"Well, Ariel Mendoza doesn't have a real coat," Brooklyn said. "She gets cold. She gets teased at school all the time, too. I think she needs this more than me."

"Are you sure you want to give it away?" Ben asked.

"I'm sure," she said, wrapping it back up. "I have two coats in the closet at home. I can just use those."

They cleaned up the wrapping paper and ribbons and sang Christmas songs. Stacie ended the party early. "Brooklyn needs her beauty rest," she said, setting up a cot in the room. "Come back tomorrow morning and we'll open more presents."

"We'll be back bright and early tomorrow," Ben said.

"You're sure Santa will still find me?" Brooklyn asked.

"I'm positive," Ben said.

Luke, Ben, and the kids returned to Helaman and went to the church, where the bishop was holding his annual Christmas party. Foster children from the area and needy families in the stake filled the cultural hall. Decorations garnished the walls, and gifts covered the stage. The kids reminded Luke of himself, when he was that age with their shabby clothes and downtrodden spirits. There was a turkey dinner with all the fixings, a musical performance by the McMurrays (a rendition of "O Little Town of Bethlehem"), and an appearance by Santa Claus, also known by the adults as "Santa Law." The bishop even had his own costume. When Ben and the kids presented Ariel Mendoza with the coat, she put it on in the hotter-than-a-sauna cultural hall, and didn't take it off the rest of the night.

After helping to clean up from the party, Luke went home. He couldn't get

Brooklyn out of his mind. The stuff about the angels—he tried to explain it logically. He couldn't. Luke resolved that when he returned the next day, he was going to ask more questions. It wasn't a scandal, but what a story it would be for his book.

At about seven on Christmas morning, Luke awoke. He couldn't wait to see Brooklyn. Just before he stepped into the shower, the phone rang.

"Luke, it's me," Ben said. He paused. Luke could tell something was terribly wrong. "I'm calling to let you know Brooklyn died this morning."

Neither spoke for several moments. The cause of death was a post-operative blood clot, Ben explained. Her heart stopped beating at 5:03 a.m.

"I don't believe it," Luke said.

"Neither can I," Ben said, voice quavering.

"She seemed so normal, so healthy last night," Luke said. "I'm sorry, Ben. So sorry."

"You know, she really cared about you. Some of her last words were about you," Ben said. "She wanted me to tell you to keep wearing your CTR ring. And to remember her. I think she knew that she was going."

After hanging up, Luke meandered around the house, pounding his fist into the walls. It was too cruel. So much for that prayer he gave in the bathroom. What kind of God would take a little girl like that away from her family?

Luke looked down at his CTR ring. He couldn't hold the tears back anymore. He hadn't cried since he was eight years old, a record he had been proud of. He hadn't cried since the last time his dad came home drunk and beat him with a belt. His dad had told him to quit crying and to take it like a man. After that, he vowed never to cry again, to show his old man. Now he was crying like Miss America. He couldn't stop. It was almost as if twenty-plus years of pent-up emotion was being vented all at once. Luke had experienced some miserable Christmases in his time, but this was the worst.

The day after, he went to the gym and started working out harder than ever. He played basketball with a group of guys, but threw around more elbows than shots. When the other players finally left, he shot hoops by himself for two hours. When he returned home, he went to his computer and started writing about Brooklyn, about the accident. That night, Ben showed up at Luke's house and presented him with a picture that Brooklyn had drawn and was saving for Christmas for Luke. It was a picture of her and the angels. Luke started to feel the tears welling up in his eyes again.

"You sure you don't want this?" Luke asked.

"I appreciate that, but your name's on it. She wanted this to be for you." Ben also returned the gift Luke had given Brooklyn. A baseball glove. Luke told Ben to give it to Jared.

Luke found Brooklyn's obituary in the local paper, cut it out, and placed it inside his quadruple combination for safekeeping.

The funeral was held a couple of days later, on a snowy morning. The chapel was filled to capacity. Even Lloyd Gruber and his wife showed up to offer their condolences to Ben and Stacie. It marked the first time in years that the Grubers had entered the church.

Luke wore a dark suit and dark glasses. He sat alone in the back of the chapel until Uncle LeVan spotted him and invited him to sit near the front with the family. Unlike other funerals Luke had been to, there was no wailing and carrying on. There were plenty of tears, but these people seemed calm and at peace. Besides being heartsick for Ben and Stacie, Luke thought he was more upset about Brooklyn's death than Ben and Stacie seemed to be. He wanted to punch a hole through a brick wall. Ben and Stacie appeared relatively composed. He hoped, for their sake, they would be reunited with their daughter again someday, though he was sure that could never happen. It was merely a pipedream. A fantasy. But whatever belief, even if it were false, could get them through this tragedy, he supported it.

Bishop Law conducted the service. Ben sat on the stand, waiting to deliver the most difficult talk of his life. He felt almost numb, still in shock that his oldest child was gone.

The congregation spilled into the cultural hall. Flowers bedecked the stand. There were hymns sung, including one by the McMurray family, and one by Brooklyn's Primary class. Sister Watkins spoke about the Lord's love of children. Ben offered some personal glimpses into Brooklyn's life and almost made it through without crying.

"You know," Ben said, "I've always believed in the resurrection. I never doubted it was true. I guess I took it for granted. All of a sudden, when Brooklyn died, it really shook me up. I had to pray for the reassurance that it was true. I had to work for it. Now I know that it is. As it was revealed to the Prophet Joseph Smith, a place is reserved for our children in the Celestial Kingdom with Our Father in Heaven. I'm inspired to live a better life, just so I can be with her again."

Bishop Law talked about the plan of salvation and his testimony of the resurrection. All in all, the Mormons put quite a spin on life-after-death, Luke thought. It sounded too good to be true.

When the service was over, Luke accompanied the family to the cemetery. Afterward, the Relief Society hosted a meal for the Kimballs in the cultural hall. Ben invited Luke to join the family. Tables were filled with food, mostly potatoes in casserole dishes, but Luke didn't have much of an appetite.

A few days after the funeral, Luke visited the gravesite. Ben pulled up in his car and stood beside Luke.

"You said in your talk that you prayed and received 'reassurance' that Brooklyn still lives," Luke said. "What kind of reassurance?"

"When I have a real problem I go to a secluded place in the canyon, near my uncle's cabin, where I can be completely alone. Then I just start talking to Heavenly Father out loud. I imagine him walking alongside me. I tell him everything that's on my mind, my innermost thoughts and feelings. And He listens. Sometimes I feel like I hear Him speak, though I don't hear anything audible. He comforts me and strengthens me through His spirit. You learn to depend on Him completely. You learn to go entirely by faith. I don't know what I would do without Him."

To Luke, it all sounded like a radical form of therapy.

Not that it was easy for Ben to go on with his life. The heartache was almost too much to take at times. He couldn't walk by Brooklyn's room without being overcome with emotion. Late at night, or early in the morning, when he couldn't sleep, he'd creep toward the empty room and pray that it was all a nightmare, that he'd find her sleeping in her Little Mermaid nightgown with half the covers kicked off onto the floor. Instead, to his recurring despair, he would see the bed made. Ben would walk inside, close the door, and sit on the bed with the pink quilt Stacie had made for their daughter's birthday and bury his face in his hands and cry. Almost every day when he returned from work, he'd find Stacie in Brooklyn's room, doing the same thing. The other children were confused about Brooklyn's whereabouts, though Ben and Stacie had explained countless times that she was living with Heavenly Father and that she was looking down upon them.

What made things even more heart-wrenching for Ben was knowing that he wouldn't even be able to baptize his own daughter—and it was so close to her eighth birthday. The only relief he could find was reading the scriptures and praying with all his soul. That was the only way he knew to combat the haunting questions of "What if?" and "Why us?"

Ben had been through this before, on a much smaller scale, each time Stacie had miscarried during the early years of their marriage. The difference was, those babies were faceless and nameless. Next to Stacie, Brooklyn had been Ben's best friend and they shared a special relationship known only to fathers and daughters.

But life marched on. He had to keep managing the store every day, fulfilling his church callings every week, being strong for Stacie and the rest of the family.

The ward grew closer through the tragedy and not a day went by without someone expressing their sympathy and telling Ben what a wonderful girl he had in Brooklyn. Luke noticed they were careful to talk about her in the present tense.

As for Luke, he found himself thinking about Brooklyn, about death, all the time. He had never lost anyone close to him, at least to death, partly because he had never allowed anyone to get close to him. But now that Brooklyn was gone, he wondered if it was worth it to let that ever happen again.

CHAPTER 28

Even though Luke wasn't a member of the Church, Brother Sweeney called to schedule him for tithing settlement just the same. Luke didn't know exactly what tithing settlement entailed, but if it was something Mormons did, well then, he figured he'd better do it. He was sure the bishop would hound him about baptism again.

"I see you've paid your tithing every month since September," Bishop Law said. "May the Lord bless you for your faithfulness. So can I consider you a full tithe payer?"

"What do you mean by that?"

"Do you pay ten percent of your increase to the Lord?"

"This is quite a substantial sum I've given to the Church," Luke said, trying not to let his frustration show. Here he was, not even a member of the Church, giving charitable contributions to the Church. Was the bishop implying he should be giving *more?* "Are you telling me it's not enough?"

The bishop smiled. "The amount doesn't matter. The intent of the heart does. Only you know if you are paying an honest tithe. As a prospective member of the Church, it's an important lesson to learn. May I share a scripture with you?"

"You may," Luke said, knowing he'd regret it.

Bishop Law put on his reading glasses and turned right to the dog-eared page in the book of Malachi.

"Will a man rob God? Yet ye have robbed me," the bishop intoned in his best James Earl Jones voice. "But ye say, Wherein have we robbed thee? In tithes and offerings. Bring ye all the tithes into the storehouse, that there may be meat in mine house, and prove me now herewith, saith the Lord of hosts, if I will not open you the windows of heaven, and pour you out a blessing, that there shall not be room enough to receive it."

The bishop took off his glasses and placed them on the desk. "I want you to know that I believe in that promise in the book of Malachi. Now may I share with you a story?"

Luke wished he had kept his mouth shut. "You may," he said.

"When Sister Law and I were first married, we were destitute. We were so poor that some nights we ate boiled water for dinner. The day I got laid off at Geneva Steel they gave me a severance check, and I was tempted to spend the whole thing on food. But my sweet wife reminded me of that passage of scripture I just read to you. So I sat down right then and wrote out that tithing check and placed it in an envelope to give to the bishop. About forty-five minutes later, a member of the ward, who wouldn't have known of our financial crisis, knocked on our door. He said he had been deer hunting that weekend and had a truckload of deer meat. He wondered if we might want some. The words of Malachi came to me again. Even though I had paid tithing all my life, I gained a real testimony of that principle that night. The windows of heaven were opened. Not only did the packages of meat fill our freezer, there was so much that did not fit in there. There literally was not room to receive it."

"C'mon," Luke said. "You expect me to buy that?"

"It's true," the bishop said with a laugh. "Just ask my wife. She spent the next year trying to find creative ways to cook deer meat. You haven't lived until you've eaten Deer Meat Casserole and Deer Meat Surprise. I ate so much deer that year I thought I was going to grow antlers. If I may counsel you, Luke, test the Lord and see. In your own way, you will be blessed beyond measure."

Luke did not like to be counseled, especially by a myopic tow truck driver. *How dare this guy tell me what to do?* he thought.

"Have you given any more thought to your baptism?" the bishop asked.

"I'm still not ready, Bishop," Luke said. "I can't join until I feel like it's the right thing to do."

Bishop Law stood up and moved his chair over to the other side of the desk and sat down, so that their knees were touching. Luke didn't like his personal space being violated like that.

"I respect your feelings," Bishop Law said, leaning forward in his seat. "The Lord doesn't want you to be baptized unless you're fully ready to commit to the gospel. May I say that I've been very impressed with your progress, and I'm grateful for all that you do in this ward. Is there anything that would keep you from getting baptized?"

"Just my conscience," Luke said, leaning as far back in his chair as he could.

"Anything you want to talk about?"

"No, not really."

"Will you keep praying and asking the Lord for help so you can be baptized?"

"I'll do what I can," Luke said.

"Remember, Luke," the bishop said, peering into Luke's eyes, "in the Book of James it says, 'A double-minded man is unstable in all his ways.' I want you to think about that."

Luke thought about it, all right. He felt his face flush, and he got the feeling he wasn't pulling anything over on this guy. It was as if Bishop Law had some sort of cosmic ability to read his thoughts. Luke realized he was perspiring in places he didn't know he had sweat glands.

The bishop offered a prayer to close their interview, then stood and squeezed his shoulder. "If you ever need to talk," Bishop Law said, "you know where to find me."

Tithing settlement, he decided, was just another wretched experience he had to go through for the book's sake. Speaking of the book, Luke didn't feel like writing much these days. He had a serious case of writer's block. He would stare at the computer screen for hours without writing. Every time he typed something, he immediately deleted it. He'd spend stretches at a time just staring at the photo of Brooklyn in his wallet.

By New Year's Eve day, Luke knew he had to get out of town. He'd been cooped up in Utah way too long and he needed a vacation. Without telling anyone, except for Kilborn, he packed a bag, gassed up the car, and started driving toward Las Vegas, which was only six hours away.

When he entered Nevada, he felt like an inmate out on parole. Best of all, there was no snow. He checked into a luxurious Vegas hotel, the most elegant suite. He deserved it, he figured, and charged the room to Kilborn. In the suite there was a little refrigerator stocked with a variety of confections as well as alcohol. For Luke, it was like seeing an oasis. He removed a mini-bottle of liquor, lifted it up close to his face and stared at it. Then the glint of the CTR ring on his pinky finger caught his eye. He thought of Brooklyn. *Wear this and it will help you choose the right,* he could hear her say. It was as if she were watching him. He left his room and took the elevator to the lobby, where he found the craps table. As he was about to place a bet, he felt someone tap his shoulder.

"Brother Manning," said Brother Monson, "who would have thought we'd be down here in Sin City at the same time!"

"Imagine that," Luke said.

Brother Monson was just passing through the casino to the buffet. The Monsons were on their way to California on vacation. He invited Luke to dinner. Once again, Luke's fun was ruined. On New Year's Eve, no less. Try as he might, he just couldn't get away from these Mormons. After taking part in an $8.99 all-you-can-eat buffet with the Monson family, Luke returned to his hotel room in time to watch the ball drop in Times Square. Oh, how he wished he were there.

On New Year's Day, Luke holed up in his hotel room watching all the college football games with the aid of his remote control. He lay on the bed, which was covered with Snickers bars, potato chips, and bottles of Pepsi.

CHAPTER 29

When the first Sunday of the new year rolled around, Luke was back in Utah and at a boiling point. He was tired of spending his Saturday nights reading the Primary manual. He was sick of counting down the days until he could go back to New York. He had had it up to here with going home teaching, performing not-so-random acts of service, spending countless hours in meetings. As far as he was concerned, being a Mormon was one big pain in the backside.

And if that weren't enough, the starting time for church was moved up to 8 a.m. for the new year. That, Luke thought, was cruel and unusual punishment. On the other hand, Sister Watkins gave him some good news. She told him she and the bishop had decided to let him and Ben teach the same class for the year, though normally the children moved up to a new class and a new teacher in January.

"You're holding them back?" Luke said. "Have I been that bad an influence?"

"Oh, no, no, no," Sister Watkins assured him. "It's not that at all. You and Brother Kimball are doing a wonderful job. We just want to maintain your continuity and familiarity with the children. We think that is especially important, what with Brooklyn passing away. The kids really like you two. The fewer changes for them right now, the better."

The church parking lot on that first Sunday morning of the New Year was like the New Jersey Turnpike at rush hour. Luke had to park in the last row, which didn't exactly perk him up. Then he walked inside the church and couldn't believe what he was seeing. On this day, the church hallways were like a mosh pit.

"What's going on?" he asked Brother McGown.

"I don't know. Do you suppose the Second Coming happened last night and no one told us?" he joked.

Luke picked his way through the masses, then slipped into his usual seat for sacrament meeting, next to the Kimballs. It was strange to see them there without Brooklyn.

The doors to the overflow area in the cultural hall were parted as families grabbed chairs and set them up. While the prelude music played, Luke looked up on the stand and laid eyes on the most beautiful girl he had ever seen in his life.

"Who," Luke asked Ben, "is *that?*"

Ben glanced up. "You mean the girl shaking hands with Brother Sagapolu? That's Hayley Woodard," he said. "She just returned from a mission to New York this week."

"New York?" Luke asked. "What part?"

"Rochester, I think."

"That's not far from my hometown. Why didn't you tell me about her before? She's got to be the Mormon Aphrodite."

"The Woodards, you may recall, weren't in our ward until the boundaries changed. I didn't even realize until recently that she had gone on a mission. I guess I just assumed she was married and had kids."

"Wait a minute," Luke said. "Did you say her last name is Woodard?"

"Yeah."

"Don't tell me she's Bruce Woodard's daughter."

"Okay. I won't then."

"But she is, huh?"

Ben nodded. Luke's infamous confrontation with Brother Woodard during that basketball game a couple of months earlier had come back to haunt him.

"Does he own a shotgun by chance?" Luke asked.

"Of course," Ben said. "They don't call him 'Grit' for nothing."

Not only was Hayley beautiful, she was a girl he could take home to Mom, if, that is, he knew his mom's whereabouts. Hayley was petite, with shoulder-length brown hair, big chocolate eyes and a smile that could light up several city blocks. She wore a simple white blouse and a Levi skirt. Luke wouldn't have thought the Mormons were capable of producing a girl that beautiful, especially from Bruce Woodard's gene pool. Of course, he reasoned, with the number of times these people procreated, the law of averages was bound to catch up eventually. Although he had read Mark Twain's comment that Mormon women were so ugly polygamy was an act of charity, he thought Mormon women, as a whole, were actually quite attractive. But Hayley was on a completely different level. Luke had dated super models, but this girl beat them all by several touchdowns. As the meeting began, Luke could hardly keep his eyes off her. Gradually, all of his troubles seemed to melt away. He even forgot for a while that he was in Utah.

"I can't believe she went on a mission," Luke said to Ben during the opening hymn. "I feel bad for those male missionaries who had to serve in the same state with her. Talk about temptation."

At one point, during the sacrament hymn, Luke made eye contact with Hayley and she looked away quickly. He knew that he had to meet her.

All of a sudden, Luke had something to live for besides making it back to New York with his sanity. Up until now, socializing with Mormon women had not even been a consideration. Mormon girls, to him, were just too plain, too boring, for him. All Mormon women seemed to want was to be barefoot and pregnant. But he was sure Hayley was different. Considering the Mormon culture's obsession with marriage, he was surprised she wasn't already snatched up. Then he reminded himself that she hadn't met someone like him yet.

When Hayley stepped to the pulpit to deliver her talk, Luke was enraptured. Her voice was melodic. Her talk was engaging, humorous, and sincere. On top of that, she shared stories about New York. He was completely enthralled at church, something he never dreamed could happen.

Luke was a master at picking up women, though he feared he would be a little rusty after not doing it for several months. Then again, meeting women was an art form for him. The fact that she had served in New York made it almost too easy—no creativity required. He had a built-in pickup line. He thought about how she hadn't been kissed in at least eighteen long months, and he would be more than happy to break that dry spell for her. Speaking of which, it had been quite a while since he had lip-locked with a girl. He was determined to go out with Hayley Woodard and kiss those irresistible lips by week's end. Luke always thought it was good to set goals.

Of course, there was one little obstacle: Brother Woodard. Grit.

"You've got to introduce me to her after church," Luke said to Ben.

"I'll do more than that," Ben said. "Maybe we can double date sometime."

"You read my mind," Luke said. "How about this week?"

"Maybe you ought to meet her first."

The introduction would have to wait, however. Hordes of people surrounded Hayley after the meeting. One of those people was a tall, handsome guy. He hugged her and kissed her cheek.

"Who is that clown?" Luke asked Ben. "Tell me it's her brother."

"Sorry, it's not her brother."

Okay, maybe there were two little obstacles, Luke thought.

Ben and Luke went to teach their Primary class, and when Luke walked inside the classroom, he instinctively looked for Brooklyn. All that was there, though, was an empty seat. Following the prayer, Oliver raised his hand. Ben and Luke figured he was playing a game by himself, as he did often, but then he started stomping his feet and grunting.

"Oliver, do you have something to say?" Ben asked.

"Where's Brooklyn?" he asked.

Ben couldn't respond.

Luke didn't know how to respond to the question either. Luckily for him, Cindy McCormack spoke up. "She's up in heaven, with Jesus and Heavenly Father and my Grandma McCormack," she said.

"When is she coming back?" Oliver asked.

"She won't be coming back, Oliver," Cindy said. "But she will be resurrected someday, right?"

Ben nodded.

Oliver crawled under his chair and started making train noises.

"You'd think it would get easier," Ben said to Luke.

After church, Ben called. "Thought you'd like to know the Woodards are having an open house at their home for Hayley in about ten minutes," he said.

"I'll be at your house in nine," Luke said. "Do you think Grit will let me in?"

"Guess we'll find out."

Ben made the mistake of telling Stacie that Luke was interested in Hayley.

"Oh, they'd make a great couple," she gushed. "They'd be so cute together. He's from New York and she served in New York. It's kismet. Let's set them up this week. I'll call a sitter. You know, this may be the final push Luke needs to get baptized. There are a lot of guys who get baptized after they fall in love. Hayley would clear up all of his doubts, I'm sure."

"Let's not get ahead of ourselves. Don't start ordering wedding invitations and picking out china yet. Let's just see what happens today."

"Okay," Stacie said, adding, "You're not much of a romantic."

Luke sprayed on an extra dose of cologne and moussed his hair again. He had thought this Mormon assignment had made him lose all interest in women. Now, he felt like a man again. His virility was definitely intact.

Ben, Stacie, the three kids, and Luke entered the Woodards' front door and found a house full of people mingling and milling about. Luke planned to do everything he could to avoid Brother Woodard and to find out about that mystery guy at church who had been with Hayley.

Visitors were carrying Rice Krispy treats and brownies on a napkin in one hand and some sort of Sprite-based punch in the other. Luke noticed Hayley from the opposite end of the living room. People were lined up to talk to her.

"Tell me about Hayley," Luke said as Ben's kids made a beeline for the refreshment table.

"What do you want to know?" Ben asked.

"Anything. Everything."

"I don't know her that well," Ben said.

"We served together in a stake calling a few years ago, so I know her," Stacie said. "She left for a mission much later than most sister missionaries. I think she's twenty-six. She already graduated in nursing from BYU."

"She's a nurse, too?" Luke said. He thought he couldn't have dreamed up a better girl.

"Now if only you can convince her to leave her boyfriend . . ." Ben said.

"Was he the guy at church that was clinging to her like Velcro?"

"I don't know," Stacie said. "Maybe he is her boyfriend."

"I'm not worried," Luke said. Ben smiled.

As Ben and Luke had made their way near the front of the line, Sister Fidrych cut in front of them.

"I've been thinking," she said to Luke.

"Uh-oh," Luke replied. He knew that couldn't be good.

"Have you ever run for public office before?"

"Afraid not," he said. "Hey, isn't that your kid spilling red punch on the vegetable tray?"

"Oh my!" Sister Fidrych yelped as she dashed into the kitchen.

Finally, Stacie, Ben, and Luke reached the front of the line.

"Welcome back," Stacie said, giving Hayley a hug.

"Thank you. It's good to see you, Stacie," Hayley said. "I heard about Brooklyn. I am so sorry."

"Thank you," Stacie said. "You remember my husband, Ben. And I want you to meet Luke Manning. He moved in across the street from us, in the Winters' house."

She extended her hand and when she touched Luke, he felt as though he were going to melt into a puddle. Not that he would allow anyone to notice.

"Nice to meet you," Luke said, smooth as ever.

"It's nice to meet you, too," she said in that lilting tone she had.

"I enjoyed your speech," Luke said. "You had some interesting stories. I moved here from New York City. I'm from Syracuse originally."

"Really?" Hayley said. "Syracuse isn't in the Rochester mission, but it's close to where I served. What stake did you live in there?"

"Luke's not a member, yet," Ben interjected. "But he might as well be. He's had all the discussions, he goes to church every week—heck, he even has a church calling. All we need to do is add water."

"We'll have to talk about that sometime," Hayley said with a smile.

Luke grinned like a snake oil salesman. This truly was going to be even easier than he thought. "How about this week?" he said.

"This week?" Hayley replied, taken aback. "Well, I don't know, I . . ."

"Say, I just had a crazy idea," Ben piped in, noticing Hayley's reluctance. "Why don't the four of us do something on Friday night?"

"Sounds great," Luke said. "Are you available?"

"Well," Hayley said, trying to think of an excuse not to be available, "I suppose so. I don't have any plans at all this week. I guess that would be fine."

"It will be fun," Stacie said.

"I'll call you," Luke said.

Hayley half-smiled as she greeted the next person in line. "Okay."

Stacie, Ben, and Luke slipped into the kitchen.

"That girl is incredible," Luke whispered to Ben.

"Uh, there's something I should probably tell you about returned missionaries," Ben said. "Especially females. Take it nice and slow. Remember, she hasn't been on a date for a long time."

"Don't worry, Ben. Neither have I. Besides, I'll be a perfect gentleman. I hope she takes it easy on *me.*"

Brother Woodard entered the kitchen wielding a knife, presumably so he could slice more ham for the refreshment table. He was wearing an apron that read, "Kiss the Cook," but he looked more like he was capable of strangling a grizzly bear with his bare hands. Ben knew Brother Woodard would go nuts when he found out his daughter was going out with Luke.

"You think Grit would refuse to let me date his daughter, all because I knocked out one little tooth?"

"I don't know. Once, when my friends and I were deacons, we were throwing snowballs at cars. We hit his pickup truck one time. He chased us down, one by one, and hung us from the branches of a tree by our coat hoods until each of our parents came. He really is the nicest guy. He'd do anything for anyone. But you don't want to cross him."

"Now you tell me," Luke said.

Ben saw Hayley's friend from church and introduced himself.

"I'm Thad Robbins," the man said. "Nice to meet you."

"Are you a friend of Hayley's?" Ben asked.

"Yeah," Thad said, "you could say that. We were in the same student ward at BYU and we dated for a while before her mission. We graduated together. It about broke my heart when she told me she was going on a mission. I wrote her every week, though. In fact, I decided to get my master's degree so I could be around when she came home."

"So you two are an item," Luke said.

"I'd like to think that," Thad said.

The guy seemed nice. So nice that Luke almost felt a little bad that he was going to steal his girl from him.

Ben felt bad, too—for Luke. He could tell that Thad was the type of Mormon guy that Hayley would probably marry. There was no way she'd be interested in Luke, he thought, even if he did get baptized. Ben thought he'd better prepare Luke for the worst.

"They probably became pretty close through letters on her mission," he said.

"If writing letters is what it takes to win her over," Luke said, "he has no chance. I'm pretty confident I can outwrite that guy. In New York, I used to average three marriage proposals a week from female readers."

Ben knew Hayley and he knew she would never marry outside the temple. He knew Luke had no chance with her.

CHAPTER 30

For Luke, Friday night couldn't have come fast enough. He knew nothing long term would come of this, with her being a Mormon and all. But why should he deny himself a little fling with a winsome Mormon girl?

He called Hayley on Tuesday afternoon to shore up their plans. Brother Woodard answered the phone. Surprisingly, he didn't hang up. When Hayley got on the line, Luke tried to make some small talk. He could tell she didn't feel entirely comfortable. "See you at six on Friday," he said.

Tuesday night, Luke joined Ben and Brother McGown to coach the ward youth basketball team. Down by five points at halftime, Luke suggested the team play a 2-3 zone. Not having practiced it much, the team looked confused and was frequently caught out of position. One of the referees, who wore thick glasses, kept calling fouls on the 6th Ward's best player, Ammon Adams, until he finally fouled out.

Luke vocalized his displeasure to the officials and Ben told him to calm down. The Helaman 4th Ward coach asked the referees to call a technical foul for Luke's frequent outbursts. "He's not even a member of the Church," the coach told Ben at half time. "He shouldn't even be here."

"Now that's a real Christian thing to say," Ben retorted back to him. "They should make you in charge of the Church Missionary Committee. What do you want, a ban on all non-members from coming into the church?"

The referee gave Luke a warning, told him to keep his mouth shut, and called a technical on the bench. Luke was quiet, for a while. But when he found out that the ref belonged to the opposing team's ward, he stomped onto the court during a timeout, although Ben tried to restrain him. "How are you going to be able to look yourself in the mirror tomorrow morning, knowing you stole one from our kids! You're blinder than Stevie Wonder!"

Both referees ejected Luke from the game, out of the gym, out of the building, and served him an unprecedented suspension for the rest of the season. Because of Luke's ejection and the technical free throws awarded to the 4th

Ward, the 6th Ward lost the game. Afterwards, Ben resisted the urge to give Luke a lesson in sportsmanship. Ben and Luke only hoped that news of his suspension didn't get back to Hayley.

To kill time before his big date, Luke visited Mable Sterling. These visits had become a weekly ritual. He would show up around noon and they'd eat lunch together—usually tuna fish sandwiches and peanut butter cookies prepared by the nurse. Mable would give him sage, Mormon-based advice about life and he'd write it down, for his book. It was like a Mormon version of *Tuesdays with Morrie* that he liked to call Wednesdays with Mable. Luke was hoping maybe Mable, being aged, would slip and let out some Mormon secrets. But he quickly realized that mentally, Mable was sharper than Laban's sword.

"I appreciate you coming over," she said.

"Don't you get visits all the time?"

"Not really. All of my children and grandchildren live out of state. The deacons come over on Sundays to give me the sacrament and collect my fast offerings. And my hometeachers come by once a month. Bishop Law stops by when he can. Other than that, it gets lonely."

She asked Luke to tell her about himself. She was impressed by his story.

"You are so close to joining the Church," she said. "I know how you feel. It took me a while to warm up to Mormonism, too. Robert and I had been married a year before I got baptized. You know, I don't think it's coincidence that you wound up here in Helaman. The Lord moves in mysterious ways, doesn't he?"

"Don't I know it."

After some prompting, she launched into her life story, how she met her husband, who introduced her to the gospel at the University of Southern California. She recalled the most minute detail of their first date, down to the perfume she wore and what they ate for dinner. She told how her husband became a mission president in Jacksonville, Florida, before he was called to serve in the Church hierarchy.

"Being that high up in the Church," Luke said as he chewed his sandwich, "he must have seen a lot."

"Oh, yes," Mable said. "He knew a few of the Church presidents well. Would you like another peanut butter cookie?"

Though he realized he wasn't getting anywhere with her, he liked talking to her for some reason. Mable was like the grandmother he never had.

"You're a fine young man," she said. "Are you courting anyone special?"

"Funny you should ask," Luke said. "I'm going out with Hayley Woodard on Friday."

"She is a delightful girl. I commend you on your choice."

"Any advice?"

"Compliment her on her hair, treat her like a queen, and get her home by eleven."

"So that's the secret, huh?"

"Worked on me," Mable said, laughing.

When the day of the big date finally arrived, it was hard to tell who was more excited, Luke or Stacie. Stacie was sure Luke and Hayley were destined to be together. Ben, of course, was more skeptical. Luke was a spiritual midget compared to Hayley. How long that kind of relationship would last, he didn't know, but he hoped that it would be long enough for them to get through dessert.

Of course, Luke wasn't thinking past that evening and that first kiss. His biggest concern was setting the right mood. He knew that, as with all women, he could charm her. Usually, he didn't have to exert himself much.

Luke arrived at the Woodards' house fashionably late. He wasn't altogether sure if Brother Woodard was going to allow him in the house, let alone to go out with his daughter. He half-expected to see the Utah Highway Patrol forming a human barricade around the front yard.

Sister Woodard answered the doorbell and eagerly invited him into the front room. Brother Woodard was sitting in an easy chair, reading the *Farmer's Almanac*. He didn't stir. Luke didn't have to possess ESP to sense that Brother Woodard wasn't exactly ecstatic about him taking out his precious daughter, who was just days removed from the mission field. Sister Woodard, on the other hand, was downright perky. She asked about Luke's plans for the evening.

"We're going to the Kimballs' cabin in Heber City," Luke said. "Ben and Stacie are already there. We'll eat dinner and play some games."

"That sounds like fun, doesn't it, Bruce?" Sister Woodard said. Brother Woodard grunted.

"Like to come with us?" Luke asked.

"I'd love to," Sister Woodard said, "but I'm sure you two need time alone to get to know each other."

Brother Woodard's hands balled up into fists.

Hayley made her way down the stairs. She was even prettier than Luke had remembered. Her hair was pulled back in a ponytail and she wore blue jeans and a gray sweatshirt. He was convinced that she could have worn a burlap sack, a sombrero, and oversized bowling shoes and still hit a 10.5 on the Julia-Roberts-meter.

"Hi," she said shyly.

"Hi," Luke replied. "You look great. I like what you've done with your hair."

Bruce shifted uneasily in his chair.

"Thanks," she said, "but I didn't do anything with it."

"Have fun, you two," Sister Woodard said.

"You'll be riding in style tonight," Luke said to Hayley as he escorted her out the door.

"Ever ridden in a Corvette before?"

"Can't say that I have," Hayley said.

Luke sensed she wasn't the type of girl who was impressed by fancy cars. She wasn't that shallow, like most of his dates in New York.

"I guarantee you'll enjoy the ride," he said.

"As long as we get there in one piece," she said.

Brother Woodard watched out the window as Luke opened the passenger door for her and helped her inside the car. As soon as they backed out of the driveway, Brother Woodard grabbed his coat, gloves, and car keys.

"Bruce," Sister Woodard said, "they don't need a chaperone." He sighed, shut the door, and put down his keys. He began pacing the living room floor.

Luke headed for Provo Canyon. Soon, he realized Hayley might not appreciate the Jimmy Buffett CD he had playing, so he turned it off. "What kind of music do you like?"

"Country," she said.

"Country?"

"Not that my-dog-died-my-wife-left-me-and-I'm-doggone-broke country," Hayley said. *"Good* country."

"Isn't that a contradiction?"

"I really missed that music in the mission field."

"Tell you what," Luke said, trying to break the ice, "you choose what music we listen to."

"You got it," she said. She started pushing buttons on the stereo and it didn't take her long to find a country station.

"Now this is *real* music," she said, tapping her toes to the twangy beat.

Luke asked her about New York and as it turned out, Hayley had served in the general vicinity where he grew up. She had even been to Syracuse a couple of times for special conferences. Luke was surprised to learn there were Mormon churches in his hometown, because he had never noticed them before. She had also labored for a few months in Palmyra, not far from Syracuse, at the Hill Cumorah Visitors Center. She told him about some of the people she met on her mission. "I probably sound silly," she said. "I'm just trying to get acclimated to life again."

Luke just loved hearing the sound of her voice, no matter what she was saying. "Please, don't apologize," he said. "I like your stories."

He was tempted to ask her about Thad, but he didn't.

"You mind if I ask you why you're not baptized?" Hayley asked. "Sorry for being so direct. I guess I'm just used to being a missionary. Stacie told me a lot about you, and I just couldn't believe that you've been going to church for months without being a member. Stacie told me you teach Primary with Ben and that you're always going to ward activities and service projects. Sounds like you're a golden investigator. What's holding you back?"

"Well," he said, trying to sound sincere, "I don't take commitments lightly. I just want to make sure of what I'm doing. Baptism is a big step."

"Yes, it is," Hayley said.

"Here we are," Luke said as he turned down a side road illuminated by the Kimballs' cabin. Ben's car was parked out front and smoke was rising from the chimney; Ben and Stacie were inside, preparing dinner. It was the first time they had been on a date together since Brooklyn had died. Candles flickered on the table. Ben thought that was a bit much, but he wasn't about to argue the point with his wife, The Matchmaker.

After parking the car, Luke opened her door and offered her his arm. Since it was her first date in almost two years, she felt uncomfortable, but took his arm anyway, to be polite. When Luke slipped on a patch of ice on the front porch, both of them tumbled into a snowbank. Luke landed next to Hayley, which he didn't mind at all, and Hayley laughed.

Ben let them in, and told them to dry off next to the fireplace. Seeing the chicken, baked potatoes, and tossed salad on the dinner table, Hayley removed a small camera from her purse. Then she took a photo of Luke, Ben, and Stacie in front of the dinner table. "It's for my scrapbook," she explained. Ben picked up the camera and snapped another picture, so Hayley could be in a photo.

Ben asked Luke to offer the prayer over the food. He was able to fake his way through it since he had a standard prayer he had more or less memorized and he could come off sounding sincere. To impress Hayley, he added a few extra lines and polysyllabic words, showing off his abundant vocabulary. Luke was pulling out all the stops on this night.

Conversation flowed during dinner. When Luke and Ben started off on a sports tangent, Hayley would offer a few insightful comments—which came as a pleasant surprise to Luke—then changed the subject. Afterwards, all four did the dishes, though they spent most of the time flicking bubbles at each other. Then they played a few parlor games. Ben and Stacie were on one team and Luke and Hayley on the other. Luke and Hayley won every time.

"We've been married ten years. You two have known each other two hours," Ben lamented. "And you guys are the ones reading each others' thoughts. It's like you're on the same wavelength."

"Oh, just sit down and play," Stacie said, smiling.

Ben began to be hopeful again, that maybe Stacie was right. Maybe Hayley would be the one to persuade Luke to be baptized.

As the evening progressed, the more Luke liked Hayley. There was just something so innocent and pure about her. She was unlike any woman he had ever met. Luke knew he couldn't blow this by trying to kiss her on the first date. Recalling Brother Woodard's disdain for him, and what Mable had advised, he had her home by eleven sharp. That was the earliest he had ever taken a girl home—at least a girl he liked. At the door, she thanked him and said good-bye, giving him a solid missionary handshake.

"Sorry," she said, "old habits are hard to break."

Never had he been turned on by a handshake before. "No need to apologize," he said. "You can shake my hand anytime."

"Thanks again," she said. "Good night."

"Good night . . ." Luke echoed. The door shut. ". . . Your Majesty."

CHAPTER 31

For the first time since arriving in Utah, Luke was happy. If only he could convince Hayley to leave Mormonism for him, he'd have it made. Luke was so infatuated, it didn't even dawn on him until later in the week that spending time with Hayley might come in handy in the book—a twenty-something woman's perspective of the Mormon Church.

Oh yeah, the book.

He had written more than half of it, he figured. Kilborn was disappointed the scandal involving the bishop hadn't panned out. But he knew Luke could find another one. Hayley's value to the project was not lost on Kilborn, either. He was hopeful that Luke could corrupt her, to prove that Mormon girls were like any other girls on the face of the earth, despite professing such high-minded standards.

During sacrament meeting a couple of days later, the bishop announced that Hayley had been called as the Primary chorister. Luke knew opening exercises was about to become one of his favorite activities. On the way to the Primary room he caught a glimpse of her that almost caused him to walk headlong into a wall.

Somehow, Sister Fidrych found out Luke had gone out with Hayley. "I think I hear wedding bells," she said to Luke. "Too bad you have to get baptized first and wait a year before you can get married in the temple."

Luke wondered what the chances were of Sister Fidrych being sent on a mission to outer Mongolia. "We went on one date," he said. "That's it."

"Well, if you're going to pursue this, you'd better move quick. You have competition, you know."

"How's that?" Luke said.

Sister Fidrych lowered her voice, which, for her, was quite a feat. "She's interested in a guy named Thad."

"I've met him," he said.

"Yeah, well, he's from Canada and he plays hockey on the weekends.

Despite that, I hear he's a really nice guy. He served a mission to Australia. He's getting his master's degree in social work."

"Thanks for the scouting report," Luke said.

"As a word of warning, those guys at BYU are hungry to get married. I know because I married one. My hubby wanted to lock me up quick when he got back from his mission. Just imagine a guy who has been waiting for eighteen months."

Hayley led the music in Primary that day and Luke couldn't keep his eyes off of her. Luke even sang audibly for the first time in church, and performed the hand actions, too.

A few days after their date, Luke sent Hayley a dozen, long-stemmed red roses. Two more days passed, but he didn't hear anything in reply. That didn't stop him from calling her for a second date. He couldn't get a hold of Hayley, though.

"I'm sorry, Luke, she's not here. She just got a job at the hospital this week, thanks to Brother Z," Sister Woodard said. "She's busy and has a weird schedule so I don't know exactly when she'll be back. But I'll let her know you called. By the way, those were lovely flowers you sent."

"I'm glad someone enjoyed them," Luke said.

He ended up leaving five messages for her, but he never did hear back. It puzzled him, since he thought their first date had gone so well. Then again, he thought, maybe Brother Woodard was erasing the messages. Or maybe this Thad character was more of a threat than he had realized. Or maybe his non-member status scared her off. At any rate, Luke couldn't believe he was getting the cold shoulder from a woman.

That was a first for him. He usually didn't have second dates because he generally got all that he wanted from women on the first date, then never bothered calling again. As frustrating as Hayley was to him, she was also a challenge—which made her all the more enticing.

Since he had nothing better to do on a wintry Thursday night, he took Ben up on an invitation to go to a BYU basketball game. He noted two rather unusual aspects about attending a game at the Marriott Center: a pregame prayer and married students holding infants on their laps. *This is definitely not your usual college basketball crowd,* Luke wrote later.

On the way home, Ben asked about Hayley.

"It's not going anywhere," Luke said.

"Why? You guys seemed to get along so well," Ben said as he drove north on I-15.

"Why do Mormons like to rush things like this?"

"No one's talking about rushing anything. Just don't give up too soon."

"We've been on one date," Luke said.

"Yeah, but you guys have chemistry. I've never seen a first date go so well."

"Better than yours with Stacie?"

"Well, not quite."

"You think she's avoiding me because I'm not officially a Mormon?"

Ben was afraid he'd ask that. Suddenly, something caught Ben's eye out the window. "Did you see that?" he asked.

"What?"

"A person! On the side of the road!"

"I didn't see a thing," Luke said. "I think you're hallucinating. How many cups of Sprite did you have at the game? I think it's impaired your vision. I told you not to drink and drive."

Ben slowed down and pulled over onto the shoulder.

"What are you doing?" Luke asked.

"I swear I saw someone back there. I'm going to check on it." Ben zipped up his coat, opened the door, and jumped out into the blizzard conditions. Luke hated it when Ben went Good Samaritan on him.

"He's nuts," Luke said to himself. "It's ten o'clock and it's about ten degrees below zero out there . . ." He had no other choice but to get out of the car and catch up with him.

Sure enough, about 100 yards away there was a scruffy, long-haired man wearing tattered clothing, lying in the snow. Ben tried talking to him, but the man did not respond. Ben and Luke picked him up, carried him to the car, and laid him in the back seat. Ben did a quick first-aid check on him, using what he could remember from being an Eagle Scout, then he and Luke jumped in the car and raced to the hospital back in Provo. The man was practically frozen. Icicles dangled from his beard. His coat was thin and ripped, and he wore a dirty T-shirt underneath. His fingers and the tips were turning white. His shoes had more holes than an Afghanistan golf course.

Once they arrived at the hospital, they were forced to sit down and wait. Then Luke heard an angelic voice.

"Ben? Luke?" Hayley said. "What are you doing here?"

"We found this man on the side of the road."

"Let me see if I can help," she said.

Within minutes, the front desk admitted the ice man, who was still shivering. Hayley wheeled him into the emergency room.

"What relation are you to him?" asked the receptionist, handing Ben insurance forms.

"A friend," Ben said.

"What's his name?"

"We're not sure."

The nurse scowled. "How long have you known him?"

Ben looked at his watch. "Ten minutes, maybe." He told her what had happened. "I'll pay for the charges."

"No," Luke said to Ben. He whipped out his credit card. "The charges are on me." He knew Hayley was just a few feet away, overhearing the conversation. Certainly that would win points with her, he thought.

"You sure?" Ben asked.

"Of course. You've got diapers and baby formula to buy, remember?"

The nurse took the credit card. "Fill out these forms, please."

Luke couldn't believe the kind of messes Ben kept getting him into. It got to the point where Luke almost hated hanging out with him, for fear of what he would have to do next.

Ben borrowed Luke's cell phone to call Stacie. While Luke finished up the paperwork, Hayley sat down beside him.

"Looks like your friend will be fine," she said. "Luckily you found him before hypothermia set in."

"That's good to know," he said.

"We'll keep him here overnight for observation." She paused for a moment. "Listen, I'm sorry I haven't returned your calls. I've been really busy here at the hospital. I'm trying to make a good impression my first week. Oh, and thanks for the flowers."

"Anytime. How would you like to go out with me on Friday?"

"I'm working on Friday," she said.

"That's okay. How about a candlelight dinner in the X-ray room?"

"Sounds interesting," she said, "but I think my supervisors might frown on that."

"What about Saturday?"

"I'm going to be a bridesmaid at my cousin's wedding in Logan that day."

"Are you free at all between now and next Christmas?"

"How about next Wednesday?" she said.

Luke smiled. "Wednesday it is. I'll pick you up at six."

Everything was right with Luke's world again.

The next morning, since Ben had to go to work, Luke returned to the hospital to check on the ice man. Doctors told Luke he had a wallet with no money and an old, expired driver's license from Michigan inside. The man's name was Phil Santangelo. That was about all they knew. That, and he had been treated and was ready to be released.

Luke went to Phil's room and introduced himself. Phil didn't have much to say. Luke thought about paying the bill and walking away, but he knew Ben wouldn't just leave the guy alone.

"Since you probably don't have anywhere to go," Luke said, "you can stay with me for a while, if you want."

"How do I know you're not a lunatic?" Phil asked.

"You're just going to have to trust me," Luke said. "I'm not as bad as I look."

Before leaving the hospital, Luke phoned Ben at the store and told him the plan.

Of course, Luke's motives were less than pure. He felt a little sorry for Phil, sure, but the overriding factor was that he thought Hayley would be impressed with him if she knew what he was doing. As he drove Phil to Helaman, he realized that never in a million years would he have dreamed of taking a complete stranger, especially one that looked like Charles Manson, to his house. You just wouldn't do something like that in New York. Then again, this wasn't New York. Naturally, Luke conducted a background search on Phil and decided to let him stay.

Phil was a interesting roommate, to say the least. First, he wasn't big on showering or grooming of any sort. Second, he ate like a starving sumo wrestler. That first morning, at about eleven, he awoke and headed for the kitchen. He ate six bowls of cereal and swallowed three raw eggs.

"I've got some raw bacon in the fridge, if you're interested," Luke said. Phil nodded appreciatively.

"When's the last time you ate, man?" Luke asked.

"I don't remember," Phil said. Then he downed two ham sandwiches, a bag of potato chips, and a full pitcher of orange juice. Two hours later, he ate lunch.

Luke had to ensure that Phil didn't find out about the book and then blab it to everyone, so he installed a lock on the door of his den. Still, having a house-guest had its perks. Luke skipped church on Sunday to "babysit" Phil. For the first time in long time, he could relax on Sunday and watch TV.

Much to Luke's delight, Hayley called him that afternoon. "I noticed you weren't at church, and Stacie told me you were taking care of Phil," she said. "That's sweet of you."

"That's just the kind of guy I am."

It was ingenious. He was becoming a hero in Hayley's eyes by sitting at home doing next-to-nothing.

"Are we still on for Wednesday?" she asked.

"I'm not letting you off the hook, if that's what you're thinking," he said.

Luke called Ben to ask if he could watch Phil on Wednesday. But the Kimballs were going to visit some relatives that night. By Tuesday, it became clear that Luke was going to have to take Phil with him on the date. There was no way Luke was going to leave him alone in his house.

"Yo, Phil, you're coming with me tonight," Luke announced on Wednesday morning while Phil dined on peanut butter and banana sandwiches.

"Where?"

"On a date."

"But I hardly know you."

"Very funny," Luke replied. "You're accompanying me and a lady friend."

"I don't want to go. I'd rather not go anywhere. I like it here."

"I make the rules around here and I say you're coming with me. We're going to a nice restaurant, although around here, 'nice' is a relative term."

"What will we be eating?"

"Thick, juicy steaks."

"What time are we leaving?"

Before leaving to pick up Hayley, Luke made Phil shower, then he mari-naded him in cologne, so he would be tolerable. Since they were roughly the same size, Luke gave him some clothes to wear and told him to get in the back seat of the car.

Sister Woodard answered the door when Luke arrived and welcomed him into the house. Luke looked around, but Brother Woodard was nowhere to be seen. Hayley came down the stairs and she made Luke's heart do a triple-lutz.

"Doesn't she look beautiful?" Luke said to Sister Woodard.

"Yes, she does," she said. "Of course, I am a little biased."

"Enough, Mom," Hayley said.

As they walked to the car, Luke warned Hayley about the creature lurking in the back seat. "Phil is going with us," he said. "Hope you don't mind."

"Mind?" she said. "Why would I mind? That's great. I'd like to get to know him better."

So much for date No. 2, Luke thought.

Hayley got in the car and immediately shook Phil's hand. Then the two started a conversation that lasted until they got to the restaurant. Instantaneously, Phil transformed from a mute into a chatterbox. At dinner, he ordered the two most expensive menu items.

"What brought you to Utah, anyway?" Hayley asked Phil as the waiter brought their food.

Phil started pouring out his soul, right there over his grade A-cut sirloin.

"Five years ago, I was a successful businessman in the Detroit area," he began. "Stock market. Real Estate. A couple of Internet ventures. Had a wonderful wife and two sons. Then a couple of deals went bad. I lost a lot of money. So I started drinking, doing some drugs to try to offset my losses. One day I woke up, packed a suitcase and left home without saying good-bye. I bought a motorcycle, joined Hell's Angels, and started riding all over the country. It was liberating. I ditched my suits, grew out my hair, got some tattoos, bought myself a leather jacket. No pressures, no stresses, no worries. I moved to Florida and started a new life. But all that did was land me in the gutter. My bike got stolen and about three months ago, I realized what a terrible mistake I had made. I decided I wanted to be back with my family. So I hitchhiked to Michigan and went to our house. Strangers opened the door. My family had moved to Utah, at least, that's what I was told. It took me a while to get here. In Colorado I was picked up by some college kids headed to California. Without any warning, they dumped me in a snowbank on the freeway. That's where Luke and Ben found me."

"We can help you find your family, Phil," Hayley said. "Right, Luke?"

"Um," he said. "Sure."

"Luke used to work as a reporter for a newspaper," she said. "I'm sure if anyone can find them, he can."

He appreciated the vote of confidence from Hayley, but once again Luke found himself volunteered for something against his will. He didn't have time for this. But he couldn't say no to her. For Hayley, he would have memorized the Articles of Faith.

"You'll really help me?" Phil asked. "Wow. You Mormons really are nice people."

"Just like it says on their brochures," Luke said.

Phil went back to his steak. Hayley excused herself to go to the bathroom.

"Okay, pal," Luke said after Hayley was gone. "What are you trying to pull? You expect us to believe that story?"

"It's true."

"Listen, I am trying to get to know this woman. You are not helping any. For the rest of the night, keep your mouth shut."

"Okay," Phil said, salting his potatoes. "Are you still going to help me?"

"I'll help you, but I can't promise anything."

Once they finished eating—Phil ate two desserts—Luke placed $100 on the table. He gave up a little more tip than usual, to impress Hayley. After they left the restaurant, the young waiter who had served them that night rushed out to the parking lot. "Excuse me, sir!"

Luke turned around.

"Sir, you left a hundred dollar bill on the table."

"I know," Luke said. "That's called a tip."

The young man's face lit up. "Are you sure? It's almost the same cost of your meal."

"Well, I liked your service. If you have a problem with it, I can give you something a little smaller . . ."

"No, that's okay. I'm not complaining," he said. "Thank you so much. I'm saving money for my church mission and this really helps. You must not be a Mormon."

"No, I'm not," Luke said.

"Not yet, anyway," Hayley added.

"That explains it," the waiter said. "Most people tip only ten percent, if that, around here. I guess that's how most Mormons are. We're conditioned to give ten percent all the time. Besides, most people aren't going to give waiters more than they give to the Lord. Mormons feel like they already give enough to the Church or something. That's why I'm so grateful for your generosity."

"You're welcome," Luke said. "Good luck on your mission."

Luke was going to do everything in his power to woo Hayley.

CHAPTER 32

Over the next couple of weeks, Luke and Hayley got together often—to help Phil. Unfortunately for Luke, it was all about as romantic as a statistics class. He longed to touch her hand and stroke her hair, but that seemed to be the last thing on Hayley's mind. And he didn't want to get slapped, though he might have enjoyed it.

Hayley seemed obsessed with the idea of finding Phil's wife and children. She told her mom she desperately missed being in the mission field, serving the Lord, and others, all day long. Working in the hospital made her feel like she was still helping people. Trying to be a good example to Luke, a non-member, and assisting Phil further filled that void in her life.

All Luke and Hayley had to work with were the names of his wife and children though Phil worried his wife may have remarried. Luke showed Hayley how to use the Internet and access government records to locate people. But they weren't having much success. They had no evidence that Phil's family was actually living in Utah.

Luke bought a suit and a tie for Phil so he could go to church. That gesture reduced Phil to tears. "You might want to shave," Luke suggested, "or someone might confuse you for Lorenzo Snow."

"Who?"

"Forget it. Just a little Mormon humor. I think I've been here way too long."

Sure enough, Phil shaved and got a haircut. He didn't look like the same man. At church, Phil followed Luke everywhere, like a puppy dog. Of course, people in the ward embraced Phil. Literally and figuratively. Brother Sagapolu gravitated toward Phil the first time he saw him. When Phil found out that Brother Sagapolu owned a motorcycle, well, they immediately became blood brothers.

Another little problem Luke had to deal with was Super Bowl Sunday, an occasion Luke had always held sacred. Of course, he knew that this year was going to be different. He wouldn't be able to go to a bar and bet on the outcome, watch the game and drink all day. No, this year he would be in church, teaching Primary. Plus, Ben had some hometeaching appointments scheduled. Luke didn't want his Super Bowl Sunday completely ruined, so he decided he would tape the pregame show and the game and then treat Monday like Super Bowl Sunday. That way, he could watch the entire thing without interruption. The trick would be not to know the outcome before he watched the tape. Luke knew that Ben and his family didn't watch TV on Sundays, unless it was some sort of church program, so it wasn't as if Ben was going to see the game and blurt out any information.

Luke set the VCR up to record as soon as the pregame show began. When Luke arrived at church, two people took his mind off the game immediately: Hayley and Lloyd. When he saw Hayley, he shook her hand as long as he could. In the back of the church, he saw Lloyd and his family. Of all the Sundays for Lloyd Gruber to return to sacrament meeting for the first time in ages—Super Bowl Sunday.

"It's a miracle," Ben told Stacie during sacrament meeting.

"The Grubers back in church?" Sister Fidrych muttered to Sister McGown. "That's one of the signs of the Apocalypse, isn't it?"

In Primary, Phil sat on one of the little chairs next to the kids and didn't say much. He even colored pictures with them.

Following church, Luke went into his den and locked the door to work on his book. Late that afternoon, he left with Ben for home teaching appointments. At the Grubers, Lloyd even turned off the Big Game before they came in.

"Whatever you do, just don't tell me the score," Luke said, explaining his plans for Monday.

This time, Lloyd allowed his family to join him for the visit. Sister Gruber seemed like a completely different woman than the one Luke had met a few months earlier. She spoke glowingly about being back in church. At first, she said, she felt like some people were looking at her funny, wondering why she had decided to return to church. But she enjoyed being back.

"I didn't realize how much I was missing out on," she said. "I missed that feeling I have at church."

Lloyd wasn't as emotional about it, but even he seemed glad he had gone to sacrament meeting that day. "It wasn't as boring as I remembered it being," he said.

When he returned home from the Grubers, Luke walked into the living room to find Phil fiddling with the remote control.

"Didn't I tell you not to touch this?" Luke demanded. Then he discovered that Phil had inadvertently recorded a BYU devotional over the tape. Luke's Super Bowl Monday was botched.

"Sorry, Luke," Phil said. "I didn't mean to—"

Before Phil could finish the sentence, Luke was out the door. He got in his car, drove up Provo Canyon and listened to the rest of the game on the radio. He knew he had to get rid of Phil soon, before he killed him. That gave him even more incentive to find Phil's family. He resolved to hire a private investigator.

A couple of days later, however, Luke was skimming the local paper when he noticed a photo of a high school basketball game. On the back of one of the player's jerseys, he thought he could see the letters S-A-N-T-A-N-G. The angle of the photo, and the way it was cropped, didn't allow him to see the rest of the name. He turned to another page and looked in the box score of the Lehi High School game. There he saw the name Santangelo. Bingo.

He called Hayley. "You're coming with me to a basketball game in Lehi on Friday," he said.

"Why?" she asked. "We've got more important things to do. We've got to find Phil's family."

"That's why we're going."

They sat in the stands and watched junior guard Tony Santangelo, who spent most of the game on the bench. Hayley brought her camera and took pictures to document the event. "He sure looks a lot like Phil, doesn't he?" she said. "He has his smile and walk."

"And the way he sits there on the bench and drinks his Gatorade, it's just like Phil would," Luke said.

"We just can't let Phil know about this yet," Hayley said.

After the game, they saw Tony and an older woman, whom they assumed was Phil's wife, and a younger boy, leave together. They followed her to her home and wrote down the address. It appeared as though they had solved the mystery. For Luke, that carried with it some good and bad news. The good news was, maybe he could get rid of Phil. The bad news was, maybe his days spending time with Hayley would be over.

Luke and Hayley debated on the way home what they should do next. They decided to return the next morning, which they did. They drove to the house and knocked on the door. The woman who answered appeared to be cleaning. She wore an apron and held a feather duster in one hand. Luke and Hayley introduced themselves.

"I'm Maggie White," she said. Luke knew that White was her maiden name. "How can I help you?"

"Do you happen to know a Phil Santangelo?" Luke asked.

Maggie dropped her feather duster on the floor. "Did he send you?"

"No, he didn't send us," Hayley said. "He doesn't know where you live. We're friends of his. We volunteered to help him find you."

Maggie stepped outside and shut the front door. "All this time, I thought maybe he was dead. Or in prison. Where is he?"

"He lives with me, in Helaman, right now," Luke said.

"I don't want the boys to know," she said. "Please, don't tell him where we are."

"We won't," Hayley assured her, "if that's what you want."

"Yes, that's what I want. Are you two Mormons?"

"I am," Hayley said.

"We've just begun a new life. The boys and I joined the Church while we were in Michigan, and we came to Utah to start over. Things have been going so well. It's taken a lot of years and tears for us to get through this. I don't want to re-open old wounds."

"We can understand that," Hayley said. "We promise we won't tell him where you are. But I want to let you know that he has changed. He is attending church. He is really sorry for what he has done. If you change your mind, give me a call." She wrote down her number on a piece of scratch paper.

"You seem like really kind people," Maggie said. "I know you're only trying to help. But don't count on hearing from me."

Hayley's heart sank. So did Luke's. He wondered how much longer he would have to put up with Phil.

CHAPTER 33

Luke attended the annual ward Valentine dance, though he was decidedly against it. Hayley had to work that night. Nevertheless, Ben and Stacie prodded him to the church.

"You mean Mormons are allowed to dance?" Luke asked.

"Sure," Ben said. "We just don't do it all that well. We've never been accused of having much rhythm. Except for Gladys Knight. Did you know she was a member?"

"Yeah, I heard," Luke said.

To Luke, there was no reason to go to the dance, other than for research purposes. All the married couples sat together at designated tables. Luke took Phil with him and they sat at a table with three or four single women, all of whom were either elderly widows or middle-aged spinsters. None of them was as interesting as Mable, Luke thought. During dinner the women chattered and doted over Luke. When the time for dancing came, they lined up to have a turn with him.

"If only I were fifty years younger," Sister Wilmsmeyer said as she slow danced with Luke to the song "Sentimental Journey." Luke was wishing *he* was fifty years younger.

By nine o'clock, when the older women were falling asleep in their chocolate eclairs, Hayley showed up, wearing a red dress she had borrowed from her mom. Hayley was the only woman Luke knew of who could wear a modest outfit and make his blood pressure go up by 100 points.

"Now's your chance," Stacie told Luke, gesturing toward Hayley. "I bet she raced over after work just to see you."

Maybe Stacie was right, Luke thought. He sauntered over and asked her to dance. She said yes. To Luke's delight, it was a slow number. Hayley kept her distance, though. You could have fit a beach ball between them. As he was about to tell her how beautiful she looked, Hayley began talking about Phil.

"I put Phil's name, and Maggie's, on the prayer roll at the temple this morning," she said. "I've been praying that somehow Maggie will agree to let Phil back into their lives. Wouldn't that be great?"

"Yeah, great," Luke said. "It couldn't happen soon enough."

"I really think Phil is a good guy, despite his problems. My mom always told me I have a gift for discerning people. I've always been able to see people's hearts, their true characters."

Sweat beaded up on the back of Luke's neck. "That's quite a talent," he said.

"I can read people for some reason. And I have a good feeling about Phil. Maybe he'll even join the Church. Wouldn't that be something?"

Luke just nodded, staring at her lips. The music stopped and their dance ended. She smiled, thanked Luke and politely excused herself. She found Phil and they talked for ten minutes. Hayley, Luke decided, was harder to figure out than multivariable calculus. Usually, he had to fend females off with a stick. But Hayley seemed almost completely uninterested in him, at least romantically. His mind examined the possibilities. Was it his cologne? Or could she read him like a cheap comic book?

Whatever the case, it was clear to him that what she wanted and what he wanted were entirely different things. When he went home that night, he deliberately tried not to think about her. He even thought it was beginning to work, sort of. A few days later, Hayley phoned frantically.

"Luke, I have great news!" she said. "Maggie called me a few minutes ago. She said she would agree to see Phil at her house. Can you believe it? She told me she's done a lot of soul-searching and fasting and praying, and felt that she should at least allow the boys to see their father. Can you believe it?"

"That's the best news I've heard in months."

Luke let Hayley tell Phil about their surprise. She told him how his family had joined the Church and was living in Lehi.

"You two are the best duo this side of Harley-Davidson," he said. Then he dropped to his knees and started sobbing uncontrollably. Hayley cried, too. She leaned down and hugged him.

Luke was insanely jealous.

"You know how I've been going to your church," Phil said. "Well, I want to become a Mormon, like my family. How do I go about doing that?"

"We can help you," Hayley said eagerly, "but first you need to learn a few things."

"I'll do it. Whatever you say. When can I see Maggie and the boys?"

"Thursday night," Hayley said.

Luke bought Phil new clothes for the occasion. Before they picked up Hayley, Luke asked Phil if he was sure about becoming a Mormon. "You have to pay tithing, you know," he said. "That's ten percent of your income."

"No sweat," Phil said. "I can pay ten percent of nothing."

As for the meeting with his family, it didn't go all that well. Maggie kept her distance. Phil was so nervous that when he walked in the house, he clumsily broke a vase that sat on a table in the entryway. Then he started crying and apologizing.

"Get a hold of yourself," Luke told Phil. "It's only a vase."

"It's not just the vase. I'm sorry about everything," he said to Maggie. "Can you ever forgive me?"

Maggie didn't say much. She just took him upstairs to a room where Tony and Gary were playing video games.

"Boys," Maggie said, "this is Phil." They barely looked up.

"He is your father," she said. "The least you can do is say 'hi.'"

"Hi," they chorused unenthusiastically, then went back to their video games.

"Don't pressure them," Phil said. "It's going to take time."

Luke and Hayley left Phil alone with Maggie and the boys, then picked him up at nine. Maggie invited him over again the following week, and the week after that. They spent time alone together and talked for hours. They saw Brother Givens, a marriage counselor in the ward, to communicate about their feelings toward each other and their past.

A penitent Phil took all the discussions—from Elder Petrovic and his new companion—in record time. He read the Book of Mormon from cover to cover. He started shaving and showering every day. He committed to baptism.

"Why don't you get baptized with me?" Phil asked Luke.

Luke shook his head. "Can't do it right now," he said.

Phil asked Brother Sagapolu to baptize him and Elder Petrovic to perform the confirmation.

"How about a double dip?" Brother Sagapolu asked Luke before the ceremony. "Like I always say, two baptisms are beddah than one."

Luke wished people would quit bugging him about the baptism thing.

Just a little more than a month after being rescued on the side of the freeway, Phil became a member of the Church. Maggie and her sons attended the service, of course. Hayley bawled most of the time and used up three rolls of film. Ben was happy the Ice Man was getting baptized, but a part of him wished he was the one doing the baptizing. More than that, he was devastated that he would never have the chance to baptize Brooklyn.

Before closing the meeting, the bishop asked Phil to say a few words. First Phil expressed his love for his family, then he removed a folded-up piece of paper from his shirt pocket and started reading a prepared statement. "What Luke and Ben did for me was truly a Christlike thing," he said. "Jesus said, 'I was an hungered and ye gave me meat. I was thirsty and ye gave me drink. I was a stranger and ye took me in.' That's what Luke and Ben did. They saved my life. Physically and spiritually."

After the service, the Kimballs hosted an open house. Ben and Stacie made barbecue beef sandwiches. Luke brought potato chips, and Hayley made fruit punch. The Davises and McGowns brought four different types of dessert. The Munchaks provided a few unidentifiable entrees.

Swayed by Phil's changes, Maggie agreed to allow him to live with them in a spare room. Luke was relieved. On the day Luke was to drive him to Lehi for what he hoped was the final time, Phil was so nervous he threw up all over the front seat.

"No problem," Luke said. "Happens all the time."

After he dropped him off for good, Luke felt free. He went to Mable's house and she was thrilled to see him. They played checkers and talked. "How are things going with Hayley?" she asked.

"Why do you ask?"

"I can tell she's on your mind."

"Who have you been talking to?"

"No one. I'm a shut-in, remember? I can just tell that you're thinking about a beautiful woman and I seriously doubt that it's me."

Luke laughed.

"Are you still spending a lot of time with her?" Mable asked.

"Yes, but we're not dating. We're just friends."

"But you want it to be more than friendship, is that it?"

"I don't know right now. It's kind of complicated."

"Honey, relationships between men and women are meant to be complicated. Why do you think God made men and women different? Why don't you take her on another date? Give her a box of candy. Tell her how you feel. I know it sounds old-fashioned, but it worked back in my day, and I'd be willing to bet it would work now."

"Maybe I'll try that."

That night, he called Hayley. "You know," he said, "now that Phil is gone, I was thinking that we've only been on one official date together."

"Two, by my count," Hayley said.

"Two?"

"Yeah, the time we went up to the Kimballs' cabin and the time when you and Phil and I went to that fancy restaurant."

"You and Phil and I? Haven't you heard that three's a crowd?"

"That happens to be one of my most memorable dates of all time."

"Really? You really need to get out more, then," Luke said. "That's where I come in. I'll concede, we've been on two dates. How about a third?"

"What do you have in mind?"

"Dinner. My place. Friday night. I'll pick you up at seven."

"Tell you what. I'll come, but I'll drive myself. I have a bunch of errands I need to run that day."

This woman is going to drive me to drink again, Luke thought.

"What should I wear?" Hayley asked.

Luke wanted to say a black, backless dress, but he caught himself. "Something comfortable."

"T-shirt and sweats, then?"

"Sounds fine to me."

With Stacie's help, Luke cooked up a candlelight dinner that would have made Martha Stewart envious. It was going to be his shot at romancing Hayley. If this didn't work, nothing would. Before she arrived, Luke dimmed the lights and had soft music playing on his CD player. When she walked in the house, wearing a T-shirt and sweats, she laughed.

"What's so funny?" asked Luke, who was wearing a T-shirt and sweats, too.

"Nothing. I've never had a guy cook for me before," she said. He presented her with flowers and a heart-shaped box of chocolates.

"That's nice of you," she said. "Thanks. What's the occasion?"

"It's our third date."

Hayley removed her camera from her purse and Luke took a picture of her holding the gifts.

"Smells good," she said. "What are we having?"

"Filet mignon. I'll bet never in the history of the world has there been a case where two people dined on filet mignon in T-shirts and sweats."

"That's not true," she said, snapping a photo of Luke taking food out of the oven. "I heard the Rockefellers did that all the time."

After dinner, Hayley helped him do the dishes. He not-so-accidentally put his hand in the water at the same time she did. He never realized cleaning up could be so invigorating. When they finished, Luke was lighting a couple of candles as Hayley relaxed on the couch. As she sat down, she felt something stab her leg. She reached down, pulled out one of Luke's 3 x 5 index cards that had slipped between the seat cushions. She picked it up and read Luke's handwriting:

> *MORMONVILLE (to the tune of Jimmy Buffett's 'Margaritaville')*
> *Slurpin' on Jell-O*
> *Watchin' all the folks go*
> *Down to the church with their kids all in tow*
> *Tappin' on my laptop*
> *On my kitchen countertop*
> *Where all these minivans come from, I don't know*
>
> *Wastin' away again in Mormonville*
> *Searchin' for that large lake of salt*
> *Some people claim that there's a Mormon to blame*
> *But I know it's nobody's fault.*

When Luke sauntered over and saw what Hayley was reading, he almost had a coronary on the spot. It was something he had penned months earlier during a bout of insomnia, for his book. He had wondered where that card had gone.

"I didn't know you rewrote folk songs," Hayley said.

"Well, uh, yeah, it's just a little hobby I have," Luke stammered.

"I always thought writers were strange. But it's quite clever. Too bad we don't have road shows in the Church anymore. I'd like to see you perform this."

Luke smiled, hoping that his cover wasn't blown. He took the card from her and tossed it on the kitchen counter. He hoped he could explain it all away. "I had forgotten all about this. . . ." he said.

"I think it's pretty good," she interrupted. "Sometimes we as members of the Church take ourselves a little too seriously. You certainly won't be like that, when you join the Church."

That was close. Too close, Luke thought. He quickly changed the subject and Hayley didn't bring it up again. She did ask to read things he had written in the past. So Luke brought her a box of old copies of the *Post*. She read his stuff intently. "You're a good writer," Hayley said. "Pretty sarcastic, though."

"Thanks."

"So what kind of writing are you working on now?"

Luke was afraid that question was coming. A part of him, taken in by her eyes and her lips, wanted to tell her his secret. But he knew he couldn't.

"I write about everything," he explained, making it up as he went. "I like to write about the beauty I see around me. The mountains. The snow. You."

Hayley looked at him incredulously. "Tone it down, Romeo."

In the flickering candlelight, they talked, about nothing in particular. During their conversation, Luke inched imperceptibly closer and closer to her, until he had his arm around her. Eventually he got so close to her, he could almost hear her heartbeat. Or maybe it was his. After a couple of minutes of sitting in silence, Luke raised his left hand and softly brushed her cheek. With his other hand, he touched her hair. Hayley sat frozen, impassive, staring straight ahead. He gently turned her face toward his and gazed into her eyes. He decided to continue until she stopped him. Or slugged him. His eyes closed, his lips approached hers.

"What are you doing?" she asked.

Luke slammed on the brakes and opened his eyes. It seemed pretty obvious to him what he was doing. He hoped he hadn't squandered this opportunity.

"Would it be okay if I kissed you?" he asked.

She didn't respond for a moment. Then she looked into his eyes. She nodded.

Luke softly pressed his lips against hers, ever so briefly. He had never experienced a kiss like that before. Then he kissed her again, a little longer and wrapped his arms around her. She hugged him back, with a little less zeal. He could feel her lift her arm and look at her watch.

"It's 11:53," she whispered. "I'd better go."

Why does this girl have to be a Mormon? he thought. *Doesn't she know what she is missing?* He escorted her out to her car and stole one more kiss before she left. As he did, Hayley looked around nervously. "Don't worry, nobody saw us," Luke said. "Except maybe Stacie. And Sister Fidrych. They've probably got the binoculars on us right now."

Hayley laughed. "Thanks for a nice evening," she said. "That was probably one of the best third dates I've ever had."

"You think the third one was good, just wait until our fourth."

"You won't have to wait long. Why don't you come over to my house for lunch tomorrow?" she asked. "This time, I'll cook for you."

"What should I wear?"

"Your best pair of overalls," she said, squeezing his hand.

"Good thing I'm picking mine up at the cleaners tomorrow."

She got into her car and left. Luke felt like a new man. He strutted into his house and pumped his fist in the air. For some reason, he didn't sleep much that night.

Luke picked up the infamous index card and laid it on his desk, next to the stack of cards that had the other verses of the Mormonville song:

> *I don't know the reason*
> *I'll be here thru basketball season*
> *With nothin' to do but write this darn book.*
> *It'll be a winner*
> *And a hit with the sinner*
> *But even for a million bucks, I think I got took.*

> *Wastin' away again in Mormonville*
> *Searchin' for that large lake of salt*
> *Some people claim that there's a Mormon to blame*
> *But I know, it's all Kilborn's fault.*

> *I did my home teaching*
> *Tired of all this preaching*
> *Sat through general conference for two straight days.*
> *Now I'm a teetotaler*
> *A regular church-goer*
> *I just might go crazy before I get out of this place.*

> *Wastin' away again in Mormonville*
> *Searchin' for that large lake of salt.*
> *Some people claim that there's a Mormon to blame*
> *And I know, it's my own fault.*

CHAPTER 34

At about noon, Luke pulled up in front of the Woodards' house. It was a warm, spring-like February day. Grass was starting to appear in patches from under the snow. He walked past the white picket fence that surrounded the rustic home and up to the porch where a welcome mat and a homemade wooden swing sat. Sister Woodard invited him inside. Hayley wore overalls and her hair was pulled back in a ponytail. He wanted to kiss her when he saw her, but she was holding a greasy spatula in front of her like a buffer.

"I'm making my specialty. Hamburgers," she said. "It's not filet mignon, but I got good at doing these on my mission. I always helped cook at the big zone conferences."

"How did you know hamburgers are my favorite food?"

"Whatever," Hayley said. "Where's Dad?" she asked her mother as they sat down to eat.

"Oh, you know how he is," she said. "Once he gets started on a project, he can't stop until he finishes. I'll take him a hamburger or two later. Don't worry about him."

Luke couldn't help but worry about him. He started looking around the kitchen for the nearest exit.

When lunch was over, Luke volunteered to do the dishes. Sister Woodard was impressed.

"You don't have to do that," she said.

"I insist," Luke said.

"I'm glad to hear that," Hayley said, "because I have some cleaning to do upstairs."

Luke finished up the dishes with Sister Woodard supervising him. When Hayley returned, she took him into the family room.

"This must be your famous scrapbook," Luke said, lifting a large album, "on this, um, uh, what do you Mormons call these types of tables?"

"We call them coffee tables," Hayley said, "just like everybody else. And, yeah, that's one of my scrapbooks."

"You mind if I take a look?"

"Looks like you've already helped yourself," Hayley said as Luke opened to the first few pages, which chronicled her two-week stay at the MTC and the first month of her mission. "I'm working on the other volumes," Hayley said. The book was filled with photos and descriptive captions. Included were photos of parts of New York he barely knew existed, like Hill Cumorah.

"This is well done," Luke said.

"That's what you said about your burger, too," Hayley said.

"No, seriously, as a newspaper man, I can tell you this is impressive."

"Thanks, newspaper man," Hayley said. "It's just a little hobby I have."

"You have any other hobbies I don't know about?"

"When I was a little girl, I was into the 4-H Club. I raised pigs, sheep and chickens, and took them to the state fair every year."

Luke couldn't believe he had fallen for a girl with a background in animal husbandry.

"Don't forget to tell Luke how you were Helaman Days Queen," her mother called from the kitchen.

"Thanks for bringing that up, Mom."

In minutes, Sister Woodard brought Luke photos of Hayley wearing the crown and sash and sitting on a horse.

"How did you get that crown to stay on your head while you were riding?" Luke asked.

"Bobby pins," Sister Woodard said. "Lots of them."

"How old were you here?" Luke asked.

"Fifteen."

"Look how pretty she was," Luke said. "Did she ever have an awkward stage, or has she always been beautiful?"

"Always beautiful," Sister Woodard said, chuckling. "Just like her mother."

Hayley rolled her eyes. "Why don't we go outside, Luke?" she said. "My mom doesn't need any encouragement from you."

She led him to the barn, where she introduced him to the sheep, cows, and horses. Luke started sneezing.

"What's wrong?" Hayley asked.

"Nothing," he said, "other than I'm allergic to everything bucolic."

"We can go somewhere else, if you want," she said.

"No," Luke said, "this is perfect." Then he took her by the waist and pulled her close. As he kissed her, the barn door swung open and Brother Woodard was standing there, holding a pitchfork. Luke saw his life flash before his eyes.

Brother Woodard glared at Luke. "Uh, excuse me," he said as he turned and walked out, slamming the door behind him.

Luke tried to jumpstart his heart. Hayley laughed. "Poor Dad," she said. "I think that's the first time he's seen me kiss a guy. It's strange, but my dad is usually so friendly with the guys who ask me out. It's almost as if he is avoiding you. I apologize. Maybe he's having a mid-life crisis. I need to talk to him about it."

"No, *I* need to talk to him about it," Luke said.

"What do you mean?"

"You don't know, do you?"

"Know what?"

"How your dad lost his tooth."

"Lost his tooth? What does that have to do with anything? I know what happened."

"You do?"

"Yeah, it was an accident during a church basketball game. It was the same tooth that our mule Bessie kicked out when I was twelve."

"What your dad didn't tell you is that I'm the one who knocked out his tooth. It was during a fight."

"A fight?"

"Yep."

"*You* did that?"

"Afraid so. Believe me, it was an accident," Luke said, striding toward the barn door. "I think I'm going to have a talk with your dad."

"That's probably a good idea," Hayley said. "I'll be in the house in case you need medical assistance."

Brother Woodard was fixing a part of the fence that left a gap for the sheep to escape through. As Luke made the long walk to where "Grit" was working, his allergies started acting up. His eyes were watery and puffy, his nose itched, and he sneezed every fifteen seconds. Hives covered his arms.

Brother Woodard saw him coming, sized him up, then resumed hammering.

"Bruce, don't you ever relax?" Luke said as he approached him.

Brother Woodard didn't so much as acknowledge Luke's presence. He merely adjusted his cowboy hat. A nail was clenched between his teeth.

"So this is where the little farm animals make their getaway to freedom, huh?"

Brother Woodard stopped hammering to check his work, then strung up some more barbed wire.

"Bruce, may I talk to you? May I call you Bruce?"

"No," Brother Woodard said.

"How about 'Grit'?"

"You may call me Mister Woodard or Brother Woodard," he said, squinting. "Whatever it is, make it quick. I've got a lot to do before sundown."

"We got off to a rough start," Luke said, handing him another nail. "I'm sorry about what happened last fall with your tooth and all. I know what you're thinking. That the only reason I am trying to apologize is because I am dating your daughter. And you're right."

Brother Woodard stopped hammering and looked at Luke. "At least you're honest."

"I know Hayley is a wonderful girl—"

"The best," Brother Woodard interrupted. "All the reports I've gotten back on you so far say you are a gentleman with her. But I don't like any funny business going on in my barn that doesn't involve the livestock. I won't interfere with anyone who my daughter is courting, as long as that anyone is a complete gentleman. No more kissing in the barn. If I catch you doing that again ..."

Luke finished the thought in his head. Something about a bull being turned into a steer. Then Luke sneezed so hard he hurt his neck and he saw stars.

"What are you, allergic to something?" Brother Woodard asked.

"Probably to you and everything else on this farm," Luke said.

"You city folk are a different breed," he said.

"This is quite a place you have here," Luke said.

"It is. It was owned by my father and my grandfather before him." Brother Woodard removed his hat and wiped the sweat off his forehead with a bandanna.

Meanwhile, Hayley and Sister Woodard were keeping tabs on them from the kitchen window.

"I wonder how it's going," Sister Woodard said.

"It looks like they're having an in-depth conversation," Hayley observed. "That may be a first for Dad."

"You really like him, don't you?"

"Of course I like Dad," Hayley joked. "I don't know, Mom. I mean, yes, I like Luke. I like Thad, too. But I don't know Luke. He can come across as so arrogant, but the more I get to know him, he's a really nice guy. He's different from every other guy I've dated. But what I can't figure out is why he's not baptized, although the last thing I want is for him to join the Church because of me. I think, deep down, he has a testimony of the Church, but he doesn't realize it. There's just so much I don't know about him."

"Today might be a good day to change all that," Sister Woodard said.

"Maybe you're right," Hayley said.

A half hour later, Brother Woodard and Luke entered the house, laughing.

"Are you okay?" Hayley asked.

"I'm fine," Luke said.

"I was talking to my dad," she said.

Hayley invited Luke on a horseback ride. Her horse was a light brown mare named Buttercup. She gave Luke a stubborn gray pony named Gus. Hayley mounted the saddle like an expert equestrian. Luke nearly fell off on his first attempt.

"I'm sorry," she said. "I guess I've got you out of your element."

"Way out," Luke said.

They followed a dirt path that cut through the Woodards' farm. After a while, they stopped, tied up their animals and sat down in a pasture near a grove of trees. Luke's eyes were red and burning. His backside was sore. He could barely breath without wheezing. But he didn't care, as long as he was with Hayley. He couldn't remember ever being happier.

"Are you okay?" she asked.

"I'm fine," Luke said. "Besides, if things get too bad, you're a nurse. I'm sure I'm in good hands."

"Have you had allergies all your life?"

"The first time I noticed them, I was twelve," Luke said. "I was at the New York State Fair and I was miserable. That's when I decided against becoming a cowboy. I just wish I had some water right now."

Using the heel of her boot, Hayley made a hole in the thin sheet of ice from a pond. She scooped up some water and flicked it on Luke's face. He grabbed some water and splashed her back. After a while, both dripping wet, they leaned up against an oak tree. She shivered.

"I can warm you up," Luke said. "I wouldn't mind. Really."

"I'll be fine," Hayley said, keeping her distance. "But thanks for your concern."

"Okay, just trying to help."

They listened to the birds chirping and gazed up at the blue sky. "So, what do you think of my parents?" Hayley asked.

"Well, now that I know your dad isn't going to lynch me, I think they're okay."

"When do I get to meet your family?"

Luke was afraid she was going to ask that. "Probably never," he said. "I don't think you would want to meet them, anyway. I haven't seen my parents in years. My dad, I never really knew very well. He abandoned me and my mom when I was a kid. After that, we were on welfare. My mom got hooked on drugs and couldn't hold down a job. Until I was eleven, we lived in an apartment in the slums. That's when she tried to sell me for drugs."

Hayley sat up. Her eyes grew as big as frisbees.

"She was on cocaine, into prostitution," Luke explained. "She must have been pretty desperate, either that or I was making her crazy. I remember she left me alone a lot. One night she met this guy at a party and she asked him if he had drugs. She didn't have any money, so she offered me in exchange. Who knew I was worth three grams of coke? Turned out, that guy was an undercover cop. I became property of the state of New York. Of course, I didn't find out about this until I was in college and did some research on the case. Anyway, they sent her to prison. To this day, I don't know what became of her."

Hayley put her hand on his. "I'm sorry."

"Not exactly a Mormon upbringing, is it?"

"But look how you turned out," Hayley said.

Luke realized he had never told anyone in detail about his childhood before. "I probably shocked you, didn't I?"

"No, I'd say mildly surprised. I've been on a mission. Nothing shocks me anymore."

"I remember when I was sixteen," Luke continued. "It was in the summer, and some friends and I stole some cigarettes from a convenience store. We were caught and I'll never forget that night I spent in jail. I knew at that moment that either I could keep doing that kind of stuff and end up in prison like my mom, or

I could change. The night in that cell was a watershed moment. It motivated me to get an education. To make something of myself. A couple of years later I was accepted at Syracuse University. At first I wanted to go into broadcasting, but I've never been a fan of happy talk during newscasts. Plus, there was no way I was going to wear makeup. After graduating in journalism, I was hired at *The Post*." Luke stopped there before he said something he'd regret.

"That's amazing," Hayley said. "Then you came to Utah and found the Church. You really have been blessed. It's amazing how the Lord has directed your life."

"Now it's your turn," Luke said, before she could start wondering about the gap between his being hired at *The Post* and his coming to Utah.

"Me? My life story is pretty dull. Except for my mission, I've lived all my life in Utah. We lived in Payson until my grandpa died and my dad took over this farm. My two older brothers had gone on missions by the time I was five. I always wanted to have a little sister or brother, but my mom never had any more children. That's why when I get married, I want to have a large family."

"Three or four kids?"

"More like eight or nine," she said. "But I'm twenty-six and the biological clock is running out on me."

"What are you talking about? Twenty-six is young."

"Not in Utah."

"Have you ever gotten close to getting married before?"

"I've been engaged twice."

Luke grinned. "I'd consider that pretty close," he said. "Now we're getting somewhere. Keep talking."

"The first time was when I was eighteen," she said, looking trustingly into his eyes. "Just out of high school. I started dating this returned missionary. I liked him and we went out for a few months. One night we drove to Salt Lake and he bought me an expensive dinner. He took me on a horse carriage ride through downtown, then we went to Temple Square.

"Out of the blue, right in front of the temple, he dropped to one knee and proposed to me. In front of everybody. He gave me a ring and everything. It was soooooooooo embarrassing. I knew I didn't want to spend the rest of my life, let alone the eternities, with this guy."

"So you said no, right?"

"No, I said yes."

"Come again?"

"There were a lot of people milling around and staring at us. What was I supposed to say? It took me a week to get up the courage to say no and give the ring back."

"How did he take it?"

"I don't know. He moved to Alaska a couple of weeks later."

Luke grinned. "I'm no Dr. Laura, but I'd surmise he didn't take it well."

"Then I went to BYU and dated quite a few guys. I hope it doesn't sound like I'm bragging. Anyway, there was one in particular that I really liked. Kevin. We dated all during fall and winter semesters. He proposed to me on top of the Kimball Tower at BYU. He put the ring inside my coat pocket and when I put my hands inside, I found it. It was all so romantic. That time, I felt good about getting engaged. He was set to graduate and go to medical school in California. In fact, he was the reason why I became interested in nursing. But something was bothering me, I couldn't figure out what. I realized I didn't want to put him through school or leave my parents. I didn't love him enough to make those sacrifices for him. Only I didn't realize that for a long time. The invitations had been sent, money had been spent, reservations had been made. But I knew I couldn't do it. A week before the wedding, I backed out."

"Ouch."

"I still feel guilty. But I just can't get married until I'm absolutely sure it's right."

"You're the Mormon equivalent to the runaway bride, then," Luke said.

Ooops.

Hayley stood up and turned her back on him.

"I'm sorry," Luke said. "I shouldn't have said that."

"It's not you," Hayley said, wiping tears from her eyes. "You're right. I guess I'm afraid of commitment or something. I just want everything to be right when I get married. All my high school friends are married and have three or four kids already. My family thinks I am too picky. But I have set a standard for the kind of man I want to marry, and I'm not going to settle for anything less. Everybody thought I was crazy for going on a mission, except my parents. Some people think the only reason I went on a mission is because I was scared of marriage. It's true that I never planned on going, but it was something I felt I had to do. I wasn't running from anything; I was running toward something that turned out to be one of the best experiences of my life. Now that I'm home, I know the pressure is on. Everyone is expecting me to get married. But I have to be in love."

"What would happen if you fell in love with a non-Mormon?" Luke asked.

"Why is it you always ask such difficult questions?"

"That's how I make a living."

"Well, to be honest, growing up I never thought I would even date a non-member, not that we think we're better than non-members. It's just that we marry who we date, and I don't want to risk falling in love with someone and not marrying in the temple. That's very important to me. I couldn't forfeit eternal life and the celestial kingdom for a 'til-death-do-us-part,' earthly marriage." She paused. "In fact, you're the first non-Mormon, and the first non-returned missionary, I've dated since I was eighteen."

"Are you okay with that?"

"So far, yeah," she said. "Sometimes I forget you're not a member. But you will be soon, right? What's holding you back?"

"I don't think I would make a very good Mormon."

"Why do you say that?"

"Weren't you paying attention when I told you my life story?"

"What happened to you with your parents wasn't your fault. Besides, all that is in the past," Hayley said. "When you get baptized, the Lord gives you a fresh start. If you're good enough in the Lord's eyes, you're certainly good enough in mine. I'm not perfect, either, you know."

"That's news to me," Luke said.

"Since you brought up stuff about us," Hayley said in a serious tone, "you should probably know that I've been seeing someone else for a while."

"You mean Thad?"

Hayley was stunned. "How did you know his name?"

"I'm an investigative journalist, remember?" Luke said. "Actually, I met him at your open house. What's up with you two?"

"I've been dating him a little since I got back from my mission. He wrote me faithfully for the entire eighteen months. Anyway, I called him this morning and told him we needed some space. He's at BYU, I'm here at home, living with my parents. It's hard. He's a great guy and I really like him." She paused. "I can't believe I'm telling you all this. But I told him that I wanted to see what happened with you and me. He was very understanding and supportive about it. He said he would give me as much time as I needed. There was a time during my mission when I thought I might marry him. I'm not so sure now. You've complicated things."

"That's one of my talents," Luke said.

"Let's just take it slow," Hayley said. "And let's not kiss in front of my father."

"Good idea."

As they rode back to Hayley's house, Luke realized he had never thought about settling down with one woman before, but she was beginning to change his mind. At the same time, he did not feel worthy of her. She was so wholesome, so kind, so pure. He was none of those things. She deserved better. Besides, he had a book to write.

Luke knew it wasn't meant to be between them. He wasn't a Mormon, let alone a returned missionary, for starters. Plus, he didn't need a child, let alone eight or nine, interfering with his career. Still, the prospect of being with Hayley was so tempting, he thought, he might even consider converting to Mormonism for her.

Luke and Hayley went skiing the next weekend. He had never been before so Hayley taught him how to snowplow. He spent most of the day sliding down the mountain on his back. How could he be expected to concentrate, what with Hayley, wearing a form-fitting snowsuit, skiing ahead of him?

Around the ward, people were starting to talk about them as an item. Everyone seemed to make it their business. Luke and Hayley heard the whispers, the wisecracks. They downplayed their relationship well and established some ground rules: no sitting next to each other at church, no talking to each other in church except for an informal greeting, no public displays of affection. The last thing they needed was Sister Fidrych announcing their engagement in fast and testimony meeting.

During enrichment night, Sister Fidrych sidled up to Hayley with curiosity in her eyes. "So, how are things between you and Luke?" she asked. She was the only one in the ward who dared ask.

"He's fine and I'm fine," Hayley said, struggling to breathe after taking a whiff of Sister Fidrych's perfume.

"I hear you two are spending a lot of time together. I don't blame you. He's very handsome. Very mysterious."

"Mysterious?"

"Oh, yeah. No one really knows much about him. No one really knows why he moved to Utah."

"What's there to know?" Hayley replied. "He was at the *New York Post* before coming out here."

"Oh, reeeeaaaaally?" Sister Fidrych said.

Hayley knew from that reaction she had revealed too much.

"Really. He came out here, where there's peace and quiet to do some free-lance writing. He wanted to get out of that New York City rat race. What's the big deal?"

"Nothing. Nothing at all. We'll talk later." Sister Fidrych sat down. Finally, she had something new on Luke Manning.

CHAPTER 35

Ben invited Luke to go to another BYU basketball game, and since Hayley had been taking up so much of his time, Luke figured he had better accept the invitation. It was a thriller of a game and it went into overtime, but Luke's mind was on Hayley. As he and Ben drove home, wondering who they would pick up on I-15 this time, Ben mentioned he had a meeting early the next morning with Brother Sweeney.

"What's up with that guy?" Luke asked. "When you ask him how he's doing, just casually, he always says, 'Best day of my life.' That's impossible. How can each day get progressively better? You mean to tell me he doesn't have bad days? C'mon. He's like one of those phony motivational speakers."

Ben looked at Luke and smiled. "There's probably something you should know about Brother Sweeney," he said. "He has cancer, but he doesn't like anyone to make a big deal about it. He's been awfully sick for several months now."

"If you'll excuse me," Luke said, "I'll remove my pair of Nikes from my mouth."

"The bishop has tried to release him from his calling but he doesn't want that," Ben said. "He thinks if he rests all the time—which is what the doctors advise—then he'll just die. The tough thing is, when he was diagnosed, he had just left a computer software firm and was trying to start his own business. He has no insurance. Every medical bill he has to pay himself. Members of the ward set up a fund at the Bank of Helaman in his name. He was embarrassed at first about it—he's not the type to want people fussing over him and feeling sorry for him. We've had some contributions and it's helped."

"So, this cancer, it's terminal?"

"That's what the doctors say, but they don't know how long he has left. It's amazing, the way he can deal with a death sentence and raise a family, in addition to all of his other responsibilities. He does a lot to keep the ward running smoothly. So when he says, 'Best day of my life,' he means it."

For the next week, Brother Sweeney's plight gnawed at Luke. He couldn't stop thinking about him, his wife, and seven children. Every time he closed his eyes, he saw Brother Sweeney, smiling, saying, "Best day of my life." How any man facing so much adversity could answer the simple question, "How are you?" like that had to be superhuman. Or crazy.

Luke awoke early one morning and went to the Bank of Helaman. He approached the teller and explained he wanted to contribute to the Bob Sweeney Fund, but that he wanted to do it anonymously. He wrote out a check for $5,000. With all the money Kilborn was paying him, that was pocket change.

The following Sunday, during fast and testimony meeting, when there was a bit of a lull, Brother Sweeney walked to the pulpit and adjusted the microphone.

"Brothers and Sisters," he began, then stared at the back of the church for what seemed at least several minutes. Tears coursed down his face, and he bowed his head to compose himself.

"They say God answers prayers through His children. And my testimony of that truth has grown this week. A doctor's bill arrived at our home recently, and I didn't know how we were going to pay it. All sorts of thoughts entered my head. A bake sale. A garage sale. A house sale. I was going to ask my kids to sell their baseball card collection. I didn't know what to do. Georgia and I didn't tell anyone about our dilemma. We simply prayed and placed our trust in our Heavenly Father. A tremendous peace came over us. We felt like He would provide. On Friday, I received a call from the bank president, who informed me that an anonymous donor had contributed . . ."—he tried to compose himself again—". . . five thousand dollars to our fund."

Brother Sweeney continued, "I don't know who did this, but knowing the type of people we have in this ward, I believe that person is here today. I wish I knew who you were, but I may never know. So please accept my most profound gratitude. The Lord will bless you for your sacrifice and generosity..."

As Luke walked to Primary, he felt like he was walking on air. Church didn't seem so bad. Especially when he knew he was about to see Hayley lead the music. In fact, waking up every morning knowing he was going to see Hayley took away much of the thrill of crossing off each day from the calendar, which was well into March. While the NCAA basketball tournament and its accompanying office pools usually captured his attention this time of year, Hayley overshadowed all that. In fact, he barely noticed the NCAA Tournament. Besides, he had his own basketball tournament to worry about.

The week of the stake championships, Ben left with his family on vacation and Brother McGown had to go out of town on business. Ben lobbied hard with the stake athletic director to revoke Luke's suspension. "He is *this* close to being a convert," Ben explained. "Shunning him from athletic events forever is not the answer."

Ben promised that Luke would be on his best behavior and that he would not speak to the officials or do so much as give them a dirty look. The stake athletic director relented. "But just one more outburst from him," he threatened, "and I'll speak to Bishop Law about making him a stake basketball official."

That pretty much left Luke in charge of the team. Ben warned him to keep his emotions in check.

Once cleared to coach, Luke tried to find out everything he could about the team. "Who's your go-to guy?" he asked Ben.

"That's one of our problems," he said. "We don't have one."

"What about that tall kid?"

"You mean Ammon?"

"Yeah, he has some potential."

"He's going through a tough time right now. His dad's in prison for embezzlement and that's really affected him, on and off the court. The bishop and I visit his dad once a week. I know Brother Adams well because we used to be ward clerks together. He got behind in some credit card payments and got desperate. He took some cash from his work. Ammon refuses to see his dad. His parents have divorced. It's a sad situation."

Luke knew if his team had any chance of winning the stake tournament, he needed Ammon Adams. During the first practice Luke held, Ammon played like his feet were sitting in buckets of sand.

"Get your head and feet in the game!" Luke hollered. "You need to post up! You need to rebound! Mable Sterling could beat you to the hoop, the way you're playing!"

Ammon yelled back and slammed the ball on the floor. Which was exactly the reaction Luke was hoping for. At that point, he ended practice and dismissed the team, except for Ammon. Luke took him into the same classroom where he and Ben taught Primary.

It took a while, but Luke got Ammon to talk about his problems. "Everyone wants me to go see my dad. But I won't do it. He's ruined my life. Every time someone sees me, they feel sorry for me, like I'm a loser, like my dad."

"First off, I don't blame you for not seeing your dad," Luke said. "I wouldn't either. Believe me, in a way, I know what you're going through. But if there's one thing I've learned, it's this: You can't confront your future until you confront your past. What's done is done. Your dad is not you. What he has done is not a reflection on you. You have to make your own statement. Be your own person. You have a lot of talent. Instead of feeling sorry for yourself and moping around, I want you to channel that frustration. When you step on that court from now on, I want you to play as though you're trying to show everyone what Ammon Adams is all about. Can you do that?"

Ammon nodded. "Yeah," he said as he got off his chair. "Thanks, Brother Manning."

"That's Coach Manning, to you."

"All right, coach."

With Hayley by his side, Luke showed up at the stake center for the first game in a suit and tie. The official—the same one that Luke had disparaged and humiliated months earlier—approached him before the game and told him that if he heard anything, no matter what it was, even a scripture, come from his mouth, he would be banned for life from stake athletic events. Luke said he understood. No way did he want to go down as the Pete Rose of Mormon basketball.

The 6th Ward won its first two games in the tournament, thanks to Ammon. He was unstoppable. He dominated inside and outside, scoring sixty-eight points in the two games. Most importantly, he looked like he was having fun.

"What's gotten into him?" asked McKay Taylor, a friend of Ammon's who served as Luke's assistant. "I haven't seen him smile like that in months."

The 6th Ward advanced to the championship game against the heavily favored, two-time defending stake champs, the Helaman 2nd Ward. It had Beau Cashman, who stood 6-foot-9 and weighed 150 pounds. He was about as graceful as a giraffe on roller skates, but his height made up for that. Earlier in the season, the 6th Ward had lost by thirty-five to this team as Cashman simply stood near the basket and tipped in all his teammates' missed shots. He had scored fifty of his team's sixty-two points. He also had blocked eighteen shots.

The night before the title game, Luke had the team over to his house for a pregame meal and meeting. He served the team pizza, wrote out the game plan on a grease board, and showed them game films of the first two games and one of the 2nd Ward's games (he had Hayley in the stands with a camcorder), as well as an inspirational sports video. By the time tipoff rolled around, Luke's players believed they could beat the Los Angeles Lakers.

Luke instructed Ammon to drive right at Beau Cashman in order to get him into foul trouble. The strategy worked. The referees called three personals on Beau in the first five minutes. With him on the bench, the 6th Ward pretty much had their way. Wasn't even close. They won, seventy-seven to thirty-two.

Bishop Law had made a friendly wager with Bishop Archibald of the 2nd Ward—the losing ward had to wax the gym floor at the church every month for the next year. With this vested interest, Bishop Law and two dozen other ward members were in attendance at the championship game. Afterwards, Luke and his team cut down the nets with a pair of scissors. Hayley, naturally, took pictures.

"The cost of the nets is coming out of your ward budget," a stake official told Luke.

"Take it easy, I'll buy them myself," he said. "I'll have new nets up by Monday."

It was the first championship for the ward—in any sport, by any age group—as far back as anyone could remember. At a party at Luke's house following the game, Luke broke out a bottle of bubbly. "I understand 1998 was a very good year for non-alcoholic sparkling cider," he said as he poured the bishop a glass. On Sunday, the bishop had the team, and Luke, stand up during sacrament meeting and be recognized for their feat. The championship trophy, the net, and a ball, signed by Luke and all the boys, were enshrined in a glass case in the foyer.

CHAPTER 36

To celebrate the improbable championship, Luke and Hayley went out to eat a few days later. While they were leaving the restaurant, they noticed thick, black smoke billowing from a building a couple of blocks away.

"That's the Baptist Church," Hayley said, running toward the burning structure. Luke called 911 on his cell phone, and police and fire personnel arrived minutes later. So did Pastor Erickson, leader of the Baptist congregation. He was devastated to see his new church, built only a year earlier, partially destroyed although relieved that no one was inside. The county fire department launched an investigation into the cause of the blaze, but Pastor Erickson had his own ideas about what had happened and he wasn't shy about expressing those to the news media.

Days earlier, he said he had seen six kids playing baseball on a grass field adjacent to the church. The pastor said he kindly asked them to leave because he didn't want any windows broken. The boys, who were all deacons and members of the 6th Ward, were reluctant to leave, but they did. Witnesses told the pastor those same boys were seen in the area not long before the fire broke out. Pastor Erickson was certain the Mormon kids were responsible for the damage.

"Isn't it enough that the Mormons have a church on every street corner?" the pastor pleaded into the TV cameras. "We have one in this entire community. And now it is gone."

Luke licked his chops. What a great chapter, he thought—a cat fight between two churches. He couldn't have contrived anything better than this.

The parents of the accused boys believed their children were innocent, but they were heartbroken by the allegations. Some members of the ward believed the six boys should not be allowed to pass the sacrament or collect fast offerings unless they were acquitted.

Bishop Law interviewed every boy, though, and believed they were not responsible, so he let them continue in their duties. "They're innocent until proven guilty," the bishop said, "in the eyes of the law. I've spoken to them and as far as I'm concerned, they're innocent in the eyes of the Lord."

The story grabbed headlines throughout the state and it was played up on the evening newscasts, even though the boys were not charged with any crime. The pastor was a persuasive man, though, and he was sure he had nailed the culprits.

Bishop Law met with Pastor Erickson for an interfaith summit and offered his chapel to be used for worship services while the pastor's congregation was displaced. He also told him regardless of the outcome of the investigation, his ward was going to help rebuild the church. The pastor took this as an admission of guilt, but the bishop didn't care how he took it. "We only want to help," he said.

Brother Cook, who owned a construction company, contributed materials. Brother Webb, a plumber, and Brother Smith, an electrician, offered their services free of charge. In all, thirty-one ward members volunteered to assist in the reconstruction. And, of course, the Relief Society brought food to feed the volunteers.

During evenings and weekends, Mormons and Baptists labored side by side. Luke volunteered because (a) Hayley had, and (b) he was hoping sparks would fly between opposing church members. Turned out, the only sparks he saw came from the electric saws.

The church was rebuilt in a matter of weeks. It turned out even better than before, some of the Baptists said. They added that their congregation had never been so unified.

Days after the building was completed, fire investigators announced that the cause of the blaze was a faulty electrical wire. Pastor Erickson held a press conference. He offered a public apology and thanked the Mormons for their assistance.

So much for an ecumenical cat fight. When it came to his book, Luke just couldn't catch a break.

The 6th Ward—and the Baptists—marshaled forces again later that month when Dale's Quik Stop convenience store, which had been purchased by a New York-based corporation, started stocking shelves with pornographic magazines. Located just off the freeway in Helaman, the store was a popular hangout for the truckers passing through.

Brother Brunansky happened to stop in the store, buying a candy bar with his son, when he saw the prurient publications on the shelves. He immediately alerted the ward, and the city, to the situation. At once, residents demanded that the Helaman City Council pull Dale's business license. The Council knew that was not an option because there was no law on the city's books that prohibited the sales of sexually oriented material. It had never been an issue before. It didn't surprise Luke that the members of the council were all people he recognized from church meetings. In fact, it would have been hard to tell much of a difference from the city council and a high council in Helaman.

During an emergency city council meeting, which opened with a prayer, dozens of Helaman residents filled the room to offer their input on the matter of preserving morality in the town. Of course, Luke had to be there.

The store owners opened the meeting contending that Helaman residents didn't patronize the Quik Stop and had documentation to prove that fifty-one percent of the store's patrons were from outside Utah—the vast majority of whom did not share the community's standards. They had a right to free speech, they argued, and they would be willing to take the city to court if their rights were violated.

Then Helaman residents took over. They were downright hostile.

"We won't allow that smut to exist in our community, period," said Brother Brunansky. "There's a reason why we call this town 'A Little Piece of Heaven.'"

Brother Munchak spoke, displaying more charts, graphs, and pie charts than Ross Perot, about the "pernicious evils" of pornography. Sister Fidrych offered her ten cents worth, too. "If we allow this, what's next?" she asked. "Nightclubs? Strippers?"

Later that week, the council passed a sexually oriented business law and a zoning ordinance that banned the sale of pornographic magazines or videos in town. Either Dale's would have to remove their pornography or move their business elsewhere. That's when Dale's lawyers had a fit. They challenged the constitutionality of the ordinance and immediately filed a lawsuit, backed by the American Civil Liberties Union. They claimed such a law violated their First Amendment rights and requested a temporary injunction to prevent Helaman officials from enforcing the law. Judge William F. Lipitz granted the injunction.

So, Helaman residents took the next step. The following day, Luke went from bystander to participant in the episode when he was roped into protesting the convenience store. The two Helaman Stakes organized shifts to picket the business. People held up signs quoting Book of Mormon and Bible scriptures. They chanted things like "Stamp out porn" and "Not in our town" for hours. Luke walked back and forth for a cause he was indifferent about. But it was a chance to be with Hayley, and it was great material for his book. Plus, he had always wanted to know what it felt like to live in the 1960s. At one point, Luke had the picketers chanting, "Heck, no, we won't go!"

That was until all the television cameras showed up. He knew he couldn't risk being recognized.

The local news stations and papers played up the story—especially when Judge Lipitz reversed the injunction. Dale's lawyers immediately appealed to the State Supreme Court. "We'll go all the way to the U.S. Supreme Court if we have to," one lawyer said.

With that sound-byte, plus footage of picketers marching around the store twenty-four hours a day—since Dale's was open twenty-four hours a day—it didn't take long before the national and international media jumped on the story, too. Dozens of reporters from various news organizations were dispatched to Helaman—including one Peter Bartholomew from the *New York Times*.

Knowing reporters from all over the country would be at the courthouse for a preliminary hearing of the case, Luke showed up at the meeting in disguise. His hair was shorter than it had ever been back in New York, and he was clean-shaven, without his goatee. He hoped he would go unnoticed. As a precautionary measure, he wore a baseball cap and tinted glasses to the hearing. He had arranged to go with Hayley, and when she saw him she stared.

"What's with the specs?" she asked.

"All the better to see with," he answered.

Luke saw Bartholomew sitting with the other reporters and tried to be as inconspicuous as possible, keeping his head down. All the reporters in attendance were jotting down every word for their stories. When the court recessed after opening arguments, Hayley stopped to talk to Sister Watkins. Luke tried to sneak out of the building. As he did, a man grabbed his arm from behind.

"Excuse me, sir, I was wondering if I could get a comment from you."

Luke turned around and saw his nemesis standing there. Bartholomew looked like he had seen a ghost. "Luke Manning," he said, "is that *you*?"

"You're quite the reporter," Luke said. "You have a fine grasp of the obvious."

"What are you doing here?"

"What kind of question is that? I know a good story when I see one."

"Funny, I haven't seen you this week and I didn't see you with the other reporters during the hearing."

"That's because I'm not your run-of-the-mill reporter. Now if you'll excuse me, I've got some work to do."

"What paper are you covering this for anyway?" he asked. But Luke had already headed for the door. He was getting more than a little nervous. He knew this couldn't go on much longer.

Meanwhile, back at Dale's, the picketers continued their protests. It didn't take long before truckers went out of their way to avoid the store just so they wouldn't have to listen to all the religious rhetoric and fight their way past the picket lines. The next day, the business agreed to stop selling porn and drop its lawsuit. It also announced its intentions to move to a different county as soon as possible. Luke was just relieved it was all over so he wouldn't have to hide from Bartholomew anymore.

Between rebuilding a church, picketing a store, and everything else they had going in their lives, Luke and Hayley had precious little time to spend together, at least alone. Every once in a while, they went to dinner and a movie, or bowling, but Hayley always had more creative, not to mention more economical, ways to have fun. One day, she dragged him to the Family History Library in Salt Lake City to do research on his ancestors. Luke did not put up any resistance.

"I don't know much about my parents," he told Hayley. "I don't know if we'll be able to find much on them."

"There are more than two billion names in the records here," Hayley said. "I'm sure your parents and other ancestors are included in here somewhere."

During their research, Luke was shocked at what Hayley discovered—the kind of skeleton in his family's closet he would never have expected.

"Luke!" Hayley said excitedly, scaring an elderly couple at the computer terminal nearby, "you're not going to believe this!"

"You found something?"

"I found more than something," she said, peering at the screen. "I think I found your great-great-great-great-great-grandfather. Ever hear of Jedediah Manning?"

"You mean Great-great-great-great-great-grandpa Jed? Nope. Never heard of him."

"He was a member of the Church!"

Luke slid his chair in front of the screen. "There must be some kind of mistake. . . ."

"No!" Hayley said. "It's all right here."

According to Church records, Jedediah Manning (1807-1859), indeed, had been baptized a member of the Church in 1844. Go figure.

"Looks like you and the Church go way back, after all," Hayley said.

As far as Luke and Hayley could tell, no other relatives, including Jed's wife and children, had joined the Church. Hayley helped Luke fill out his family group sheets.

"Isn't this fun?" she asked.

"More than Mormons should be allowed," Luke said.

Surely there had been some type of clerical error. He decided that when he returned to the East, he would do some more research on this Jed Manning and set the record straight. He didn't have time at the moment. His book took precedence. And time was running out.

CHAPTER 37

Ben showed up at Luke's house one Friday night at 6:45, dressed in a suit. "Can I ask you for a favor?" he asked.

"As long as it has nothing to do with shoveling snow."

"Not this time. Stacie and I have been planning all month to go to ward temple night but our sitter just called and canceled. If you wouldn't mind, if you're not doing anything, could you stay with the kids for a few hours? They're all in bed. It will be a piece of cake."

"You must be desperate," Luke said.

"How'd you guess?"

Luke agreed to do it, since Hayley was working and he had nothing else to do. Plus, he figured he could take his laptop with him and write while he was there. As soon as Ben and Stacie left, before Luke could even unpack his computer, Jared and Megan sneaked out of their beds and crept into the kitchen, begging for a drink of water. They returned moments later, wanting a story. The third time, they asked for ice cream. He didn't see how a little treat could hurt, so he granted them that request, too.

Just as he removed the chocolate syrup from the refrigerator, he heard the baby start to whimper, which rapidly progressed to hysterical screaming. He told the kids to stay put, and went up the stairs to Rebecca's room. Upon opening the door, Luke almost collapsed from the stench and staggered backward into Ben and Stacie's room. After a couple of minutes, he re-entered with a towel around his nose and mouth. Peeking into the crib, he saw a green substance oozing from the baby's diaper, like something out of *Alien*. Caught in a sheer panic, Luke called Sister Woodard and explained the emergency.

"You're in luck. Hayley just walked in the door," she said. "I'll send her right over."

Hayley had gotten off early from work, and when she arrived at the Kimballs, she heard the baby howling and saw Jared and Megan chowing down, unsupervised, on ice cream. They had chocolate syrup all over the counter and floor. She told them not to move and went searching for the No. 1 problem—Luke. She found him in the hallway, frazzled almost beyond recognition. He was sitting on the floor outside of Ben and Stacie's room, in a catatonic state, staring at the ceiling.

"Luke," she said, "are you feeling all right?"

"I don't know," he said, sounding like a post-traumatic stress disorder victim. "I think my olfactory senses have been permanently damaged."

Hayley rolled her eyes and went to work. She cleaned up the baby, gave her a bath, tossed the dirty sheets in the washing machine, put on new sheets, gave the baby a bottle, and laid her back down. Then she went downstairs, scrubbed chocolate stains off of the kids, the walls, the furniture, the toaster. After that, she tucked the children to bed and read them a story. With a cold compress on his head, Luke followed her around, watching everything.

"You saved me," Luke said after order was restored. "This is exactly why I'd make a lousy father."

"You just need practice, that's all," Hayley said. "Those are the types of problems I can't wait to have someday."

It all served as yet another reminder why he would never be able to have a long-term relationship with her. And he couldn't help but feel, somehow, like he was going to be missing out. She made even domesticity seem attractive.

Ben and Stacie returned home by ten. "How did things go?" Ben asked.

"Piece of cake," Luke replied.

The night was still relatively young and to show his gratitude, Luke told Hayley he would take her out. "We can go anywhere you want," he said. "You name it."

"Really?"

Luke nodded.

"Then let me drive," she said, grabbing his car keys. She started by tuning the radio to a country music station.

"Where are we going?" Luke asked.

"It's a surprise. I don't want to give it away."

"Will I like this surprise?"

"Probably not."

She was right. Moments later, they arrived at a Helaman dance hall. Outside the building was a sign that read "Country Night." Inside was a group of men wearing cowboy hats, tight Wranglers, and belt buckles the size of dinner plates.

Within forty-five seconds of arriving, Hayley was asked to dance by some guy named Wyatt. She was twirled, spun, dipsey-dooed, and swung around like a ragdoll. Luke noticed all the guys drooling over her. Almost every one of them danced with Hayley, putting their grimy paws all over her hands, back, and waist. Breathless, she came over to where Luke was standing, in a corner. He was drinking a Pepsi.

"C'mon," she said, grabbing his arm. "It's fun."

"I don't think my insurance covers this," he protested.

He took the floor anyway and Hayley showed him a few moves. But it was no use. He country-danced like Herman Munster in moonboots. When they stopped to rest, Hayley was laughing. "Wasn't that great?"

"Yeah," he said, "if you're into vertigo."

At 11:45, Hayley suggested that they leave and that drew no argument from Luke. As he drove her home, she thanked him for going, then fell asleep, her soft cheeks glowing in the moonlight. Luke didn't claim to know the secret to happiness, but he knew he didn't need Mormonism or any other "ism" to find it. He had found his, sitting in the passenger seat.

All he knew was that bliss wasn't going to last much longer.

CHAPTER 38

The first weekend in April, Hayley invited Luke to go to Temple Square for the Saturday morning session of general conference. It was hard for Luke to believe, but six months had passed since the last conference. Trouble was, each general conference session seemed to last six months to Luke. But this time, he was going to be at the LDS Conference Center in person, which he figured was the least he could do for his book's sake. Plus, he was going with Hayley.

As they left early that morning, Hayley put a tape called *Saturday's Warrior* in the tape deck to listen to on the way to Salt Lake.

"What is this?" he asked warily.

"This is required listening if you're a member of the Church, or a soon-to-be member of the Church."

"As long as it's not country music," he said.

They ate breakfast at a restaurant in downtown Salt Lake City, then walked around the visitors' center on Temple Square, where Hayley showed him the giant Christus statue. By then it was time to go to the Conference Center. They wended their way past people carrying signs along the streets outside the Conference Center, protesting LDS views on abortion and homosexuality. He saw tables set up with people passing out brochures, calling the Mormon Church, and Mormons, to repentance.

Following the first session, Hayley couldn't stop talking about Elder So-and-So's talk and the symbolic meaning found in this scripture or that. Luke mostly nodded and looked pensive, even though he hadn't a clue what she was talking about.

They sat near an immaculately landscaped flower bed on Temple Square and marveled at the Salt Lake Temple. "The stones they used to build this are made out of granite, taken out of the canyon. It's incredible. Without computers or high-tech machinery, they were able to build this. My parents were married here and so were my grandparents and great-grandparents."

"I suppose you want to carry on that tradition."

"It's been my dream since I was a little girl," she said. "What about you? What's your dream in life?"

Luke blurted out the first thing that entered his head. "To spend one summer attending a baseball game at every big league ballpark."

Hayley forced a partial smile. "That's it?"

"That would be quite a feat."

"Oh," she said. "Isn't there more to life than that? Don't you want a family someday?"

Luke had painted himself into a corner. "Like I've told you, I don't know if I'm cut out for fatherhood," he said. "Getting married and having children has always been the last thing on my mind. It's hard to get used to the idea."

Now he had done it. Hayley looked down and didn't say another word.

Then, out of the blue, as Luke was trying to figure out a way to smooth things over, he heard a familiar voice say, "What are you still doing in Utah?"

Luke wanted to grab for an airsickness bag. It was Peter Bartholomew. Again.

"What's the deal, Luke? Are you a Utah resident now?"

Luke tried to think of something clever to say. But nothing was coming.

"After being in that piddly little town, Helaman, a while ago, I decided to do a three-part series on the Mormon cult, so the *Times* sent me back out here," Bartholomew said, eyeballing Hayley. "I find it more than coincidental that I've run into you here twice in a month. Do you live here or something? Don't tell me you've converted to Mormonism."

"I've got nothing to say to you," Luke said.

"There's something going on here," Peter said. Then he turned to Hayley. "Hi," he said, shaking her hand. "I'm Peter Bartholomew, *New York Times*. Luke and I . . ."

". . . are finished talking," Luke said, standing up and taking Hayley by the arm. "We've got to get out of here."

"I'm going to find out what you're doing here," Bartholomew called out as Luke and Hayley walked briskly toward the conference center.

"Who was that?" Hayley asked, looking back at Peter. "And what was he talking about?"

"We worked for competing papers in New York," Luke explained. "That guy is bad news. You can't trust him. He'd take any bit of information, or misinformation, and jump at the chance to destroy me or anybody."

As soon as those words left his mouth, Luke realized he could have been describing himself. Luke knew Peter would stop at nothing to find out about his being in Utah. He needed to finish his book, and quick. He couldn't afford to take any chances, and if Bartholomew found out what was going on, he would certainly expose him.

Luke and Hayley didn't see much of each other for a week or so. Part of the reason was simply that they were both so busy. Mostly, things had turned awkward. Luke knew Hayley was an intelligent girl, despite her affinity for country music, and that she was probably growing frustrated with him. Not to mention suspicious. The more time he spent with Hayley at this point, the more counterproductive it would be. They could never be together, that much was obvious. So why waste any more time? On the other hand, he also knew that breaking up with her would be like cutting out his heart with a steak knife.

On Wednesday, he went to Mable's.

"How are things going between you and Hayley?" she asked.

"Not well," Luke said, pushing Mable in her wheelchair into the kitchen. "We're spinning our wheels, so to speak. Choose whatever analogy you'd like. I don't think either of us knows where to go from here."

"For what it's worth, I'm sure you two make a handsome couple," she said, placing her hand on his. "I hope things work out for both of you. You know, when Robert and I were dating, he received a lot of pressure to stop seeing me from people, since I was not a member of the Church at the time. They were appalled that he would date a non-member. But he stuck with me. He patiently answered all my questions about the Church. He didn't pressure me to join and that made all the difference. If it weren't for him, I may never have found the gospel. The most important thing is to be honest with each other. Robert and I had no secrets. We knew everything about each other. Don't keep anything from her."

Luke knew Mable was right, but there was no way he could be completely honest with Hayley. Still, he decided he and Hayley should talk. It was time for both of them to move on with their lives. He had a book to finish, she had a happily-ever-after and an all-expense-paid trip to the celestial kingdom waiting for her. Luke felt like a cad. He was postponing her life, her marriage, her children. Besides, he didn't deserve a woman like her.

Luke arranged for them to get together. Hayley suggested a hiking trail up Provo Canyon. They were both unusually quiet during the ride there. Luke had planned what he was going to say, as much as it would kill him to say it. He hoped she would take it well.

"Is there a place to sit at the top?" Luke asked as they climbed up the steep terrain.

"Are you tired already?" she asked.

"No, but from the looks of this trail, I will be soon."

Just then, Luke tried to plant his foot on a rock, which gave way. So did his ankle and he took a nasty tumble down the trail. Hayley reached him and had him remove his shoe. His ankle was swollen to the size of a tennis ball.

"We'll have to get you home and put some ice on it," she said. Then she helped him up. "Lean on me."

"My pleasure," Luke said.

Luke placed his arm around Hayley's waist and she put her arm around him to help him keep his balance as he hopped down the hill to the car. At that moment, he realized how nice she smelled. How soft her hair was. He knew breaking up would not be easy and he knew it would be uncomfortable for both of them, having to see each other at church on Sundays. Hayley drove him back home and put his ankle in a bucket of ice. She left and came back with dinner for him and then wrapped up his foot with an ace bandage.

"You'd better stay off this for a couple of days if you can," she said. "It's only a sprain, but the longer you rest it, the better off you'll be."

"Thanks for taking care of me," Luke said.

"Just doing my job," she said brusquely.

For a moment, watching Hayley care for him, he let his mind toy with the idea of being married to her. He thought about how wonderful it would be to come home to her every day. Her mere presence turned his old house into the Taj Mahal. He wondered what their children might look like.

"I'd better go," Hayley said. "I've got to work early tomorrow."

While Luke rested his ankle for a couple of days, he came to his senses. He knew their relationship had to end. He picked up the phone and invited Hayley over for dinner. His mobility impeded, he ordered Chinese food. As soon as she arrived, Hayley asked Luke about his ankle.

"It's almost as good as ever," he said, showing her how the swelling had gone down.

"I'm glad," Hayley said.

Luke's plan was to eat a nice, relaxed dinner, talk, and then, somehow, he would delicately tell her that they shouldn't see each other anymore. It had worked fairly well once before with a woman he had dated in New York. But Hayley foiled his plan right off the bat.

"I don't have much of an appetite tonight," she said. "We need to talk." Luke hated those four little words and he hated even more that sound in her voice.

"Okay," Luke said. "Why don't you start?"

"I don't think we should see each other anymore," she began. "We're so different. We both want different things out of life. I think it would be better if we dated other people. What do you think?"

"I think I couldn't have said it better myself," Luke said.

"I'm glad you feel that way because I wanted to let you know I'm moving to Provo to live in a single adult ward," Hayley continued. "I think it would be for the best. I'm moving into my apartment this weekend."

It was like a sucker punch. Luke hadn't seen this one coming at all. Certainly her leaving would make things easier, but he also knew it meant he would probably never see her again.

"You need any help moving?" Luke asked.

"No, thanks," Hayley said. "I don't have a lot of stuff. My dad's going to help me." He limped over to the door, where she stood. "Well, I guess this is it." Hayley nodded. He kissed her on the cheek.

"Good-bye, Luke," she said as she turned and walked to her car.

"Bye, Hayley."

Then he watched the prettiest girl he ever saw drive down the street and out of his life.

Luke didn't feel like eating, either, so he called Ben and asked him if he and Stacie wanted Chinese food. Ben happily accepted it, but left behind one fortune cookie. Later that night, though he wasn't in any mood to celebrate, Luke commemorated his ten-month anniversary of arriving in Utah by drinking a bottle of non-alcoholic sparkling apple cider left over from the basketball team's stake championship. Then he opened his fortune cookie.

"Don't let the opportunity of a lifetime pass you by," it said. Luke didn't believe in fortune cookies or nonsense like that. He preferred to think that the message referred to finishing his book. He had two months to turn it into a masterpiece.

CHAPTER 39

Luke figured the best way to deal with this breakup was to plunge himself into his work. He spent the morning in front of his computer, but nothing came to him. As a diversion, he got into his car to run some errands. The radio came on and it was playing country music. Luke quickly changed the station. At least now he wouldn't have to listen to that cowbell-inspired cacophony anymore.

He was weary of writing about the Mormons, about their beliefs and ideologies. Besides that, everything reminded him of Hayley. He thought up almost every excuse he could not to write. He resorted to mowing his lawn, and Ben's, just to avoid it.

After months of being alcohol-free, Luke felt he deserved a drink. It was time to put out the flames of a romance that had crashed and burned. If that didn't cure him of writer's block, nothing would. Over the previous months, everything had started to build up inside—Brooklyn's death, the pressure of finishing the book, the run-in with Bartholomew, the fact he had been in Utah more than ten months and hadn't uncovered even one scandal, and the split with Hayley. He was on the verge of turning into a basket case. Only an ice-cold alcoholic beverage could soothe his frustration, he thought, and he had just the one in mind. A six-pack of beer. That was all he would need. No one had to know about it. He rationalized that trying to obtain a drink without getting caught would be good research for his book. Plus, he had made it this far and only had about eight weeks left before the assignment was over.

That night, Luke got on the freeway and headed south, not stopping until he was in a town called Santaquin. He figured no one would know him there, so he found a mini-mart and grabbed a six-pack. He looked around, hoping no one would recognize him. After paying for the beer, he asked the cashier to place it in a plastic bag. His heart was thumping. He felt as though someone were watching him, as though he were stealing it. For a moment he was tempted to open a can while driving, but he figured there were laws against such behavior. And for all he knew, in Utah it was probably a felony punishable by death.

Racing home, he couldn't wait to chug a refreshing can of beer for the first time in several months. His excitement was doused, though, when he pulled into his driveway and saw McKay Taylor, who had been Luke's assistant on the ward basketball team, sitting on his front porch.

Luke left the beer in the car and approached McKay.

"What's up?" Luke asked.

"Got a minute?"

"Sure," Luke said reluctantly.

"I just need to talk to someone."

Luke wanted to tell him to find a shrink. "Okay, talk."

"I'm turning nineteen in a few months," he said. "And I am miserable."

"Aren't you a little young to be getting depressed about birthdays?"

"It's not that. I'm just having a tough time because everyone thinks I should go on a mission. Ever since I was born, my parents have planned on me going when I turned nineteen. I thought I would, too. But I've got a gorgeous girlfriend, a scholarship to BYU, and a great summer job. My girlfriend, Sue Beth, would probably get married if I went on a mission. I told my parents I wasn't going and they were crushed. I've talked to the bishop about it, but I wanted to talk to you about it, too."

"Me?" Luke asked. "Why me?" After all, the only meaningful conversations they had had in the past had to do with 1-2-1 zone defenses and fast breaks.

"You're cool. You've been out in the world. You didn't go on a mission, you're not even a member of the Church, and look how you turned out. I know that you talked to Ammon and it turned his life around. I need some advice. Everyone just thinks that if I don't go on a mission, I don't have a testimony. Everyone will look down on me. I'll be a social outcast."

Luke felt a little sorry for the kid. "I'm not going to tell you what to do, but we can talk," he said. "Let's go for a drive."

McKay smiled. "You've got the coolest car in Helaman," he said.

As they walked toward the Corvette, Luke remembered the contraband in the front seat. "Wait! Um, I've got some junk there in the passenger's seat. Let me grab that." He hastily picked up the sack of beer and held it tight against his jacket, hoping McKay didn't see the contents inside. He slipped it in the garbage for the time being.

As they drove around Helaman, Luke listened to McKay rattle on about himself. "I think my parents will disown me. Why can't they respect my choice?"

Luke was in no position to give this kid advice about his life. He wondered what Ben would say. He wondered what Mable would say. Mustering all the wisdom he could, Luke finally spoke up, saying what *he* would say.

"Well, that's the key," he said. "It's your decision. You're the one who has to decide what's best for you, regardless of what anybody else thinks. As long as you know you're doing the right thing, nothing else matters. Forget what everyone else says. You'll never get anywhere in life doing what you think other people expect you to do."

"My parents keep telling me that the prophets have said, 'Every worthy young man must serve a mission.' What if a mission is not for me?"

"Then don't go," Luke said. "Look, you know what's best for you. If you go to make others happy, you'll be unhappy. I remember Ben telling me that one of the worst things he encountered on his mission was malcontent companions who didn't want to be there. Why go and be some unwanted burden and pain in the butt for someone who really wants to be there? What a waste of time that would be."

McKay soaked it all in.

Luke took him to a malt shop and they ate ice cream and played pool. After that, he dropped McKay off at his home. "Thanks for the talk, man," McKay said.

"Anytime," Luke said, hoping the young man wouldn't take that literally.

When he returned to his house, he went to retrieve his beer from the garbage can. But Ben walked up his driveway, holding a large bag.

"Hey Luke," he said, "our garbage can is full—I've been doing a lot of spring cleaning around the yard. Do you have space in your garbage can for this?"

"What's in there?" Luke asked.

"If you have to know, it's full of dirty diapers. I hope you don't mind. It stinks a little. But the garbage man comes tomorrow."

Luke opened the can and Ben dumped in the odoriferous sack. So much for Luke's beer party.

"Thanks," Ben said as he left.

Luke gazed wistfully into the garbage can and the fumes from the garbage bag prompted a flashback of the night he babysat Ben's kids. No way was he going to take that beer out now. So he went to bed. *A six-pack*, he thought, *was a terrible thing to waste.*

Several weeks later, Luke received a phone call from McKay. "Brother Manning!" he said excitedly. "I just wanted to let you know I received my mission call to Japan. I want to thank you for your advice."

"Advice? I thought I told you to do what *you* wanted to do."

"I did. I saw what you were getting at. I had to learn for myself that the only way I could be truly happy is if my will is in harmony with the Lord's will."

"That's what you got from our talk?"

"More or less," McKay said. "I did some hard thinking. I prayed a lot, too. I realized a mission is something I want to do."

Swell, Luke thought. *Now I'm going to be held responsible for sending kids on missions.*

Around that same time, Lane also called. "I don't know if you remember me or not," said his old drinking buddy.

"How could I forget? You're the Mormon rebel from the U of U."

"Not anymore," Lane said. "I wanted to call and tell you that I'm a changed man, dude. You remember that night we went drinking up the canyon last fall? Well, a couple of hours after we dropped you off, my friend rolled our car five times out in the desert outside Wendover. I guess you could say God woke me up by putting me in a coma. I came out of it and I'm repenting of my mistakes. I can't go on a mission, but I want to share the gospel and I wanted to start with you, dude. Do you want to learn more about the Church? There's no obligation."

No obligation? Luke thought. He knew better. "Well," he said, "I really don't have time this year. But I'm glad to hear you're not comatose anymore. Congratulations. I guess you won't be celebrating with a beer."

"No way, dude," Lane said. "I'm done with that stuff. Hey, if you ever want to talk, about the Church or anything, you have my number, right?"

"Right," Luke said, though he had thrown it away months ago. These Mormons were just getting weirder and weirder. He needed to get out of Utah.

CHAPTER 40

Ben and Stacie were growing worried about Luke. They rarely saw him and when they did, it looked like he was losing weight. The Kimballs invited Luke over for dinner, but he had a dozen excuses why he couldn't go. When they heard about his breakup with Hayley from Sister Fidrych, they felt bad that Luke hadn't told them himself.

"I bet he's going through a rough time," Stacie told Ben. "He probably needs to talk about it."

"Guys don't want to talk about it," Ben said. "He just needs some time alone. Then he'll be his same old self again. He's been through a lot these past few months. This might actually be a good thing for him. Sometimes people need to be humbled a little before they get baptized. Maybe this is what Luke needs. He has to realize, on his own, that until he gets baptized, things are going to be tough for him. I know he knows the Church is true. I just can't understand why he won't get baptized."

With Stacie's endorsement, Ben bought season tickets to BYU football games as something for him and Luke to do together in the fall. Ben was planning to wait until a couple of weeks before the season and surprise him. In the meantime, Ben invited him to go golfing. Luke went, though he seemed unusually quiet. Definitely not the same Luke that Ben knew. It was on the ninth hole that Ben finally got up the nerve to ask him about Hayley.

"Do you still think about her?"

"Sometimes, but it was never going to work. We're too different," Luke explained before tapping in a putt from five feet away. "She's better off in Provo, with all those returned missionaries. I'm a little old for her, anyway."

As for Luke, he had a date every night with his computer. Somehow, he managed to regain his writing touch again, and he spent almost every free moment writing the last third of his book. It was about four o'clock one Tuesday afternoon when his computer started making a gagging sound and his mouse froze up. Then the monitor went blank.

When he restarted the computer, he discovered the files from the past two months were nowhere to be found. Luke tried three or four different tricks to try to locate them, but they had been obliterated. All 240-plus pages. He cursed up a storm, enough to fill three Swearing Jars. He paced. He took a long drive up the canyon. He kicked himself for not saving multiple copies. He kicked the wall, leaving a large indention. The home owners would not be pleased.

By 9:30, Luke had tried almost everything he could think of, including calling a computer support hotline. The customer service people gave him a couple of places where he could take the computer, but they made no promises that the missing files could be recovered. The process could take weeks, they said. Luke didn't have weeks.

He resigned himself to the fact that he would have to call Kilborn in the morning and tell him the devastating news. All that work, gone. He would have to start over. He knew how Martin Harris must have felt when he lost the Book of Lehi.

The thought of having to rewrite all those pages, which were floating around somewhere in the ozone, with such a stringent deadline already crashing down on him, made him physically ill. At 10 p.m., there was a knock on the door. It was Brother McGown, dressed in a sweat suit.

"I was jogging by and saw your lights on and thought I'd stop in," he said.

Luke was not in a chatting mood, seeing as how his last few months of work had vaporized. Still, he remembered that Brother McGown worked for a computer company and invited him inside. As his home teacher, Brother McGown was always asking if there was anything he could do to help. Luke figured this was his chance to take him up on the offer.

"Do you know much about data recovery?" he asked.

"I'm no expert," Brother McGown said, "but I've been known to find lost information before. Why? Did you lose something?"

Luke hesitated, knowing that he didn't want anybody in Helaman to see those files when and if they were ever found. But this was an emergency. His biggest concern was salvaging his work.

"My hard drive is toasted. I have a lot of work on there," he said. "If you could help me . . ."

"I'd love to help," Brother McGown said eagerly. "Isn't that the worst, when you lose a bunch of files? That's happened to me a few times, too. Once, I lost fifty-four pages of my personal journal. It was just terrible. Did you lose something important?"

"You could say that."

For the first time, Luke escorted a person to his inner sanctum, his den—after he quickly stashed all the notes, documents, and books about the Mormons. Brother McGown made himself right at home, turning on the computer and fiddling with the screen and the keyboard. Meanwhile, Luke paced the floor like an expectant father.

After forty-five minutes, Brother McGown announced, "I'm going to have to call in the reserves on this one, Luke. This is not good. I'm not saying it's hopeless, but this is a little over my head. May I borrow your phone?"

"Who are you going to call at this hour? It's after ten o'clock."

Brother McGown laughed as he dialed a number. "Steve would do anything for a brother in need," he said.

"Steve?" Luke asked. That was all he needed—more people getting involved. Hymns and a prayer would surely follow.

"Steve Fidrych will know what to do," Brother McGown said. "If there's anyone who can restore your hard drive, it's him. He's a genius when it comes to this stuff."

"You mean Sister Fidrych's husband?"

"Yep. He does this stuff for a living. If he can't do it, no one can."

Luke's worst nightmare was coming true. Sister Fidrych was a one-woman 50,000-watt radio station. If the files were ever recovered, and if she found out, she would blow his cover. No matter what happened, he figured, he was in trouble.

"Look, it's late and I hate disturbing people . . ." Luke said.

"Don't worry about it. We'll get this thing figured out. We're happy to help. This is what your hometeachers are for."

Not only did Brother Fidrych show up, so did Sister Fidrych, who had a neighbor stay with her kids. Sister Fidrych was sporting green-tinted facial cream, her hair was in curlers, and she was dressed in a bright teal robe and fuzzy white slippers. She held an edited copy of *Titanic* in her hand. "Do you mind if I watch this?" she asked. "These recoveries usually take a while."

As soon as Luke said yes, she went directly into the kitchen to make Postum with a mix she had brought from home. She began asking questions about what information he had stored on the computer.

"Just a couple files," he said.

"I bet it's something important."

"How'd you guess?"

"You know how I've been trying to find out where I know you from?"

"Yeah . . ."

"Well, Hayley told me you used to work for the *New York Post*. I got on the Internet and the other day I found out you were the one that did the big gambling story about Governor Sharples in New York. Then it hit me! I saw you on TV last spring, talking about it with Katie Couric. Why didn't you tell me? That's where I know you from!"

"Congratulations," Luke said. "I'm very happy for you."

"So, can you tell me what you're doing here in Utah? Just between us? You're working on a special project, right? Something about UFOs in Southern Utah? Or sea monsters in Utah Lake?"

"Can I get you a donut?" Luke asked.

"Love donuts."

"I've got glazed, powdered, and the cream-filled kind. What would you like?"

"All of the above," she said.

By the time Luke returned from the kitchen, Sister Fidrych had fallen asleep on the couch. Those sleeping pills he had placed in her Postum when she wasn't looking apparently had done the trick.

Two other ward members arrived well after midnight, and suddenly Luke's den had turned into a ward activity. He tried not to panic when he saw them dismantling his computer and intermittently saying, "Uh-oh, this doesn't look good."

Luke couldn't believe these people. In a few more hours they all had to go to their jobs, and were still working diligently. He had a newfound respect for computer geeks. On the other hand, *if they only knew what they were trying to save,* he thought, *they probably wouldn't be so enthusiastic about helping.* Sister Fidrych remained asleep on the couch in the living room, which allowed the crew of computer troubleshooters to work twice as fast.

It was a little past 5 a.m. when Brother McGown turned to Luke. "Let's hope this works. Say a little prayer."

He turned on the computer. In a matter of minutes, a list of his files, including the one titled "Mormonville" popped on the screen.

"You found it!" Luke yelled, pumping his fist. Then he grabbed the four men and engaged in a prolonged group hug. While he was indeed thrilled to know his work wasn't gone, it was his desperate attempt to distract them from the name of the files. Fortunately for Luke, the men were sleep-deprived and practically loopy. Brother McGown asked Luke to open the files to make sure everything was okay.

So he did. "MORMONVILLE" appeared on the screen.

"Mormonville?" Brother McGown said. The room went silent.

Luke closed the file quickly. He was glad Sister Fidrych was snoring on his couch at the time.

"Looks like everything's in order. Thank you," he said. "I'm taking you all out to breakfast to celebrate. I'd take you in my Corvette, but you wouldn't all fit." Luke knew that Sister Fidrych alone would have taken up the entire back seat and part of the trunk.

After waking up Sister Fidrych and coaxing everyone out of the den, Luke had them pile into the Fidrychs' van, which looked like a giant bread box on wheels. They went to an all-night dining establishment on the edge of town. While eating French toast and scrambled eggs, Brother McGown asked Luke, "Out of curiosity, is that file we recovered some sort of project of yours? It looked like a book."

Luke wanted to plant an apple fritter in his mouth.

Sister Fidrych perked up. "Book? What book? So, Luke, you are writing a book?"

"Something called *Mormonville*," Brother McGown said.

"See! I knew he was up to something big," Sister Fidrych said. "Tell us what you're working on, Luke. You can tell us, since we're the ones who helped you recover it."

Luke had to think fast. He remembered the Mormons' fetish with record-keeping and he decided to use that to his advantage. "A journal is a personal thing. How would you like someone asking about your journal?"

That shut them up. Brother McGown apologized and didn't say another word about it. Sister Fidrych didn't either, but Luke could see the wheels spinning in her head.

Luke learned an important lesson from the incident. One, that he had to create multiple backup files—which he did at the earliest opportunity—and, two, that he needed to be more careful, being so close to the end of his adventure in Utah. He only had thirty days left, and he only hoped Sister Fidrych, not to mention Peter Bartholomew, wouldn't figure everything out before then.

CHAPTER 41

Ben heard about the successful recovery of Luke's missing files—from Sister Fidrych, of course—and he decided to drop by the next day. Before answering the door, Luke quadruple-saved his book, as he always did after The Incident.

"This might sound like a strange question," Ben said, "but how long to you plan to stay in Helaman?"

"You're right. It is a strange question," Luke said, wondering what Sister Fidrych had told him. "Why do you ask?"

"Since the Winters will be home from their mission in the fall, I was wondering what your plans were. Stacie and I have talked about it, and if you plan to stay here in town, you're more than welcome to move in with us. You can stay in the basement. We'd love to have you."

Like that would ever happen, Luke thought. He couldn't tell Ben that he was just weeks from leaving town. "Thanks for the offer," he said.

"Just let me know. By the way, are you doing anything on Friday?"

"What, another service project?"

"Not this time," Ben said.

He explained he was going to a reunion of sorts at a pizza place in Provo. It was one of the haunts Ben and his freshmen roommates used to frequent when they were going to BYU. They were convening there on Friday night for a little celebration/commemoration. The following week, one of Ben's old roommates, Jeremy, was getting married in the Salt Lake Temple. Jeremy was the last of the four longtime friends to get hitched. Plus, Ben's old roommates had heard about Luke and said they wanted to meet him.

"So you're inviting me to a Mormon bachelor's party, then," Luke said.

"I guess you can call it that," Ben said.

"That means no girls jumping out of cakes, I take it."

"That's a pretty safe bet. Sorry to disappoint you."

Luke accepted the invitation. He thought it might make another good story for his book.

Ben picked Luke up at 6:30 that night, and as soon as Ben and Luke entered the Provo city limits, Luke couldn't help but think of Hayley.

When the four former roommates met at the appointed hour, they greeted each other with hugs in the restaurant lobby. Luke, meanwhile, pretended that he was with another group. After taking their seats at a booth, the quartet started swapping missionary tales. They also relived stories about their college days together, peppered with inside jokes. Luke thought sacrament meetings were boring. This was worse. Luke thought if one of those guys started one more story with the phrase, "My companion and I were knocking doors when . . ." he was going to knock heads together.

They were pretty typical Mormon guys, Luke thought—crisp, clean, no caffeine, and completely boring. All in all, they were quite innocuous, except for Kyle. From the outset, Kyle had two strikes against him in Luke's estimation: he was an attorney and he was from California. Kyle mentioned that his wife wanted to move to Utah County, but that he was violently against it.

"What's so bad about Utah?" Ben asked.

Is that a rhetorical question? Luke wondered.

"First, I wouldn't make as much money here. Second, I couldn't stand living and working here. Everyone thinks the same here, especially in Utah County. And third, Mormons here are so judgmental. You'll agree with me, right, Luke?"

"I'll have to take the fifth on that," Luke said. "If I say something, I might have to walk home."

"Uh, Kyle," Ben said, "do you realize you're talking to a bunch of Mormons who happen to be from Utah County?"

"You know I don't necessarily think of you guys in that same way."

"Necessarily?" Ben said.

"You have to admit, you're spoiled by all the temples and churches so close by. You're rarely tested or challenged. These mountains shelter you, not to mention blind you, to what's out there in the real world. You don't have to deal with real people here. It's like a Fantasy Land. It's easy to live the gospel in Utah."

"Easy?" Ben asked.

"Yeah," Kyle responded. "You guys don't even take advantage of what you have. Mormons here drive by multiple temples on their commute to and from work every day but actually do a session only a couple of times a year. I know people around the country who drive for hours every month to go to the temple.

Non-members in Utah think you have an elitist attitude and look down on them. You have no tolerance for anyone or anything different from you. You guys have this holier-than-thou attitude."

"We look down on non-Mormons, huh?" Ben said, his glasses fogging up he was getting so steamed. "Is that why some of the highest-baptizing missions in the Church are in Utah? Luke isn't a member, but he is one of the best members of our ward. Luke, when you moved here, did you feel looked down upon?"

"Not at all," Luke said. "Of course, I am a little over six feet tall."

"Don't be so defensive, Ben," Kyle said. "It's not your fault. Utah Mormons are programmed to be this way. Mormons are just stronger outside of Utah than inside because they have to be."

Ben felt the hair on his arms rising to attention.

"I'd be willing to bet many of the best members of the Church live here in Utah," Ben said. "The prophet and apostles come to mind, for starters. If Utah's such a terrible place, why do so many people come here? And you know the main reason Utah County is growing so fast, don't you? It's because of the slow leak in California."

Luke had never seen such hostility out of Ben. Usually Ben had all the spunk of a bowl of Corn Flakes. Luke, like everyone else within earshot, sat back and enjoyed the verbal fireworks.

"Take it easy, Ben," Kyle said. "This is a nice place. I know there are a lot of good members of the Church in Utah. I like Utah. My point is, it's not the real world. In the real world there's all sorts of things—crime, violence, lotteries, racial diversity—that Utah Mormons are naive to. You guys just bury your heads in the sand."

"You keep referring to 'The Real World,'" Ben fired back. "Isn't that a show on MTV? Is that the way you want things to be? We shouldn't have to apologize for it being the way it is in Utah. We're supposed to be establishing Zion, remember? No matter where we live."

"Ben, if you ever lived outside Utah, as a non-missionary, you'd under-stand," Kyle continued. "You grew up in Utah County, where all your friends, teachers, everyone, was LDS. What about opposition in all things? When I was in high school, I was one of only five LDS kids in my school. Everyone knew we were Mormon and so we were watched closely. For the most part, people respected our beliefs. But some went out of their way to say and do things to make us feel uncomfortable. Like when they'd pass around *Playboy* in geometry class. Or a coach would unleash a string of expletives just to see how I'd react. And the beer parties thrown after football games. Kids drank and smoked and slept around all the time. And dating? There were only two Mormon girls in my high school, and one was, well, let's just say she was a sweet spirit. Since we didn't date non-Mormons, I sat home for almost every high school dance. I couldn't go to my Senior Prom. All you Mormon guys have to do for a date is go down the ward list. You don't realize how easy you have it."

"I feel for you. I do," Ben replied, "but just as I can't completely understand what it's like living outside Utah, you don't understand what it's like to grow up as a Mormon in Utah. In many ways, believe it or not, it can be tougher."

"This ought to be good," Kyle said.

"Fitting in is a big thing for teenagers," Ben explained, "but so is standing out, being different. In Utah, since the majority of people are LDS, many kids try to stand out by going against the grain. We had kids, even LDS kids, who smoked and drank and did other stuff. When you live the gospel here, you're one of many in a crowd. Those kids knew they weren't going to ruin the Church's reputation by breaking the commandments. The bottom line is, it's not easy living the gospel no matter where you live. I respect Mormons who live outside Utah, but I get tired of them bashing Utah. Especially when so many of them end up here anyway. I believe that God's influence is stronger here than anywhere else because there are so many faithful members of the Church and so many temples. I also believe it's where Satan's influence is greatest for that same reason. This is the Lord's stronghold, so it only makes sense that Satan is working as hard as he can here, too. Remember that prophecy how in the Last Days Salt Lake City will be one of the most wicked cities in the world? There's a lot of gray area here and Satan thrives on that. He wants us to ease up and relax. That's the challenge we have."

To close his sermon, Ben took a sip of root beer. Luke wished he had brought his tape recorder.

Kyle smiled. "Those were some pretty good arguments," he said. "You could have quite a future as an attorney."

"No thanks," Ben said. "Haven't you heard that lawyers will end up in outer darkness?"

While eating pizza, Jeremy, Lance, and Kyle asked Luke questions about his impressions of Utah and about Mormonism and his life in New York. He toned down his responses, of course.

"Enough about me," Luke finally said. "This is Jeremy's party, isn't it?"

"You're right," Lance said. "For Luke's sake, I'll explain things from the beginning. When we were all freshmen living on campus, Jeremy took this Marriage Prep class. Except Ben was the only one who knew about it. Jeremy claimed there was no other religion class available, so he made Ben swear not to tell a soul. Ben promised to keep quiet. And he did, of course. Jeremy had his textbook for the class and he would hide it under his scriptures in his room. Then one day, a couple of weeks into the semester, we were horse-playing and Kyle knocked Jeremy backward and all his books went flying onto the floor. Kyle knelt to help pick them up and noticed the Marriage Prep book. Jeremy couldn't hide it anymore. It's an unwritten rule—freshman guys don't take Marriage Prep. Kyle and I couldn't quit laughing and we told everyone we knew. I'm surprised it wasn't published in the *Daily Universe*. Jeremy was teased mercilessly. Half the girls in our ward invited him to study hall, the other half shunned him because they thought he wasn't going on a mission.

"At the end of the semester, Jeremy, in an attempt to exact revenge, put the marriage prep book in Kyle's suitcase before he left to go home. Well, we all went on missions and Kyle kept that book the whole time as a memento of his freshman year. When Ben got married—the first of us to do so—we gave it to him as a gift, and we all decided the book would be passed on to whoever was the next to get married, and the next and the next. The last one to get married would have to keep the book displayed forever in a prominent place in his living room. No exceptions. The last one is stuck with the book forever. There's a curse attached to the book, too: his firstborn son will become, like him, a Menace To Society. Here we are, eight years after we established the ground rules, and the last of us is finally getting married."

"To borrow some lines from the scriptures, this book has made one eternal round," Kyle said. "The last shall be first and the first shall be last."

"So, we proudly present to you, Jeremy Smith, the dreaded Marriage Prep book," Lance said. "You'll have plenty of time to read it."

Everyone at the table clapped—again attracting stares from the rest of the patrons and employees in the restaurant. "Thanks, guys," Jeremy said. "If I had known this was going to be so embarrassing, I probably would have canceled the wedding and set my sights on becoming a ministering angel."

"Tell us how you met your fiancee," Ben asked.

"I never found a wife at BYU, but it wasn't for a lack of trying," Jeremy said. "When I graduated I should have received a refund on my tuition. After I got my bachelor's degree, I enrolled in graduate school at BYU. Still no wife, just a lot more debt. So I stayed in Utah County, went to umpteen singles wards, went to stake dances with thousands of eligible girls, signed up for dating services, logged on to LDS Internet chat rooms. Who knows how much time and money I spent in an effort to get married? Meeting women was not a problem. Finding the right woman was. I probably dated ninety percent of the unmarried women on campus, and I finally realized I was merely spending money on other men's future wives. It got discouraging. Especially when my hair started receding past my ears. Then, one morning, while I was at the temple I met this gorgeous girl, a returned missionary. I talked to her for about an hour."

"Your fiancée?" Lance asked.

"No. She told me about her equally gorgeous roommate. *She's* my finacée. That was four months ago and we've been together ever since. I found my eternal companion, and it didn't cost me a dime."

While Luke was polishing off the last piece of pizza, he saw Hayley walk into the restaurant with Thad. She was flashing that smile of hers and looking very happy. Luke tried to hide behind a menu. A part of him was jealous of Thad, another part was happy for her.

Ben decided they had better go. It was 9 p.m. and the party was wrapping up anyway. After all, everyone had wives and kids or a fiancée waiting for them. Except for Luke. He and Ben sneaked out of the restaurant after paying the bill.

"Looks like Hayley's having no trouble moving on with her life," Luke said to Ben while they drove back to Helaman. *Of all the pizza places in Provo,* Luke thought, *she had to walk into that one.*

One week later, during a break from writing, Luke went to Ben's grocery store to pick up some Snickers and six-pack of Pepsi. He turned the corner when he came face-to-face with the prettiest girl he'd ever seen. Again.

"Hayley," he said, feeling his heart beating again for the first time in weeks. "How are you?"

"Hi, Luke," she said nervously. "I'm fine. And you?" Then she dropped a cake mix and it hit the floor. They bent down at the same time to pick up the box, and Luke noticed a sparkling diamond on her left ring finger. Hayley turned red.

"This looks new," Luke said.

"Oh, yeah, um, well, I'm engaged."

Luke felt his heart almost stop cold.

"So, who's the lucky guy?" Luke asked.

"Thad," she said almost apologetically.

"Congratulations. I'm happy for you. When's the big day?"

"August 21."

Luke was glad he would be out of Utah by then.

"I really need to go now," Hayley said, walking away. "Thad is waiting for me in the parking lot. It was good to see you."

"Good to see you, too."

And just like that, she was gone again. Luke really had nothing against Thad. The more he thought about it, the more he realized how perfect Thad was for her. They were both returned missionaries. They both were raised as Mormons. They both wanted a quiver full of children. How could Luke possibly compete with that?

Eight more days, and Luke knew he wouldn't have to worry about running into Hayley Woodard ever again.

During Luke's final week in Utah, sleeping and eating became leisure activities and he didn't have much leisure time on his hands. When he wasn't writing, he was cleaning and packing. All Luke wanted was to finish the book and get out of town. He couldn't wait to get his life back.

Kilborn e-mailed Luke his flight plans and information about his hotel reservation at the Ritz-Carlton in New York. Luke was to leave on Sunday afternoon and meet with Kilborn Monday morning. Woody Elfgren, meanwhile, would come up from California with some movers to take the TV, computer, and furniture that belonged to Halcyon Publishing out of the Winters' house after Luke's departure. Luke planned to leave Helaman like a thief in the night, although he knew that was the cowardly way out. There were some people he needed to say good-bye to before he left.

Saturday, Luke went to Mable's house. "Oh dear," she said, "is it Wednesday already?"

"No," he said. "I came to tell you that I'm leaving."

"That was a quick visit. Okay, see you Wednesday."

"No, Mable, you don't understand. I'm going to New York tomorrow and I'm not coming back."

"Dear, don't go away just because a relationship didn't work out. There are plenty of other nice Mormon girls around. Take my great-grand daughter, for instance . . ."

"I'm not leaving because of a woman," Luke said. "It's complicated. Maybe I'll explain it to you someday."

"You might want to hurry. I'm ninety years old, remember."

Luke smiled, leaned down, and gently hugged her. "You take care of yourself," he said before walking out the door.

"Don't forget to write," she said.

From there, he went to the cemetery to visit Brooklyn's grave. He placed a bouquet of bright yellow daffodils on her headstone and told her good-bye.

That night, he decided he'd better see Ben. He didn't know what he was going to say, but he owed him an explanation. Ben, after all, had become his best friend.

Ben and Stacie had just put the kids down to bed. Ben came outside and they started talking and shooting baskets in the driveway. Luke wanted to tell him the truth, but he couldn't bring himself to it.

"You're a good man," Luke said as he sank a nineteen-foot jump shot from the petunias.

Ben rebounded the ball. "You're a good man, too," he replied. "Are you okay? Is there something you want to talk about?" He hoped it was something about baptism.

"No, not really."

Ben stood at the free throw line and dribbled a couple of times. "Well, I'd better go in," he said. "I've got to get up early to get the kids ready for church. I'll see you tomorrow."

"Yeah," Luke said as he passed the ball back to Ben. "Tomorrow."

Luke went home for the last time and turned on his computer.

CHAPTER 42

Fighting the burning sensation in his eyes after nearly twelve straight hours without sleep, Luke tapped out the final keystrokes at sunrise.

Unlike the previous chapters of his book, he didn't e-mail the final ones to Kilborn. These he decided to hand-deliver. He saved the file on three separate disks and printed a hard copy. His book was finished. It was time to go back to New York.

Luke didn't feel anything close to what he had imagined he would. During his year spent in exile—er, Utah—he had often dreamed about the moment he completed his book and it was nothing like this. He had imagined himself popping open a champagne bottle and dancing a little jig on the kitchen table. Or running naked down Main Street in Helaman. But he wasn't in the mood for either of those things. He just wanted to leave.

His flight to New York departed at 2:30 that afternoon. As tired as he was, he couldn't sleep. He finished packing and carried his bags and boxes to the garage, where he set them in the backseat and the trunk of the car. Before showering, Luke put on a CD from his Frank Sinatra collection, to one particular song:

Start spreadin' the news, I'm leaving today
I want to be a part of it, New York, New York . . .
These little town blues are melting away
I'm gonna make a brand new start of it, in old New York . . .

As he listened and sang along, he turned on the faucet and grabbed a bowl and filled it full of hot water. He placed his hand inside and poured liquid soap over his pinky finger. Then he pulled and twisted and yanked until the CTR ring Brooklyn had given him came off. *That's gonna leave a mark,* Luke thought. He placed the ring in a large box with his other Mormon-related paraphernalia, then looked out his kitchen window and thought about how he would miss the mountains.

Then, something—habit, perhaps—compelled him to put on a suit and tie and drive the car, filled with his luggage, toward the church just after 10 a.m. Sacrament meeting had just barely begun. He stopped briefly at the Kimballs' home to put the Swearing Jar on their front porch—there was about seventy-five dollars in quarters in there. Luke stuck a note on the jar: "I hereby bequeath this money to Jared. I figure he can use this loot for his mission. Luke."

The moment he stepped inside the church, he felt his innards tighten up. Why he was there, he didn't know. Brother Sweeney was walking out of the clerk's office as Luke headed down the hall. He shook Luke's hand. "Good morning, Brother Manning," he said enthusiastically. Luke knew it was the last time someone would be calling him by that title.

"Hi," Luke responded. "How are you?"

"Best day of my life."

Luke smiled as he heard those words for the final time.

He sat down in the seat the Kimballs always saved for him. Ben and Stacie smiled warmly. Jared jumped on his lap. The congregation was already finishing the opening hymn, "Oh Say, What Is Truth?"

During the sustaining and releasing portion of the announcements, Luke half-expected Bishop Law to call his name. Instead, the bishop asked Brother and Sister Gruber, who were sitting on the back row, to stand. The ward members turned to look. Brother Gruber had accepted a call to serve as a home teaching coordinator and Sister Gruber had been called to be a Primary teacher. The bishop made one more announcement.

"I see that Hayley Woodard and her fiancé, Thad Robbins, are here with us today, visiting from their ward in Provo," he said. "We'd like to welcome them. Most of you already know that this delightful couple will be getting married later this summer in the Salt Lake Temple."

The congregation turned, again, to gawk at Hayley and Thad. Luke couldn't bear to look.

After the sacrament, the bishop bore his testimony about prayer. "We all have our own Gethsemanes and Valley Forges in life. Like our Savior and like George Washington, we have to pray fervently," he said. "You can't offer a fifty-cent prayer and expect a million-dollar answer." Then he turned the time over to the congregation. Luke popped off the pew and headed to the pulpit.

"I've never done this before," Luke began, adjusting the microphone, "and I'm sure many of you are surprised to see me up here. But I can assure you that none of you is more surprised than I am."

Luke looked into the eyes of all those trusting faces smiling back at him. The Kimballs. The Grubers. The Sweeneys. The McMurrays, who took up a whole row by themselves. Oliver was standing on a pew, waving.

"My purpose for being up here today is to tell you that I'm not who you think I am," Luke said.

Nobody knew whether to chuckle or to gasp.

"While it's true my name is Luke Manning and that I am a freelance writer from New York, almost everything else about me that you know is false."

Not a sound could be heard in the chapel. Even the infants stopped crying. Luke felt like he had just told the Primary children there was no such thing as Santa Claus. Ben squeezed Stacie's hand, praying that this was an object lesson, or at least had some logical explanation.

"About fourteen months ago, I was hired to write a book about the Mormon Church," Luke continued. "That's the reason I moved here. It was all a facade. Many of you referred to me as a 'golden investigator.' Well, I was fool's gold. As if you needed to be told at this point, I am not a good person. I was a wolf in sheep's clothing. I came here to infiltrate the Church and write about my experiences among you. Your lives, your hopes, your problems will all be exposed in my book. In case you're wondering, it will be published and released in four months."

"I knew it!" Sister Fidrych said, nudging her husband, "Didn't I tell you he was up to something like this?"

Bishop Law folded his arms and looked straight ahead. Brother Sagapolu bowed his head. Ben was sure this must be a very bad dream.

Luke couldn't bring himself to make eye contact with Ben. Hayley stood up and excused herself from the meeting, with Thad trailing behind. Luke was glad Hayley finally knew the truth.

"As you can probably guess, it isn't the most flattering book, if you're a Mormon," Luke said. "I'm going back to New York this afternoon, so I have a plane to catch. For those whom I have offended, which is probably everybody in this building and the eleven million plus Mormons worldwide, I'm sorry. You are fine people and I appreciate your friendship during my time here. I'm truly sorry it had to end this way."

With that, Luke stepped off the stand and marched out of the chapel. He got into his car and drove to the Salt Lake International Airport as fast as the law would allow.

CHAPTER 43

When Luke arrived at the airport, he left the car in long-term parking for Woody to pick up. *I'm going to miss that car,* he thought as he checked in his bags. On the flight to New York, Luke slept most of the way. He checked into the Ritz-Carlton that night and went to bed for a few hours. Early Monday morning, Luke opened the curtains and gazed upon New York City. *It sure feels good to be back in Babylon,* he thought.

A black stretch limousine took Luke to the Halcyon Books Building. There, in a conference room, he found a festive atmosphere as balloons and streamers dangled from the ceiling. Kilborn had a 100-watt grin on his face. He shook Luke's hand vigorously. "Congratulations," he sang, then slapped him on the back. "You survived and look no worse for the wear."

Luke handed Kilborn a disk containing the final few chapters.

"This is a time for partying, not working," Kilborn said. "Here, have a drink."

"It's a little early to be drinking, even for you," Luke said.

"You're back in the real world now, son," Kilborn said. "C'mon. Loosen up. Have a drink. It's over!"

Luke grabbed a champagne glass and took a swallow. A handful of editors and execs were on hand at the catered affair. Displayed on the walls were mockup covers of his book with the words *My Year Among The Mormons* emblazoned in red letters across the top. Luke still didn't like that title, but he didn't care at that point. The cover featured an artist's rendering of Luke standing next to the Salt Lake Temple. Press agents told Luke their plans to book a number of talk shows in upcoming months.

It was quite a shindig. Not that Luke noticed. He left after twenty minutes. The last thing he wanted to think about was the book, and the Mormons, so he sneaked out the door. That afternoon, Luke went car shopping; he'd grown accustomed to having his own transportation in Utah and couldn't imagine going without. By nightfall, he had packed his new Corvette full of his possessions and headed to Greenwich and his new house. As soon as he entered the Greenwich city limits, it occurred to him that he was in Steve Young's hometown. He just couldn't get away from the Mormons, try as he might. Everything seemed to remind him of the Mormons.

His house, which sat on two acres of land, had an elaborate alarm system and phones in all five bathrooms. Even the toilets had sensors and flushed automatically. The place was huge. It was big enough to hold a Kimball family reunion, Luke thought.

After a couple of days of getting settled—not one visitor stopped by—he returned to New York City and checked back into the Ritz-Carlton. He spent the afternoon thinking about his future. What would he do? Luke had so many options in front of him—he could go back to newspapers or continue to write books. It was one of those dilemmas he enjoyed having. Plus, he couldn't wait to collect his second $500,000 check.

But first things first. Luke went to Shea Stadium to watch the Mets play for the first time in what seemed like eons. In the fifth inning, his cell phone rang. It was Kilborn.

"Can I call you back?" Luke asked. "There are two on and two out. The Mets are rallying."

"I need to discuss your book with you tomorrow morning," Kilborn said. Luke wanted to concentrate on the game, but the man *was* paying him $1 million. So he agreed to see him.

"Fine," Luke said. "I'll be there at nine."

"Eight," Kilborn grumbled.

The next morning, Luke returned to Halcyon Publishing. This time, no balloons or streamers, or smiles from Kilborn greeted him.

"There's a big problem with the last few chapters of your book," Kilborn said, lighting up a cigar.

"Could you be more specific?"

"Sure," he said. "It stinks."

"Jack, don't sugarcoat it. Give it to me straight."

"Those last chapters on that disk—tell me they are a joke. You almost sound like you're writing a public relations brochure. I can't sell a book like that. If you want to plead temporary insanity, I understand. Everything up to the last few chapters is great. We need you to do some extensive rewriting. Maybe that cowgirl you dated got to you. Whatever it is, your tone at the end is different from the rest of the book."

"Jack, I wrote what happened. What you want me to do is a rip job. I'm not rewriting a word. I don't write fiction. It's my first-person account of my year with the Mormons. That's what we agreed on. I stand by my work."

"Then we'll just have to send you back for a while then and find some more things to write about."

"I'm not going back, Jack."

Kilborn stood up and wagged his finger at Luke. "You don't understand. I'm not asking or requesting that you go back. You *will* do it. It's in the contract." Kilborn took the document out of his desk drawer. "You don't have any other choice. What happened to you while you were in Utah? Did the Mormons brainwash you or something?"

"No, they didn't brainwash me. I've written the truth," Luke said. "Isn't that what you said you wanted, the truth? Besides, I already told those people about the book."

"You did what?" Kilborn asked, slamming his fist on his desk. "You've made things awfully tough on yourself. Your contract explicitly states that we have exclusive rights to edit this manuscript. We've invested a lot of money into this project. You're going to keep working on that book until it is done to my satisfaction."

"I did what you paid me to do," Luke replied. "I spent a hellacious year in Utah. I invaded the Mormon society, I earned their trust. Do you realize how many countless hours I spent going to meetings and providing gratuitous service to others? I shoveled so much snow I don't think I'll ever be able to stand straight the rest of my life. I went practically a whole year without beer and women. I've had enough. Yes, the Mormons have a questionable history, which I outlined in the book. But there's no Great Scandal lurking beneath the surface. For the most part, they are good, honest, hard-working people doing what they believe is right. I'm done with them and I'm done with this assignment."

"You've lost your edge. Your Mormon friends have duped you," Kilborn said. "Your neighbor, whatever his name is . . ."

"You mean Ben?"

"Right. You paint him like some sort of modern-day hero at the end of the book. He works in a grocery store, for crying out loud. He obviously has never heard of birth control. His daughter's death was God's way of telling him he has too many kids."

Luke lunged across the desk and grabbed Kilborn by the bolo tie. "If you ever say anything about him, or his kids, again, I'll shove that cigar down your throat."

"Let go of me!" Kilborn yelled, pushing him away. "You've just proven my point. You've become one of them. You broke the cardinal sin of journalism. You became emotionally tied to your subjects. I think you really believe you are a Mormon."

"I'm outta here," Luke said, heading for the door.

"You're not going anywhere!" Kilborn bellowed, chasing Luke down and stepping in front of him. They stood toe-to-toe. "You don't get it, do you? I own you. You have no bargaining power here. I'm paying you one million dollars to write this book. You agreed to it. You signed the contract. You will finish the book the way I want it done."

"And if I don't?"

"I'll personally make sure you get blacklisted in this town. Plus I'll sue your Mormon-loving butt for breach of contract."

"Look, I'll save you the trouble," Luke said, pulling out his checkbook and a pen. "I'm tired of your games."

"What are you doing?"

"This is a check for $500,000," Luke said, scribbling away. "I'm returning your money and you can keep your other half million. You no longer own me." He handed Kilborn the check. "By the way, I wouldn't try cashing that for a couple of days, if I were you."

Kilborn was stunned, but he wasn't going to let Luke off that easily.

"You think that's going to cover all the expenses we pumped into this project? Any royalties you would have received from the sale of this book will be garnisheed to pay for your expenses. I'm going to make sure you never make a dime off this book. By writing that check, you've forfeited all your rights to it."

Luke dropped the check on Kilborn's desk. "Consider this relationship severed," he said on his way out.

As he left the Halcyon Books Building, he simultaneously felt like the most liberated man in the world and the dumbest. Finally, he was rid of Kilborn, the man who had been torturing him for more than one year. On the other hand, he had just walked away from one million dollars.

Luke secretly wished Kilborn would call back and renegotiate. But he knew that wasn't going to happen. He had just earned Kilborn's everlasting hatred.

When Luke returned to the Ritz-Carlton, the manager came to his room and told him he was being evicted. "Sir, Mr. Kilborn canceled your reservation," he said. "Please pack up and leave immediately."

In the space of thirty minutes, Luke had gone from affluent to almost indigent. He looked in his wallet. He had no cash, just a few credit cards and a picture of Brooklyn. Luke sold his car and bought a clunker of a vehicle with four bald tires, an engine that sputtered and windshield wipers that didn't work. The car had engine trouble and a flat tire fifteen minutes after he bought it. Where was Brother Gruber when he needed him?

Luke schlepped his way to Greenwich and hired a real estate agent to sell his home. Fortunately for Luke, it sold in a couple of days. He paid off his loan and deposited the rest of the cash to cover that check he had written to Kilborn. Luke returned to New York City again but this time he wasn't checking into any five-star hotels. Instead, considering his bank account was on the verge of flat-lining, he had no other choice than to check into a budget motel and put the charges on a credit card. Except for a lumpy bed, a leaky ceiling, a full complement of rats, and a window with a view of an alley littered with trash, it was a very nice place.

What bothered Luke as much as anything was Kilborn's comments. Had he gone soft? Had he allowed himself to become Mormonized? Luke figured once he found a job, everything would be normal again. He knew that he could rebuild his career. First, he would grow back his goatee. For now, he buoyed himself with examples. Didn't Donald Trump, as much as Luke despised him, resurrect his empire in this very town? Didn't the Yankees, as much as Luke despised them, rebound from almost fifteen years of futility to become a dynasty once again? That's exactly what Luke aimed to do himself. What he needed was to get his old column, and his old life, back. He brazenly walked into the newsroom of the *New York Post*, where he received a chilly reception from former co-workers and was forced to wait in the lobby for about forty-five minutes. When he met with the managing editor, Luke's hopes of getting back on with the paper were quickly dashed. He got the infamous and disheartening line: "We're going in a different direction."

"We have a new columnist we're happy with," the slick-haired editor said. "There's no room for you. Ownership has put a ceiling on new hires. I'm sorry, Luke." But Luke could tell he really wasn't sorry. He probably enjoyed seeing Luke grovel.

That was Luke's first clue that recapturing his old life might not be easy. Of course, he knew Peter Bartholomew was going to hear about this.

Luke sold his car for food money and wished he hadn't given away his Swearing Jar filled with quarters. He updated his résumé and e-mailed it to national magazines and big newspapers up and down the Eastern seaboard. When he didn't hear from anyone after a week or so, he made follow up calls to numerous editors to whom he had sent his résumé. Most of them didn't remember having received it. Besides, they didn't have any positions available.

Luke wasn't used to this kind of rejection. Using every connection he could think of, he contacted a variety of weeklies and magazines. It was as if everyone had forgotten about him. It was always the same response: "We'll be in touch if anything becomes available." That was bad, especially since his money supply was dwindling. His view of that dumpy alley dotted with homeless people out his window was turning into a metaphor for his life. Luke feared he was on the brink of becoming a homeless person himself.

One afternoon, Luke answered his cell phone. "Hello?" he said.

"I hear you're staying at a hotel that makes Beirut look like Paradise. It got minus-five stars in *Hellholes Monthly*."

"What do you want, Bartholomew?" Bartholomew had found Luke's phone number on a résumé that was floating around New York.

"I just wanted to catch up on old times with an old rival."

"I'm hanging up now."

"I wouldn't if I were you. After I saw you in Utah a couple of months ago, I started putting things together. The *Times* sent me back to Utah last week. I really enjoyed talking to all your friends in that thriving metropolis of Helaman. I'm working on this story about your stay in Utah. Would you like to comment on your book or the Mormons in general? Or the fact that Jack Kilborn is going to sue you?"

"You're bluffing."

"Oh, am I? I know everything about *My Year Among The Mormons*. I've talked to Ben Kimball, Hayley Woodard, Sam Law, Susan Fidrych. Boy can *she* talk. I've got a file cabinet worth of information about your little junket to Utah. I've got excerpts from your book. I'm giving you a chance to tell your side. Are you going to talk to me or not?"

Luke hung up and tossed his cell phone against the wall. Suddenly, he knew how it felt to be on the other side of the journalism fence.

Two days later, Luke walked out of his hotel room and scanned the headlines in the local papers, as usual. He never bought papers since he didn't have the money. On that particular day, though, above the fold on the front page of The *New York Times* he saw a picture of Sister Fidrych posing next to the church back in Helaman. Below was a story under the following headline:

Too Good To Be True:
Ex-Post Reporter Dupes Mormons in Utah Town

Luke bought a copy of the paper. When he returned to his room, he began reading.

By Peter K. Bartholomew

HELAMAN, Utah—As we sit together on the freshly cut grass in front of an unimposing, red-brick church, Susan Fidrych is in disbelief. Her eyes become moist. It's midday here in the heart of this ultra-conservative, predominantly Mormon town. The scorching-hot sun is beating down and cows are mooing nearby as she describes the betrayal inflicted on her Mormon congregation by a one-time "brother in the gospel" who turned out to be a modern-day Judas.

Many others here in this sleepy bedroom community—the same one that caused a national uproar a few months ago when it successfully stopped a convenient store from selling pornographic material—feel betrayed as well after learning they had been deceived by New York City journalist Luke Manning. These members of the Mormon Church naively accepted Mr. Manning into their close-knit society and unwittingly allowed him to perpetrate a premeditated sham in order to write a tell-all book—due to be published soon—about them, their lives, and the beliefs they hold sacred.

"Why would he, or anyone, do this to us?" Ms. Fidrych asks. The answer is simple and as old as that New Testament story about Judas Iscariot: he did it for the pieces of silver—in other words, the money.

Helaman (pop: 4,076), nestled at the foot of the Wasatch Mountains, is about forty-five miles south of Salt Lake City, located in a state that is without question the Mormon Capital of the World, as approximately seventy percent of Utahns belong to the Mormon Church, also known as the Church of the Latter-day Saints. In Helaman, that percentage approaches ninety-five percent.

One year ago, a Mormon congregation here eagerly welcomed a new, non-Mormon neighbor to their church. Though Mr. Manning never officially joined the Mormon faith through the rite of baptism, he attended meetings and activities on a regular basis during the year he spent in Helaman. In fact, Mr. Manning was assigned to work with the children at the church.

"He was always there anytime someone needed help," recalls Ms. Fidrych, who lived a block away from Mr. Manning and belonged to the same congregation. "But from the first time I met Luke, I had my suspicions about him. I mean, young, single men from New York City don't just move to Helaman without a reason. I thought maybe he was running away from something. To me, it didn't add up. But he seemed so nice and seemed to have a genuine interest in the Church. He was too good to be true."

Mr. Manning was contacted by the Times, *but he refused to comment.*

As part of his reporter's act, Mr. Manning became good friends with a neighbor, Ben Kimball, a grocery store manager. And he was involved romantically with a twenty-six-year-old woman, Hayley Woodard, who is also a member of the congregation.

Weeks ago, members of the Helaman 6th Ward discovered to their shock and horror that Mr. Manning, a former New York Post *reporter, had hoodwinked them all. It wasn't until the day he returned to New York City that Mr. Manning publicly confessed—during a church meeting, no less—his real purpose for living in Utah. During the previous twelve months he spent in Helaman, he had been chronicling their lives and his experiences among them with the aid of notebooks and tape recorders, without their knowledge. The outgrowth of his work is a book tentatively titled* My Year Among The Mormons, *scheduled to be published this fall.*

News of the book's imminent release has hit Mormons here hard, and the book itself will surely have long-term repercussions on the eleven-million member church worldwide.

"With a history that many religion experts consider curious at best and spurious at worst, Mormons are already hypersensitive to criticism," says Columbia University religion professor Dr. David Busenbark. "This book is bound to make them much more so. Myself, I'm looking forward to reading this book. What intrigues me about it is that it will lay the religion bare, not from the skewed perspective of bitter ex-Mormons with an axe to grind nor from the perspective of a religious scholar. Luke Manning lived among those

people. It's not the first mainstream book about Mormonism, but it promises to be the most entertaining. It may have a profound influence on how the world sees Mormons."

Official Mormon Church spokespersons say they were not aware of the book and declined comment.

"We really thought he was our friend," Ms. Fidrych says. "Sure, we feel hurt," she adds, dabbing her eyes with a handkerchief. "He violated our trust. He could have robbed us all blind, taken us for all our material possessions and it wouldn't hurt as much as this does."

The Times *obtained a copy of several chapters of* My Year Among The Mormons. *After reading portions of several scathing chapters that were made available to her by the* Times, *Ms. Fidrych shook her head. "It's still hard to believe we've been exploited this way," she said.*

In the book, which is written in first-person, Mr. Manning refers to Utah as "a drab, saint-ridden desert" and describes the people as "self-righteous clones who can't, and don't like to, think for themselves." He chronicles the events of a year of his life inside the Mormon Church, which claims to be a Christian organization. While the Mormon Church is one of the fastest growing denominations in the world, its doctrine is so blatantly divergent from other Christian churches that those Christian churches refuse to be categorized with the Mormons.

Included in the manuscript are chapters about the Mormons' reported obsession with angels, their polygamist roots, and a long history of discrimination against Native and African Americans. One chapter discusses how the Mormon Church fosters a right-wing philosophy that encourages many of its members to hoard food and weapons in preparation for Armageddon. Some Mormons, according to Mr. Manning, believe they will someday assume control of the United States government.

Woven throughout the book is Mr. Manning's extensive descriptions of his experiences with members of the Mormon faith. Samuel Law, a Mormon bishop, was Mr. Manning's ecclesiastical leader during his time in Utah. Mr. Manning wrote about his suspicions that Mr. Law peddled drugs.

When contacted at the church where he presides, Mr. Law calmly denied those allegations. When asked if he and the other members of the congregation would consider suing Mr. Manning for libel over his book, he said the thought "had not crossed his mind. . . ."

At that point, Luke stopped reading. Instead he wadded the newspaper into a ball, stomped on it, and threw it away. He cringed at the thought of what his book might look like once Jack's army of bloodthirsty editors got through with it.

The next day, there was a follow-up story:

'Brainwashed' Reporter To Be Sued By Publisher?

While members of the Mormon Church deal with their disillusionment regarding a tell-all book written about their lives, the author, Luke Manning, has problems of his own.

The New York City journalist could be facing a lawsuit from publishing giant Halcyon Books for breach of contract, the Times *has learned. Halcyon hired Mr. Manning to write* My Year Among The Mormons, *but was not satisfied with a couple of chapters of his final manuscript.*

Ultimately, the conclusion of this tale could be decided in the courtroom. Halcyon officials are preparing a breach of contract lawsuit that would prevent Manning from receiving any further remuneration for his work.

Halcyon spokesman Miles Singleton said Mr. Manning was commissioned to write the book and was paid a $500,000 advance. Mr. Singleton contends his company spent $250,000 to put Mr. Manning up in Helaman for one year.

Jack Kilborn, vice president of Halcyon Books, hired Mr. Manning to write the book. He emphasized that overall he is happy with the way the book turned out. Still, he added, changes must be made to ensure accuracy.

Asked about the chances of Mr. Manning completing the book to Halcyon's satisfaction, Mr. Kilborn replied, "We have irreconcilable differences. I've been in this business for thirty years and I've never had a would-be author pull something like this. When we hired him, we considered him to be one of the best journalists in the country. Now? I wouldn't trust him as far as I can throw him. I can't imagine any reputable news organization or publisher hiring him after this debacle. You want to know my opinion? I think those Mormons brainwashed him. They must have worked some of their voodoo on him, perhaps in one of their secret temple ceremonies. That's the irony of the thing. He thought he had hoodwinked them, but, in the end, they hoodwinked him. That's reflected in his writing toward the end of his book—he became sympathetic to their cause, the same cause that he bashes in the rest of the book. When he came back, he was not the same person he was when he left. They turned this arrogant reporter into a cowering chicken. It's further proof that the Mormons are nothing more than a cult. I hope this book gets into the hands of everyone in the world, so that when they see those clean-cut Mormon missionaries at your door, they'll think twice before letting them in."

When contacted by the Times, *Mr. Manning declined to discuss the book or possible litigation.*

The only party that stands to benefit from this soap-operatic scenario is Halcyon Publishing, that is, if it can turn My Year Among The Mormons *into a runaway best-seller. Ironically, the publicity and controversy surrounding the writing of this tome could produce astronomical profits for the book-publishing empire. At least, that's what Halcyon Books is banking on.*

Mr. Kilborn emphasizes the book will still be released, even without Mr. Manning's cooperation, in the coming months. "Some of his research was faulty, but that will be remedied by the time it is published," he vows.

Mr. Manning has since returned to New York. But when he tried to reclaim his job at the Post, *it elected not to re-hire him.*

That week, Bartholomew made the rounds on all the network news programs, talking about his stories and about Luke's book. Later, Luke got on the Internet and saw that Bartholomew's articles had been picked up by the wire services, and ran on the front page of all the Utah-area newspapers. He was sure that back in Helaman, people were preparing to tar and feather him.

CHAPTER 44

Babylon, it turned out, wasn't at all how Luke remembered it.

Every once in a while, he'd hear the staccato of gunfire or people yelling. Mostly, he stayed in his seedy motel room, waiting for his cell phone to ring, waiting for someone to rescue him from the abyss.

Famished, he pulled a ball cap low over his face one afternoon and wandered into a soup kitchen. While he stuffed bread into his mouth, someone recognized him. "Look," a man said, "it's that newspaper guy."

After eating, Luke returned to his apartment and sequestered himself for three straight days. He didn't shave or shower. He stayed in bed, watched TV, slept, and stared at the unidentifiable brown stains on the ceiling. A year earlier, he was one of the hottest reporters in the country. Now, he wasn't sure where his next meal was going to come from.

Luke's stomach was rumbling, but it wasn't just from hunger. Everything was going wrong. The hotel manager stopped by one morning to inform him that he had exceeded the limit on all of his credit cards.

"Do you have another way to pay?" the manager asked.

He didn't.

"In that case, I'm going to ask you to leave. Today."

"I've got nowhere to go," Luke said. "I need a little more time."

"Okay. I'll give you until 8 p.m. to check out."

Luke opened the dusty curtains and saw the smog hovering overhead. The grayness enveloped him. What if he just ended his agony? As far as he could tell, there wasn't much to live for. He opened the closet door and reached for a box on the shelf that stowed some heavy-duty allergy medicine. Swallowing a handful of those pills, he thought, would be his ticket out of this debacle. As he tipped the box to get it down off the shelf, something heavy fell out and clocked him square on the forehead.

While rubbing his sore cranium, he saw that five-pound quadruple combination laying on the ground. He kicked it across the room, and almost broke his foot. Why he was still lugging that thing around, he didn't know. But, to Luke's surprise, it reminded him of a happier time. Then his eyes caught his name LUCAS DAMON MANNING engraved on the front of the case. He sat down and unzipped the case. On the inside page was a note from Ben, dated Sept. 2.

Luke,

Congratulations on your baptism and becoming a member of The Church of Jesus Christ of Latter-day Saints. Think of this book as the road map to help you return to the presence of Our Heavenly Father. Within these pages, you'll find peace and the answers to all of life's questions.

With love,

Ben, Stacie, Brooklyn, Jared, Megan and Rebecca

Luke shook his head. *Even from three thousand miles away,* he thought, *Ben can still find a way to preach to me.*

He opened to a random page in the Book of Mormon and found a copy of Brooklyn's obituary. On that same page, he found a verse, underlined in red. Luke had marked selected verses every once in a while to give the impression to ward members that he had actually read them. Why he had underlined this particular scripture—Mormon 9:21—he didn't know. But he read it.

Behold, I say unto you that whoso believeth in Christ, doubting nothing, whatsoever he shall ask the Father in the name of Christ it shall be granted him; and this promise is unto all, even unto the ends of the earth.

Luke shut the quadruple combination. The rest of the day, as he prepared to leave the motel, he couldn't help but think about those words. How could a man who supposedly lived on earth 2,000 years earlier *help* him? How could a man who lived on earth 2,000 years earlier *know* Luke Damon Manning? And how could such a promise be given to everybody? If nothing else, one thing was certain: Luke knew, sitting in that squalid hotel room, he was definitely at the ends of the earth.

He was desperate. What did he have to lose? A double-minded man is unstable in all his ways. He could use a little stability, he thought, and he had lost everything but his last dram of dignity. Down to his final out in life, he called upon a pinch hitter.

Luke decided to make a deal with God.

The only way he knew how to talk to Him was the way the Mormons had taught him. He knelt on the filthy floor, folded his arms, and closed his eyes.

It took him about five minutes just to get any words out of his mouth. "God, I tell You what," he began ungracefully, "it seems I'm in some trouble here. I don't know where else to turn."

Luke knew he had better be careful how he dealt with God, because he knew whatever he promised to do, he would have to live up to it. "If you give me a job," he implored, "I will read this Book of Mormon. That's a big sacrifice for me, but in exchange for gainful employment, I'll do it. I'm desperate. By the way, I'm kind of in a hurry. I'm being booted out of this place in a couple of hours. In the name of Jesus Christ, Amen."

Just as Luke expected, there were no heavenly apparitions. No voices from the skies. There were no flashing lights—unless you count the neon signs outside his window advertising X-rated entertainment. He felt nothing. Ben and the missionaries had always talked about feeling something when communing with God, but Luke didn't. But, hey, he gave it a shot. If God helped him find a job, then his biggest problem would be solved. He would repay Him by reading the Mormons' book. No big deal. And if God didn't help him find a job, at least he would know without a doubt that Mormonism was a bunch of nonsense, and he could use the Mormon scriptures to start a bonfire to keep him warm during his homeless sojourn on the streets of New York City.

While he packed, he hoped his cell phone would ring and deliver some good news. It didn't happen.

Before leaving the hotel, Luke found a metal shopping cart with two wobbly wheels in the alley. He placed his belongings inside and started pushing it down the street. As he went, he rummaged through garbage bins behind restaurants looking for scraps of food.

So much for the Mormon God, Luke thought.

Ben always told Luke that Heavenly Father was mindful of all of his children at all times and listened to every prayer uttered by one of them. So what about Luke? He figured after all he had done, he didn't deserve an answer from God.

Late that night—he didn't know exactly what time because he had already pawned his watch—Luke found a copy of the *Post* on the ground. He sat down on a park bench, read a little of the *Post* and a little out of his Book of Mormon.

When he got tired, he laid down on the bench and spread the paper over him. The quadruple combination he used as a pillow.

The next morning, Luke awoke to the sensation of a Saint Bernard relieving itself on his leg. Luke's neck was kinked from lying on the scriptures, and he could barely turn his head to the left. Since his life was a dung heap of sorts, he contemplated doing a swan dive off of the Brooklyn Bridge. Then his cell phone starting ringing. After digging through a box, he found it on the fifth ring.

"Hello?"

"Luke?"

"Yeah."

"This is Jerry Schwartz."

Jerry Schwartz? He hadn't talked to him, or thought of him, in years. When Luke had last seen him, Jerry had been working as an editor for the *Syracuse Herald-Journal*. Jerry had hired Luke as an intern during his college days.

"It's been a long time," Luke said, trying to figure out how Jerry had found him.

"Indeed it has," Jerry said. "How's my favorite intern?"

"I've been better," Luke said, looking at his wet pant leg.

"So I hear. You know, I used to read you every day when you were with the *Post*. I sent you a few e-mails, but you never responded. I was wondering what had happened to you this past year. You turned into Amelia Earhart. Then I read that article in the *Times*."

"Well, you should know that not all of that stuff you read in there is fit to print. Nor is it all true."

"Why didn't you talk to the *Times* and give your side?"

Luke exhaled. "In hindsight, I should have. It was a mistake."

"I don't think any less of you, if that means anything," Jerry said. "You know how those New York media types like to do hatchet jobs."

Luke knew. "How did you find my number, anyway?"

"I was attending an editors' conference in Fort Lauderdale a couple of weeks ago, and a man in front of me dropped a stack of papers on the floor. I reached down to help him and your résumé just jumped out at me. I asked him if he was going to hire you and he said no. I tried to tell him about you, but he said his paper was in the process of laying people off, not hiring. So I asked him for your résumé and he gave it to me. Anyway, I've had it for about a week. I was sitting here at the office and for some reason, I felt like I should call you."

God must have a wicked sense of humor, Luke thought.

"I'm glad you did," Luke said.

"Have you found a job yet?"

"No. Still looking."

"Any strong leads?"

"No," Luke answered, shooing away a pigeon from his shopping cart.

"Would you consider coming back to Syracuse?"

Luke hadn't sent Jerry a resume for a very good reason. The last place he wanted to go back to, besides Utah, was Syracuse. He never thought he would go back home, but, of course, these were desperate times. "I'd consider it," he said.

"We're in the middle of a budget crunch ourselves, but if you're willing to move down a rung, at least in terms of circulation and salary, we'd love to have you. I've already run it by management and they're willing to bring you aboard. If you come out here tomorrow, to let management know you're serious, you should be able to start soon. You can stay with me until you get settled. How about it?"

"Well," Luke said, "this is embarrassing to admit, but I'm in a tough spot right now, financially."

"No problem," Jerry said. "I'll wire you some money."

After they worked out the details, Jerry told Luke to catch a bus to Syracuse that day. "I'll be waiting to pick you up tonight."

Jerry's phone call had to be happenstance, Luke thought. He tried to find a loophole. The *Syracuse Herald-Journal* wasn't what he had in mind—he was thinking more along the lines of the *Boston Globe* or the *Washington Post* or the *Baltimore Sun.* But, given his situation, he was in no position to argue. He didn't exactly feel he could back out of a deal with God.

"Okay," Luke said, looking into the sky, attracting the attention of people rollerblading through the park. "You win. If You had something to do with getting me this job, well, I thank You. While you're at it, if You could help me find something a little higher on the pay scale, I'd appreciate it. I promised I would read this Book of Mormon, and I will." He picked up his quadruple combination, sat down on a park bench, and turned to the end. "I'll read all 531 pages. Even if it kills me."

Luke collected the wire from Jerry and went to the bus depot, with his suitcases and boxes. As he waited for the bus, he opened the Book of Mormon, took a deep breath, and dove headlong into the first chapter of Nephi. "I Nephi, having been born of goodly parents. . ."

In his book, Luke had made a reference to what Mark Twain had called the Book of Mormon: "chloroform in print." Now he found that it, at least temporarily, took his mind off his problems. As he took his seat on the bus, Luke vowed that he would be back, working and living in New York City someday soon. It was bitterly ironic, that he was returning to Syracuse this way, a disgrace. But going back to Syracuse wasn't his best option. It was his only option.

CHAPTER 45

On the trip to Syracuse, he read the first 150 pages of the Book of Mormon. He wished Ben or Brooklyn had been there with him if only because he had so many questions. Why would God tell someone (Nephi) to kill another person (Laban)? How could Laman and Lemuel not believe, even after seeing an angel? What did they have, rocks for brains? And what was this business about the great and spacious building? And this whore that sat upon many waters? As for the Isaiah chapters, Luke hadn't a clue what they meant.

He recalled the many talks and lessons he had heard about the characters in the book, the people Brooklyn always talked about. While reading, he could see why the Mormons acted the way they did. He finally understood why the Mormons had frequent flier mileage built up from all the guilt trips, courtesy of those so-called ancient prophets.

Jerry picked Luke up at the bus depot, as planned. While traveling to Jerry's house, childhood memories flooded Luke's mind. He had never thought he would return to Syracuse, unless it was accepting a prestigious award from his alma mater. Instead, he was right back where he had begun. The place hadn't changed much, from what he could tell.

Jerry's wife, Linda, fixed Luke a nice meal that night and Luke ate like a starving coyote, much as Phil had his first day in Luke's house in Helaman. Jerry and Linda tried not to stare. Afterward, Jerry ushered him to a spare room. Tired from the long drive, Luke was tempted to go right to sleep, but, to make good on his promise to God as quickly as possible, he pulled out his scriptures. He started reading something about a king's wife denying her husband's death, explaining that to her, he "doth not stink." Which reminded Luke that he was beginning to stink himself. So he showered.

The words that stuck out to him the most, the ones he noticed over and over, were that if people obeyed the commandments, they would prosper. That sounded good to him, considering his circumstances. But did he want to prosper, if it meant not having any fun at all?

Linda had breakfast waiting for Luke in the morning, though he politely turned down the coffee. "I've got you an interview with the publisher today," Jerry said. "It might take some time to sort things out, but I'm confident we'll get you hired soon. I hope you don't get bored while you wait. We have an extra car here. It belongs to my son, who is on a study abroad program in Spain this summer. You can use it while he's gone."

Luke thought Jerry and Linda were so nice, they might as well be Mormons.

After breakfast, Luke went to talk to the publisher, who opened with, "So you're the guy who wrote a book about the Mormons."

Luke nodded.

"How many wives did you marry while you were out there?" the man laughed.

Luke pretended to laugh, too, just to humor the man. The publisher promised him a job within the next few weeks. "By then," he explained, "we'll find a place on the staff for you."

Meanwhile, Luke hated owing people. He felt like a foster child all over again. Knowing it would take a few weeks before he could start full-time at the paper, Luke decided he had better find temporary employment. Jerry loaned him enough money to put down first and last month's rent on an apartment and some cash to buy food. There was a grocery store near his apartment. He went in to buy some cereal and frozen pizza and noticed a "Help Wanted" sign on the door. Luke found the manager.

"I'd like to talk to you about the job opening," he said.

"Have experience?" the manager asked.

"Plenty."

"Ever been a cashier?"

"No."

"Ever bagged groceries before?"

"A couple of times."

"Willing to work graveyard? We're open twenty-four-hours-a-day."

"Absolutely."

"Weekends?"

"Yes."

"Okay," the manager said. "You're hired. Can you start tomorrow?"

"What time do you want me here?"

Luke received his own blue apron with a tag that had his name on it and started his first shift—11 p.m. until 8 a.m., Friday through Tuesday. He thought of what Ben would do if he were around managing things. Inspirational thoughts with every receipt probably wouldn't go over well here, Luke thought. He bagged groceries, stocked shelves, and responded to clean ups. When no one was around, which was much of the time, he would grab the hose from the produce department and cool himself off from the oppressive summer heat. He kept reminding himself this job was only temporary. During the lulls, which were constant, he resisted the urge to sleep. On his "lunch" breaks, at about 3 a.m., he'd read a few verses of the Book of Mormon.

Not long after he received his first paycheck, Luke heard loud voices through the walls of his apartment one afternoon. The young boy next door had asked his mother for a soccer ball for his birthday. She had slapped her son and shouted at him, saying she had no money for any toys.

Luke remembered having a similar discussion with his mom when he was six or seven.

That night, Luke went to a department store and found a soccer ball. It wasn't a cheap purchase, at least for someone making minimum wage. Then he had the bakery at the store make a cake with the boy's name on it, just as he had done for his home teaching families back in Utah. Putting the gift in a box, along with some balloons and party favors, he placed the ball and the cake in front of the door after the boy had gone to school. After he rang the doorbell, he slipped inside his apartment. After a few minutes, all he heard was the mother crying. Luke listened later that night as she, the boy, and a few of his friends celebrated and ate some cake. Luke watched out his window as the boy played with the ball in the street, and a familiar feeling came over him, just like the times he had helped shoveled sidewalks, or had lifted Oliver up to get a drink out of the church drinking fountain, or written that check for Brother Sweeney.

Happiness couldn't be that simple, could it? Luke wondered.

As Luke read his Book of Mormon that evening, he found the following passage: "I tell you these things that ye may learn wisdom; that ye may learn that when ye are in the service of your fellow beings ye are only in the service of your God." A man named King Benjamin had uttered those words. King Ben immediately became Luke's favorite Book of Mormon prophet.

The next day, Luke found a soup kitchen. He brought some food from the grocery store and even served the homeless people in line. It was payback for the time he ate at the soup kitchen in New York City.

It had been a while since Luke had done any writing, and he wanted to make money at it. He figured he could do some freelance writing until he was hired on with the Syracuse paper. The idea for his first story came from some information about his ancestors that he found stuffed in his quadruple combination. The most intriguing part, of course, was Jedediah Manning, his Mormon great-great-great-great-great grandfather. He decided his first project would be a first-person account about becoming acquainted with Jed. Since he had plenty of time on his hands during the days, he went to Jedediah's hometown of Liverpool, a small suburb just outside of Syracuse.

Luke found a phone book and started calling all the Mannings in town. There were three. Two hung up on him. The third gave him the name of AnnaLee McGelvy. "She's always had an interest in dead people," the stranger said.

Luke called Mrs. McGelvy.

"Yes?" she asked.

"My name is Luke Manning and . . ."

"I'm not interested."

Click. Luke called again.

"Ma'am, if you'll just give me a moment . . ."

"I'm not going to buy anything."

"I'm not going to sell you anything. I was just wondering . . ."

Click.

Luke found her address and walked over there. He entered through a wrought iron fence to the ancient brick home. Luke knocked on the door and waited for five minutes. No response. Then he noticed the curtains moving. He knocked again. "Mrs. McGelvy," he shouted through the door, "all I would like is to talk to you. I don't want money. I'm a writer and I'm trying to do some research on my great-great-great-great-great-grandfather, Jedediah Manning."

After waiting a few more minutes, Luke turned and started to leave when the door creaked open.

"What do you want to know?" asked a gaunt woman with bifocals.

"I understand you might know about Jedediah Manning and I was wondering if you could tell me about him. It's for an article I'm working on."

"I'm his great-great-great-grand daughter," she said proudly, adjusting her shawl. "Why should I trust you?"

Luke pulled out his family group sheet. Mrs. McGelvy studied it for a moment.

"Where did you get this?" she asked.

"The genealogical library in Salt Lake City."

"So you're a Mormon," Mrs. McGelvy said warily.

"Not exactly," Luke said.

"Well, I guess I can talk to another descendant of his," she said. "For a few minutes. But no funny business."

"I won't even crack a joke," Luke said.

He followed her inside as she shuffled slowly to the living room. Dozens of black-and-white pictures covered the walls. As Luke sat down on the couch, up came a cloud of dust.

"I appreciate your time, ma'am," he began. "You appear to be the resident expert on the Syracuse Mannings."

Mrs. McGelvy placed a patchwork quilt over her legs. "Yes I am," she rasped. "In fact, this is the very house that Jedediah Manning built himself."

For the next two hours, she told him a captivating tale about the Mannings' struggle during the potato famine in Ireland and their eventual arrival to this country. Jed, she explained, had four children, two sons and two daughters. Luke was the great-great-great-grandson of William Manning and Mrs. McGelvy was the granddaughter of Martha Manning. "I guess that makes us distant cousins," Mrs. McGelvy said.

"Well," Luke said, "I guess we're not that distant anymore."

He listened and wrote down almost every word she said. After a couple of hours, she guided him to the basement and to a box filled with faded documents, papers, and photos. Mrs. McGelvy handed Luke Jed's journal and he started reading. He was a talented writer, Luke thought. And here he had always believed his writing talent was the result of a mutant gene.

Because Luke showed so much genuine interest, Mrs. McGelvy became more than accommodating.

"Could I get a copy of that family tree?" she asked.

"Have this one," Luke said.

"Would you like to borrow Jedediah's journal?"

"You would let me do that?"

"Nobody else seems to care about it," she said. "And you seem like a nice young man."

"I'll guard it with my life."

Upon returning to his apartment, he read the entire journal. At age forty, Jed had converted to the Mormon Church. In those pages, Jed expressed his love for the Book of Mormon and the prophet, Joseph Smith. Mary, his wife and a devout Protestant, didn't want anything to do with the Mormon Church, however. He wanted to join the Mormon handcart migration to Utah, but Mary refused to go along. So he remained in Liverpool and raised his family. Jed wrote often about his strong desire that his wife, and his children, would one day accept the true gospel of Jesus Christ. Mrs. McGelvy told Luke that he had saved the life of a young girl who had fallen through the ice at a nearby pond. Jed contracted pneumonia and died two weeks later. As far as Luke knew, that was the end of his ancestors' Mormon connection.

For so many years, Luke had felt isolated and alone. Thanks to Mrs. McGelvy, he had been introduced to his family. Discovering his roots made him feel like Alex Haley, and that reminded him that it was Hayley Woodard who had clued him into genealogy in the first place. And she was the last person he wanted to occupy his thoughts. He didn't need to remind himself that she would be married in a matter of days.

Luke received additional help from the LDS Church genealogical website, www.familysearch.org, and he finished the article in about a week. He gave Jed's journal back to Mrs. McGelvy and presented her with a copy of the article. He thought it was one of the best things he had ever written. He mailed it to a number of publications.

Digging up information about Jed inspired him to do additional research about other relatives, though not all the news was good. He found out dying young ran in his family. His great-grandfather, his grandfather, and a number of uncles had died before the age of forty. Accessing information about his father, Luke found out that he had been killed ten years earlier in a car accident. He was thirty-nine at the time. Luke figured at age thirty-three, his days on earth were numbered.

All this—not to mention his return to Syracuse—made him curious about his mother, Sheila Manning. Luke had gone more than twenty years acting as though she never existed, but now he started to wonder about her. Last he had heard, she was incarcerated. Maybe she was still in prison, he thought. He figured it was worth finding out. One afternoon, he drove past the apartment complex where he and his mom had once lived together. Seeing that place reminded him of how far he had come in life, and, at the same time, how far he had fallen.

A couple of months earlier, Ben and Stacie had given talks in sacrament meeting on Mother's Day. They had spoken so glowingly of their own mothers that, for the first time in years, Luke had wondered about his. Flipping through a Syracuse metropolitan phone book, Luke found a Sheila Manning listed. On his day off, he decided he would pay her a surprise visit.

But the more he thought about it, the more anxious he became. After all those years, he had built up a reserve of anger the size of Alaska. Many times growing up, in his mind, he had lashed out at her. He had formulated a diatribe, in the event he ever saw her. Those words resurfaced quickly. Perhaps unloading on her would make him feel better.

Luke arrived at the address, a housing project in the slums. He didn't have an apartment number for her, so he approached the first person he saw, a black woman wearing a halter top, chain-smoking cigarettes.

"Do you know where I could find a Sheila Manning?" he asked.

The woman looked him up and down. "Are you a cop?"

"Do I look like a cop?"

"Never can tell," the woman replied.

"Look, I'll give you ten bucks if you can tell me which apartment is hers."

"Make it twenty dollars and you have a deal."

Begrudgingly, he removed a hard-earned twenty dollar bill from his wallet and handed it over. She placed it in her halter top.

"She used to be in apartment 397," the woman said. "She moved out a couple of months ago."

"Where is she now?"

"They took her to some nut house. It was kinda sad. From what I heard, she was working at an all-night diner as a waitress. She never talked to anyone around here. Kept to herself. Anyway, one night she starts throwing dishes and silverware out of her window and onto the street. The police came and cited her for disturbing the peace, which was kind of funny since there hasn't been any peace around here in years. She was a strange woman. Then a couple of weeks later, the police show up again and find her in her apartment, unconscious. I heard she overdosed on something. They took her away to some insane asylum. The one at the university. That's the last I heard of her."

Then the woman threw the butt of her cigarette on the ground and stamped it out with her foot. "Are you a friend of hers?" she asked.

"No," Luke said. "I'm her son."

CHAPTER 46

A couple of days later Luke went to Upstate Medical University's Psychiatric Unit, in search of his mother. He didn't know what to expect.

"Can I help you?" the receptionist asked.

"I hope not," Luke said. "I hate rubber rooms and strait jackets."

The receptionist didn't even crack a smile.

"I'm here to see Sheila Manning," he said. "She's my mom."

"Dr. Orvitz is with a patient right now, and he's booked up through the rest of the afternoon. If you'll please take a seat, I'll tell him you're here."

Just then, the doctor walked out of his office. With him was an overweight man biting his fingernails. When the doctor found out Luke was there, he postponed his next appointment and took Luke into his office.

"So, you're Sheila's son," he said.

"That's what it says on the birth certificate."

"You may be the key to helping her," Dr. Orvitz said. "She suffers from severe depression and has attempted suicide twice. I've made a little progress with her and the medication has helped. It seems many of her emotional problems stem back to when she lost you."

"Lost me?" Luke said. "You make it sound like I was a house key. She didn't lose me. She tried selling me."

"I'm aware of that. She's hurting emotionally from that ordeal."

"Big surprise there," Luke said.

Dr. Orvitz removed his glasses and leaned forward. "I'm sure you're hurting emotionally, too. Maybe you'd like to talk about it."

Luke laughed. "I'm not signing on to decipher ink blots and lie on your couch and tell you my troubles."

"So, what brought you here?"

Luke shrugged his shoulders. "I don't know. Curiosity, I suppose."

"If you're coming here to berate Sheila, then I won't allow you to meet with her. You have no idea how much she's gone through."

What about what I've gone through? Luke wanted to say. But he let the thought pass.

"We met while she was in prison and I've invested years of work in her," Dr. Orvitz continued. "You mean everything to her. Now, I don't know what motivated you to come here, but I would ask that if I allow you to see her, you will not talk about the past, at least not until she's ready. Any negative feedback at all from you could undermine all the work I've done with her. If your motives are pure, then you can see her. But one negative word, it's over. Is that clear?"

"Crystal."

"Give me a week or so to prepare her for this," he said.

When the week was up, the doctor called Luke and told him to return to the hospital and to bring his best smile. "I'm not sure how she'll react," the doctor said, "but I think seeing you will help."

Dr. Orvitz led Luke through a thick door with a computerized lock and down a checkerboard-tiled hallway. They walked down the corridor until the doctor stopped and peeked through the window of a room. He knocked and opened the door.

"Sheila," he said in a jovial voice, "someone's here to see you."

Luke stared at the woman in the bed. She was 48, going on 78. Her skin was wrinkled, her eyes sunken, her hair disheveled.

"This is Luke," the doctor said.

"Long time, no see," Luke said.

Sheila looked straight ahead at the wall.

"Just talk to her," Dr. Orvitz said to Luke. "She'll respond when she's ready."

With most subjects off-limits, he started talking about baseball and movies. She barely blinked.

"Sheila, you get your rest," the doctor said after a while. "I'll bring Luke around again soon."

For the next couple of weeks, Luke faithfully went to the hospital every day during visiting hours and launched into a monologue. Why he kept coming back, he wasn't sure. He wasn't so much talking *to* her as *at* her. He told her about his college days, his career, his trip to Utah, the Mormons, his book about the Mormons. He told her about Ben, Brooklyn, Brother Sweeney, and Hayley. Then one afternoon, after he had run out of things to say, he turned his back to leave and heard:

"Lucas, don't go."

She was the only person who had ever called him Lucas.

Luke returned to her bedside.

"Thank you for coming all these days," she said in a quiet voice. "At first, I thought you were going to get angry with me and I wouldn't blame you for that. What I did to you was terrible and wrong. But you've been such a gentleman. I want to tell you how proud I am of you."

It was Sheila's turn for a soliloquy and Luke listened. She told him about a fifteen-year-old girl who came from a rich family. The girl got pregnant at a party in high school and was scorned by her very strict parents. She wound up marrying the father, who couldn't hold a job; after seven miserable years, he left her for another woman. She had no way to support herself and her son, so she turned to prostitution and found comfort in alcohol and drugs—until that fateful day when she asked an undercover cop if he wanted to buy her son in exchange for drug money.

With these words, Sheila broke down crying. She sobbed so loudly, Dr. Orvitz ran into the room to find out what the problem was.

Luke continued his visits to the hospital. Dr. Orvitz told Luke this was the best therapy she had ever received. She had opened up more over a three-day period than in all the years of sessions with Dr. Orvitz combined.

After a while, the doctor allowed Sheila to leave with Luke for a few hours at a time. They went to movies, took long walks, and talked. She told him how she used to pray for him while she was in her prison cell and how, years later, she used to clip his articles when she had the chance. She told Luke about when he was a baby. "I'll admit I've made mistakes, but I've never been prouder in my life than I was the day you were born, Lucas," she said. "I loved you from the moment I saw you." She recounted stories about Luke as a child, things he didn't know about himself, things he had forgotten.

"That must have been horrible, being in that prison," Luke said as they sat near a fountain at a park.

"I was there five years, but it seemed like fifty," Sheila said. "I've made a lot of mistakes in my life. Lucas, do you believe in God?"

He was taken aback by the question. "Do you?"

"I think there is probably a God, but there's no hope for me. How could God love someone like me?"

"C'mon," Luke said. "Of course God loves you."

"How do you know?"

Truth was, Luke didn't know for sure. But he knew about some people who did.

"The Mormons believe there is a purpose to life," he said. "They believe we are God's children and that he wants us to become like Him. They say God is literally the father of our spirits and the whole reason we're on earth is to be tested so we can return to Him."

Luke couldn't believe the words that flowed of his mouth. He felt like a missionary.

"Do you believe that?" Sheila asked.

"I don't know," Luke said, "but it sounds good."

"Even if that's true, I've blown my chance in life. How could I ever be accepted by God, after what I've done? Sometimes, I have these dreams. It's dark and I'm walking through a dark tunnel of some sort. I am just wandering, feeling my way around, when suddenly I see this bright light. Then everything I've ever done wrong plays back in my mind. The light disappears and I'm in the dark again, alone."

"If Dr. Orvitz hears you talking like that," Luke said, "they'll never let you out of that hospital."

Sheila lay down on the grass and put her arm over her eyes. Luke had an overwhelming urge to help. "There's a book I know of that might help you," he said.

"Thanks, Lucas, but when I was in prison I read every self-help book ever written."

"Probably not this one. It's called the Book of Mormon."

"What is it about?"

"The Mormons believe that Joseph Smith received some gold plates from an angel named Moroni and translated them," said Luke. "The book is supposedly the record of an ancient people who inhabited America hundreds of years ago. Crazy, huh?"

"Almost as crazy as I am," she said. "Where can I get a hold of a copy?"

"I think I can dig one up in my apartment."

"I appreciate your concern. You know, until you found me, I figured I had nothing to live for. Now I feel like I have something to live for."

"That's good, because you're not going to die. You're not getting out of this so easily. I'm going to talk to the doctor, and you're going to live with me."

"You would do that for me?"

"Sure," Luke said with a smile. "I need help paying my rent."

Sheila was skeptical about Mormonism, but she was willing to give it a look. As she read the Book of Mormon, she had questions about the book's plot and its strange words, like Liahona and Rameumptom.

"And why do things come to pass so much?" she asked.

"They just did back then," Luke answered.

It was as if Luke was the parent and Sheila was a four-year-old child with a question every second. If he didn't know the answer to a certain question, which happened a lot, he would tell her so. He wished Ben was around to help.

"Maybe you ought to meet with the missionaries," Luke said.

"No, thanks," Sheila said. "I heard somewhere they brainwash people."

Meanwhile, Dr. Orvitz said the improvement Sheila was experiencing was clinically inexplicable. She was sleeping through the night and eating regular meals for the first time in years. She was far from cured, he warned Luke, but he was hopeful she could recover and live a normal life. With the understanding that she would live with Luke—and that he would take care of her—the doctor decided that within a few days, she could leave the hospital. "You're like a one-man support group for her," Dr. Orvitz said. Luke promised to make sure she took her medication and stayed away from alcohol and drugs.

About that same time, Jerry called Luke and told him that the *Herald-Journal* was ready to hire him. So Luke gave up his apron and nametag for a computer and notepad. It was thrilling for him to return to a newsroom setting, even though fellow reporters looked at him askance his first day.

"So you're the guy who wrote the book about the Mormons, huh?" said a reporter in the cubicle next to him. "How many wives did you snag while you were out there?"

In a case of cruel irony, Luke was assigned to the religion beat, meaning he would have to write two to three stories a week for the Saturday religion section. When he received his assignment, he groaned inside, but he wasn't going to complain openly. It would be good to have a steady paycheck again, to be writing again. That, and it was nice not to have 3 a.m. lunch breaks anymore. Or cleanups on aisle six.

When Sheila moved into Luke's apartment, he had everything ready—her own room with flowered curtains, her own closet and television. She hugged her son and thanked him.

Meanwhile, their conversations about Mormonism continued daily in their modest living room.

"It says here in the Book of Mormon that when we're resurrected, we'll be restored in perfect form," Sheila said. "Do you suppose that means the women will look like Christie Brinkley and the men will look like Brad Pitt?"

"I wouldn't bet on it," Luke said. "But if that's the case, it may be worth getting to heaven to find out."

"Not that I could ever get there, but what do you think heaven's like? A bunch of people playing the harp?"

"The Mormons say we will live with our families," Luke said.

"Really? Maybe I could find a nice Mormon guy and settle down with him and live in heaven." She laughed.

"Sure, but I'll warn you up front: Mormon guys are pretty boring. And forever is a long, long time."

"Maybe you'll find a nice Mormon girl, too."

"Naw," Luke said. "There was only one I was ever interested in. And she's getting hitched soon. Tomorrow, in fact. Not that she's on my mind or anything."

"Maybe they'll have sports in heaven."

"I wouldn't bet on that, either. From what I know about pro athletes, most of them won't make it to heaven."

"What do you have to do to get there?"

"You have to repent and get baptized."

"What's with this repentance? How can there ever be forgiveness for me, for the things I've done?"

Luke shrugged his shoulders. "I don't know. The Mormons think so. Maybe you ought to talk to the missionaries."

He wanted to tell her that the missionary discussions were dreadfully boring—same with church meetings—but he didn't want to discourage her. "There's a way you can find out for yourself if this stuff is true, according to the Mormons."

"Really? How?"

Luke picked up the Book of Mormon and turned to the promise, found in Moroni.

"And when ye shall receive these things, I would exhort you that ye would ask God, the Eternal Father, in the name of Christ, if these things are not true; and if ye shall ask with a sincere heart, with real intent, having faith in Christ, he will manifest the truth of it unto you, by the power of the Holy Ghost.

"And by the power of the Holy Ghost ye may know the truth of all things."

Sheila thought about those words for a moment. "Does that mean I can ask God if this stuff is true and he will answer me?"

"That's what the Mormons say."

"Do you believe what the Mormons say?"

"Like I told you before, it sounds good, in theory."

"You spent a year living with them and that didn't convince you of anything. You really believe you can say a prayer and learn *'the truth of all things'?"*

"I don't know," Luke said. "Why don't you read the Book of Mormon and pray about it."

"I will if you will."

Luke had already finished the book to make good on his deal with God. Reading it again couldn't hurt. Anything to help his mom.

Long after he brushed his teeth and got into bed, he was still thinking about Moroni's promise. He had read those verses several times before, but he had never really considered what they were saying. That night, Luke retrieved his notes and read what Ben, the missionaries, and Bishop Law had said on that topic. All the time he was in Utah, he had dismissed that promise completely.

This time, he gave the Mormons the benefit of the doubt. What if they really did know the truth? As Ben had told him once during one of their conversations, "You can't know for yourself unless you study it for yourself. When people say that Mormonism is false, what proof do they have to back it up? I know the LDS Church is true because I've read and prayed about the Book of Mormon. I have my answer. And nobody can take that away from me."

Luke put down his notes and took out his quadruple combination. He looked through the Doctrine and Covenants and the Pearl of Great Price until he stumbled upon a section titled "Joseph Smith—History; Extracts From The History Of Joseph Smith, The Prophet."

Of course, he had heard the story of Joseph Smith on at least a dozen occasions, but as he read those passages, it was as if he were hearing it for the first time. He read about the First Vision and the apparitions of the Angel Moroni. If it were all true, this stuff about Joseph Smith, the Book of Mormon, and the plan of salvation, it would be a big story. Stop-the-presses big. The biggest story in the history of the world. To think that Jesus Christ and God the Father came down from heaven to restore the gospel and the true church on the earth. To think that it all happened somewhere near his hometown. Just an hour away.

Luke could not resist. If his mom was going to learn about the Mormon Church, the least he could do was help her do some research.

CHAPTER 47

When Sheila awoke at 6:30 a.m., Luke was already dressed and sitting in the living room, fidgeting.

"What's wrong?" she asked.

"Get dressed. We're going to Palmyra this morning."

"Where?"

"Palmyra. It's about sixty miles west of here. The Mormons call it 'the cradle of the Restoration.' We're going to investigate the Joseph Smith situation."

"Isn't he dead?"

"Yes, but the Mormon Church owns land where he lived, where he said he saw his vision. Let's go check it out."

Sheila smiled. "I'm always up for field trips."

Luke already had his work for the week done, so he knew no one at the office would be looking for him on a Friday. By 8 a.m., they were on the road to Palmyra in a used car he had purchased from another reporter at the paper.

Naturally, during the drive there, he couldn't help but think of Hayley. When Luke pulled into the Hill Cumorah visitors' center and was greeted by a sister missionary, he imagined how Hayley must have looked and acted. He imagined non-Mormons converting on the spot for her. Luke saw a short film, asked a few questions, and signed the guest registry. Then Luke and Sheila walked to the top of Hill Cumorah to look around. As soon as he arrived at the top, Luke stood motionless. His mother joined him.

"You feel something?" he asked.

"That's the wind," she replied.

They walked along a pathway toward a monument that featured a statue of the Angel Moroni. "This Angel Moroni is on all the Mormon temples," Luke explained to his mother. "He's quite the celebrity to the Mormons. Even has his own tie tack. They don't believe in or worship saints, but Moroni is the closest thing the Mormons have."

They gazed across the verdant valley below and Luke tried to imagine Joseph Smith receiving gold plates from an angel. *Why couldn't God send me an angel?* Luke wondered.

Then a bus full of tourists from Utah showed up. One man asked Luke to take a group picture of them surrounding the monument.

"On the count of three, say 'Moroni,'" Luke said before snapping the photo.

To escape the crowd, he and Sheila drove to the Martin Harris Farm, then to Joseph Smith's farmhouse, where they took a tour and listened to a presentation and signed another guest registry. Afterward, they visited the Sacred Grove.

"How do you feel?" Luke asked as they entered.

"I'm getting hungry," Sheila said, then added, "How do we get out of here?" as they veered off down a pathway. "I hope we're not lost."

"This is one place I wouldn't mind getting lost in," said Luke, who soaked in the serene surroundings.

They walked reverently through the grove. Luke recalled what he had read about the appearance of God the Father and His Son to Joseph Smith. He wondered how many of those trees were around when that happened.

When they exited the wooded area, they saw the spire of the Palmyra Temple rising above the tree line in the distance. They visited the temple grounds and strolled around there, too. The entire time he had to keep reminding himself he wasn't in Utah. That was the only other place he had experienced the same kind of feeling.

As they drove home, Luke was lost in thought and Sheila started perusing her Book of Mormon. He noticed her reading something intently.

Suddenly, Sheila interrupted the quiet drive to Syracuse, almost causing him to drive off the road. "Listen to this!" she exclaimed. "There's this story about a guy named Alma. It talks about all the sins he committed, how he tried to destroy the church and how he was visited by an angel. He says, 'I was racked with eternal torment, for my soul was harrowed up to the greatest degree and racked with all my sins. Yea, I did remember all my sins and iniquities, for which I was tormented with the pains of hell; yea, I saw that I had rebelled against my God, and that I had not kept his holy commandments.'

"Lucas! This is just how I've felt!" She continued reading aloud.

"'Yea, and I had murdered many of his children, or rather led them away unto destruction; yea and in fine so great had been my iniquities, that the very thought of coming into the presence of my God did rack my soul with inexpressible horror. Oh, thought I, that I could be banished and become extinct both soul and body, that I might not be brought to stand in the presence of my God, to be judged of my deeds. And now, for three days and for three nights was I racked, even with the pains of a damned soul. And it came to pass that as I was thus racked with torment, while I was harrowed up by the memory of my many sins, behold, I remembered also to have heard my father prophesy unto the people concerning the coming of one Jesus Christ, a Son of God, to atone for the sins of the world. Now, as my mind caught hold upon this thought, I cried within my heart: O Jesus, thou Son of God, have mercy on me, who am in the gall of bitterness, and am encircled about by the everlasting chains of death.'"

She looked up from the book, her eyes filled with tears. "Listen to this part! 'And now, behold, when I thought this, I could remember my pains no more; yea, I was harrowed up by the memory of my sins no more. And, oh, what joy, and what marvelous light I did behold, yea, my soul was filled with joy as exceeding as was my pain!'"

Sheila underlined the verses with a red pencil Luke had given her. He had received it from Ben. "I'd give anything to feel that way." After several moments of silence, she asked, "Lucas, I know I don't deserve it, but will you please forgive me for what I did?"

Luke didn't know what to say. "That was a long time ago," he said, changing lanes.

"I know I could never make it up to you. But can you find it in your heart to forgive me?"

"Yes," Luke said. "I forgive you already." As he uttered those words, he felt a chip he had toted around the past twenty-plus years slip off his shoulders. All those hateful words he had once planned to say to his mother vanished from his mind.

"Thank you," Sheila said as she held on to Luke's arm. "Thank you. I love you, Lucas."

"I love you, too." It was the first time he could remember saying that to anyone in his life.

"You know," Sheila said, wiping the tears from her face, "maybe I will listen to the missionaries after all."

When they returned home, Luke looked up the number for the local Mormon missionaries. He dialed it, got an answering machine, and left a message.

What bothered him, though, was all this talk about angels. Joseph Smith received visits from plenty of them. Alma was a bad guy when he received his. Even Brooklyn had been with angels after she was hit by that car. *Why not me?* Luke thought.

He started reading everything he could about prayer, in hopes of finding some tidbit of information about how to receive a visit from an angel. In one book he had brought back with him from Utah, it said a Mormon prophet had spent eighty-five entire nights on his knees in prayer.

"Consecutively?" Sheila asked when Luke told her as much.

"No. Eighty-five different nights he says he prayed from the time he went to bed until morning. It says it right here."

"Who did that?"

"President Spencer W. Kimball."

Kimball. It figured. Must be a relative of Ben's, Luke thought. Ben was the only person he could imagine doing something like that. How could someone pull eighty-five all-nighters—praying, of all things? What, Luke thought, if he spent one night doing that? Maybe an angel or two would show up. Then he wouldn't have to wonder anymore.

Before retiring, Luke ate a big meal, drank a can of Jolt cola, and placed his sunglasses on the nightstand. *Maybe,* he thought, *God would send an angel.* He knew it was going to be a long night. Then he picked up the Book of Mormon again. Now that he had seen where Moroni had deposited the plates, the idea of angels and visions seemed a little more plausible in his mind. He re-read Moroni's promise and turned out the lights. He knew he should experiment with Moroni's promise, but he didn't feel ready. Or worthy. Still, it was a promise he could not resist. It was time to strike another deal with God. This time, the stakes were higher.

Luke noticed the time on his alarm clock. It was 10:07 and he set the alarm for 6:07 a.m. Eight hours. If he could pull it off, he thought, it would at least qualify him for an honorable mention in the *Guinness Book of World Records.* Luke figured that if he mentioned all his misdeeds and mistakes, at least the ones he could remember, that would take up most of the time. But to be convinced that Mormonism was true, Luke needed some hard evidence. An angel, perhaps?

Luke knelt by his bed on the wood floor, bowed his head, folded his arms, and started praying the way he was taught by the Mormons—addressing Heavenly Father. While struggling to utter his first few words, he remembered Kilborn had once told him to "bring Mormondom to its knees." Funny, he thought, that it was Mormondom that had brought him to his knees.

Luke thanked Him for Jerry, his job, his mother, his car, his apartment, for the Book of Mormon. He continued talking for what seemed like hours, until he hit a verbal dead end. Luke peeked at his alarm clock. It was 10:15. Eight minutes had passed. Luke already had a headache and his bed was beckoning. Out of frustration, he slugged his pillow. Why was he torturing himself like this? He had a decent life now. He had a job. Why mess with it?

Still, he kept trying. Groping for the right words, he asked God if the Book of Mormon and the Mormon Church were true. No answers came. Just silence. So he kept repeating his requests, more and more urgently. Soon, he felt physically exhausted and completely spent, as if he had just run a marathon. But for what? He remembered the story of Enos from the Book of Mormon, how he "wrestled" with God in prayer. Luke felt like something, or someone, had him in a half-Nelson. He was on the verge of being pinned.

Luke's knees felt as though he had undergone double ACL replacement surgery. None of his words were even penetrating the ceiling, as far as he could tell. Maybe God didn't answer prayers, he thought. At least, not *his* prayers. He felt so ridiculous, talking to himself. This prayer stuff, he thought, was highly overrated. He got back into bed and drifted off to sleep.

CHAPTER 48

Luke slept in until noon. After a breakfast of champions—cold, leftover pizza and a Pepsi—he turned on a baseball game. Yet instead of balls, strikes, and double plays, all he could think about was Joseph Smith, President Kimball, and Ben. They all had talked to God, or so they had said. Why couldn't he?

Meanwhile, Sheila cleaned the house, went to the grocery store and called on some help-wanted ads. By 5 p.m., Luke was still sitting in front of the TV.

"Are you feeling okay, Lucas?" she asked.

"Yeah, why?"

"No reason, other than you haven't moved in five hours."

Luke rubbed his knees, still sore from the previous night. Looking out the window, he saw a tow truck rumble down the street. "You can't offer a fifty-cent prayer," he remembered Bishop Law saying, "and expect a million-dollar answer."

Ben had told Luke that he would go off by himself in the woods and talk to God sometimes. Luke stood up and stretched.

After Sheila went to bed, he put on a jacket, grabbed his car keys and a flash-light, and headed out the door. As he drove west, he remembered that Ben had taught him to think of God as literally His Father, a real person who actually takes time out of His busy schedule to listen to the prayers of His children. Brooklyn used to pray as if He were in the room. So Luke decided to talk as if God were a person. A friend. A father. Not some unapproachable, abstract object. Since he never really had a father, he imagined God, the person, as being a combination of Ben and Bishop Law, only a lot older.

Luke kept driving until he arrived at the Sacred Grove, then parked the car. If there was one place God might send an angel to tell him the truth of all things, this was it, Luke thought. He gazed up at the clear, star-filled sky and listened to the crickets chirping. Nobody seemed to be around, so he turned on the flashlight and started walking. He entered the grove, took a deep breath and introduced himself to Heavenly Father, as if He were standing there, and the words just flowed. As he walked, he talked. Luke told Him his life story, though he figured He already knew it all. For hours and hours, he emptied the contents of his soul in that grove of trees—his successes, his failures, his fears, his hopes, his dreams. When he got tired of walking around, he'd kneel by a tree and continue talking aloud.

Time ceased to exist. Before he knew it, dawn was breaking, and the birds were singing. He closed his prayer. On the one hand, he was proud of his accomplishment—he had spent an entire night talking to God. On the other, he was disappointed that he saw no angels. Still, despite the fact his throat was parched, he felt at peace. He felt happy though he couldn't explain why.

As the sun rose above the horizon, Luke drove back to Syracuse and caught himself singing Mormon church songs. Maybe it wasn't coincidence, Luke thought, that the birthplace of Mormonism and the birthplace of baseball, in Cooperstown, N.Y., were separated by only a couple of hundred miles.

When he opened the apartment door, he found Sheila in the kitchen, frying hash browns.

"I didn't even know you were gone," she said. "Where have you been?"

"I just needed to take care of some business."

"What kind of business can you take care of at this hour?" Sheila asked.

Luke stumbled groggily to the bathroom. He needed a nap, but he didn't really feel tired. He looked in the mirror at his bloodshot eyes. While shaving, he swore he heard a voice.

Go to church, it said. He opened the bathroom door. "Did you say something?" he asked Sheila.

"No, Lucas. I'm just finishing breakfast for you when you're ready."

Luke shaved off his goatee and hopped into the shower. Then he heard the voice again.

Go to church.

Great, he thought, now he was hearing voices, just like in *Field of Dreams*. At least, Luke thought, the voice wasn't asking him to build a church.

Luke figured sleep deprivation had taken its toll. He looked at a calendar above the toilet. It was September 2. It had been exactly one year from the day that he was supposed to be baptized into the Mormon Church.

Dripping wet, Luke heard the voice again as he reached for a towel.

Go to church.

Luke dressed and when Sheila saw him, in a suit and tie, and without a goatee, she almost dropped a plate of scrambled eggs.

"Have you ever heard voices, ones inside your head?" Luke asked her.

"No," she said. "I've felt really depressed in my life, but I've never heard voices before. Why do you ask? Lucas, are you hearing voices?"

"I don't know," Luke said.

Luke grabbed the phone book. He had seen a Mormon Church in Liverpool, where Mrs. McGelvy lived, so he looked up the phone number and found out when sacrament meeting started. He put Brooklyn's CTR ring on his pinky finger for the first time since leaving Utah.

"I'm sorry," he said to Sheila, "I'm not going to eat breakfast this morning." Before he could tell her why, he announced, "We're going to church today. Can you be ready by 8:30?"

"Are you feeling okay?" she asked.

"Yes, in a weird sort of way. Are you coming with me?"

"Of course," she said. "Just let me throw on a dress and some shoes."

As he and Sheila traveled to Liverpool, he gave her a crash course on Mormon church meetings. "And whatever you do," he explained, "don't clap after the songs, even if they're really good."

"What's this?" Sheila asked, picking up a gray envelope that was sitting on the dashboard. It had Bishop Law's name and a Helaman address on the front.

"It's for tithing," Luke said. "It's like paying rent to God."

Finally, they found a sign in front of the church building proclaiming, "THE CHURCH OF JESUS CHRIST OF LATTER-DAY SAINTS. Visitors Welcome." When Luke walked in the doors with Sheila, he felt like as though he were back in Helaman. Carrying his quadruple combination, Luke led Sheila to the chapel. A man and his wife greeted them and introduced them to the bishop.

"Welcome, Brother and Sister Manning," he said. "I'm Bishop Paxson. I'm glad you're joining us today."

Luke actually didn't mind being called "Brother." In fact, he kind of liked it.

"You two are members of the Church, right?" the bishop asked.

"Not in a literal sense," Luke said, handing him the tithing envelope, representing ten percent of the money he had earned since leaving Utah. Confused, the bishop ushered them to front-row seats.

"My mom would like to meet the missionaries while she's here," Luke told the bishop. "She wants to take the discussions." While motioning the missionaries from across the room, the bishop almost tore his rotator cuff.

The ward members were just like the ones from Utah, except they talked faster. Speaking of fast, the missionaries reached the front of the chapel, sat down, and introduced themselves in ten seconds flat.

The bishop opened the meeting by welcoming everyone out to fast and testimony meeting. Luke provided a quiet, running commentary on the proceedings to help Sheila understand what was happening. After the sacrament, Luke listened the testimonies of a dozen ward members. One mother accompanied a young boy, probably Brooklyn's age, to the pulpit and explained that her son wanted to sing his favorite Primary song instead of bear his testimony.

"We are as the army of HE-LA-MAN!" the boy sang. It gave Luke goosebumps.

With about five minutes left in the meeting, for reasons Luke couldn't understand, he walked to the pulpit.

"I haven't done this for a while and the last time I did this, it didn't go over too well," he announced to the congregation of strangers. "The past eighteen months or so, my life has been in spin cycle. Down has been up, up has been down. It all started when I met the Mormons. They befriended me. They gave me baked goods. They bugged me. I never had any time for myself. They asked me questions, invited me to parties, put me to work. In other words, they became like family to me. In return, I betrayed them. My fondest wish is that I could tell them how sorry I am. But I can't. I will never see them again. It wasn't until I left them that I realized I envied what they have. What you have. One friend is a guy that's my age. He has a great wife and great kids. What I wouldn't give for that. But, since I've been gone, I've learned something else. Not only does God exist, he knows *I* exist. That's been a—"

Luke paused as he noticed an attractive figure enter the back of the chapel. He watched the prettiest girl he ever saw sit down on the back pew.

"Hayley?" he said into the microphone.

The congregation turned around. Red-faced, Hayley Woodard waved.

"Excuse me, I see an old friend back there," Luke said, stepping off the stand. Bishop Paxson didn't know what to do, so he closed the meeting.

Luke's knees quaked as he made the walk to the back row, with all the ward members watching him. He sat down next to Hayley. She gave him a firm missionary handshake.

"You know," Luke whispered after a pause, "the only time I see you anymore is at fast and testimony meetings."

Hayley smiled.

"What are you doing here?" he asked. "Don't tell me you're on your honey-moon."

"No," she said softly. "Thad and I broke off our engagement weeks ago."

"Really?" Luke replied, trying not to sound too happy. "I'm sorry about that."

"It's okay. Things weren't going to work out," she said, her voice trailing off. "I had to get out of Helaman. I had some money saved up, so I decided to return to my old mission stomping grounds."

They sang the closing hymn together, though neither of them paid much attention to what they were singing. Following the closing prayer, the ward members introduced themselves to Luke and Hayley. Sheila made her way to the back and kissed Luke's cheek.

"Hayley," Luke said, "I'd like you to meet Sheila, my mom."

"Your *mom?*" Hayley said in disbelief. She turned to Sheila. "It's a pleasure to meet you."

"Likewise. I've heard so much about you," Sheila said. "You two probably have a lot to talk about."

The missionaries invited Sheila to the Gospel Doctrine class they taught. "After that, you can attend Relief Society," one of them said.

"When you're done," Luke said to her, "meet us in the foyer."

"Okay," Sheila replied, "but I believe the word is pronounced, 'foy-eh.'"

"Not in Mormonville," Luke said.

CHAPTER 49

Luke and Hayley found themselves alone in the chapel. He couldn't believe he was face-to-face with her. There had been too many coincidences for this to be mere coincidence, he thought.

"So," Luke began, "how long have you been out here?"

"In New York? A couple of weeks. How are you doing, anyway?"

"You wouldn't believe it if I told you. I could write a book about what I've been through the last couple of months. I even worked for a time at a grocery store."

"I'm sure Ben will be happy to hear that," Hayley said with a grin. "You look tired. But it sounds like you're doing well."

"I am now. You look great."

"Thanks. You, too."

"How's everyone at home?"

"Some things have happened since you left. Brother Sweeney died a few weeks ago. His wife had 'He Made Every Day The Best Day Of His Life' engraved on the headstone. Bishop Law says even he didn't realize all that Brother Sweeney did for the ward, until now. Oh, and I have some good news, too. Stacie and Ben are expecting a child in the spring. They say if it's a boy, they're naming it Luke."

"Yeah, right."

"I'm not kidding."

"Obviously, either they have amnesia or they have not read that *New York Times* article."

"No, they read it. We all did. Sister Fidrych made copies of it and attached it to the ward newsletter. Not that we put much stock in the article. You were right about that reporter. He's a little weasel. He came out and tried to interview us all, and we referred all interview requests to Bishop Law, except for Sister Fidrych. But you know how she is. The reporter invited her to dinner, asked her some questions, and she just started talking. She didn't mean any harm."

"How did you find me, anyway?"

"You are not an easy man to track down, but I guess your investigative skills must have rubbed off on me. Jack was of no help, of course."

"Jack? Jack who?"

"Jack Kilborn."

"You talked to *Jack?*"

"I talked to a lot of people about you the last couple of months. Not long after you left Helaman, I called Brother and Sister Winters, in Nauvoo, and asked if they had a permanent address for you. They said they didn't know you and that the checks they received every month came from a guy named Jack Kilborn with Halcyon Books, in New York City. So when I flew into New York, I looked him up."

"And you got in to see him? How?"

"I was in the lobby of the Halcyon Books building, standing at the elevator, when I saw this girl wearing a Young Women's Medallion. You just don't see those in New York City. I introduced myself and asked her if she was LDS. She said yes and that her name was Audrey Kilborn. Jack's daughter is a member of the Church! Can you believe that?"

"Barely," Luke said.

"Anyway, Audrey told me that she was starting to work for her dad during the summer as an editorial assistant. Jack was upset about her being a Mormon but she was trying to smooth out their relationship. They decided never to talk about religion. She told me about how you gave back all that advance money, a half a million dollars, because you didn't want to change the book the way Jack wanted it. She even got me an appointment with Jack. Boy, is he mad at you."

"Yeah, I heard."

"He said he had done everything he could to make sure you never worked in New York City or for another big newspaper again. By the way, Audrey doesn't think he'll actually sue you. In fact, he's so frustrated about the whole thing he may not even publish your book at all. He is the rudest person I have ever met. I asked him where you were, and he suggested I check the gutters. Audrey and I called every hotel we could find in the phone book. We called all the newspapers in New York City. I almost gave up on finding you. So I drove out to Rochester and visited friends and families I knew from my mission for about a week. Yesterday, I went to Palmyra, and the visitors' center. I glanced at the guest registry and saw your name and that you had been there the previous day. I also found out that you lived in Syracuse."

Luke laughed.

"It gets better," Hayley continued. "I drove to Syracuse last night and stayed at a hotel. I tried finding a phone number for you, but you weren't listed. So I bought copies of all the local papers. I went through every page of every paper until I found your byline. I called the *Herald-Journal*, but no one answered. I drove around until I found the newspaper offices downtown. Everything was locked up. This morning, I woke up and checked out of my hotel. Since today was Sunday, I decided I needed to find a church to go to. No one could tell me where a Mormon Church was, so I just sort of drove around until I found this place. It was as if I were led here."

"Did you hear a voice, by chance?" Luke asked.

"Excuse me?"

"Forget it."

"I walked in and was standing in the foyer, reading the bulletin boards, when I heard you talking. I was shocked, at first. But I probably shouldn't have been. I knew the Lord would help me find you."

"How long are you here for?" Luke asked.

"Until tomorrow. I've got to drive back to New York City first thing in the morning. I've got an afternoon flight out of LaGuardia. At least we can hang out together today. I can't wait to tell everyone back home."

"Why? So they can know where to forward my hate mail?"

"What are you talking about?"

"After what I've done? I'm sure that everyone in the ward would like to see me dead after I dropped that little bombshell on all of you."

"Yeah, that was definitely one of our most memorable sacrament meetings of all-time. That was quite a farewell you had. After you walked out the door, the whole place started buzzing."

"I can only imagine," Luke said. "I feel badly about the way everything ended up."

"It doesn't have to end, you know."

"What do you mean?"

"I mean it's not too late. That didn't have to be the final chapter."

"I'm not following you."

"Can you wait here for a minute?" Hayley asked, standing up. "I've got something for you."

Luke was a captive audience. If she had told him to wait there until the next general conference, he would have done it.

Soon Hayley returned with a large book. "This is yours," she said, dropping it in his lap.

"What's this, one of your scrapbooks?"

"Open it."

The cover was thick and dark blue. The title page read, "To Luke Manning, Love the Helaman 6th Ward." Inside were pages of Hayley's photos of Luke, plus drawings and letters from members of the ward.

"You don't think you're the only one who can create a book, do you?" Hayley said with a grin.

Luke flipped through it. "There must be seventy-five pages here," he said.

"Seventy-eight, actually."

"Did you compile this?"

"I had help from Ben and Stacie and the whole ward, really. A couple of weeks after you left, Bishop Law decided to set up a table in the foyer at church for people to write you letters. Usually, that's an event reserved only for missionaries at Christmas time."

The first part of the book included contributions by Primary kids, featuring drawings of everything from an Ark to Zion. Oliver apparently used the entire box of crayons on his picture, though underneath it, a teacher, probably Ben, had written, "I love you, Brother Manning."

Luke found pages and pages of letters from the adult members of the ward. Among the excerpts:

Bishop and Sister Law: "Luke, we want you to know how much we care about you. Please understand that we don't harbor any ill will toward you. The Lord loves you and we love you. We miss you coming over for dinner and brightening our days with your smile and sense of humor. You're like the son we never had."

Mable: "You're very special to me, like one of my grandsons. I guess I was the first to learn you were leaving us and the last to know why. My Wednesdays aren't quite the same without you, though now I get visits from ward members almost every day."

Ammon: "Thanks for all your advice and help, everything you taught me about basketball and about life. I'm visiting my dad every week. It isn't easy, but things are going better. I hope things are going good with you."

Brother Gruber: "You and Ben were definitely the best hometeachers we've ever had. Thanks to you two, we're enjoying the blessings of the gospel again. The wife and I are going to the temple again soon. Go Raiders!"

There were also letters from Brother Z, the McGowns, Sagapolus, Davises and even the Munchaks, to name a few. There didn't appear to be a letter from Sister Fidrych.

So much for being the most hated man in Helaman. Instead, these people were acting like he should run for bishop. Toward the end of the scrapbook, he found a letter from Ben. Luke wasn't sure he wanted to read it, but he did.

Luke,

I hope this letter finds you doing well. You might be interested to know that my golf game, thanks to your lessons, has improved this summer.

The other day Stacie and I were cleaning Brooklyn's room when we found a diary of hers under her mattress. One of her entries, dated August 22 of last year, talked all about you coming to one of her soccer games. "Luke is so nice. He gave me a piece of gum and told me if I scored a goal, he would buy me an ice cream cone. I didn't score a goal, but he bought me an ice cream cone anyway. I am glad he is my friend and that he will be baptized soon."

I'll admit, when you told us about your book, I was hurt, then disappointed, then angry. But I've given this a lot of thought over the last couple of months. You will probably think I'm crazy for saying this, but I really, truly believe that you came to Utah for a reason. And it wasn't to write a book. The Lord wanted you to become a member of the Church. It was all part of His plan. I believe that you know that the gospel is true. You weren't living a lie, at least not once you started becoming active in the Church. In John 7:16-17, the Lord says, ". . . My doctrine is not mine, but his that sent me. If any man do his will, he shall know of the doctrine, whether it be of God or whether I speak of myself."

You did God's will and I don't believe it was an act. Maybe at first it was, but not at the end. You just went about it all backwards.

I know you aren't perfect. None of us is. That's why we have the Church in the first place—to make us better people. Don't think the Lord won't forgive you because of what you've done in the past. He has the power to help us overcome all. Most importantly, you must remember, this isn't the

Mormon Church. It's the Church of Jesus Christ.

You'll never know what having you for a neighbor has meant to me and my family. You're like a brother to me. I don't know where you are or what your situation is right now, but please don't shut us out of your life. If you ask me, you belong here in Helaman. You are always welcome to bunk out at our place. Our basement is small, but we would love to have you back. At least call or write. Please.

Your Brother,

Ben

Luke tried to blink away a tear. His entire body was flooded with a peaceful feeling. He looked at Hayley and he suddenly realized God had sent him an angel as an answer to his prayer, after all. Everything clicked. He might have missed out on his million-dollar fortune, but he knew he had received his million-dollar answer. This stuff about Joseph Smith and the Book of Mormon and the plan of salvation—it *was* the biggest story in the history of the world.

"What's this?" he asked Hayley as he turned to the book's final page.

"It's a CD with a song the McMurray family recorded about you. It's called The Gentile Among Us. It's a catchy little tune."

"Can't wait to hear it," he said. He closed the book. "Did you write me a letter, by chance?"

"No," she said. "I'm just the messenger."

"Ben thinks I should go back to Utah. Do you have an opinion on the matter?"

"It's up to you. Sounds like a good idea. How is the ward basketball team going to win another championship without you?"

"Hayley, I'm sorry I wasn't honest with you. I really am."

"I always knew there was something you weren't telling me," she said. "Ben and Stacie and I have talked about it a lot and, like them, I believe that the person you described back home in sacrament meeting doesn't exist anymore. After you left Utah, everyone in the ward decided to conduct our own little investigation of you. Those of us who knew you best held a special meeting, which eventually evolved into a potluck dinner. Anyway, we were amazed by how many people in the ward turned out. We sat in the cultural hall and we took turns talking about all you had done in our ward. That's when we found out that it was you that gave all that money to Brother Sweeney's fund—the bank president, who is in the stake presidency, told us. We found out that you visited Sister Sterling—Mable— on a regular basis. The Grubers talked about having returned to full activity to the Church, thanks in large part to you. The Taylors said McKay probably wouldn't be serving a mission if it weren't for you. And there's Phil. Without you, he might not have found his family and joined the Church. Then I come out here and find out that you've reconciled with your mom. And you're wearing your CTR ring, I see. The fact I found you here, at church, going to the pulpit during fast and testimony meeting, no less, that wasn't fake. It's further proof that you've gone through quite a transformation. Everything I've seen and heard only confirms that you are a good person. You're coming to church, and not because of some project. I'm no lawyer, but if you were accused of being a Mormon in a trial, there would be plenty of evidence to convict. I hate to break this to you, Luke, but you're as Mormon as the Tabernacle Choir."

"You think? After all I've done?"

"Absolutely."

"I know this is off the subject," Luke said, "but what about us?"

"I don't know," she said. "I know people back home miss you."

"Have *you* missed me?" Luke asked.

"I don't want you to come back to Utah for me. That would be a mistake."

Hayley was as stubborn and inscrutable as ever. But that was only two of the hundreds of things he adored about her.

"But if you did come back," Hayley added, "I guess I would consider starting over. A first date, perhaps?"

That's when Luke began to think seriously about living in Utah. Visions of service projects, minivans, sacrament meetings, and diapers danced in his head. *Am I insane?*

No, in love. Not only with Hayley, but the thought of starting a new life without pretense or pride. Of being, gulp, a full-fledged Mormon. *Maybe Utah is the place,* he thought.

"If I do go back," he said, "how would I make a living?"

"You know, we do have newspapers in Utah," Hayley said. "I think the *Helaman Times* is hiring. If that doesn't work out, I'm sure with all of your experience in the grocery business, Ben would probably consider bringing you aboard."

Just then, Sheila returned from Relief Society and told Luke she had an appointment set for the following Tuesday with the missionaries.

"How would you like to go to Utah for the discussions?"

"That's a long way to go to listen to the missionaries, isn't it?" Sheila asked.

"What I mean is, how would you feel about moving to Utah?"

"Are there cute men there?"

"Don't get too excited. Most of the men your age in Utah are already married with seven kids. And polygamy is not an option."

"I kind of like this church. I'd like to meet a nice guy, too. Hayley, do you think that's possible, at my age?"

"Are you kidding?" Hayley said. "With the Lord, anything's possible."

"I like this girl already," Sheila said. "What are we waiting for? Let's go to Utah."

CHAPTER 50

A couple of weeks later, on a Saturday morning, after Luke had given his two-week notice to his employers at the *Syracuse Herald-Journal* and had thanked Jerry for all of his help and had presented him and his wife with a copy of the Book of Mormon, Luke and Sheila took a plane to Salt Lake City.

When they arrived at the Salt Lake International Airport, Hayley was there waiting. She helped load all the possessions Luke and Sheila owned into the back of her father's pickup truck. Then Luke and Sheila squeezed into the cab with Hayley, who drove them directly to the ward house in Helaman.

Luke and Sheila had taken the discussions together with the missionaries in Syracuse. Sheila committed to baptism, but she was still a little unsure. She wanted to watch Luke get baptized first.

Once they arrived at church, Hayley took Sheila into the chapel to sit by her and her family.

Ben was in the bathroom, dressed in spotless white. "You can't use that ruptured appendix excuse this time," Ben said, hugging Luke. "If only Brooklyn were here to see this."

"Actually, I'm pretty sure she's here, somewhere," Luke said.

After Luke changed into his white clothing, he and Ben entered the chapel. The place was filled to capacity. Everywhere he looked, he saw familiar smiling faces.

Mable was sitting in a wheelchair in the back, next to an oxygen tank. Elder Webster, and his fiancée, had arrived from Idaho for the occasion. Elder Petrovic, who had become an Assistant to the President, was there too, with his companion. Phil and his family, who were preparing to be sealed as a family in the Mount Timpanogos Temple, sat toward the front.

Bishop Law conducted the baptismal service. Lloyd Gruber spoke on the first four principles and ordinances of the gospel. The Primary children sang "We'll Bring the World His Truth." Then Ben escorted Luke to the baptismal font. There was room for twenty-five people to watch the baptism. Brother McGown, who had replaced Brother Sweeney as the ward executive secretary,

301

arranged for the baptism to be shown on closed-circuit TV in the chapel, so all the ward members could watch, too.

Elder Webster and Elder Petrovic served as the witnesses. Ben and Luke stepped into the tepid water. Once situated, Ben raised his arm and pronounced the sacred words of the baptismal prayer. "Lucas Damon Manning, having been commissioned of Jesus Christ . . ."

At long last, Ben performed his first baptism. When he finished, he didn't want to leave the font. It was as if all his past failures in missionary work were washed away in that water, too. Afterward, Stacie—who was great with child, and, yes, it was a boy—took a couple of photos of her husband and Luke. One of the pictures would be for Elder Burghoff. *The conversion story would take a little longer than a few sentences to explain, though,* Ben thought.

Bishop Law confirmed Luke a member of The Church Of Jesus Christ of Latter-day Saints. At the end of the meeting, Sheila asked Ben if he would baptize her soon. "I'd be honored," he replied. "Thank you."

When the meeting ended, a long line of people formed to congratulate Luke. There were plenty of hugs, smiles, and tears. It was like one giant reunion. By late that afternoon, the last of the well-wishers had gone. Bishop Law closed up the building as Luke, Sheila, Ben, Stacie, and Hayley looked on.

"By the way," the bishop told Luke, "we never did release you from your calling."

"That's right," Ben interjected with a laugh, "and I think it's your turn to teach tomorrow."

"You Mormons don't waste any time, do you?" Luke said.

"You mean *we* Mormons, don't you?" Ben said.

As they walked out of the church and to the parking lot, Luke had one arm around his mom and one around Hayley. Luke kissed Hayley on the cheek.

"How do you feel?" Hayley asked.

"Heck," he said grandly, "this is the best day of my life. So far."

That night, he and Sheila moved into the Kimballs' basement, agreeing to stay until they found a place of their own. On Monday, they would start looking for jobs. Luke wasn't exactly sure what the future held, but at that moment, it didn't matter. He had almost forgotten that he had missed out on his Pulitzer Prize and his one million dollars.

That book he wrote about the Mormons—he still regarded it as the worst assignment in the history of journalism. *And,* Luke thought, *it is the best thing that has ever happened to me.*

About the Author

Jeff Call lives in Cedar Hills, Utah, with his wife, CherRon, and their five sons. He served an LDS mission to Chile and later graduated with a bachelor's degree in journalism from BYU.

Jeff is a sports reporter for *The Deseret News*, and is also a regular contributor to *BYU Magazine*. *Mormonville* is his first novel.

9 26575 76186 6